# Gotham Chronicles

# Gotham Chronicles

## The Culture of Sociopathy

T. Byram Karasu

ROWMAN & LITTLEFIELD PUBLISHERS, INC.
*Lanham • Boulder • New York • Toronto • Plymouth, UK*

Published by Rowman & Littlefield Publishers, Inc.
A wholly owned subsidiary of The Rowman & Littlefield Publishing Group, Inc.
4501 Forbes Boulevard, Suite 200, Lanham, Maryland 20706
http://www.rowmanlittlefield.com

Estover Road, Plymouth PL6 7PY, United Kingdom

British Library Cataloguing in Publication Information Available

**Library of Congress Cataloging-in-Publication Data**

Karasu, Toksoz B.
    Gotham chronicles : the culture of sociopathy / T. Byram Karasu.
        p. cm.
    ISBN 978-1-4422-0817-9 (cloth : alk. paper) —
    ISBN 978-1-4422-0819-3 (electronic)
    1. Young women—Conduct of life—New York (State)—New York—Fiction. 2. Young women—Sexual behavior—New York (State)—New York—Fiction. 3. Young women—Family relationships—New York (State)—New York—Fiction. 4. Interpersonal relations—Fiction. 5. Personality disorders—Fiction. I. Title.
    PS3611.A7773G68 2011
    813'.6—dc22                                                          2010032825

∞ ™ The paper used in this publication meets the minimum requirements of American National Standard for Information Sciences—Permanence of Paper for Printed Library Materials, ANSI/NISO Z39.48-1992.

Printed in the United States of America

Dedicated to the late historian Christopher Lasch,
who anticipated the culture of sociopathy.

# Acknowledgments

I am indebted to a number of gifted people in the preparation of this book. Foremost I want to thank Jonathan Sisk, senior executive editor at Rowman & Littlefield Publishers, Inc., who recognized the social significance of this project. I would also like to thank Elaine McGarraugh, production editor, who masterfully guided the progress of the book and Kathy Dvorsky, who meticulously copy-edited my manuscript; to Darcy Evans, editorial assistant, Acquisitions, who enthusiastically solicited endorsements.

I am most appreciative of Noam Fast, M.D., for his skillful editorial assistance; Hilda L. Cuesta, for her extraordinarily competent and diligent efforts; Josephine Costa, for her organizational skills in facilitating complex administrative endeavors; Tina Marie Bonanno for her infinite resourcefulness; and Angela Toscano for her technical wizardry.

I would especially like to thank my wife, Sylvia R. Karasu, M.D., who has given me her generous and invaluable assistance throughout the course of my work and for her enduring and loving support.

# -I-

There was no genuine love, there was no genuine hate; there were only genuine interests—interests in money, success, sex, and power. At the dawn of the second millennium, these excesses and unchecked exaltation of selves were celebrated by all the social, legal, political, and financial cuddlings.

The place was New York City.

In the last quarter of the past century, New York City, which in the vernacular of the region means Manhattan—the rest of the city's boroughs dismissively called "bridge and tunnel"—became a sanctuary for narcissists, benign and malignant, and a hothouse for cultivating indifference to all the known values and principles of previous generations. Upper Manhattan, especially the area running west to east between Fifth and Park Avenues and south to north between 59th and 96th Streets, was the ultimate Manhattan—the Rectangular Kingdom.

In contrast, Lower Manhattan has always been an enviable destination for creative people—artists, actors, writers—and social drifters. They entertained—or hoped to entertain—the high citizens of Upper Manhattan; and they earned enough money to pay the rent for their walk-up studio apartments in seedy row houses and crumbling old buildings.

Frequently, quite frequently—to make a living—these creative individuals resorted to waitressing, housekeeping, and other service jobs, competing with illegal immigrants. They didn't mind, as long as they had the time and freedom to pursue their artistic endeavors—at least, that is how they justified their lifestyles.

But some threw their towels into the creative ring and actually became bartenders, personal trainers, yoga teachers, spiritual guides, and masseuses. Some others hung their shingles and declared themselves psychotherapists.

Those in the masseuse subgroup walked a fine line; they—usually beautiful women—visited the homes of these citizens of the Upper East Side of Manhattan wherein occasionally they received offers from their clients that were at times offensive and at times extravagant, if not destabilizing.

Mallory Coldwell, a twenty-two-year-old, attractive brunette from Westport, Connecticut, had possessed the steadiness of a high-wire walker. While a student majoring in English at New York University, she had learned, and then practiced, deep massage and Rolfing therapy to support herself—her father had agreed to pay only her tuition. Her modest clientele—mostly NYU faculty members and their spouses—were very impressed by her ability to relax them and to unearth their long-buried memories through skillful affliction of severe pain on their internal organs, arms, legs, or necks and backs, especially on the fourth and fifth lumbar vertebrae. When all else failed to relax her treatment-resistant patients, Mallory would supplement the treatment with pot brownies she had baked. Through her clients' praises—"it is cheaper than going to a psychoanalyst" and "she is also equally cold and distant"—she earned the nickname of Ice Doc.

Mallory, who graduated from NYU the previous June, wanted to pursue her only genuine interest: writing. Instead of becoming a teacher in one of those "faux high schools" in the boroughs, and thus not having enough time or solitude required for writing, she decided to continue to earn money through offering her services as a massage therapist. She would work as little or as much as she needed, and she would devote the rest of her time to becoming a writer.

*⟨⟩*

# -II-

$M$y name is Mallory.

I have to write my story: The violation of humanity demands its narration; historically it had always been the case: Philomela sings her rapist's crime; Count Ugolino narrates the story of how he was forced to eat his children's corpses; the Bible retells the incest between Lot and his daughters.

Once I was myself, before I had my periods—a gawdy girl—I dreamt of strawberry ice cream melting into fears; and snow days drifting into innocent sins. I didn't know why, but I felt guilty—I sang unmelodious songs in tuneless cries and walked with muted steps; I looked at arrogant breasts and throbbing crotches with virginal disdain and apologetically gave out hushed-down scents. I was lonely.

Then one day I was no longer myself. I bled to wild inebriation a full-bodied lush woman; I threw my unshackled lust into sullied laps and into endless breaches. I know that I was guilty of being unlovable. I sang carnal warning, walked breast forward (the lustiest conceit); I gave out hormone-addled perfumes and never absolved in orgasmic laughters.

I have always been anxious, but not anxious enough to stop myself to be crucified to sex—indetermined sex. I had been so disappointed by the norm—sexual and otherwise—that I took unknown forms, unknown to me. Rudderless, I plunged into an ambiguous course—yes, there were obscene touches, malignant caresses, fearful felicities and false pangs, and also throbs of intoxications with phantom scents—all lonely feats. No, I wasn't simply lonely.

My name is Mallory, and I am unhappy. But it is never enough for me to be simply unhappy—I need to be ungrounded. It isn't that I am in need of some misfortune, but if that is what it takes to be in my emotional home, then so be it. Marijuana does that, without creating much mayhem; so does the feeling—just the feeling—sexually abused (within consensual space); man with greed of desire does that. Nevertheless, I do wish to maintain my right to be fucked and despised. Are these all signs of freedom, or am I like the character in Poe's Descent into the Maelstrom, commenting on my own destruction?

3

# -III-

When one of Mallory's grateful clients—an aging professor of history—recommended her services to John Levine, one of the board members of the university who couldn't sit still in meetings because of his back pain, Mallory's life drastically changed. She could earn more money from one client on the Upper East Side than she could from ten on the Lower East Side.

Mr. Levine, a wealthy man in his late seventies, was a survivor of prostate cancer. Four years ago his prostate had been surgically removed; doctors believed that the disease was contained in the capsule—a biopsy of regional lymph nodes was free of malignancy. Two years later, however, a routine backache work-up showed cancer metastases on his vertebrae. Now he was receiving a regimen of hormone therapy—"chemical castration," he called it—to which he reacted with tales of sexual bravado: "I am a poster boy for quick recovery from postsurgical complications, holding in and holding up."

Wherever Mr. Levine went, whether at a meeting of one of the various boards he belonged to, or at his favorite "hangout," The Harmony Club, he never failed to mention this young and beautiful masseuse he had found. He intoned about how strong and competent she was, how much better she was than all the chiropractors he knew; how her long, magical fingers would rub away his pain. "She is professional, very professional," he would say, emphasizing the *professional*. There, he would wink to other guys (while not so carefully hiding from women around him); and in case the men didn't get it, he would display a mock salivation.

Two of Mallory's major clients, Max Hathaway, a hedge fund manager, and Mrs. Jeanny Weisman, the wife of an assistant district attorney, Jeffrey Weisman, also came through such promotional bragging of Mr. Levine. Within a year of graduation Mallory terminated all her other clients and no longer accepted new ones. Working for these two men and Mrs. Weisman provided enough income for her needs—she accepted only cash.

Max alone would have been sufficient—he was extremely generous—but Mallory didn't want to put "all her eggs in one wallet," not because he had made the relation sexual from the first call on, but because he was utterly disrespectful of her profession. Otherwise seeing him five to six hours a month would have covered all her expenses. Mr. Levine and Mrs. Weisman paid her regular fees. This did not make much economical sense, but she felt sorry for Mr. Levine—he had to be dying—so she couldn't leave him; she liked Mrs. Weisman, who was genuinely interested in receiving massage and Rolfing, and who also was safe to sell pot to in her dwindling market.

Mallory scheduled biweekly two-hour sessions with each of them. They were all disappointed. None of them believed that she wanted to make just enough money to survive so that she could write. Each of them interpreted her relative availability in their own ways: Mr. Levine suspected that she couldn't tolerate his faint smell of urine more than twice a month; Max accused her of promiscuity—she might need male variety; Jeanny was convinced that Mallory was having homosexual panic!

⚬⟋⟍⟋⟍⟍⟍⟍⟍⟍⟍⟍⟍○

In reality Mallory's needs were truly modest. She bought her clothes from thrift shops, wore no makeup, and owned no jewelry. She didn't go to restaurants and ate little, and then only organic vegetables, fruits, canned wild salmon, and nuts—mostly Indian 401 raw cashews and almonds. Her favorite dinner was Gruyère cheese and French baguettes. She had stopped taking drugs (mainly marijuana) and drinking any alcoholic beverage a year ago; she didn't drink soda or even bottled water. She preferred to filter her own water from the tap. Mallory washed, dried, and even cut her own hair. She took care of all her cotton dresses and underwear at the Laundromat. She mostly wore sneakers and owned only four pairs of shoes—her two gay neighbors jokingly questioned whether she was a woman at all.

Mallory lived in a studio apartment on the fourth floor of an old, dilapidated building on Orchard Street on the Lower East Side. Each floor was divided into two apartments (one small, one large), except the first floor, which was occupied by a hat store, selling only fedoras. A gay couple shared the other apartment on Mallory's floor: Peter, a tall and well-toned and tanned forty-two-year-old who looked like he'd just jumped out of a Polo ad of the Ralph Lauren Company, where he worked as an assistant designer, and Dave, a bold, short, and heavy thirty-one-year-old who was always looking for a job. Frequently they invited Mallory to dinner. Dave loved to cook.

The rest of the apartments in the building were occupied by mostly single, middle-aged, and older people, whom Mallory occasionally ran into walking up or down the stairs and exchanged a few pleasantries, or simply listened to their complaints about the building. It was either too hot or too cold; the stairs were too narrow, steep, and dark; and cockroaches and mice ran all over, undeterred by all their efforts.

The manager of the building, Mr. Lazarro, never wanted to hear such "trivia"; he was known to throw out tenants who bugged him too much. His enormous head and bulging eyes were quite convincing of his intent: "You are damn lucky to have a roof over your head," he would mock the complainer, and he would dare them, "If you don't like it, leave." No one did, for the low rent corresponded to the lowly state of the building. Mr. Lazarro lived in Queens and would show up early on the morning of the first day of each month to collect rent in person; otherwise, he expected the tenants to fix their own apartments and designate the care for the communal areas among themselves.

Mallory had no complaints as long as the place was quiet, and it was—eerily quiet, inside and outside. This was especially true at night, when the whole neighborhood was deserted—Mallory's favorite time. She would write until dawn and then go to sleep and wake up around noon. Her clients preferred appointments at the end of the day—except Max, whose appointment time was mostly at noon and irregular. So in the afternoon she was free to do little chores or go to yoga or Kabbalah classes—and, of course, write.

Mallory's first novel—she had submitted a few sample chapters of the manuscript—was returned unread by a number of publishers in New York. The novel was a story of incest, narrated by a teenager—the twin sister of the victim. A graduate student, Hamilton Thurman III ("Ham"), her teaching assistant from New York University, gave her some advice: Get an agent and write about a subject that you know emotionally. Mallory knew the subject.

ᘒᙏᙉᕲ

# -IV-

*M*y name is Mallory, and I am not—I don't really know who, or what I am; or what I want. Yes I do, the latter: I want to be loved (erase that—how pathetic, how banal, how trite, and how pitiful!).

Let me lower down the flag a bit: What I want is "my being" to be recognized. All my adolescence I wanted so badly to be noticed, even if as a weird one, that I used to say peculiar things out of context in a given social situation. I would inform my audience with a sense of urgency that marriages among cousins or uncles and nieces are unnecessarily prohibitive, for there are no real negative genetic consequences, especially given the progress of preventive medicine.

"Is someone getting married?" was the common reply; then I would deliver a torrent of information about "the utter absurdity of one of the most potent ideas"; those are the ideas that I would pick here and there from books.

In college, I got more literary in my disruptive attention-seeking to the point of condescension. For example, I would say, in parrot accent: 'Talk, talk, that's all you do." Of course not many English majors read Zazie in the Metro and got to know her parrot—Laverdure.

Eventually, by the time I was a senior at NYU, I recognized that I was Bellow's Herzog—all that ineffectuality, the failure of best potentials were demonstrated in my existence.

# -V-

Mallory got off the subway at 77th Street and Lexington Avenue and briskly began to walk to her appointment with Mrs. Weisman on East End Avenue. She was a few minutes late; she was always a little late to all her dates—personal and professional. Was it her inability to organize her schedule better or her chronic mixed feelings? But could she be ambivalent about everyone? Everyone seemed to be on time except that Ham—he would be late a half hour or even more, to the point that she would wonder whether he'd show up at all. "How dare he? Well, I guess I need him more than he needs me; this must be the essence of relations—business, love, even friendship."

Ham was not only Mallory's mentor in writing, he was also her wholesale supplier of marijuana. He could easily sell to anyone, so her buying didn't constitute a major power. He never asked for a date or even a massage, so she had nothing special to offer to him, and that was his power—the son of a bitch. She resented that.

The doorman opened the door. "Good afternoon, Mallory...you are fifteen minutes late again!"

"Fuck! Even doormen on the Upper East Side are obsessive neurotics! And he calls me by my first name. I guess I am one of their servants." Already worked up from thinking of her neediness of Ham and his dismissive attitude, Mallory was trying to contain her rage—a good day to Rolf someone, she muttered.

*I have been living in emotional hibernation—I don't relate to others; in fact, people are scarcely real to me. Of course, I am hardly real to myself. My mind seems to have many disorganized episodes of otherness—one walks in the haze of hollowness; another at the thin edge of insanity; yet another in a dark-toned amnesia—all sinking me to infertile anxiety and depression.*

# -VI-

The Rectangular Kingdom of the Upper East Side of Manhattan was surrounded—from the east, south, and north—by townhouses and postwar high-rises that were occupied by the Kingdom's support system: delicatessens, bakeries, supermarkets, stationery stores, beauty parlors, tailors and dry cleaners, shoe repair shops, bars, restaurants, doctors' offices, and banks.

Above the main floor of these buildings—on better ones—lived upper-middle-class professionals: physicians, psychiatrists, dentists, architects, art dealers, junior executives, and lawyers who expressed their intellectual superiority to the high citizens of the Rectangular Kingdom but still never failed to advertise their close affiliations. Some surely believed that they had chosen the wrong professions; with their intelligence and hard work they could have easily belonged to a private equity firm, made a bundle, and lived in the Kingdom.

Business lawyers were the most frustrated. They asserted that all those business tycoons and investment bankers couldn't do a damn thing without their legal advice or protect themselves from inevitable lawsuits. Criminal lawyers who were confined to prosecuting thieves and murderers in the boroughs were fuming because the rich and powerful considered them a mere extension of the police department. The only recourse for these "lowly" district attorneys was to target members of the Kingdom themselves. The idea of subjecting them to the investigative process was not only the ultimate revenge for DAs but potentially also the only way of getting out of that legal ghetto. They dreamed of running for high office by bludgeoning the wealthy and powerful in public, in newspapers and on television, for betraying the public trust, thus making a name for themselves and establishing the platform of tough and honest "sheriff"— they were all waiting for a *Bonfire of the Vanities* moment.

Although the forty-seven-year-old assistant district attorney Jeffrey Weisman had escaped his colleagues' financial fate—his father was a wealthy man—he remained loyal to their mood: resentful and frustrated and unduly ambitious. Jeff had inherited certain traits from his prickly, acerbic, and unmannered father: He was an aggressive, merciless, and determined prosecutor who would not mind crossing the ethical and legal boundaries to bring about convictions against his targets. He would browbeat and even threaten lawyers of defendants to submit to his pre-judged decisions; he was intoxicated with his power.

The only person whom he couldn't frighten was his own wife, Jeanny. If anything, Jeff was intimidated by her. She came from a Waspy family whose money had run out long ago, yet she maintained a sense of owner-ship of America. Jeanny's parents unsuccessfully tried to discourage her from dating Jeffrey while they were both at Columbia Law. After their marriage, her parents accepted Jeffrey on their own terms as being an "All-American Jew."

But Jeffrey's fear of his wife had even deeper roots. Jeanny was like his father in that she was chronically dissatisfied, irritable, depressed, and anxious. This made Jeffrey feel both guilty and helpless. All this put him in the role of a solicitor with her—for a smile, sex, interest in his job—and an apologizer for anything that may have gone wrong in their lives: her genital herpes (even though he was sure that both had it at the time of their first sexual contact), their eleven-year-old daughter Ellen's ADD, and their thirteen-year-old daughter Samantha's promiscuous behavior. To be home for her husband and children, Jeanny quit her law career. She accepted Jeffrey's pursuit of power with a sober forbearance.

Marriage to Jeff placed Jeanny pointlessly at odds with herself. She was so badly misunderstood by her husband that all her sense of purpose dis-solved. To be a wife and mother of two children and living in artificial luxury only generated a raw unhappiness in her—a sense of being lost with no hope to be found.

For a while, Jeanny thought only total madness may pull her out of what seemed to be infinite emptiness, that craziness may take the lid off her hibernating soul and put an end to the banality of her impasse. She didn't want to commit suicide—an underwhelming result for herself—she just wanted to be free from sanity and its requirements. Only mari-juana offered some transitory oblivion.

Her raising her children Jewish and attending all those high holidays with Jeffrey's parents, whom she hated, sank her deeper. This once-promising, young, healthy, and beautiful lawyer who used to pulse with self-confidence became physically and psychologically shriveled.

But Jeanny was not a complainer...if only her back didn't ache so much! The doctors at New York Hospital found no structural causes for her pain. They advised her to do certain exercises to strengthen her abdominal muscles, take hot baths, learn relaxation techniques like yoga and meditation, and get massages. Every doctor she consulted inquired whether she was under any stress, which she denied. Nor did she follow any of their advice. She especially eschewed massage, which she considered a form of decadence practiced by somewhat questionable characters. Occasionally she looked at *New York* magazine's personal services pages; there were many advertisements of masseuses that always hinted at something more: "by a beautiful lady," "happy ending," "the ultimate satisfaction," and "you'll come again." But when Mr. Levine spoke so highly of a masseuse—a New York University graduate and an expert in Rolfing—who helped him with his back problem, she decided to give it a try. One concern that Jeanny couldn't alleviate until she met the masseuse was, what if she was one of those butches who "molested" women under the disguise of deep massage? "They inflict so much pain elsewhere in your body that you forget your original pain!" wrote one article.

⁂

When Jeanny met Mallory for the first time, she almost fainted. Mallory was no butch. On the contrary, she looked exactly like Dina—her only semihomosexual experience from her college years—but even more beautiful: same gentle body with its sensual curves, same green eyes, and same shiny straight hair. Jeanny was on the thin and muscular side while Mallory was fleshy, curvaceous, and undulating. "How could such fine hands give deep massage to anyone?" she thought.

When Mallory put her elbows on both sides of her lower back, Jeanny began to cry. She didn't exactly know why—it wasn't really hurting that much. Just to cover up she let out a little scream: "Ouch."

"Talk to me," whispered Mallory in her ear. She knew that her elbows were not that sharply lodged.

"Talk to you?" Jeanny felt a little embarrassed.

"Yes, or talk to yourself aloud," Mallory pressed.

"Oh, just an image of an old friend popped up in my mind; we have not seen or talked to each other for a very long time. I am rather surprised that I could be crying over a lost relation after so many years, especially because I don't cry so easily to begin with. A touch lower on the left side, right…right there! My goodness, what is that?" Jeanny asked.

"A knot. The lost relation? What was her name?" Mallory inquired.

"Oh, her name was Dina. Why? Does it matter? How do you know it was 'she' and not 'he'? Am I having some sort of analysis, facedown, with a hands-on analyst?" Jeanny asked defensively.

Mallory had learned not to respond to every question.

"Turn over and bend your knees; now this might hurt a little." Jeanny obeyed. Mallory took her right leg above the knee and began to slowly push it toward her body. For her age, Jeanny had quite shapely legs,

Mallory thought—slim and toned. But why was her buttock sagging? Mallory kept pressing Jeanny's leg.

"What was the nature of that lost relation with Dina?" Mallory continued.

"Is this how the CIA makes people confess their crimes? It was just a…a college experiment—an emotional lesbianism. When she wanted to make it sexual too and I didn't…well, she left me for another girl. You must have had a similar experience with girls or boys," replied Jeanny, her face scrunched up.

Now Mallory was on Jeanny's left arm. She felt her breasts were small and floppy; she must have nursed her children.

"I ran into a young girl with short hair in the hall as I was coming in…"

"Oh yeah, Ellen," Jeanny interrupted. "She is my younger one; she was at the tutorial. She is a handful—struggling in school, you know—math, English, plus she is always talking in class; fidgeting, dropping things, fighting with others. The school psychologist tested her. She has a high verbal IQ and a low performance IQ—a form of ADD; I don't know; no one in my family had such a problem."

"Turn over; and the older?" Mallory asked.

"Samantha…Samantha. I don't know what your generation was like at that age, but when I was her age—she just turned thirteen—I didn't even kiss a boy; she is doing everything and with everyone. The school actually gives free condoms to 'sexually active' students. Can you believe that? My mother emphasized throughout my teenage years and long after to preserve myself for my husband. When I tell Samantha about this, she just laughs: 'Oh, Mom, you are so out of it!'"

"Well, you are done, Mrs. Weisman," Mallory said.

"Oh, please call me Jeanny; let me get your money." Jeanny jumped off the table and carefully counted and recounted the money. She got a little too close to Mallory and tilted her head right; Mallory thought she was going to give her a kiss. No—Jeanny shook her hand gently and gave her the money.

෧෴෴ඏ

# -VII-

*I* never lie, but I don't always tell the truth either; when it comes to my writing, its truth becomes the very reason for my existence. Matisse advises that one should exaggerate in the direction of truth—a novel would waste the truth. I exaggerate in the direction of intellectual deliverance because of my literary limitations—bringing about a phantom union between artifice and verisimilitude.

The strained voice that I am using in my novel here belongs to a teenager with a profound shallowness, who juxtaposes her life experiences in abrasive fashion, and then awkwardly dances on the debris.

# -VIII-

As Mallory approached her building, she saw a young boy on a bicycle delivering pizza to David, in front of the door.

"No cooking dinner tonight, huh, Dave?" she teased him.

"Yeah, Peter is away with some Polo people for a shoot; I hate cooking just for myself."

They began to climb the squeaky stairs; by the time they reached the fourth floor, Dave was out of breath. "Would you like to join me or have a couple of slices of pizza to eat on your own?" he labored to say.

"Thanks, but I better buckle down and try to do some work. I have an appointment with Ham tomorrow, the fellow that I told you about—one of my teachers from NYU; anyway, he is editing my novel. I'll take one slice, though, if you are not going to save it for later."

"Oh, please." Dave, huffing and puffing, entered his apartment and put one slice on a plate for her to carry to her apartment. Mallory quickly got undressed and put on her Gap sweatshirt and pants while eating the pizza. She pulled her chair closer to her writing table and turned on her computer: "my manuscript—the litter of betrayal."

***

*I wonder. What do men think I am thinking when I am under them, while they are hitting their pubic bones against mine, with escalating speed and force. I hear the pounding of their hearts—they're breathless. Drips of their sweat fall on my body, on my face—it is creepy; then with a howl or two, followed by a seizure-like convulsion, they throw their full load on me.*

*Men definitely look pitiful after orgasm. Didn't Aristotle say copulation makes all animals sad?*

*Then they look apologetic, not for their weight—that is actually strangely comforting—but for something they have done. Is it for having discharged in me or on me? I can understand why a male spider would not, could not fight against* being eaten by the female after copulation—this is definitely some sort of guilty act that invites mortal punishment.

So what am I thinking when this is going on besides feeling vaguely angry? Mostly I am thinking of something else, but that is also true when they are talking to me; I am not really part of any of their transactions with me, not really there.

൭ᴍᴍൄ

# -IX-

Above 100th Street sprawled the community of Harlem, which was divided into Spanish Harlem on the east and Harlem proper on the west. Above 135th Street, Harlem meandered into Washington Heights and Inwood, which were closer in many aspects to the neighboring borough of the Bronx than to Manhattan. There, lived middle and lower–middle class citizens without whom the Rectangular Kingdom could not have functioned: teachers, psychologists, social workers, maids, nannies, taxi drivers, garage attendants, doormen, plumbers, cleaners, electricians, repairmen, police officers, firemen, sanitation men, salesmen, store clerks, dog walkers, deliverymen, nurses, aides, and security guards.

On the Upper West Side, especially between Columbus Avenue and Riverside Drive, in an area with two medical centers—St. Luke's and Presbyterian—and a major university, Columbia, there was a peculiar "unmelting" pot of inhabitants: Blacks, Puerto Ricans, Dominicans, Koreans, Yugoslavians, and a spattering of Whites—mostly the faculty and students of the university.

For the past six years (since his sophomore year at Columbia University), Ham—Hamilton Thurman III—had been renting a room from a Bosnian family, a mother and son, who lived on one floor of a rundown brownstone building on West 108th Street off Amsterdam Avenue. This ruggedly handsome poet, now a graduate student and a teaching assistant in the English Department of New York University, chose to stay with the Bosnians partly because he felt comfortable with them but mainly because the idea of looking for people tolerant of his habits was too much for him. Twice in the past he was asked to leave his place because he smoked too many cigarettes and too much weed. The Bosnians—the son, Ahmed, and his mother, Vakfiye—smoked like chimneys; she even tried a little marijuana but couldn't understand what the fuss was all about.

Ham was dreading his lunch meeting with Mallory—a recent graduate of his department whom he had mentored during her senior year. Ham served as the informal editor for her writing. She was also one of his clients for weed, but she didn't seem to be a total pothead—he was sure that she was reselling, because she always had a lot of cash.

Ham would have preferred only to be her weed supplier, because he didn't want to hurt her feelings with his critique of her manuscript. Writers never appreciate honest comments on their work. All they want is unqualified praise and a subtle conveyance of awe in appreciation of their geniuses. He recognized Mallory's talent but felt that her obsession with a single subject as the driving force for her writings was too limiting. Furthermore, that topic—incestuous ambivalence—had to be reserved for the dark alleys of first-person narration rather than the "authorial I," which Ham told her a couple of times. She kept violating the fundamental principle of the subjective showing by aesthetic telling, thus distancing herself from the immediacy of the experience, and thus from getting published.

Not that he considered himself such an expert in getting his work into print. Every major publishing house and most independent and university presses had turned down his book of poetry, *The Rage of My Soul*, with "platitudes" such as "your command of English is remarkable, but..." One editor even had the audacity to scold him for using too many adjectives and adverbs. Should his work then be reduced to nouns and verbs: "Fuck you"?

Upon his literary agent's advice, Ham tried to "be visible," as a conventional writer's wisdom advised: Two of his poems appeared in the snobbish *New Yorker*, but he couldn't win a single poetry competition, not even a consolation recognition from the Wick Poetry Center, the *Spoon River Poetry Review*, the *Crab Orchard Review*, and Tupelo.

Actually, he abhorred even the idea of submitting his poems for competition. To him, a poetry competition was an oxymoron; was poetry becoming a sport, or more like the Westminster Dog Show? There was even a prestigious Walt Whitman Poetry Prize! Whitman must be turning or burning in his grave. No, no, no, "No rhyming."

But the poetry publishing "business" was different from that of novel publishing. No one made money from of it, least of all, the poets. The best-selling poetry books printed fewer than five thousand copies; no one read any of them from cover to cover, of course, for good reason; every poet had one song to sing. All one needed to do was open the book randomly and read one of the poems; you'd have read them all.

Maybe there was still some chance, he hoped, as long as his agent didn't return the manuscript. The ringing of the phone stopped his reverie—it was Christine, his agent. "Speak of the devil," he muttered.

"Ham, I am returning your manuscript; no publisher has expressed any interest; if anything I am getting negative reviews, not just generic and neutral rejection letters. I am sorry. We are both wasting our time and energy; do you want friendly advice?"

"Not really." Ham's voice slid away.

"Well, nevertheless; I think you should get a teaching job and still dabble in poetry, if you want. You see, I have been in this business longer than you have lived; I have seen many successes based on the different takes. For example, Aram Saroyan, who is considered a concrete poet, says poems aim to be things as well as words, to be looked at as much as read. Now it is hard to look at your poems without getting blurry eyes. Forget reading them; they lay on the page clumsily—ill-sorted collections of letterings and spaces, poorly matching pieces deforming the intended whole."

Ham felt himself shrinking into the sofa; he was hardly able to hold on to the telephone.

"You see, Ham, you have to define yourself; you are neither romantic like Keats or Stevens nor experimentalist like Gertrude Stein—hello, hello…Ham…Ham…oh, well."

Ham was sinking into a hollow lassitude. He lit a joint, took a few tokes, and lay down on his couch, which was covered with many kilims. Did he have a song to sing? A single song? Maybe he didn't. Was that why Columbia's graduate program rejected him—an alumnus and son of one of its own professors?

৬৩৩৩৯

# -X-

Ham hurried to the Chinese restaurant—Hunan Balcony—on 98th Street and Broadway. Mallory was already there; the rest of the place was half-empty.

"I'm sorry, I got this community service thing; I had to talk to students about the horrors of addiction at PS 146 in East Harlem; it takes two transfers to get here."

Not only was he half an hour late, he was also lying. He felt a tinge of shame—a poet lies?

Mallory cast her eyes away.

"Actually, I fell asleep. I am sorry."

Mallory was never put off by his lies, nor was she impressed by his honesty.

"You got the shit?"

"Yeah, yeah." He put a squashed brown bag on Mallory's lap.

"The same?"

"The same, eight."

Mallory casually gave him a white envelope.

"So, you only got a community service rap? Most people go to jail for that."

He wondered whether she was happy about his light sentence or disappointed by it.

"Yeah, two hundred hours, though." He sought her eyes. Not there. Mallory always looked away, far away somewhere over his shoulder. For a second, a flashed glance would meet his eyes, and then she would be "gone" for another ten minutes.

"This guy, Assistant District Attorney Weisman, happened to be an undergrad student of my father; they became close friends. I think he is the kind of son my father would have liked to have. He asked, 'How is the senior?' Then he lectured me for an hour about how grateful I should be for the opportunity that life provided me; how I should be trying to deserve to be the son of my illustrious father; some bullshit like that. Then

19

he dismissed the case on some technicality that I couldn't fully compre-
hend except that the police had no fucking right to stop and search me
on the street; everyone smokes on the Upper West Side, for God's sake.
Thankfully, I had only three joints in my pocket, not anything like that,"
he pointed to Mallory's large straw bag made of organic materials.

"Did you say the assistant DA's name was Weisman?"

"Yeah, Jeffrey Weisman; Dad thinks this guy will go far, very far, may
even be a mayor, senator, or governor. He may even be the first Jewish
president of the country. Do you know him?"

For a moment, he thought that Mallory might be a supplier for the assistant DA, but he wasn't the type.

"No, no. Only from headlines at the newsstands."

What a small world, she thought. Mallory was staring at a couple on
the west side of Broadway, across the street; they had been kissing for at
least two minutes, totally indifferent to onlookers.

"I hate newspapers," declared Ham. "They always tell you about certain events and people as if they are all unique experiences. It makes no
difference who or how many persons died in a Bronx fire, who got shot by
an off-duty policeman, who got raped—they are all interchangeable—and
then there is national and international news, which are totally unrelat-
able. The mind of a writer cannot be subjected to the kind of generic mis-
information that spawns synthetic emotions."

He had to stop this litany, not because Mallory was not listening, but
because there was no point to it; sooner or later he had to talk about her
novel. Ham looked at her; Mallory was still looking out. She was as beautiful as she was inaccessible behind her frosty walls.

"For someone who doesn't read newspapers you know a hell of a lot,"
Mallory uttered, still looking at the couple across the street who were
now engaged in some intense conversation. She wondered why Ham
never had asked her out for a date after all this time; fucking students was
one of the fringe benefits of being a teaching assistant—in fact, the only
benefit.

"I cannot seem to move ahead with my novel; I feel covered with darkness. Do you ever feel that way?"

Ham regained his teacher's posture: "Well, as Doctorow once said,
'writing a novel is like driving at night; you only have to see as far as your
headlights.'"

Food arrived. Ham rolled his moo shu pork into two big pancakes, devoured the first one, and drank a whole bottle of Heineken before Mallory
began to open her chopsticks.

"I love Chinese vegetables…. So, did you get the chance to see the
second draft?" Mallory asked while trying to pick up a slippery bamboo
shoot from her plate.

Ham's dreaded moment had arrived. He thought that Mallory, whose hysterical intellect was clouded by a spiritual hangover, could tolerate only muted critique. Anytime he was a little too honest, she fell back to her "out-of-focus face," gazing at certain points far away. She would suddenly transform into her other self—prim distancing—and talk with an equally distant and censorious voice; her casual grace would be replaced with a taciturn spastic indifference. He had to gauge his cadence.

"Anyhow, I looked at my review of the first draft; that remains unchanged. The part of your book that deals with the incest story told—in a disjointed diary form, I must add—by a teenager is very engaging. There your diction and your style match that of a young woman—events are narrated with an air of pseudo-insouciance. The young girl is wallowing in her helpless confusion with a peculiar flavor of sadness that rings true, and the reader gets the story, in spite of its fitful presentation.

"Then there is another voice—an incongruous one that is superimposed on the story in a rather jittery narrative form by a young woman with precocious insight, who seems to be ambushed by life; she manages to maintain her savage humor in the midst of all that *sturm und drang*. The diction here is that of a poet by default, à la Robert Lowell, but the style is more like a bull in a philosophical china shop.

"This intellectual, philosophical part of your manuscript is not only discordant with the story line, it is also discontinuous with each of its own segments. It seems like you start with a potentially fecund idea and end up getting stuck in the literary equivalent of a cul-de-sac."

Seeing Mallory's clawing eyes, Ham retreated: "Well, let me just add quickly that there is much, much improvement from the first. The title, *Lost Illusion*, is, I presume, an homage to André Maurois—the undisclosed title of every novel?"

"Ham, please skip the bullshit preface."

"No, I mean it. There is textual cohesiveness in this draft, and the story line moves with an engaging pace. You write with a formal style but with honesty and passion. You have a strong narrative line. You have fascinating, complex, and memorable characters whose choices, decisions, and actions are consistent with their emotional states; the nature and the purpose of the conflict build steadily with colorful language and snappy dialogue. You heighten the sympathy for the protagonist, you keep the reader gripped, you keep intensifying suspense even in total intimacy. You...you really deliver what you promised to your reader."

Mallory bristled.

"All this for a ninety-page manuscript?...Ham! Am I still in your fucking class, Literature 101?"

He swallowed another rolled pancake, gulped down the rest of the second beer, wiped his mouth with a paper napkin, pushed his chair from the table, pulled his drooping shoulders back, and looked at her for a full minute. This time Mallory's eyes were coldly fixed on his.

"I didn't read it!"

Mallory's eyes went vacant.

He was waiting for her to say something, even to yell or curse, anything. Her gaze shifted again to a distant look. What was she thinking, he wondered; how could a face be so unreadable?

"Here's the thing. It isn't that you couldn't rewrite a better version of these chapters; it is the premise itself, Mallory—the question of believability. I mean...look, for example, maybe your protagonist isn't imagining things, misreading some events, or has a very rich fantasy life, or is not paranoid; that is okay, but then a third-person omniscient voice must shadow the first-person narrative, to cast a doubt on the protagonist's sanity—that is when your frame is set to trump facts, à la Lakoff."

Mallory gently dropped her chopsticks on her half-eaten plate.

"Am I missing something here?" Ham grumbled.

By now he was hoping to get out of the restaurant without getting slapped.

"Furthermore, the father's inflicting sexual crimes on his own teenage daughter must generate some powerful emotions in her twin sister, your heroine, like empathy for her, rage against the father, or a perverse yearning for the same for herself; or some activities to try to stop it. How could she be so emotionally indifferent?"

Mallory gave a quick look at the billfold that the waiter brought, threw down two $20 bills, and closed it.

"Please call me when you read the second draft as is and also let me know how much I owe you."

Mallory glided out of her chair, collected her bag and her coat, and stood by the table. Ham lifted his head to look at her as if saying "Yes-s-s-s?"

She was deep in her thoughts without paying attention to the awkwardness of the situation. They were from the same stock! She was admiring his thick, thatchy-blond hair, undulating down to his broad shoulders, and his solid square jaw, almost divided in half by a deep cleft, like her father's.

Ham wondered whether she was waiting for the real question. All right, then…

"Let me ask you this, Mal. Is the incest story of your protagonist…oh, umm, is that autobiographical? That is the only possible explanation for the artifice of your character's indifference—taking an emotional distance from the event—a sort of protective shield against feelings."

His upturned light-blue eyes, which commonly reflected a genuine interest, were a little hesitant.

"Didn't you say in your lectures that the first novel is likely to be more autobiographical than autobiography?" Mallory said. "Furthermore, I hope you mean artful by 'artifice' and not deceptive."

Mallory took a few steps and turned around: "If you grew a mustache you would look like General Custer."

As she walked the length of the restaurant toward the Broadway exit, all heads—men and women—turned to stare at her. Her hips were rolling in soft harmony with her outturned elbows; her arms swung back and forth, bouncing her breasts together. Once she approached the door, she threw her coat on her shoulders as her long, silky hair slid over it. A cool breeze from outside rushed in. Now the restaurant was totally silent.

ᏀᎳᎾ

# -XI-

*I could have been a poet, but in high school, teachers' making me practice on meter and rhyme turned me off. Although I feel like a poet folded into prose, I still could write, but now poets turn me off. They lack the very poetic decorum that they complain the world of literature is missing—unaware of their own Kafkaesque intrusion to the lives of innocent people with their bizarre and inscrutable minds.*

*Poets are sort of mutinous characters, insulated and helpless—they can't support themselves with their métier—at best they may get teaching positions and bore students with their idiosyncratic take on literature.*

*Male poets have strong feminine undertones, female poets have masculine overtones, but they are all like European aristocrats whom Thomas Paine described as being "the drones, a seraglio of males (and females) who neither collect the honey, nor form the hive." I am at least now collecting the honey—I'll keep collecting until I reach the "fuck you" point—and my novel will be my hive.*

# -XII-

Mallory's phone rang.

"Hi, did I wake you up?" Patricia asked tentatively.

"No, my considerate sister, you just interrupted my work. For your information, I usually wake up by noon, and it is almost one o'clock; for goodness' sake, stop being so sarcastic. We know, we know, you wake up at 6 a.m.; what do you expect, you are going to be a doctor."

"Mallory, please, I don't think so; I don't want to be a doctor. I hate medical school. It is torture—each class is harder than the next one. I may be good at basic sciences, but I don't like them; plus I don't want to work that hard all my life. You should see the geeks here that I am surrounded by—Jews and Asians. After all-day classes and lectures they stay in the library till midnight and the whole weekend. I just can't do that. I go to my room exhausted; I don't even have time to see my dentist. You know, Mallory, I call you for a little sympathy, and you…you are so cold, just…I don't know…"

Pat had a stable of high-grade emotions, self-pity in the lead.

"Listen, I am sorry. In December we talked about your quitting and in January you were high on dissecting a male cadaver. I mean, you know, quit if you are so miserable." Mallory moved to hang up on her but heard her sobbing.

"I would have if it weren't for Dad; he spent all his savings to send us to college and now me to a medical school. Plus he's so proud that I got accepted to Yale without any connections; how could I do that to Dad?"

"Fuck him!" Mallory exploded and quickly restrained herself. She tried to banter: "Don't take me literally, my dear sister."

"Oh, is that what this is all about again? Why is it that you've become so convinced, actually, *obsessed* is the word, that Dad sexually abused me? In the past occasionally you had made some cracks about Dad and me, and I thought you were just jealous. But now it is getting out of hand. If you really think that, why did you wait until after Mom died?"

"Incidentally, Pat, you know that Clinton may be disbarred because he lied for having had sexual relations with 'that woman' and continued to insist that his answers were technically correct?"

"What are you saying, Mallory; that my denial of your accusation about me and Dad is only technically correct? I am, in fact, lying? And what is that 'disbarred'? Are you threatening me? Are you going to spread your paranoid nonsense to my school, and the medical board? What do you want, you crazy bitch?"

Patricia hung up the phone.

൜ഝഩ൙

# -XIII-

*I* *didn't exactly know what I really wanted from Pat—maybe the truth?*
*As to Pat's second question—"why did you wait until after Mom died?"—I*
*didn't want Father to take his anger out on Mom; I also didn't want to risk losing*
*his financial help before I graduated.*

*I was also afraid of my father; he was a scary and unpredictable man. He had*
*bragged about his fights in the military; how he put an officer into a coma, his*
*solitary confinements for barroom brawls. On Sunday afternoons he cleaned*
*and polished his guns—he had a collection of Smith & Wessons, Berettas, and*
*shotguns—in the living room, no less!*

*Once he chased one of Pat's dates out of the house with a gun—because the boy's*
*crotch was wet! Any boyfriend that Pat brought home had to be arm-wrestled or*
*interviewed until Father had found something to be ridiculed. Pat wasn't so*
*bothered by such outrageous behavior from him.*

*Meanwhile, I was free to do anything I wanted. I stayed out late on dates and*
*came home drunk, openly flirted with boys in front of him; I even took them to*
*my room—no questions were asked. Father was oblivious to me, and Mother had*
*become irrelevant—not that she hardly functioned as a parent in prior years. By*
*the time we were in high school, her mind was more or less gone—she was diag-*
*nosed as suffering from the early stages of alcoholic dementia.*

*My father's continuing indifference to me throughout my high school years*
*pushed me, I believe (or is that a rationalization?), into more and more drinking,*
*smoking pot, staying out all night with friends.*

*Many summer nights police brought me home for drinking on Compo Beach*
*and swimming with just underwear on (how is that different from wearing a*
*bikini?). I was only cited for disorderly conduct, but no serious consequences fol-*
*lowed, because Westport police were very friendly with Dad—a newly retired Air*
*Force officer, a many-generations' Westporter, a supporter of the Police Athletic*
*League, and a volunteer in the fire department—a tough guy with whom they*
*could talk guns and wars.*

*The fact was that I was smart enough to get good-enough grades without much*
*studying; writing sophisticated articles for the school's newspaper and being the*

twin sister of the most industrious student, I got away with all these. "Oh, that is Mallory"; the "wild colt" was the usual permissive reaction to my antics; that is, until one late evening in the bathtub, I swallowed a bunch of Tylenols and sliced my wrist with a kitchen knife.

I wanted to die; or at least, I didn't want to live. For me the world was insufferably dark—pitch dark; was it always that way? I don't know—it just hit me on that despair-filled night; I wanted to slash open the veins of my domestic self-pity; to drown drunken, coloring my longing for the same; to unlock the damning embrace of unvirtuous lies; and then, maybe to captivate my absolute innocence, again. Oh, this is too melodramatic—too studied! Maybe I didn't want to die; I simply wanted to kill someone.

Apparently Pat had found me fully clothed, sleeping in reddish water. After my stomach was pumped and my wrist was patched up at Norwalk Hospital, I was transferred to Silver Hill for psychiatric evaluation. I was told that when Dr. Richard Heshe questioned why I was trying to kill myself, I had replied that my father was sexually abusing my twin sister. But the following day, fully recovered, bright, and cheerful, I recanted everything I had said and dismissively attributed my story to my intoxicated state with alcohol and marijuana. "Oh, pot makes me paranoid." Dr. Heshe had had no reason to keep me in the hospital. The following day, I was back to school as if nothing had happened; well, worse, nothing happened.

⌘

# -XIV-

Today was the second Tuesday of the month. The time, five o'clock—the hour and the day of Jeanny's massage therapy. She was pacing in the library, already undressed—half-covered with an unbuttoned white Ralph Lauren cotton man's shirt.

"Where the hell is she? Not only did she cut sessions to once every other week, she doesn't even come on time," she angrily muttered.

"Maria! Did you call Mallory to confirm the appointment?"

"Yes, Madam, I did; I left a message."

Maria, the Brazilian housekeeper, was another person like Jeff, who was deadly scared of Jeanny; she wasn't sure whether she'd called Mallory or not. Fortunately, at that very moment the doorman announced that Mallory was coming up.

Jeanny's mood immediately changed.

"Okay, Maria, you can go now; don't let the kids come in here and interrupt my massage."

Maria scattered.

"Oh, hi, Mallory—my goodness, you look pretty. Mallory, how do you remain so thin? And your…your belly, gee; I guess you never had children—that helps. But I wasn't that flat even before I got pregnant. I keep putting on weight in the wrong places; no diet seems to help. You must one day tell me how you keep yourself so fit."

"Well, I am ready, anytime you are." Jeanny jumped on the table and lay facedown. Mallory quickly took off her jacket, threw it on a chair, rolled up her sleeves, and put her elbows on the lumbosacral junction of Jeanny's flat back.

"Ouch, ouch!"

Mallory took Jeanny's right arm with her left hand, rotated it ninety degrees, and pressed against her right shoulder.

"Oh God, Mallory! What a strong hand; are you left-handed?"

Mallory shook her head confirmatively and twisted her left leg thirty degrees outwardly, bent her knee, and kept pushing in.

"Wow! My dear! I said last time I sort of like pain. I meant psychic pain, but even then I am not a masochist, you know."

Mallory thought Jeanny was a lesbian—a femme—even though she was quite aggressive. She knew a few butches; they were mostly medium height, big-breasted, meaty from shoulder to hips without much indentation at the belly and chunky legs to follow.

"So, who gave you the first psychic pain, that girl at Duke?"

"Yeah, she had your looks, your aloofness; after we broke up she wouldn't even say hello to me. Meanwhile all the other girls avoided me; maybe they thought I was a lesbian. I wasn't. I liked boys too much. Oh, that hurts," Jeanny purred.

Now Mallory's fists were lodged between Jeanny's two shoulder blades. The door of the library opened a crack, and Jeffrey stuck his head in.

"I just wanted to say hi," he said with a sheepish voice.

"Hi…hi…fine; Jeffrey, you are interrupting our session!" Jeanny was furious.

Mallory caught Jeffrey's sneaky eyes for a second as he quickly closed the door.

"You know, the last few months he has been coming home early on Tuesdays; I bet it's just to run into you. If he ever calls you, you've got to let me know."

Mallory had noticed Jeffrey's clumsy attempts to talk to her in the few short encounters they'd had.

"Why would he call me?" Mallory replied with the most innocent voice she could muster.

"Oh, for the same reason that a married man may call an attractive woman."

"His own wife's therapist?" Mallory said, as if shocked.

The session was over. Jeanny stepped down from the table and put her shirt back on; she was trying to find her wallet in her Gucci bag.

"Did you ever see that movie? I cannot remember its name, where Woody Allen plays the husband of a therapist, Mia Farrow? In one of their hilarious scenes, he gets the telephone number of one of her patients from her chart and starts dating her. When Mia's character finally finds out and confronts him by saying something like you just said—"How could you date my patient?"—he responds, "Well, where else can I meet other women?"

Jeanny handed Mallory ten $20 bills.

"You see, Jeffrey is like that character. Last year he tried to seduce our weekend housekeeper, Paula; she was also from Brazil, but not like Maria; she was a young and good-looking sexy kitten; he gave her extra cash and little gifts here and there. Soon the girl began to have her hair done, got her nails polished, smelled like she was dipped in Chanel No. 5. So I ended up firing her—a double loss: competent help and a pleasant companion."

As Mallory was getting ready to leave, Jeffrey showed up in the hallway.

"I am really sorry; I heard you talking. I presumed you had finished Rolfing. May I ask, what exactly is Rolfing? I mean the theory behind that."

Jeanny noticed the same crooked smile on Jeffrey's face that he had when speaking with Paula—the mouth veers to the left, upper lip pulls up a little more than the lower lip, opening an ugly hole in the corner. Simultaneously the left eye squints—not a wink, but the same invitation to a conspiratorial relation.

Mallory took a teacherly serious posture: "Well, the practice of Rolfing is based on the theory that our musculoskeletal system is the depository of all emotions, especially negative ones—the earliest memory being in the body's deepest recesses. The best way of understanding Rolfing is to experience it once."

"Come on, Jeffrey, the woman has to leave," Jeanny interjected.

Jeanny could hardly contain herself; she quickly ushered Mallory to the door, patted her on the back, and whispered, "Bring some of your brownies next time."

Maria hollered, "Mr. Weisman! Mr. Max on the telephone." Max Hathaway was his financial and political advisor. Jeff was grateful for the distraction—he escaped Jeanny's wrath.

"Hi, Max, what's up?"

"Jeff, do you know Judge Judith Gishe?"

"Supreme Court Justice? Yeah. Why?"

"Well, she is presiding over Giuliani's case. If you get her to bar Judith Nathan from Gracie Mansion, that would break the camel's back. Rudy is teetering; one more humiliation and he'll pull out of the Senate race. The Republicans have no credible substitute candidate; if you run as an independent you'll beat Clinton; otherwise that scavenger will eat the meat while leaving the carcass unperturbed."

"Max, Max, Max, slow down. First of all, what is today? Tuesday. On Friday, Giuliani will announce his decision to quit the race, all right? He doesn't need any further push; it is done."

"You are kidding; how do you know?"

"Max, I do; slow down. I don't believe, and Hamilton agrees, that I can put together a campaign to run as an independent; nor can I beat Clinton's formidable machinery, so forget it. Listen, while I have you on the phone, why do you keep buying Halliburton and so much of it? Every energy company's shares are going up, while Halliburton's is going down."

"Jeff, listen, you stick to law and let me handle the money; you see, they are all rallying except the second-largest oil-service company; what does that tell you? They are buying back their own stocks. So they'll hold back the price of the stock until they run out of cash, then they will let loose. It is a safe game to play. Halliburton is in the construction and engineering business; only insiders would know what is cooking or whether anything is simmering. Furthermore, the international market is always behind the domestic one—two-thirds of Halliburton's revenue comes from overseas. Of course, shmucks like you buy stocks that are going up, and meanwhile the insider is getting ready to dump them and make a big killing. Do you understand now?"

"Sons of bitches! Do those insiders report these trades to the SEC?"

"Here you go again. Jeff, would you stop with this sheriff-of-the-town mentality? The directors and officers of Halliburton are as smart as you are; they'll never own more than 9.9 percent of the class A securities—that is the threshold for reporting; okay? Bye."

ᑎᗰᑎ

# -XV-

Ham was right, Mallory thought. Her writer's block might be related to her being afraid of what she is about to reveal: thoughts of killing her father.

*Six months ago following the interment of Mom in Willowbrook Cemetery, we all came home, and people were gathered around the breakfast spread, eating, chatting, and laughing. I went upstairs, opened Dad's "brass knuckles closet" in the master bedroom, and picked up one of his revolvers from his gun rack—a stainless steel Beretta—I pushed the cartridge in, with bullets for twelve rounds, disabled the safety mechanism, and put it in my bag.*

*I walked down to the living room. Dad was casually chatting with the minister and a few firemen. I patted the gun; it was cold and solid. I could finish this drama of my life right now, I thought, in just a matter of seconds: shoot him a few times and then put the gun in my mouth and pull the trigger.*

*Mrs. Grayson, in her seventies and our only longtime neighbor, hurried across the room to hug me; my hand was still clutching the gun. "Oh, sweetheart, I am so sorry. Your mother was so good to me." Then others came one by one, offering their condolences. My sister was still in one corner and crying. I hesitated—he'll be a victim after all that, instead of being prosecuted as a criminal? No! I quietly slipped out and walked all the way to the train station—jittery.*

# -XVI-

*T*he train—a Metro North commuter, half-empty at the Westport railroad station—got plenty crowded by the time it reached Greenwich. A sleek black guy in his thirties squeezed himself between an elderly man and me. He was wearing a light-blue double-breasted suit. A heavy gold chain, hanging down to his midsection, was attached to an equally ostentatious gold cross. As he sat, pulling back his pants and displaying bright yellow socks, he turned to me with the informality of an old acquaintance.

"The crowd of Saturday's matinee!"

I behaved as if I were too engrossed in my book to hear him.

"Soul to Soul, ha! Who wrote that?" The man reached over and turned the cover of the book. "Gary Zukov! A Russian?"

I pushed his hands and firmly said,"No! He is an American, and I would appreciate if you could just leave me alone."

"Okay, okay. Just one thing. I am a very well-known agent; let me give you my card if you need some work or want to taste some real soul food, soul to soul, you know." He smiled, pleased with his wittiness.

I took his card and put it in my bag just to get rid of him, while wondering whether he was a literary agent. I quickly disabused myself of that possibility; how desperate was I going to get? When the train stopped at 125th station, the man got up.

"This is where I get off. If you ever need lots of money or anything, I mean it...so you've got my number." He danced to the door, then to the platform while waving to me as if we were close friends.

After the train pulled out of the station I looked at his card:

Mr. Lord Washington, M.W.P.

C.E.O. and President

Universal Escort Service, Ltd.

I thought that M.W.P. might stand for Master Whore Provider!

# -XVII-

*T*he following Sunday, "gun-cleaning day," Dad called. First he was casually inquiring: "Mallory, one of my guns is missing. Did you see anyone going up to the bedroom, by chance? I have to report it to the police; it is a registered gun. Before I do that, you know...it is a crime to possess a gun without a license, especially a gun that is registered in someone else's name."

The more I stayed silent the testier he became. "Especially in New York; are you off your rocker? The illegal possession of a handgun? You go to jail for that, and let me tell you for a very long time."

Mallory decided to placate him.

"Come on, Dad, didn't you tell me the city is dangerous and that I should have something in the apartment?"

"Yeah, but I was talking about mace or pepper spray, not a semiautomatic revolver, idiot. And that gun is not an ordinary gun; it is a collector's item. Furthermore it is my gun; if you are determined to have one, buy your own."

"How about I buy this from you, Dad?"

"Do you have any idea how much that gun costs? Buy a small Smith & Wesson; it is easy to load, unload, and clean; and it is gentle on the trigger."

I realized that he was beginning to negotiate, so I decided to make an offer.

"How about if I gave you $100 for it?"

"No way; I am coming tomorrow to get it...are you listening?"

"How about $500?" I upped the price sharply.

"What? Where could you have that kind of money? I thought you were merely getting by since you graduated. That thing, 'Dolphing,' whatever it is called, pays off that well? My God! If so, why then don't you help out your sister? I mean, her tuition alone is just impossible."

I realized that I got him.

"You know, Pat is visiting me next month, so I'll give her $1,000; $500 for the gun and $500 toward her tuition. And I'll give $500 a month till she finishes medical school."

"Well, that is very generous, Mallory. You are really something. But listen: Don't leave the cartridge in; it is not made of stainless. Its ongoing contact with the gun will slowly degrade both; when you need it, it may not function. All right, sweetheart; be careful, though."

⟨᷍᷍᷍᷍⟩

# -XVIII-

That was the day Mallory had decided to return Max Hathaway's obscene call.

She picked up the phone a few times and put it back. She kept pacing in her room; the floor was making too many creaky noises. She lay down on her bed, looking at the crumbling ceiling—half of the plaster was gone and the other half was in different stages of decay. She badly wanted to smoke pot. She has been clean for over a year; she promised herself to remain totally lucid, but the urge to change her state of mind was overwhelming. "I need it, I need it," she kept saying to herself.

The moment she lighted one she regained her ease. Now she was seeing three-dimensional gray cloud sculptures floating toward the ceiling. She chuckled; nothing is what it seems to be.

Which one is worse? she contemplated—having sex with one man for life who would support "his dearest wife's hobby," usually reluctantly—or having sex with a few men, as needed, who would gladly pay you to support your creative endeavor? According to experts, passion in marriage ends in a few years anyway; women just put up with their husbands' needs if they cannot get it elsewhere. Plus "divorcing johns" is never a mess—an emotional and financial knock-down, drag-out event. The girl just has to say no. At worst, she may have to change her telephone number, and that's it. Mallory felt elated by her critical evaluation of a woman's dilemma; she dialed "Max's" cell.

"Yep!"

That is an abrupt way of answering the phone, Mallory thought.

"Yep to you, this is Mallory; you got my number from John Levine and left that porno message!"

"Oh, yes, of course; listen, I am here with a few people. May I call you in an hour or so?"

"Well, please do, yippidy do."

The few people whom Max was with in his office were Jeffrey Weisman, Professor Hamilton Thurman II, and Mr. John Levine. Having dispensed with the idea of running against Hillary Clinton for the Senate, they were discussing whether Jeff could play a role in Al Gore's presidential run.

"The attorney general, of course," said Max.

They all thought that was a possibility.

"I've got four seats for Gore's Tuesday talk at the historical society," Max announced. "Let's contribute generously to his 'prosperity' campaign."

"That is definitely an attractive slogan," added Hamilton. "After all, the country has been quite prosperous during the last eight years."

"I think we found the right mission," Mr. Levine added. "It is within the Democratic Party and an appropriate step for Jeff to be the attorney general."

They all huddled together conspiratorially.

⊙༡༡༢༠

# -XIX-

In the Rectangular Kingdom lived (among a few scattered old-monied families, whose wealth diminished daily) many adrenaline-soaked, tough multimillionaires; the type that ate nails for breakfast: real estate speculators, news media moguls, securities traders, investment bankers, Madison Avenue power brokers, private equities giants, and hedge fund managers. They were mostly white, self-made individuals who negated their backgrounds and distanced themselves from their "failed families" and from their socially marginalized "growing up" years. Some even altered or changed their names to smother the past and create their new identities.

Everyone there understood instinctively (or learned painfully fast) the mores of the Kingdom. While rigorously denying this about themselves, they were eager to accuse and gossip about others' ruthlessness, shameless social climbing, classless self-promotion, and disgracefully excessive lifestyles.

Max was one of those successful hedge fund managers who lived in a triplex on Fifth Avenue. At the age of forty-four, after a four-year stint at Goldman Sachs, he left—took a few talented brethren with him—and set up his own hedge fund firm. He was so successful that he was nicknamed "Quant"—Quantum—by his Wall Street competitors, a term reserved for extraordinary high rollers.

⟨ᴙᴛᴛᴜᴑ⟩

Before the car even came to a full stop, Max jumped out of his massive Mercedes-Benz sedan at the corner of 60th Street and Fifth Avenue. His driver, already accustomed to his boss's impatience, quickly hit the brakes and looked at him in the mirror, trying to anticipate the next order. Max shouted as he walked away: "George, you don't have to wait; just go home and turn the car phone off. I'll stroll a little in the park." The driver appreciatively bowed his head.

It was a warm, sunny April afternoon. The blooming Japanese cherry trees competed with the pink blouses of out-of-town high school girls spilling out of two enormous buses onto Fifth Avenue. Max launched himself into the middle of these laughing and giggling adolescents and stood there. The girls carried on as if he did not exist. How could they not notice him? Max wondered—a short, overweight, balding middle-aged man with heavy dark eyebrows—a bear in a perennial garden. A tall girl braised his right ear with her elbow as she combed her long blond hair. No apology, she kept going. Another girl lifted her skirt to rearrange her pantyhose. None of them looked at him—really looked. A few blue eyes quickly scanned and dismissed him. Max breathed deeply, expanding his nostrils: Oh, yes, that alien smell—young women's sweat.

Max was surprised that he remembered exactly where he first experienced that smell. It was thirty years ago. He was fourteen. The volleyball coach picked him along with five other short male players to scrimmage against the girls' team. After the match was over—the girls defeating the boys in consecutive games—the coach gathered them all into an adjacent room and outlined his critique of both teams on a blackboard. The girls and boys were flirting and arguing the finer points of the coach's evaluation. The informality of their insulting exchanges and the self-confidence of their banter intrigued and disturbed Max.

But there was something else that threw Max off balance: a sharp odor coming from the side of the room where the girls were clustered—it wasn't pleasant or unpleasant; it was alien. The proximity of six wet and smelly adolescent females was disorienting. Max thought he should say something but didn't know what? The only thing he really wanted to know was, "what is that smell?" To Max's disappointment, the coach never asked him again to play with the girls' team.

By now the pink blouses had entered Central Park, though Max's bitter memory lingered. He tried to cheer himself up; after all, he had a date at the Plaza Hotel with a beautiful young graduate of New York University. Still, his mood kept sinking. Whom was he kidding? She was a whore operating under the pretense of offering massage therapy.

He hesitated in front of room 703. He rang the bell and waited. No answer. He rang again and rapped on the door. He put his ear to the door. There was a woman's voice cursing! He sniffed that old alien smell; Max believed in the infallibility of smell memory. There was a beautiful girl behind the door—a girl he'd had no chance of dating in high school.

An old waspish couple passing in the hall gave him a disapproving look. Max wondered if he had the room number right. What if that couple called security? Why was this woman so angry? The door opened, and Max stumbled into the room.

"Hi, I'm Shechinah. You must be Max Quant...what a strange name; is it a nickname or your *nom des affaires*? I'm sorry for having kept you waiting, I was on the phone with my twin sister, I just couldn't..."

Max interrupted her: "No, no, I didn't wait for that long; is that your Hebrew name?"

"Oh, no; Shechinah is the receptive female goddess."

He was mesmerized by what he was seeing. For her, he would have waited hours; in fact, he had been waiting for her his whole life.

The goddess she was—a slender woman, with the narrowest waist he had ever seen, accentuating all her curvatures. Her hips seemed to sit atop two long stems; her full breasts, unsupported by a bra, spilled over the V-neck of her white blouse and eased upward into her long neck, which was dressed in her sandy-brown hair—her whole body breathed sex.

For a single instant she locked her green eyes on Max's stunned face; they were as cold as they were beautiful. How could a woman like her be a call girl?

"There are two of you?" Max barely believed that even one woman like her could exist.

"She doesn't work for masseuse services, if that is what you are asking. It is not a familial trait. In fact, she is a medical student at Yale. And what do you do, Mr. Quant?"

"Please call me Max; my real name is Max Hathaway (he stressed the *Hathaway*). I don't want to play a game."

"Hathaway, huh? Okay then, well, Max; my earthly name is Mallory. What sort of leaps do you take to justify calling yourself Quant?" It was easy for Mallory to control her conversation with her clients, for they were mostly preoccupied with sexual thoughts.

"No, no, no, that's what others call me, because I had some success in the hedge fund business, that's all. There are hundreds of hedge fund guys; they all make serious money."

Max knew how to underplay himself to emphasize the full impact of his importance.

"Are there different kinds of Quants? Like mini-quants, major-quants, or mega-quants?"

Mallory didn't know how to play a call girl. In fact, this was the first time she'd ever accepted an appointment in someone's hotel room. She usually went to her clients' apartments, where, if the client were a male, she ensured there would be more than one person at home.

Mallory knew her own profession well—not just the physical aspect of massage; she could also get her clients to talk for a full hour without really listening to them. Instead of the "hmm-hmm" or the encouraging type of noise that psychotherapists make, whenever there were silences—she knew enough about psychotherapy—Mallory would press her elbow into her client's joints or on nerve endings; after a quick "ouch," the person would begin to spill material.

She was a little scared to be in the hotel room with Max, no matter how rich or successful the guy might be—there were lots of creeps out there. She tried to calm down by reminding herself that after all he'd been referred to her by Mr. Levine.

Mallory never had sex with her clients. Nor had anyone dared ask for sex, actually. She occasionally deflated pleading erections with her hands, but everyone treated her cautiously, even those who received such therapeutic masturbation. Only Max behaved, from the first call, as if she were a whore, period; and she liked it, to her surprise. She liked the simplicity and straightforwardness of the request. Max stripped her down to her sexuality—the bare essence of male and female encounters. But she'd made it clear on the phone to Max that she'll not have intercourse. He, in return, reassured her that the only thing he wanted was "to give her a massage!" Mallory presumed that he also wished to be masturbated. That was a deal she could live with—a highly profitable one.

She knew that all her male clients wanted her to masturbate them. The wish was understood by both parties—unstated but expressed in a precise script: erections in clients, avoidance of genital areas by her, and maintenance of tension by mutual awareness of each other's intentions.

Max watched Mallory crossing her legs in slow motion; her skirt glided up, showing her luscious inner thighs—whitest pink, no wrinkles, never ending.

Max wasn't sure whether she wanted to know where he stood in the Wall Street hierarchy—was he the silverback gorilla, or just another ape? And why was he not getting sexually excited? Was it because he feared all women for hire—the con artists of entrapment—or specifically her, for she looked like the ultimate embodiment of prurient danger?

No, neither, he concluded. After so many years and so many women, he was still intimidated by beautiful women.

He slid his hungry eyes toward the outer edges of her white panties. Well, he paid for it. Still, he didn't want to look too hungry and deprived; after all, he was…he couldn't finish his thought. He was what, exactly? He had a good education but he had no fine breeding. But he had money and lots of it. And this, this young, beautiful creature, with obvious provenance, wanted it. So let the transaction take place; enough with self-damning rumination.

"There are lots of mini-quants whose minis were further cut down on the eighth day of their existence, and there are those…" Max trailed off, quickly realizing that it wasn't safe to brag about his "endowment," for sooner or later there would be a moment of truth. Max wasn't circumcised, but he wasn't that well endowed either, so he reverted to his anti-Semitic posture.

"I heard that a mother would grind and cook the foreskin of the baby's penis and eat it; can you believe that?" He paused for effect: "Oy, gevalt" drained out of his lips. "Whatever that means!" Max hissed, realizing that he'd almost railroaded himself into failure of the ethnic litmus test.

Max's anti-Semitism was no more real than his being for or against anything; it wasn't real or unreal—it was suitable for the occasion. He was in the habit of making anti-Semitic comments or telling Jewish jokes in the company of non-Jews; he was always surprised that only rarely would those people join him in his Jew-bashing.

"Oh. Gross!" Mallory was intrigued with the story.

Max got up from the sofa and walked over to the window overlooking the General Motors building across the avenue. Mallory watched his profile, which resembled that of Jeanny's husband, Jeffrey; Max was a coarser, shorter, and chubbier version of him—the same bulging forehead and sharp lines around the squinting dark eyes, the short distance between the tip of his elongated nose and his meaty wet lips. Both men were tense, their conversational style mildly, and unnecessarily, contentious. Both had that peculiar smile at the end of each of their phrases that said "I am powerful, therefore I am entitled."

Mallory had never met someone with such a stench of success. He was dressed like an old man: pinstriped dark-blue, double-breasted suit; high-rising pants held up by thick, bright, yellow, ornate suspenders woven from woolen box cloth; slanted gold clip holding a silk tie at loose knots on a cutaway collar.

He had this high-alert face with wide-open pupils, zeroing in on her with a restless and distrustful look. He seemed to be a simple man with uninteresting complexities who comfortably spewed banalities as if they were highly profound revelations.

"I could have bought that goddamn building for a song in the nineties," Max said, burping. "That is one of my regrets in life; I wanted to bypass the regular avenues and take it even for less. You see, greed is not good in spite of Gordon Gekko's famous declaration. Do you go to movies?"

"Not often."

"You've got to see this movie, *Wall Street*. People think I look like Michael Douglas." Max threw a short glance at Mallory, to see if her impression of him changed; she was looking out.

Mallory managed to suppress a snigger.

"I've seen other movies of Michael Douglas; yes, you do look a bit like him from the front, but I think Paul Newman is more handsome. I used to see him occasionally at the Westport Pizzeria on Main Street."

Mallory immediately regretted making such a comparison, but she couldn't suppress her revolt for this man's naked narcissism. But this wasn't a social conversation, and she was violating the number-one principal of massage therapy: flatter the man, no matter how absurd it might sound.

"Well, I agree with you on that. Mike's father, Kirk Douglas, in his heyday was even handsomer and more talented than both of them."

Max seemed untroubled by Mallory's comment, and if anything, he was indulging in the father-son difference. He kept talking, giving all sorts of examples of the machismo of Kirk Douglas. He came back to the couch and sat close, very close to Mallory; he put his right hand on her left knee, sliding her skirt further up, and he kept it there.

"Have you seen *The Greatest Show on Earth*?"

She hadn't. Mallory thought this deal wasn't going that well. Was he older than he looked? Why was he talking about movies from whenever? Was she failing in her first attempt to be a call girl? Maybe she wasn't sexually exciting? Should she revert to her comfort zone and give him a massage? Maybe he was just a voyeur.

"Listen," she said. "You want to take your jacket off and relax a little? I'll get you a drink. There is beer, wine, and vodka in the refrigerator. What's your favorite? Oh, I meant, what is Michael Douglas's favorite drink?"

Mallory again regretted this little game; this time, she thought, she was insulting him.

Again, Max seemed unfazed. "I don't drink. You know, you are really funny. I don't know what he likes to drink, but I can guess what he likes in women."

"Well, can I…?" she bit her sentence off with the fear of making another mistake.

"Come on, out with it," Max said with a false scowl and began slinking around the room.

Mallory could only stare at him with a strenuous perplexity.

"I'll tell you what you can do. Here is your three G's." He pulled a roll of hundreds from his back pocket and put it on the coffee table. "Now, for the next two hours or whatever time is left, I will undress; you do the same, and I'll give you the massage of your life. That is it."

In a few moments, he was completely nude. Mallory began to disrobe slowly and deliberately—partly to waste as much time as possible, thus shortening the actual sexual encounter and partly to excite Max. She didn't want to fail.

Eventually Mallory took off all her clothes and stood right in front of him. He had a devouring look in his eyes.

"What is that red string bracelet?" Max tugged on it.

"It is a tie to the recycling of departed souls, ensuring one's immortality."

Max sneered: "And how do you do that?"

"By paying God in the form of contributions; every Friday night I stop by the Kabbalah Center for a few minutes, donate my money—that is it."

Max was laughing. "You've got to be kidding; and who is that person, the conduit to God? Don't tell me it's those Kabbalists from Queens, who hawk their spirituality for dummies? Unbelievable! Leave it to Jews. I know that orthodox couple: Philip Berg, whose real name is Shraga Grunberger, is an insurance salesman, and his wife used to be his secretary! You believe in that kind of shit? I thought you are a smart woman."

"You know, lots of smart women believe in Kabbalah: Demi Moore, Donna Karan, Roseanne Barr, Madonna."

"I think they are all schmucks; I wouldn't mind pulling Madonna's strings, though." He chuckled, "So you are a Kabbalist?"

"Actually I am a Febionitic."

"What?"

"You've heard of Ebionitic?"

"No."

"Well, Ebionitic is a Jew who follows Jesus and who believes in the Sermon on the Mount and decides to live in poverty. Febionitic is the reverse: a Christian who believes in Moses and would like to live in luxury, eventually."

Max was getting unnerved—he didn't know why.

"There we have something in common. I didn't realize all these years I have been living the respectful life of Febiloisi..."

"Febionitic," Mallory corrected.

Mallory lay down next to Max, who was shivering but tumescent.

"Are you cold?" she pulled the cover over them.

As soon as Max inserted his fingers, he ejaculated all over her and the bed; then he rolled over and fell asleep.

Mallory listened to his loud, truculent snoring for a few minutes. "Some massage!" She muttered. Was what just happened sex? Or was it a metaphor for something else—metafornication?

Mallory wiped his discharge from her thighs and abdomen with the white, fluffy Plaza Hotel towels. She mulled the notion of taking a shower, but decided to get out of the place before he woke up. She was disappointed and confused. The whole thing was neither as exciting nor as scary as she thought it might be. It was just boring. Three thousand dollars, for what? For a full-hour massage of sagging arms and legs, digging her fingers into bulging abdomens, cracking her knuckles in hairy chests, she got only $200. That was the confusing part. People weren't paying for her time. It was very specific; for body/mind relaxation they would pay less than 10 percent of what they would pay for sexual excitement.

She quickly got dressed, took the roll, and left. From the elevator to the lobby and from the lobby to the door other men were staring at her; it seemed they were waiting for an opening to initiate conversation.

⊙ⅢⅢ◎

Max woke up shortly after she left. He had this habit of falling asleep as soon as he came. He would sleep only for half an hour or so, but it was always a deep sleep with vivid dreams. This time, he dreamt of being in an operating room where doctors and nurses were removing his prostate, but from his stomach. One of the doctors was Rudy Giuliani, who kept saying, "It is cancer, it is cancer." Max wondered why they were not putting him out. He dismissed the dream as related to Giuliani's recent announcement that he had been diagnosed with prostate cancer; nevertheless, he decided to visit a urologist, Dr. Scherr, soon.

Max turned around. Mallory was gone, but he didn't mind that; in fact he liked it.

He thought about his wife, Norma. She always wants to cuddle and talk afterward. She complains about his insensitivity to her needs, that he uses her simply to discharge himself on and that it isn't much different from his using a toilet to pee in—not even *a toilet*, she says, because he never even tried to hide his dalliances.

⊙ⅢⅢ◎

After she left the hotel, Mallory crossed over to 60th Street, entered Central Park, and sat on one end of the long benches. She crossed her legs under her and took a long breath—the park had its own distinct aroma, she thought, and quickly dismissed the thought; she was trying to simply experience the sensations, not to think of them.

At the other end of the bench, a disheveled old Asian woman surrounded by pigeons was holding grains of corn in her upturned palms. The old woman smiled at Mallory; she had a few scattered teeth. White, brown, whitish-brown pigeons were all around her, taking little flights, turning around and landing very close to her, even walking at her feet. Mallory couldn't focus on her inner decipherings. She couldn't help but wonder why the woman wasn't throwing any corn at the pigeons, which were in a state of frustrated frenzy. She must be one of the schizophrenics that Manhattan State Hospital dumps on the streets under the humanistic pretenses of patient's rights and deinstitutionalization.

Mallory returned from her refuge of silence: "How about giving them some corn?" she ventured out.

"Do you know how to feed pigeons?" The old woman smiled again, still holding both of her palms up.

"What is there to know? Just throw the damn corn." Mallory hated withholding people.

"No, no. It is not that simple. You see, it took me three months in a Japanese temple to learn it. If you go after them with grains in your hand, they'll run away; but if you sit still, they'll come and eat in your hand."

Mallory was impressed; this crazy-looking woman was teaching her a life lesson.

"People are like pigeons. Once I was at your age and…" she couldn't continue. The noise of a passing bunch of young girls in pink and white uniforms overwhelmed her voice; they were in a joyful and playful mood, talking, yelling, tripping each other, and laughing. Mallory recognized their uniform and cringed. One of the girls made eye contact—a dull pain lodged in Mallory's throat—while two bigger girls pushed each other onto the bench; they fell on the old woman, spilling her corn on the ground. The pigeons scattered.

꧁꧂

# -XX-

*I believe I represent the commercial individuality of this decade, if not the coming century, the way that Willy Loman represented the postwar man—he only wanted to be liked and loved. I don't care about either; I just want to be paid and left alone.*

# -XXI-

I am the younger of nonidentical twins; my sister Patricia is six hours older. We were born in Westport, Connecticut. Our father, Matt, was an officer in the Air Force; our mother, Vanessa, a stay-at-home mother. They were a handsome couple: He was a blond, 6'1", with broad shoulders and a perfectly square jaw exuding confidence and charm; she was a 5'6" brunette, once a homecoming queen, but looked aged and shriveled and confused. As parents, during our growing up years, they both were absent—he was always away on some assignment, she was often drunk. Our maternal grandmother, Nana, whose colonial house we lived in, took care of all of us—sort of.

As a child I wasn't growing at the same rate as Pat. Even though I was two pounds lighter at birth, doctors reassured my parents that I would eventually catch up with my sister. Nana's feeding me extra ice cream, eggs, milk, vitamins, and a few sips of my mother's Budweiser made no difference. Pat always looked a few years older, smarter, funnier, and happier than me. Not only our parents, but teachers and neighbors all alike were drawn to Patricia; it seemed as if they tolerated me, occasionally throwing a few crumbs of praise my way: "but Mallory is polite and nice." I wanted to be neither.

When we were eleven years old, Nana died, and Dad had to take us with him to his new assignment: Incirlik Air Force Base in Adana—in southeast Turkey, bordering Iraq. We lived in a highly protected military housing complex, without much contact with the natives; all our needs—schools, shops, movie theater, playground, clubs—were contained in this hot, desertlike land wherein even asphalt melted in the summer. We mostly remained indoors. The noise of cheap air conditioners in our little cardboard houses competed constantly with the rumbling sounds of cargo airplanes or the roar of F16s landing or taking off.

In spite of all that, at first, I was happier. Dad was home almost every day, and Mom stopped drinking. But that didn't last. She began to drink again, and this time not just beer; she developed a taste for the strong, anise-smelling Turkish drink raki. Consequently, she spent most of her time in bed or on the phone with drinking and card-playing friends—wives of the officers at the base. Meanwhile,

Dad began to come home very late, or not at all. Frequently, I would awaken in the middle of the night to a commotion; Dad would be yelling at Mom and throwing things around. From my own little room behind the kitchen, I would watch them and shiver. I would hear Pat, who slept in the living room on a pull-out sofa in the middle of our parent's battleground, begging him to stop. Then Mother's heartrending cries would follow.

In Turkey, Pat grew even faster; she was almost a foot taller than I was. She looked like my much-older sister and behaved like one. She got up early in the morning, prepared breakfast, and forced me to eat—"Do you want to grow up or not?" she would scold me. Mom never saw us off to school—she was in bed, nursing withdrawal headaches from the night's heavy drinking. At night Patricia would heat TV dinners for us, though again I would hardly touch the food. At night she would help bathe our drunken mother and put her to bed. Then she would come to my room to chat. Pat would share a few thoughts with me about growing up; we'd measure her breast size, count her pubic hairs, and giggle. That was my favorite time of the day.

After Pat had tucked me in, I would stay awake for hours; around one o'clock or so, I would fall asleep for a few hours. At four o'clock every morning I would wake up with my heart violently beating against my chest. I wasn't having a nightmare, for I never dreamt. My teachers had noted, "She nods off in class; self-comparison with her sister might be depressing." They recommended that "the twins be split"; and I be sent to a boarding school.

The military doctors consulted with the specialists in Adana Hospital; I was tested and retested. After an exhaustive investigation, doctors threw up their hands, gave the diagnosis of "idiopathic growth inhibition," and called it a day—a medical day.

A local Turkish doctor, Dr. Oz, from the village of Yavuzlar, which bordered the base, and whom Mom visited often—I thought she was having an affair with him—injected me with pituitary extract from sheep (at least that is what he said it was) and gave me buds of homegrown hashish to eat, one or two every night before bedtime.

Dr. Oz also believed that piercing the ears of young girls awakened their sexuality, therefore their growth. The verity of his convictions aside, he wasn't that good at piercing ears—he had to make two holes in my left lobe to match the one on the right. Mom had full confidence in this young doctor who hardly spoke any English and couldn't explain the rationale for all his peculiar remedies. The military doctors at the base considered him a dangerous quack.

Shortly after Dr. Oz's intervention, certain changes began occurring in me. I fell asleep as soon as I chewed the second poppy and had to be yanked out of bed by Pat for breakfast. I also developed a zest for spicy Turkish food: lahmacun, a pizza of ground lamb, and Adana kebab, skewered pieces of lamb, and luscious desserts, helva, candy made of honey and sesame seed paste, and baklava, a delicate pastry made with layers of phyllo dough, nuts, and butter and sweetened with honey.

*There was an informal, but highly organized, food delivery system to the base from Yavuzlar. Teenage Turkish boys took a special pleasure in my interest in local food and were happy to deliver anything I wanted, any time of day and night. Other Americans were mostly interested in buying charcoal for their barbecues.*

*More significantly, I began to dream. In fact, I felt as if I were dreaming all night, every night. First for a few months, my dreams were all about Westport, my old hometown, mostly scenery—pines and snow. I dreamt my father was coming home after being long gone, patting me on the head, and then picking Pat up and carrying her to another room, closing the door behind them. I dreamt often of my school, Coleytown Elementary: Each time the school bus would forget to pick me up, I would wait in the cold, all alone. Mr. Lindeman, one of the teachers who liked me—if not the only one—would give me a ride home. Now, this last bit—the school bus and Mr. Lindeman—I couldn't remember if it was a dream or a memory. But all the same, every morning I would wake up a little groggy, nevertheless always in a good mood.*

*In our last year in Turkey, my dreams had become stranger. I would dream that Dad and Pat were naked in bed together in the living room; he would be moaning while caressing her head, which moved up and down on his lap. I was upset that I wasn't upset for having such awful dreams, and if anything, I was excited. I began to touch myself—Wow! That really felt good. In the past I tried to imitate Pat's playing with herself, but I got quickly sore and lost interest. I didn't understand why she was doing that all the time. If that is how one grows up, I had thought, I'll never. But now it was totally different. I thought that I could really get addicted to this strange feeling in no time. In the mornings I would forget all about these dreams; I wouldn't even mention them to Pat. But these dreams kept coming back, almost every night, and were beginning to upset me.*

*Meanwhile, more dramatic changes were occurring in me. Within the last eight months I shot up three inches in height, put on fifteen pounds, and began to have regular and abundant periods; my breasts swelled—this "shy, reticent, boyish girl turned unabashedly sexual," was the word. I was flirting with any man whom I had any contact with: servicemen, officers, teachers, delivery boys, and they all reciprocated; only Dad remained indifferent to me.*

*Meanwhile, Pat was unhappy with my fast growth and my competition at the base. But worse, in contrast to my developing into a full-figured young woman, it seemed she stopped growing. For the period of my gains, Pat remained at the same height and began to lose weight.*

*Meanwhile, my dreams continued. Now the characters in the dream—I guess my father and Pat—were in some struggle: She was, at best, reluctant, and at worst, fiercely battling with Dad, who in turn was cajoling, bribing, or threatening her. I could no longer play with myself. I decided to stop my dreams. But how would I wake myself up from a dream? I asked my half-dazed mother, who replied tersely: "Don't."*

CＴＴＬＳ

# -XXII-

Since John Levine's wife had died about a year ago from ovarian cancer, Junetta lived in a small apartment in the maid's quarters and ran his household with the help of a cook and two half-time day workers. John and Carol Levine had lived on one floor of the same Fifth Avenue building all through their fifty-two-year marriage. They never had children—she had bilateral ovarian atrophy. Carol didn't trust the idea of adopting children. She strongly believed that most of them had genetic problems: "Who on earth would give their children away—except alcoholics, drug addicts, truants, and unsavory characters? Even the best adopted children will turn on you when they reach puberty; they will reject you as their parent if you make some demands, accuse you for having bought them from their nice but poor parents," she always lectured whenever the subject came about.

In her later years Carol used to say, "Now I am glad that I don't have children—all those problems. Just John is enough to take care of."

Throughout their married life, Carol took really good care of John; when she died, John was inconsolable—he never thought he could survive without her. All the statistics were in favor of her living another ten or fifteen years after his death. John might have been in the habit of making innuendos about his prowess and telling off-color jokes, but in reality he strayed only once from Carol; he was physically and mentally completely loyal to her.

John—a gracious gentleman—was always in a good mood, even during Carol's last two years; he never thought she would die—she would be just sick, and that was okay, as long as she was alive.

When she died, a number of women in their "postmenopausal years" came to his rescue. In fact, during the shiva calls, two of Carol's friends confessed their lifelong love for him; others brought his favorite foods from the most expensive restaurants that do not customarily allow takeout—even his well-known prostate cancer didn't discourage his suitors. John had no interest in these women or in their foods; he just wanted to stare at the five volumes of albums that Carol put together about their years together and cry. Junetta tried to appease him, "Mrs. is in heaven...she was a good woman, in heaven now, waiting for you."

For John, who didn't believe in heaven, life without Carol was a hell. What waited for him was eternal grief. Only Mallory brought him some joy.

꧁꧂

# -XXIII-

"Well, hello, Mallory! Glad to see you." He put down the *Wall Street Journal* and took off his glasses quickly.

Today he was wearing a brand-new outfit he'd just bought from Paul Stuart—tight-fitting, light-camel corduroy pants, a matching-color cashmere sweater over a pink sport shirt, and a pair of dark brown moccasins. He was experiencing a strange stir within himself, a vaguely clawing sentiment he barely remembered—not all that pleasant—a mixture of inner ache and disquieting aliveness.

"Are you still single?" he asked with an exuberant smile. "I wish I were twenty years younger; I would have married you instantly. I don't know whether you would have or not. Ha, ha, ha...you know the story of that Jewish fellow, a sort of loser, announces to his mother, who has been nagging him to get married—'Mom, I decided to marry Sophia Loren'— 'Wow, *mazel tov*, sweetheart,' she replies. 'Who is she? Is she Jewish? Her mother must be kvelning.'

"'No, no, Mom, never mind her mother; even she doesn't know it yet.'" Ha, ha, ha. John again was laughing so hard that he almost choked coughing. When Junetta ran to see what the commotion was, he shooed her away.

"Mr. Levine, you are not even undressed; don't you want a massage?"

"Sweet Mallory, all in good time." He tried to get up. "I shouldn't sit on this couch; it is too soft and too deep."

Mallory extended her hand; John happily grabbed her wrists and pulled himself up. "I'll see you in the library in five minutes." This was a change of venue. The table for his massage was usually set up in the living room.

Mallory walked into the library—an enormous hall, even for a full-floor apartment. The carved-cherry wood-paneled walls were interrupted by glassed-in bookcases; two ornate lamps sat on a long, bulky oak table surrounded by dark burgundy leather chairs. The polished white and red floor tiles reflected two oversize chandeliers and recessed incandescent lights. The ceiling simulated the daytime sky with a few floating, light clouds.

The bookcases were filled to the brim with volumes of books: the complete works of Thackeray and James Whitcomb Riley, Charles Dickens, Leo Tolstoy, Nietzsche, Stevenson, *The Letters of Emily Dickinson*, three large books of Leonardo da Vinci, *The Plays of Eugene O'Neill*, Chambers's *Encyclopedia*, *The Dialogues of Plato*, *History of England in XVIII Century*, *History of Herodotus*, Gibbon's *Rome*. Mallory had to stop reading, feeling a little dizzy.

Mr. Levine must have been observing Mallory from the door. "Well?"

"This is like a mini Rose Reading Room of the New York Public Library, Mr. Levine." She walked up to him.

"Funny you should say that. I actually tried to replicate it. Fred Rose was a friend of mine. We shared the hobby of origami; give me a dollar."

Mallory dipped her hand into her bag.

"Any paper money will do"

Mallory pulled up a $20 bill. Mr. Levine turned aside as if to hide but didn't; his hands shaking, he folded and unfolded the bill and finally offered her a rose.

"My, my, that is impressive. Thank you."

Mallory carefully placed the rose on her bag.

Mr. Levine, smiling, shuffled in; he slowly stepped onto the wooden ladder and fully clothed, placed himself facedown on the massage table.

"You have an impressive collection of rare books."

"Ha! I thought you might feel more at home in the library than in the living room and may decide to come more frequently. Ohh, ohh...the library was Carol's idea. She took down the walls between several rooms for which we had no use; not that we had any use for such a library either—we never sat and read here. I usually read in bed until I fall asleep, usually about ten to fifteen pages of light stuff; you know, the kind of books you pick up at airports."

Mallory sniffed a smell, similar to Mitchell's men's department in Westport, where she worked one summer.

She kept looking at the far end of the library, where a sliding ladder made from burnished cherrywood was stationed. She imagined getting on and sliding back and forth the length of the library, but furniture was in the way, so it must never have been moved from where it was. "Lately, though, when I pick up a book and try to read where I left off on the previous night, I cannot follow—even though I make a little note on the last line; so I end up reading the same ten pages every night again and again. If you ask me what I read last night, I swear I cannot tell. You think I am developing Alzheimer's? I don't remember people's names; even the names of friends of forty, fifty years. I don't even try anymore. So I have some generic salutations: 'Hi, old boy!', 'How is my dear friend?', 'You guys know each other?' I say if I introduce two people, hoping that one will say, 'Hi, I'm Shalom Shlomo,' and the other, of course, will have to tell his name.

"The only thing I don't forget is jokes, especially the ones that you could have a hearty laugh with. Speaking of...can you tell the difference, Mallory, between female pigeons and male ones?" Mr. Levine asked with his typical mischievous smile.

"By their appearance?" Mallory played along.

"No, actually you cannot tell which one are females by looking." Mr. Levine managed to deliver the punch line in the midst of convulsive laughter: "It is by their willingness to put up with sex. Ha, ha, ha."

For Mr. Levine, to make everything in life a joke was a sort of dialectical necessity. In reality, all wasn't breezy and good cheer. He could not remain engaged in any serious discussion without feeling that he might be boring people with his rustic common sense.

Mr. Levine knew that he was not as street smart as Max, neither as sharp as Jeff, nor as witty as Hamilton. Compared to the women, John was less masculine than Ann; Jeanny was more refined than he, and Norma was more innocent. As for Mallory, however, she was an angel; and Carol, the only woman he thought he knew in his life, turned out to be the most obscure. Unfortunately, what he discovered in her diary had stained his feelings for her final years, which meant that now he inevitably reduced his life to comedic acting.

What he thought would be role-playing in transit eventually became a permanent way of being with others—as if the last few years had not been real. Wherever he was, whomever he was with, he was on stage continuously, improvising a funny role that would fit the social landscape of the moment. But at the end of each performance, no matter how brilliant and well received it was, he would become anxious and unhappy; he concluded that the unrealness was the cause of his depression. But no matter how hard he tried, he could no longer be himself.

⚭

# -XXIV-

$S$ome men fall in love with me—I know the symptoms—obsessive phone calls, paranoid jealousies, totally wrong gifts, and premature ejaculation. Others claim that they love me—I know the symptoms of that too—highly structured relations, demand performance, excessive generosities. Beware of all love-bearing men, I say. They are all self-devoted. When they say "I love you," they really mean "I want to possess you."

# -XXV-

Tonight Mallory's neighbors, Peter and Dave, were celebrating their seventh anniversary and she was the only guest, with a date or "whatever" if she wanted. Mallory decided to ask Ham, who reluctantly accepted the invitation with a condition that they would not talk about her novel. Mallory was curious as to how Ham would interact with this gay couple.

She bought an organic potted orchid and hurried home. It was a hot and humid July evening. Ham was sitting on the steps all dressed up in a beige cotton suit, white button-down shirt, and white Converse sneakers all soaked in sweat—he was holding two small bouquets of daffodils. "One is for them, the other is for you," Ham said, and even gave her a salty kiss on the cheek.

Mallory was pleasantly surprised with all that, but mostly with his being on time. Mallory put her orchid down carefully, lifted her head up, and cocked it to one side, with a grand gesture of her arms.

Ham felt in imminent danger of soupy poetry.

She began to recite:

For a breeze of morning moves,
And the planet of Love is on high,
Beginning to faint in the light that she loves
On a bed of daffodil sky…

"Wow. Tennyson, right?"

Ham did a double take; had he been underestimating this girl? he wondered.

"In my teens I wrote poems about flowers," said Ham, smiling. "My parents mockingly called them 'garden poems.' When I told them every major poet wrote about gardens, such as Milton, Virgil, Ovid, Homer, Chaucer, Blake, Keats, Stevens, Frost, Graves, Shakespeare, Wilde, Emerson, Thomas Hardy…they accused me of showing off."

Mallory also thought he was and couldn't resist a little of her own: "Han-Shan, Oshima Ryōta, Hafiz, Rumi, Ts'Au P'I."

"Who?"

"The author of *Lotus Lake*; you've never heard of him?"

"Not just him, the rest of the names you mentioned, except Rumi."

Ham was totally thrown off; he kept talking.

"You know collections of poems called flower-garland anthologies? I think it was Marianne Moore who said all genuine poems reveal imaginary gardens with real frogs in them. In Rumi's work the female body is represented as a cloistered garden. Okay, I better shut up."

"What kind of poems are you writing now, Ham? Or would such a question be considered poetically meaningless?"

"No, but any attempt to define what I write annuls it; therefore, I am reduced to a provisional mode of writing—I keep searching for the auditive appearances of my inner tumult."

Mallory said, "I see"; she didn't at all.

Ham himself was aware of his own sputtering nonsense—the worst kind of pairing dialogue.

He quickly changed the subject.

"This is some deserted neighborhood; there are no lights, no shops open, no restaurants or bars, no people! Aren't you afraid of coming home at night alone?"

Mallory recognized the unease in Ham's face; no matter how hip he thinks he is, he is still the son of a bourgeois academic couple, she thought. "No, this is a very safe place. There hasn't been a robbery or anything like that since I moved after my junior year; well, maybe one, just before I found the place. Actually it happened to the girl who lived here before; she had been working for an escort service. According to Peter and Dave, she regularly entertained her clients here; one night her beau—a friend of the landlord—beat her up very badly for some reason. The following day she disappeared."

The story was hardly comforting.

Ham followed Mallory up to her apartment—he saw a totally bare room. The walls were naked, except where spiderwebs formed a permanent gallery; no bookshelves, no prints or any other kind of art objects. There was a mattress on the floor, bed covers strewn around, one cheap wooden chair, a desk, and a wide-open, almost empty closet—a few dresses and coats and a few pairs of shoes. A long extension cord plugged into a socket at one end of the room, passed under the mattress, and climbed onto the desk, connecting to the computer. Wide, irregularly cut pieces of duct tape were holding the cord—and dust balls—to its crawling path; the place could not have been uglier and more impersonal.

If the brand-new Dell computer weren't flashing scenes from some foreign country, he would have thought the occupant had abandoned the place in a hurry.

"Aren't you bothered with all these spiders?" he asked placidly. "Do you want my lady Vakfiye to come here and give it a top-down cleanup? She does keep my room spotless, in spite of my sloppiness."

"Oh, no, I do clean the place; it is just the spiders and their webs that I leave alone; you see, Ham, well, you understand, of course, you are a poet."

"No, not really. I don't. Are you cultivating, or rather, raising spiders?"

"I knew you'd get it; I am not destroying them or their habitat. That alone helps them to preserve the sacred quietness. I fear the impermanency of their silent movements; spiders secure the transformative power of existence without being present."

"Oh!" Ham managed to say; he was often accused of being bizarre in his thinking, but this, this assignment of transformative existence to a creature, was beyond even his comprehension. She was like another version of his father. Was she afflicted with some sort of spiritual illness?

"Do you feed them too?"

"I just keep my windows ajar—sometimes my door too—even in winter; so they catch flies. Ham, you look...I don't know, you look like you've never heard of Jainism. You are a poet; you must have."

"No. What is that?"

"It is an ancient sect devoted to austerity and gentleness toward all creatures."

Ham had to show her the incongruency of her shrine: "Aren't flies deserving of the same compassion?"

"Yes, if they were less noisy. Please sit down." Mallory pointed to the chair, while picking up the covers from the floor.

"I don't have a vase, but this will do." She put the flowers in her coffee mug and placed it on the windowsill.

Ham didn't want to pursue the hole in her Jainism; he looked around. There were a few *Week in Review* sections of the *New York Times* and only two books sitting at her desk: *The Zohar* and *The Power of Kabbalah* by Yehuda Berg. Ham picked up Berg's book: "Endorsed by Madonna?" Mallory sensed the drift in his voice.

"*The Zohar* names no author! Well, it is urtext, like the Bible; the original one is attributed to Moses de León of the thirteenth century. Some others claim that it goes back to the second century—to a sage named Simeon Ben Yohai."

Mallory never ceased to surprise Ham—here was a well-educated woman with a literary mind, taken with some theological kitsch.

"What interested you about Kabbalah?"

"Oh, its concept of God; God is evoked as a receptive female presence."

Ham was not unfamiliar with the desperate attempt to escape the feeling of powerlessness.

"This bracelet is directly connected to Rachel's tomb," she said.

Ham was thumbing through *The Power of Kabbalah*: a chapter on the DNA of God! Hm-m-m…"Where do you keep your other books?"

"Nowhere. I gave all my books away and I no longer buy new ones. Books clutter my mind and even worse, they demoralize me: So many writers! Do you know that this year 275,000 books were published! So what if I publish a book? There are another 275,000 people like me, this year alone. How significant is that? Do you think there are 275,000 readers? I mean real readers, not book buyers or perusers; actual readers of a book from cover to cover, never mind the contemplators of it?"

Ham was wondering whether Mallory was also a call girl like the previous tenant, in addition to being a dope dealer. What would her gay friends think of him? A john or her pimp? On the other hand, why would a call girl live in such a dump?

"I wouldn't mind being one of the 275,000," he said. "What are these scenes on the screen?"

"Oh, they are from Turkey; aren't they beautiful? Now this one, not this," she struggled a little with her computer, "just a second, yeah, this one is a small fishing village on the Mediterranean coast less than one hour away from where we lived—white sands, half-mile deep, and long empty beaches. Our Turkish driver used to take us there for picnicking and swimming. The whole village would come to watch us, even women, clothed from head to toes in black robes, on those awfully hot days mind you, just to stare."

Mallory realized that Ham was staring at her, puzzled.

"Okay, let's go over; you'll really like them."

⚭

Peter and Dave's apartment was in total contrast to Mallory's. It was three times larger and clearly the showpiece of an interior designer. A small marble foyer opened to a large living room, and the dark oak floor was partially covered by an antique Persian rug. The shiny black color of the walls was hardly visible through the closely hung male erotic posters and paintings. A stainless steel coffee table was flanked by a soft red leather sofa, while at the other end of the room, a stainless steel dining table and six stainless chairs covered with white velvet were lined up in perfect order.

Peter, who was eligible for discount purchases at Ralph Lauren, was dressed in its Purple Label suit, shirt, and tie—he looked like one of those

Polo models. David, who always shopped in men's outlet stores, was wearing light brown pants, a dark brown jacket, and a green T-shirt with some faded lettering on the front.

Peter shook hands with Hamilton and gave an air kiss to Mallory; David hugged them both enthusiastically and noisily.

"Oh my God, he is gorgeous…oh, girl! Where did you find him? I want him; he is mine!" he screamed.

They all laughed.

Dave baked wild salmon for the occasion; he prepared a separate salad with eggs, macadamia nuts, and black olives for Mallory. He opened a bottle of 1998 Pinot Noir from MacMurray Ranch; Mallory stayed with filtered city water.

When Dave brought in his signature dessert—flourless chocolate brownies topped with caramel ice cream—Peter got up and buttoned up his double-breasted jacket.

"I have never been happier than these last seven years; David taught me to love and be loved. In the past, I always confused the sexual attraction of handsome guys with genuine love. I must confess that I've had my share of beautiful men, but…"

They all booed.

"But I was always depressed, even in the middle of those hot love affairs. Until I met David, other feelings eluded me: contentment, affection, caring, cuddling, the comfort of knowing that there'll be someone always there when you come home; or if you don't come home, someone who will look for you; someone you share your thoughts, worries, and joys with; someone to rely and to depend on when needed; someone who knows you, what you are thinking, feeling, doing.

"Of course, we do make love, but don't be put off by all these pictures on the wall and our mirrored bedroom ceiling; our love is tender and generous. I am grateful to God for giving me David, my friend, my lover, my life-witness."

Ham and Mallory were both stunned. They'd never heard such a testimony between their parents. Mallory offered a brownie to Hamilton, and he took a big bite out of it.

Dave threw his hands up: "Who knew! With goys you never know whether they are depressed or angry, or whether they are happy or hungry; so all those cuties you fucked didn't make you happy till God gave you a mother, ha! You are like Adam."

Expecting the confusion in the eyes of his audience, Dave obliged: "You know the story, right? Adam apparently was always unhappy. Finally God had had it with him. He said, 'What is the matter with you? You are here in Eden. I gave you perfumed flowers, ripened fruits, cool fountains; I gave you fresh air and fertile soil; I gave you lovely animals to play with.

I even gave you this beautiful Eve, and you still sulk!' Adam replied: 'Yeah, but you never gave me a mother!'"

Ham and Mallory politely laughed.

Peter wasn't amused: "And Jews? Why do they always tell elaborate stories to make a simple point?"

The atmosphere got a little chilly.

Mallory got up: "Peter and Dave, you have been the closest friends to me since I moved here. I just want to express my appreciation for your kindness and your generosity. May I wish you many, many more years of togetherness. Here is to you."`

She took a sip from her water. The others bottomed up their glasses. Mallory looked at Ham, as if "say something."

Meanwhile Ham was troubled by Mallory's pedantic toast; he was wondering how a person could recite an obscure poem on the spot, as she did earlier, and then say things that one tolerates only in a Hallmark card for someone's grandparents. Then he realized the room was totally quiet; all eyes were on him. What does one say for the seventh anniversary of a strange gay couple who are either fiercely intimate or about to split?

He pushed his steel-framed chair back, the way his father always does when readying himself to impart a peculiar wisdom or a profound gaffe.

"Actually I am embarrassed to be here. I had no right to intrude into your intimate world; I am not even Mallory's date; I mean a real date. I accepted her invitation just to play a normal person for a change: dress up, bring flowers, sit down at the dinner table, and have a proper conversation. But in reality, I am totally ill-equipped for social life. I don't even know what you all are talking about! Whenever I want to write about relationships, it always comes out as false, unless I pretend to be someone else—like a rageful person..."

A deafening silence followed.

"So would you like to hear a poem from my never-to-be-published book of poetry? *The Rages of My Soul*?"

Peter looked horrified; Dave looked sad. Mallory was comforted: She could definitely live with this guy.

All three shook their heads encouragingly to recite his poem.

There was a young girl
with a censored face
and an empty frame;
she lived an unlinear life—
bearing neither joy
nor sorrow—but
stood restless and told frugal tales
of betrayal and sexual menace;
she was armed with singular tears

and a deliberate
weary mind and thickened soul;
she weaved yawns to carnal desires
and swore leaden to
self-sentenced vices;
yet all that weighed her down
enfolded her past—hideous or dubious—
bewildered,
she forgave her future
without respite;
one day she ripened her demise and
was gone, forever; leaving only
infinite debris.

Then Ham slowly got up and left the apartment.

All three looked at each other. Dave said, "My dear, you could have him."

Mallory apologized for bringing him to their celebration and retired to her room feeling energized to write.

ତ୍ରୁଧୁ

# -XXVI-

*I* think poets are passively coy, full-time whiners; for they are the stepchildren of literature—they are not really wanted—tolerated only by other poets. The dictum of "I write, therefore, I am" doesn't apply to them because they deny that what they do is writing; and they may be right, for they seem to suffer from some sort of syntactical disorder—more successful ones being even worse.

In public, poets are pulsed with almost delusional self-belief, accompanied with untamed whims and impulses; but in private they are strangled with well-justified self-doubt.

In poetry the word may not expire, but the poet does. An emotion claims its voice—a portentous one—and tosses out the poet. The poem becomes a property of universal monologue, especially if it is about extraneous subjects. Then the poet succumbs to mining lighter veins, becoming more juvenile and unbearable by every stanza.

# -XXVII

*A*t Incirlik for every American officer's home, a Turkish soldier (they were *called emireri*) was assigned to serve the family's needs—to drive them *downtown or within the compound, do little repairs in the house and other chores, or whatever. The job may sound too demeaning, but in fact it was a highly desirable and prestigious one. It required that the soldier had to speak some English and be in possession of a special professional driving license; it meant knowing how to fix minor problems in Jeeps (that was the car) like changing the tires or oil and how to clean the carburetor and spark plugs, etc., so as not to be stranded in unfamiliar places.*

*Presentable soldiers, especially those with connections, tended to land these cushy jobs. There also was another potential extra benefit, mostly rumored and joked about: sleeping with the lonely and bored wives of the officers.*

*Twenty-year-old Zeki was our emireri. He was a Kurd from Gaziantep. Not many Kurds had influential relatives, so I presume he got the job on merit. Zeki (meaning* intelligent *in Turkish) was street smart, spoke good-enough English, and was a professional chauffeur in civilian life—two years of military service was mandatory in Turkey. As to presentability, he raised the bar quite a bit.*

*Zeki was a dark, solid, and handsome man; his black eyes were shaded with equally black long eyelashes. He had such an innocent smile that disarmed even my father, who looked down on Turks as a primitive tribe of the Steppes, without any civilization—not like Arabs or Persians. "But this kid is different." He kept saying, "I wish someone could help him go to a school or something." He never considered himself a potential "someone."*

⌘

*I asked Zeki to drive me to Dr. Oz. "By yourself? No, Miss, I am not allowed to take children off the base without their parents," he said in an apologetic voice.*

*"You are allowed to fuck officers' wives?"*

*Zeki was ashen.*

*"Ms. Mallory, don't say things like that; you are a nice girl. What kind of language is this? Please don't ever repeat this to someone else; I never slept with your mother, God forbid. I am a good Muslim, you see; in this country having sex with someone else's wife is considered a big sin. The people—the whole cemaat— would gather and stone both me and your mother."*

*This unbelievably calm man was literally shaking in his boots.*

*"No, they won't; my mother is American, no one can stone her; they may fire you, though."*

*Zeki forgot the little English he knew; now he was speaking in Turkish.*

*"Ms. Mallory elin pim, buni yapma bana."*

*I didn't need to understand his gibberish to know that he was pleading mercy.*

*"Well, you have the choice, don't you? You can tell my father that I ordered you."*

*"I bring doctor here?"*

*"No, no, you bring me to him and now!"*

*Anytime I talked to Zeki, my English also deteriorated.*

*I jumped into the backseat of the Jeep.*

*Zeki got in…"Allahallah!"*

*As we approached the gates of the base, Zeki told me to tell the guard that we are going to pick up my mother from the doctor's office.*

*I was so jubilant with my victory that I knew no guard was going to suspect any wrongdoing going on. I knew most of them anyway.*

*We stopped at the exit; I smiled at the guard. "Hi, we are picking up his mother."*

*I couldn't believe that—I said his mother!*

*The guard opened the gate.*

*Zeki's neck and shoulder were soaked with sweat dripping from his head.*

*We pulled in front of Dr. Oz's office; a dozen Turkish children in white, black, and yellow outfits surrounded us, laughing and yelling something.*

*"They want Chiclets, Miss."*

*Well, I had none. Some patients were lying on the ground, some sitting on the steps; some others were waiting in their tractor-trailers. The place looked like a disaster first-aid center. I walked in, and the corridor was packed with sick children, women, and elderly people; they were carrying gift packages—homemade pastries, yogurt, fruit, eggs, and live chickens.*

*How could one doctor take care of so many people? There was no receptionist or nurse. Zeki knocked on the doctor's door and just walked in. A few minutes later he came out with the doctor. I had not seen him since his prescription for how to wake up from an undesirable dream.*

*"Hello, you are bigger, okay! Dreams are okay?"*

*He quickly ushered out an elderly man and eight other people—the patient's family, who accompanied him. The man had apparently been kicked on the head by his horse.*

"Don't ever get behind your own horse!" Doctor Oz advised me. Did he mean literally? Does that mean that it is okay to get behind other people's horses? Or was he speaking metaphorically, dropping an obscure wisdom as Turks seem to do?

I asked Zeki to leave the room.

"The soldier says you came alone. Why?" he opened his eyes wide.

"Yes, I have a question that I couldn't ask in front of my mother. If I get pregnant from my father, what would happen? Like, would you help me abort the fetus?"

Dr. Oz's face was all scrounged.

"You are having sex with your father? You are pregnant?"

"Yes," I replied casually.

"You see, this is a difficult situation: Number one, if your father is having sex with you, he would be held legally responsible. The second, this is even getting too complicated for me; you are a minor. You cannot get an abortion without your parent's approval. And what about your mother?"

Dr. Oz was clearly at a loss.

"She doesn't know anything."

"Your father is aware that you are pregnant?"

"I have not told him yet."

Dr. Oz began to pace silently in his narrow office; when he stood in front of me, he looked into my eyes.

"How do you know you are pregnant?"

"I missed two periods."

"This is bad, this is really bad. Please lie down on the table and take your underwear off."

All of a sudden a great fear and shame came over me. While I was trying to figure out my sister's potential options—should she get pregnant—I was railroading myself to lose my virginity to a medical examination. But I couldn't stop it. I took my panties down. I was watching him putting on gloves. This is it!

"Let's first take a look at it. This won't hurt; just relax and spread your legs a little bit more."

This was the first time a man was touching my vagina; he pulled the lips aside. The doctor's hand was on my crotch; I felt a tingling deep inside me.

"You are sure he fully penetrated, Miss? Your virginity is intact; there is no tear whatsoever. I have to examine your uterus from your rectum; now this might be a touch uncomfortable."

I was relieved and also disappointed in some strange way. The tingling went away.

The doctor came back and spread some Vaseline on my anus and then inserted his finger slowly and gently all the way in.

I passed gas loudly twice; I was mortified.

"Oh, I am terribly sorry," I whispered.

*Dr. Oz was oblivious to the noise and the smell. One of his hands was in my rectum, the other on my abdomen, pushing against each other. The tingling came back with a vengeance and pitched; I felt like my vagina was enlarging, as if its walls were pressing my belly, my sides, and my back. Could it burst? A moment arrived I couldn't stand anymore; I wanted to scream. Then the walls of my vagina came together in a series of spasms; I had to put one hand on my mouth and the other on my eyes.*

*A splash of words from Dr. Oz took away my spasm.*

*"Well, you are not pregnant either. You have a small, normal uterus. Furthermore, it seems you are either beginning or ending your period. So I don't understand; okay, you can get dressed."*

*I wanted to stay for a little while longer.*

*"Okay, Miss Mallory, you can get up."*

*Finally I pulled myself together and hurried toward the door, while Dr. Oz was trying to be heard: "You've got to discuss the whole thing with your mother, Miss Mallory."*

☾〜〜☽

# -XXVIII-

**M**r. Levine waved and came in. "Listen, kids, how come we are always just us? I mean, don't you have other friends?"

Norma and Max Hathaway, Jeanny and Jeff Weisman, and John Levine were to have one of their regular dinners, today at the Thurmans'. Jeff called these his "cabinet meetings"—he had political aspirations.

"Of course we do," leaped Max. "In fact I like large cocktail parties the most, where everything is noisy and clamorous. You can meet lots of people—friends and strangers—exchange a few pleasantries, and move on. No prodding questions, no lengthy monologues, no heavy discussion; there 'how are you?' just means 'hi'; you are not expected to listen and to talk about other people's problems."

"I too like cocktail parties," said Jeffrey.

"Not for the same reason, though," Max Hathaway grinned. "You convert every social setting into social combat; you position yourself in a corner of the room with a few of your retainers and hold court."

"He does the same thing in small gatherings," Jeanny said.

Jeff was undaunted by their imputation: "We get together with other people too, but this eight—sorry, now seven—is our most intimate gathering. This round table of eight has a royal provenance—Louis XIV, who set the trend for intimate dinners of closest friends where they can be totally transparent without any fear of its consequences."

Jeanny smiled down, "Are we having a conversation or another deposition?"

"Actually the number is six," corrected Hamilton: "The Sun King's round table."

"Who knew," said John, "that the Sun King and we had so much in common."

At the Thurmans', dinners comprised take-out Indian, Chinese, or Japanese foods; the guests, who were well-off, lightheartedly considered their visits to the Upper West Side sort of missionary outings.

As the dinner was ending, the topic shifted to the major news of the day: the mayor's infidelities and the public announcement of his intention to divorce his wife.

"What is wrong with this man; is he lacking moral sense? Why would he announce his divorce in a news conference? How humiliating it must be for poor Donna," Ann remarked in a sharp breath.

Max, gesticulating laboriously, made a harsh, descending sound.

"And in Bryant Park no less, a kind of place for announcements of happy events," added Jeanny.

Norma stood up to say something, but Max pulled her down to her chair.

"I heard about some of his escapades too," said Jeff with a censorious tone. "What I don't understand is why, after all this, he would be interested in marrying a forty-six-year-old woman with a teenage daughter?"

"What about him? A young prince charming? A post–middle age variant of his original obnoxious self," said Ann.

"Nothing so mysterious about it," offered Mr. Levine. "When you are young and strong, you look for a lover. When you are ill with prostate cancer, you look for a caretaker woman; especially if she is a nurse. Except that the son of a bitch is giving prostate cancer a bad name."

"Prostate cancer animus," said Hamilton.

No one paid attention.

"She is a small-town Catholic girl from Philadelphia," said Norma Hathaway with a shrill voice. "She managed to become a nurse, and then she nursed a wealthy Jew into marriage; now she's a hoity-toity society woman. Jewish guys, when they get rich, fall for unfettered shiksas whom they didn't have a prayer with in high school."

Hamilton looked around, baffled: "Did she use the word 'unfettered'?"

Ann frowned: "Such an unambiguous condescension!"

"Oh, I read that somewhere," replied Norma self-pleasingly; she flashed open her crocodile-diamond Birkin bag and pulled out a pocket-sized thesaurus. "It means…"

"Shut up, Norma!" Max yelled.

"Listen; let's talk a little about the political implication of Giuliani's pending divorce and his cancer. I think this is the opportunity we have been waiting for, Jeff. Giuliani cannot survive this double jeopardy; Catholics, Orthodox Jews, and upstate New York wouldn't support him for the Senate seat. Now we have two morally tainted candidates: Giuliani for…for being…"

Hamilton finished his sentence: "for being a serial Catholic."

They giggled.

Max continued, "Hillary for being a partner to a, a…"

Again Hamilton came to help: "simultaneous philanderer."

They all laughed, Hamilton positioned to unleash his brilliance: "In times of Thoreau if someone had committed some heinous sin and partially repented, he set about reforming the world, like going to missionary work in Africa. In our times, atoners enter into politics; if they are already in there, they run for even higher office."

Jeanny's face was all scrunched up.

"Yeah, I was surprised that the president of the United States would have oral sex with a young intern in the Oval Office and get away with it."

Max said, "Please, John, come to the rescue; this is your specialty... were you surprised?"

"Well, I was surprised" answered John, "not for the same reason Jeanny was; I was surprised because the Lewinsky girl is Jewish. As far as I know, Jewish women don't give blow jobs unless they are part of a prenuptial scheme."

They were all laughing so hard that it was difficult to hear him talking— John, who was oblivious to the scene, continued: "You may have heard the story of a Jewish wedding. As soon as the rabbi declares to the bride and the groom, 'You two are now officially husband and wife,' she claps her hands with great relief: 'Today I gave my last blow job.'"

Max and Jeff were on the floor laughing hysterically, Jeanny and Ann looked shocked, and Norma said: "You know, John, not every Jewish girl is so peculiar."

"John, you are such a...gentleman, why do you tell such off-color jokes?" asked Jeanny.

"Off-color?" Ann jumped in. "Obscene, lewd, sexist...yes, why?"

"Why? Listen, sweethearts, when you do a lot and well, you don't talk about it. If you do a little, you talk a lot about it. That is true for sure in moneymaking. But if you don't do it at all, then you joke about it.

"But seriously, you all know the domestic flame has a four-year life, like a car battery; except it cannot be recharged. Sometimes you and your spouse were not a good sexual match to begin with and then you look for solutions—not that I know what makes a good match."

"Compatible perversions," said Hamilton.

"You are just being outrageous," said Ann tersely.

Max threw a placid glance at them: "Giuliani is no Kennedy or Jefferson or Roosevelt, for God's sake. He has been an unsparing prosecutor. He has been called Eliot Ness incarnate with carnivorous ambitions; a yard dog. He has arrested Wall Street executives in their offices and had them handcuffed outside the buildings just to make spectacles."

"Let's get back to your earlier point, Max; are you suggesting that I should run for mayor?" said Jeff.

"We have the money and the connections." said Max.

"Look, you have three options," explained Hamilton. "You could run for mayor on the Democratic ticket, you could run for governor or for the Senate on the Democratic ticket, or you could go for any one of them as an independent. But before we go any further, Jeff, I am going to ask you, in front of everyone, a question that only someone who really cares about you would dare to ask."

A tense silence followed.

"Do you have any skeletons in your closet?" Hamilton was serious. "As you know, the higher up the monkey goes the more you'll see his ass." They all laughed.

Jeffrey looked totally comfortable: "Wow! Hamilton, I would have expected such an obscene transgression from John; but from you—the eloquent intellect..."

They all chuckled.

"To be serious, I think Giuliani has more fun in life than I do."

Jeanny joined in, "Oh God, Jeff is so square; look at him. He doesn't even own a closet, never mind skeletons."

They all burst into laughter.

"Speaking of nurses and caretakers, John," Jeanny continued, "why don't you marry Mallory? She is such a nice person and is so devoted to you."

"Those old guys who marry young chicks for sex are in for some unpleasant and unseemly surprises."

"What sort of surprises?" prodded Jeff with a perverse glee.

"Come on, Jeff, you are a Talmud *chachum* of life."

"What is that?" said Jeanny. "Now we are all getting curious."

"That he is a wise student to know it is better to leave certain things alone."

John hastily embarked on telling a joke.

"You've got to hear this little story: A guy my age decides to marry a girl in her twenties. His friends try to discourage him. He asks them, 'What is your problem? I mean, what are you worried about?' 'Well,' they say, 'don't you ever think of dying?' He replies, 'Of course I do; what am I supposed to do about it? If she dies, she dies.'"

All three guys kept laughing in spite of stern gazes from Ann and Jeanny.

"Vices tend to get worse with age," John said apologetically.

As they prepared to leave, Jeff grabbed Max's arm: "The Paine Webber–UBS deal will be sealed in a few weeks; any thoughts on that?"

"Not financially; but if Bush becomes president and if he picks Don Marron as treasury secretary, well, too many ifs... Oh, I almost forgot I am going heavy on Halliburton stock; if Cheney gets defeated, he'll come back as CEO. But if he grabs hold of the government, boy, we'll have a windfall; either way we couldn't lose."

They all looked pleased with each other.

༄༅

After they got back home, Norma and Max retired to their bedroom to watch TV—their favorite downtime. They usually didn't talk much. Max would surf channels while Norma slowly and gradually fell asleep after begging him to lower the sound a little bit—he never did.

For Norma, life wasn't easy to pull into a safe focus—the whole world conspired to hurt her, except salesmen and women. She seemed to invite either aggression or dismissal, partly because of her overt display of richness—garish outfits, oversize jewelry—and partly because of her incessant high-pitched chattering in the tone of C minor. Max always put her down, and frequently in front of other people—he even encouraged their children to gang up on her and mock her.

Norma was awkwardly put together. She sentimentalized everything—marriage, children, husband, friendships, dinners, and especially anniversaries. She remembered everyone's birthdays and sent gifts with syrupy notes: "May you live a happy and healthy life. Love, Norma." In some ways she had the unadulterated innocence of a young deprived girl.

She went to college—okay, it was a community college—but remained crassly illiterate; she even studied the dictionary to enrich her vocabulary after one of her professors told her that Théophile Gautier (she made sure not to forget this name) became a poet by reading a dictionary. Once she dared to mention this to Hamilton (she was totally intimidated by him). He applauded and added another writer who also read the dictionary to keep his prose marmoreal; he wrote the author's name down (Walter Pater) for her to look up. She hated Hamilton.

"How much money would you be putting up for Jeff's running for an office?" she dared to ask Max.

"Well, it isn't like that; there are direct and legal contributions for any election that are *bubkes*, and there are indirect ones like bundling; now that is serious money. So on and so on, we are talking about millions."

"Millions! Max, why? I mean, why don't you run yourself with all that money; he isn't that special; is he?"

"I could definitely be a better governor, let me tell you. I can give speeches at a moment's notice; I could make mega decisions on the spot. But you see, we don't have the required provenance that Jeff and his family have."

"We don't have their what?"

"That is what I mean, 'the provenance, the provenance.' This *Stella* painting, which is hanging in our living room: Who owned that before?

Do you know? You don't, because you don't care about the 'provenance' issue; but everyone else does."

"What has that got to do with the painting, Max? You weren't owned by someone else."

"Are you a moron? What if you and Jeanny sat down to an interview with, let's say…with Larry King; what do you think people would say? Oh, I think Norma would be a better First Lady? Jeffrey Weisman is from a prominent and wealthy family, married to a lawyer, working for peanuts in public service. I? I managed to escape the Bronx, making money by hook or by crook and married for love of money. You see, I don't fool myself, Norma; you gave me two wonderful kids. Well, sort of; if we get divorced, you take Robert. I'll take what's-her-name, our daughter; because Robert got all these nutty genes from your side of the family. Wasn't it your grand-uncle who spent all his life in a mental institution? The Hathaways were middle-class working people, poor but totally sane; that is it, good night."

"You married me for my money?"

"I said the love of money; I, of course, loved you too!" with an agitated voice.

"It is also my fault that you are not the mayor? Is that what you are saying?"

"Norma, I said good night, didn't I?"

"Well, what is in it for us, if Jeff becomes mayor?"

"Lots of things; you have no idea. We'll be even richer. Now just go to bed."

"You don't want a little hanky-panky? You know, it is our anniversary."

"I am too tired, Norma. I am sorry; some other time, okay? Good night, now, and I mean it."

⚬➟➟⚬

Hamilton and Ann didn't talk long after the guests left; both seemed troubled with the events of the evening.

"I feel dirty; I need to take a long shower and be scrubbed down," Ann paused and sighed. "Hamilton, I told you many times, anytime I am with these people, I feel icky; they are all about money. At least take advantage of our connections with Max and John, the way that Jeff has, and make some money instead of keeping it in a checking account. Have them invest for us. Have you noticed at the end of every dinner, before we break up, the three men huddle and talk strategies for investing while you stay with the women? Why don't you join them and at least listen and maybe participate?"

Hamilton laughed: "You think I should weigh in on the stock market with my wealth—all of $2,600?"

"Well, they know that we don't have much money; people like us with limited income also buy a few stocks here and there. At the firm all our young associates, who make less than we do, are always reading the *Wall Street Journal*. You are smarter than all these people; if you put your mind to it, I know you will make lots of money for us."

"You want lots of money?" Hamilton wondered.

Ann sighed again: "Well, wouldn't it be better if we had a weekend house, travel without watching every penny we spent? I mean, what do you have against being rich?"

"I have nothing against being rich or even against rich people, provided that they finance and produce tangible goods—harvesting food or manufacturing usable things; but I have a lot against—that is putting it rather mildy—the speculating, trading, or making money by financing finance."

"If so, how do you justify your assisting Jeff to buy his way into a public office; are you all that much indebted to his father for giving us the mortgage? For years you have mentored him; isn't that enough? Maybe you enjoy being a grateful supplicant, a subordinate; I don't."

"I like Jeff, and I thought you and Jeanny were friends."

"Yes, we are; Jeanny is a fine woman. I am talking about the rest."

"The Jews!"

"Only the vulgar ones."

"You considered my 'Knicker-Bocker' friends vulgar too."

"Yeah, when they got drunk and obscene."

"Speaking of vulgarity, weren't all your discussions geared to exploring—and not so subtly, if I may add—how to get some renovation contracts?"

Ann screwed up her lips: "How about your colossal gaffe—asking Jeff in front of everyone, including his wife, whether he has any skeletons in his closet; especially when the subject was extramarital dalliance."

"Now, in this symbolic context, you may reconsider 'the meaning of subordinate.'"

"Listen, I don't care about your signs and symbols; you were simply out of order; thank God he didn't even flinch and Jeanny came to your rescue. Otherwise it would have been a very awkward situation, and you would have been summarily evicted from your precious apartment."

⌾⟋⟋⟋⟍⟍9

Jeff and Jeanny drove Mr. Levine to his apartment and took the elevator with him up to his floor.

"Thank you, kids, for the ride; you don't need to do that."

"It is nothing, please. John, just a brief question: At the dinner table you agreed that 'we have the money and connections,' but you didn't say, 'Jeff, run for it.'"

"You are right; the reason is whenever I have given advice about marriage or career, I've ended up regretting it. Politics has elements of both—that is something that the two of you must think over very carefully. Goodnight, Jeanny, Jeff."

On the way down the elevator Jeanny said, "Jeff, you should find better consultants. I don't know how Hamilton could be a good career advisor; I like him a lot, but he is a reckless man. His only expertise is to catch every opportunity to impart a labored witticism, and John is no better. Why are you are so intent to get his view? John is so much out of politics and everything else, except getting a massage from some cute girl."

"And you were recommending that the poor, out-of-it old guy should marry her?"

"It was a joke, Jeff; he got it and made it even funnier."

The elevator door opened on the ground level; a large guy—drenched in alcohol and holding an unlit cigar—and his wife, who was laughing hysterically, rushed in, tripping on each other before the Weismans got out.

The man unskillfully turned to his wife and loudly said, 'If you keep throwing stones, one will fall on your head; it is a Swedish proverb.'

The door of the elevator closed. Jeff and Jeanny stood there for a second, astonished.

"Who is this guy? Was he talking to us?"

Jeff vaguely remembered him. "I think he is one of the officers of UBS."

"So Jeff, do you really need to ask anyone whether you should run for an office? You know those stones may fall on my and our children's heads too?"

✺

# -XXIX-

At eleven in the morning, the phone blasted Mallory awake.
"Damn, shit! I forgot to turn it off." She scrambled to find her cell.
"Hello!"

"Hi, this is Jeffrey," a strong voice boomed.

"Who?"

"Jeffrey Weisman."

"Oh, hi."

Was this the same meek guy with the utmost deference for his wife?

"You sound so different on the phone; what's up?"

"Well, I was wondering whether we could get together for a drink or coffee."

"Why?"

Mallory, of course, knew what he wanted, but she wasn't sure what to do with him. Could she replace Max with him? Jeffrey was definitely a finer man.

"$2,000 for an hour, plus hotel and car expenses."

Since her encounter with Max, Mallory felt comfortable about taking money for sex.

"$2,000 is okay, but may I come to your place? I cannot go to hotels; I am easily recognizable."

"Well, you may not want to come to my apartment, if you knew its condition."

"Is it a doorman building?"

"No."

"Good. Do you have a bed?"

"I have a mattress on the floor."

This time Mallory was not only entering into prostitution but also breaking one of its major taboos: *taking johns to where you live.*

# -XXX-

After the birth of their second daughter Jeff felt coldly freed from the guilt of having sex with other women. The therapist, whom he briefly tolerated, told him that his sexuality and aggression—his two innate drives—were so powerful that they were great threats to his social and psychological equilibrium. "A professor at Einstein, my ass," Jeff ridiculed him. The psychiatrist didn't understand that a man like himself was capable of splitting emotional and sexual intimacy, depersonalizing and encapsulating sexuality while living a normal life. The ideal of having romantic, sexual, and emotional intimacy with one woman was an unnecessary, if not impossible, burden put on a normal man's mind by the merchants of pathology; he wasn't going against his inner self—he was for it!

The last ten years or so, Jeffrey had been hiring call girls whenever he was out of town for business (real or concocted) or even picking up "walkers" on 8th Avenue for a quick blow job in his car. He didn't really like either alternative: Call girls varied in quality, and there were always middlemen who demanded certain information like a credit card, even though he paid cash. The potential for blackmail was ever present. Pickup girls, though free from that, carried their own risks, mainly dirtiness and occasional surprises: Once the girl turned out to be a cross-dresser.

The worst was when he picked up a police decoy—in retrospect she looked too good to be true. They let him go (while chuckling) once they found out who he was, on the condition that he never drive down 8th Avenue again. He narrowly escaped a humiliating arrest and the publicity that could have cost him his job; all his future career aspirations would have ended, and his wife might have left him.

Nevertheless, the impact of these "close calls" didn't last too long. After a few weeks' interval, he returned to the scene with an even greater pounding inevitability—he kept sidling up to the fire, even on 8th Avenue.

This Mallory was just the best solution: an educated, beautiful young woman—a piece of benign meat; no middleman and no doorman. Just perfect.

As Jeffrey walked up the creaky stairs of Mallory's building, the dismally lit floors sagged and groaned; with each step dead air bounced back from the worn-out, filthy carpet. The faint notes of a piano sounded totally out of place—it was actually a disturbing sensation.

He was sure that no one who lived in a place like this would recognize him. He was anxious or a little out of breath—fourth-floor walk-up? Jeff remembered that he always got a little edgy and disconcertingly foggy before every new sexual encounter.

"Was it 4A?" Jeff noticed the mezuzah on the frame and assumed that it must have belonged to a previous tenant. The door was ajar. He hesitated for a moment, then stuck his head in.

A girl was sitting still on her crossed legs, in the middle of the room—her body seemed hovering a few inches above the floor—while letting a moaning sound out of her slightly parted lips. She was barefoot, wearing cut-off jeans and a T-shirt.

"Are you okay?" asked Jeff.

The girl didn't answer but stopped moaning; she lifted herself up as if pushing the ground down and whispered, "*Namaste.*"

"Oh, I understand, that must be your mantra, right? Sorry, I guess I interrupted your meditation."

"*Namaste* means 'my divine honors your divine'; I wasn't meditating. I was in the pose of *chaturanga dandasana* to vibrate to the interconnectedness of all life—human, animals, and nature." Mallory said in a carefree manner.

Her gaze was cast at some distant point.

"Only a few inanimate things—a mattress, a chair, a table, a couple of books, and the *New York Times*? I thought you were joking," Jeff said with a fake smile.

"There are no inanimate things; furthermore, I never joke. Did you bring the cash?" she said frostily.

Jeffrey was taken aback with her attitude; after a brief, anxious pause, he took an envelope out of his pocket.

"Yes, here, all $2,000."

Mallory put the envelope on top of the table.

"That small object nailed on the frame of the door was supposed to travel with the owner; had the person before you skipped town in a hurry?" Jeff asked.

"No, no; she was murdered. That thing is a mezuzah—you must know."

Jeff wasn't sure whether he correctly heard the casually uttered word *murdered*; maybe she was joking. Either way he didn't want to pursue that line of inquiry—it could have spoiled the mood.

"And you know what is in it?"

"Well, of course; a handwritten rolled scroll of parchment inscribed with a section of Deuteronomy."

"Then why; I mean…"

"Well, as the famous scientist Niels Bohr says, 'it works even for people who don't believe.' Furthermore, it isn't about being religious; Kabbalah is an antireligious religion offering earthly bliss."

Jeff thought this was an existentially orphaned, emotionally lost woman, preyed upon by a vulgarized form of Judaism—a McMysticism. Well, as long as that didn't interfere with her having sex with him.

They were looking at each other as if "are we done with the talking?"

"You do realize that this will contaminate my relationship with your wife?"

"Do you have to continue with her?"

Mallory took her jeans off without answering his question.

Jeffrey had been with many call girls and prostitutes but never had such a contentious exchange with any one of them; especially once the financial matter was satisfactorily settled. Occasionally, girls objected when he wanted to have anal intercourse, but even then, it was just a question of how much more money was to exchange hands.

"Let me ask you a question. Why would you pay money to have sex with a stranger when you have a beautiful woman at home and free?"

"Because I can!" Jeff replied, gritting his teeth. "Incidentally, did you say free? Free? As your Mr. Levine always says—man pays one way or another. Well, anyhow, my wife is beautiful and nice but we don't have sex…even the idea is disturbing. Mallory, I live in a household full of women—they are sisters, mother, daughters to each other—a female tribe; I am emotionally marginalized there and sexually inhibited. Do you understand that? To me, all three of them are incestuous objects. Never mind having sex with my wife, I can't even masturbate in that apartment."

Mallory thought there was good material here for a story.

"So why don't you get a mistress or a girlfriend? You are sexy, rich, and powerful; aren't there some young lawyers or interns around?"

Jeffrey was getting irritated, and he pierced her with his stare.

"You majored in literature, right? So you read what Demosthenes said thousands of years ago: 'We keep our mistresses for our delights, concubines for daily needs of our bodies, wives who tamp down sexual desire, to breed legitimate children and have loyal soldiers and housekeepers.'"

He continued in a brisk and self-assured tone: "The mistresses and the love affairs are detrimental to a marriage. I don't want to have psychological entanglements with another woman and get my marriage into trouble. You see, I pay call girls to save my marriage. I don't want to fall in love with someone or some woman to fall in love with me. You know how your favorite client Mr. Levine defines eternity? 'Between you come and she goes.'"

Jeff expected at least a smile on Mallory's face; there was a seething anger.

"Stop heaping scorn on me. This is a charged alternative to my boring marriage. I have no illusionary desires—love, affection, permanence, loyalty—but I have one real desire: sex."

Mallory took her panties and T-shirt off and lay down on the mattress. Jeff saw only a red bracelet. Images of a high school crush flashed, followed by rage and self-pity.

"Would you please close your eyes?" Jeffrey asked. "You are watching; or turn over."

Mallory moved to facedown position, sticking out her backside like an offering; she was enjoying this. He was big and solid. Jeffrey tentatively rubbed her cheeks, then put his finger slowly into her offered ass.

"Can you do that with your penis?" she said. "Tantrixal."

"Tantrixal?"

Jeff was willing to do it, in any axial fashion she wanted.

"Tantric sex is slowing down the orgasm, especially for man; for their orgasm brings the lovemaking to a snorry end. It is suspended elongation of time, sexual equivalent of that beauty in Proustian moments, or a 'wa'—perfect harmony."

It didn't turn Jeff off that Mallory was talking as if she were a teacher in a sex-education class—nothing could have as the time slowed down.

⟅⟆

Jeffrey walked down Orchard Street quite elated. Mallory was a solution beyond his wildest imagination. With those wide cheekbones, long and delicate neck, classically proportioned, symmetrical face, and ravishing body, she was terrifyingly beautiful and lasciviously innocent—she was sort of unaware of all this.

Jeff interrupted himself: Was she intentionally playing down, and if so, why? What was that Proust reference all about? He wished she wouldn't quarrel and intellectualize so much. Otherwise this was unbelievable; no question. Under different circumstances, she would have been someone he could easily marry. Now, as it is, she had her own place that was remote, quiet, and highly private. But most importantly—they had similar sexual interests that other women, including his wife, considered perverse.

⟅⟆

# -XXXI-

*I* *enjoy sex when it isn't sex—that is, when it is not typical intercourse. First, I have to feel good about myself—having written a good piece of work would do it; secondly I need men to serve me with their tongues, hands, and forearms. When the wall between my vagina and my rectum is rhythmically massaged from both sides, in audible strength, I get that erotic pleasure—a state bordering between feeling hostility and profound intoxication.*

# -XXXII-

Jeffrey Weisman was the only son of a powerhouse couple. He had a sister, Cora, who was four years older. His mother, Nadine, was an attractive, sought-after socialite; his father, Gabriel, an investment banker—a self-made man who built a fortune by restructuring mortgages for middle-class houses in the boroughs. Gabriel, after having worked with his father until his death, took the company to a greater scale by using the same technique in Manhattan in the 1970s. Thirty years later, he was a wealthy man beyond even his father's dreams. His parents were also well-known philanthropists, Nadine in cancer research and Gabriel wherever he could plaster his name on it.

Jeff grew up in a household where his every need was met and his every wish was granted—either by his parents or by the permanent staff in their Park Avenue apartment or in their waterfront mansion in Palm Beach.

Jeff was born prematurely at three-and-a-half pounds, in spite of his mother's being kept in bed and receiving weekly progesterone shots during the first trimester. He had spent four weeks in Mount Sinai Hospital before he was cautiously discharged. The rotation of twenty-four-hour, seven-days-a-week nannies had to wear antiseptic gloves and carry Jeffrey on pillows; he grew wide.

The fact was that he had gotten ill often and had recovered very slowly; Jeffrey lived in semi-isolation until the time of kindergarten. Even then, his after-school contacts with other children were severely curtailed—not that many kids sought him out as a playmate; if anything he was the butt of fat jokes. The scratching of his inner thighs, which became red and inflamed, kept him from many physical activities. They became infected from continuous rubbing against each other.

Jeff was also a bossy little kid; he demanded attention of teachers and obedience from other kids. Failing that, he'd come home and throw temper tantrums and then hide in his room for hours. His parents, who tried everything to ease his pain, felt totally helpless. This went on for years, until his junior year at Dalton High School, where everything came to a head. Jeff had gotten obsessed with the most beautiful girl in his class—Melinda.

Melinda's not paying any attention to him fueled Jeff's obsession; he began to vomit after each meal with the hope of losing weight. He never did, due to his binge eating in between or after his vomiting. When the gossip—Jeff is desperately in love with Melinda—reached the office of the superintendent, Mrs. Marantz, she called them in, separately. Jeff totally denied the allegations, while crying profusely; Melinda remained indifferent.

Mrs. Marantz, in a conference with Melinda and her mother (the father had left them when she was two years old), made a request for Melinda's sympathy in the form of a good-natured relationship with Jeff—whose father was a major contributor to the school—to which she agreed. Melinda even went one step further. She ate her lunch in the cafeteria with Jeff; she sat next to him in the library; she even gave him a red plastic bracelet to jiggle whenever he felt upset—"It helped me," said Melinda. But when Melinda went to Jeff's lavish bar mitzvah party at the Metropolitan Museum of Art with her new boyfriend, Brian—a senior and a basketball star—all hell broke loose.

First, Jeff tried to monopolize Melinda on the dance floor; when she refused, he accused her of betrayal by bringing an uninvited person to the party and then asked Brian to leave. When Melinda decided to go with her boyfriend, Jeff latched on to Melinda's arm to stop her, but instead tore the sleeve off her dress. As Melinda and Brian ran down the steps of the museum, Jeff begged her to come back while still clutching her torn sleeve.

⚬⚭⚬

Jeff was a total disappointment to his father. Gabriel, along with his own father, sweated blood with pride and dignity to get where he was, while his son was an overweight "schlemiel" chasing a "skinny shiksa" from a broken family without money and breeding.

But by the time Jeff reached age seventeen, he was no longer the loser his father thought him to be; he was one of the brightest kids in the school. After his delayed puberty, Jeffrey grew tall and muscular; he excelled in basketball and running; he was assertive and aggressive except with his father, who still considered him an inadequate son.

Jeff got accepted early to Columbia on his own merit, but his father gave the university $1,000,000 prior to the decision and informed him of the fact. Jeff finished college magna cum laude and was recruited by Columbia Law; yet again, his father preempted the victory by becoming a member of the university's board with the implicit promise of becoming a major donor and fund-raiser. At every possible occasion he dropped names, especially that of John Kluge, who was rumored to have $12 billion—implying a close relation and potential major gifts to Columbia.

So Jeff never knew whether his acceptance to schools was earned or bought by his father; he grew up insecure and always doubting himself. He was also insecure regarding the interest of girls—mostly Jewish and eager to marry into a wealthy family. He believed more in the indifference of gentiles, especially that of Jeanny, who'd slept with almost everyone in the law school except with him. The more he pursued her, the more she avoided him; he wasn't going to repeat the Melinda scenario, so one day he caught up with her on campus while she was walking past, obviously aware of his intention.

"Hi, Jeanny. Is it my nose, my balding head, my religion, what?"

Jeanny, without slowing down, said, "Hello, Jeffrey. What are you talking about?"

"Come on, you know I have been trying to have a date with you, even just lunch or a movie; would you please stop for a minute?"

Jeanny slowed down; turned toward Jeff, and said, "How about dinner tonight?"

"Okay, fine," replied the now-puzzled Jeff.

"I'll meet you at seven o'clock in front of the main gate," she said and picked up her pace.

Jeff watched her walking away hurriedly. Now how could that be? This woman for months had made a special effort to avert her eyes from him and responded to him with the briefest possible sentences, devoid of any interest. How was it that now she was offering a dinner date? For a moment Jeffrey wondered whether his father had anything to do with that. Even he couldn't do that, Jeffrey thought; or could he?

⟨ﻬﻬﻬ⟩

At 7 p.m. sharp, Jeanny showed up in the same outfit that she'd been wearing earlier. Jeff was expecting her to "fancy up" a little; he himself got all dressed up for the occasion and made a reservation at Tavern on the Green in Central Park. Jeanny was oblivious. She wanted to go to Lenge—a Japanese restaurant on Columbus Avenue. Jeff, who was taught by his parents to avoid sushi, sashimi, and raw stuff in general because it was full of mercury and/or other chemicals, hesitated for a second then asked her to give the cab driver the address.

After a few sakes, Jeff relaxed and found California rolls rather delicious; he kept talking about his job offer at the district attorney's office—that he had the option to go into his father's lucrative business but wanted to serve the community. Jeff was trying to figure out which of these career paths she would find more attractive.

"You want to come to my place?" Jeanny asked in the tone of "do you want another sushi roll?"

"Ah, oh, yes, great, of course," he mumbled.

As soon as they got to her place, Jeanny removed her clothes in a non-sensual way. Jeff, half amazed at his luck, half confused, but highly excited, threw her onto the bed—Jeanny was just lying under him, wincing with each thrust as if she were in pain. Jeff thought maybe he was being a little too aggressive.

"I'm sorry, did I hurt you?"

"Oh, no, not at all," replied Jeanny, "it was okay."

∽∞∾

# -XXXIII-

*B*y the time we were in high school back in Westport, Mom couldn't tell Pat and me apart, no matter how differently we were dressed (Pat mostly in dark, I in all other colors); we wore different hairdos (Pat's shoulder length, mine very short), but still Mom had no clue. She began to call our housekeeper Nana, Mom's mother's name.

One day Mom and I were alone in the living room, just the two of us, slumped on the sofa. She was drinking Bud; she turned and looked at me as if I were a stranger.

I waved to her, "Hello-o-o!"

"You know, I knew a girl who looked exactly like you," she said with an acid grin. "When we were in high school. Her name was Pat too. She and I were best friends, until I caught her with my boyfriend Roger; they were drinking beer and making out in his bedroom, where I was to meet him."

I hesitated; would it be too cruel to pump her to find out what she knew about my sister and Dad?

"How come you don't remember what you ate this morning, but when it comes to your high school years, you have such a clear memory?"

"Oh, yes, actually I have even better recollection of still earlier years."

"Do you remember our years in Turkey well?"

Her usual guileless smile dissipated. She stared at me with a pained expression and then yawned.

I thought I might not get another chance; she was definitely deteriorating.

"So your story of your boyfriend Roger, and your girl friend Pat's betraying you, is that something like Dad and me?"

She again looked at me—she didn't know me—and then she opened her mouth as if she was about to say something; nothing—her mouth stayed open.

"Well, is it?" I finally broke this strange silence.

"Is it what, Pat?" she spoke with blame-filled intonation. "Do I have to spell it out for you? You and Roger, yes, you betrayed me. You were my best friend, for God's sake. How could you?"

Mom began to cry—no ordinary cry; she was howling. She began to pull her hair and throw chunks of it on the floor; her scalp was bleeding.

"Mom, Mom, please; stop it. Where is your medication?"

*I ran into her bathroom and opened her medication drawer. We were to give her Valium whenever she got agitated. I brought her three pills with a glass of water. In the midst of all her agony, she compliantly chewed and swallowed the pills and drank a whole can of beer. She continued her litany against Roger and Pat for another half an hour until she slowly faded into sleep.*

*I put a pillow under her head, took her shoes off, put her legs up on the couch, collected all the hair from the floor and put it into a garbage bag, poured some beer on her scalp, and pressed on it with a towel.*

*Pat showed up.*

"What is going on here? Why is she so wet? What have you done? You look awful yourself. What is it? Did you fight?"

"No, no, calm yourself down; she got a little confused, began to pull her hair. I gave her the medication; she is fine. Let her be."

*I left Pat with Mom, put my jogging stuff on, and began to run on Easton Road, north.*

❦

# -XXXIV-

~❖~

Mallory's second rendezvous with Max was more peculiar than the previous one. She had been waiting for him since twelve o'clock; she had ordered room service—Caesar salad, whole grain toast, and fruit—and took a nap. Around three o'clock Max showed up: "I am terribly sorry; of course I'll pay for all your time." He threw a bundle of $100 bills on the bed and his bloated body into a chair.

"Mallory, I got a little problem and maybe you could help." He pulled out a handkerchief from the back pocket of his pants and blew his nose. "Did I tell you the last time about my son Robert? No? Okay, well he is fourteen; a big kid for his age—physically, not any other way. His bar mitzvah was an ordeal; he has ADD, hyperactive something or Asperger's syndrome, you name it. Last night I came home late; I went to his room to say good night—I do every night—and I found him asleep in front of his computer. The computer was on; he must have downloaded a porno flick—no, no, don't be quick to react. It was a boy-to-boy porno; yeah, two guys sucking each other."

Mallory was wondering where all this was heading.

"So you wonder whether he is gay?"

"Oh, no, not gay; no way; here is the thing. You see, when I was his age, I also played with boys, you know what I mean, sort of experimenting; it was easier. Girls had never put out then; at best you could kiss them. If a woman were available, of course I would have preferred to have sex with her."

"So don't worry, he is also experimenting."

"No, no, it isn't the matter of worrying; you see, I am in the business of fixing things, not worrying. I am like my father that way. It is in our genes."

A grin lingered on Max's face.

"I thought you were an orphan kid, adopted by a Jewish couple," Mallory said.

"This isn't the time to get into the nature versus nurture stuff, but my father fixed my problem. How? One day he saw me in the garage with another boy—we were masturbating each other. The same day, he took me to his shop on the Lower East Side, on Orchard Street, where he had a hat store—the front was the sales area, the back was the accounting business—the two were separated with a curtain. In the back worked a Polish woman; she was a bookkeeper, I would say in her thirties. Elena— a grown-up woman, a beautiful woman—big breasts. So my father went back alone for a few minutes and came out; without saying a word he pushed me in. Now that I think back, she must have been his mistress. So this woman Elena had sex with me right there behind the curtain, on a sofa—it took less than two minutes, and that was it. I never touched boys after that."

"Did you say that the hat store was on Orchard Street?"

"Yes. What has this got to do with the price of kosher dill?"

"The price of kosher dill?"

"Never mind, we are getting off track. How about doing me a favor and making my son a man? I would handsomely pay for it."

Mallory was still wondering about the Orchard connection—how could that be? There was still a hat store there; did Max own the building and the hat store? Is it possible that he knew that she lived around there? What if he was involved with the previous tenant—the call girl—and her disappearance? Or was this a pure coincidence and her "paranoia" was kicking in, as her sister calls it?

"So what happened to the hat store?"

"Are you thick? This isn't about women's hats, Mallory; with the money I'll give you, you can buy as many hats as you want from Saks Fifth Avenue. What I am asking…"

Mallory recovered a little bit. "You are asking me to fuck your son."

"Yes; long and short of it," he said with a snicker.

"Can we do it in the same hat store?"

"You know, you are bizarre. Is that supposed to be some symbolic shit or what? I don't even know whether there is still a hat store there or not, or who owns it. I haven't been there for years. Why not here?"

"Sex with an underage kid is…especially in a hotel where everyone knows you and now me."

"Not as a commercial transaction, especially with the consent and under the supervision of the father."

"Oh, you'll watch. Did your father watch you fucking Elena?"

"No, no, I'll hide somewhere or take an adjacent room. Don't worry about the details; please do this favor for me. I'll do anything you want!"

"Maybe."

"I've got to go; please say yes."

"I'll think about it."

"What is that contemptuous look? I don't do that to you. In fact, I admire you. You are a very savvy businesswoman—you sell yourself and still keep it."

"No, I don't sell myself. I do sell my time for a limited encounter," Mallory replied. "Well, I guess we both exploit each other."

Max began to feel uneasy; he was concerned that this sort of honesty could spoil his fun.

"Actually, I guess we both give pleasure to each other, right?"

As Max readied to leave, he couldn't help adding, "Furthermore, fucking a fourteen-year-old boy could be fun, ha, ha."

Mallory stood by the window overlooking the fountain in front of the hotel and tried to figure out why Max's proposal was so confusing. She used to fuck sixteen-year-old boys, but then she was sixteen herself. She couldn't even remember what that was like. It was a haphazard activity: no one was in charge. Now, as a woman, how would she even go about having sex with a kid? Would she have to undress him? Wash him? Would she lie down and beckon him or pull him on top?

ᎧᏯᏜᎧ

# -XXXV-

*T*eenage boys would fuck anything, including each other. I was very popular with them as a legitimate alternative; boys were not that choosy either. Any hole would do, even a rolled-up hand. It took just a few minutes for them to come. I just let them, so that we could have a good time. Otherwise, their preoccupation with whether they'd get "lucky" or if I would "put out" at the end of the night interfered with having spontaneous pleasure—pitiful. Also, I had to time it well in order not to face a rebound; most recovered within a few hours and their eyes became glassy again. It was okay with me, but by the time I was just warming up, they'd finish and want to talk. About what? Mostly about their parents—puke!

ᏮᎥᎥᎥᎧ

# -XXXVI-

"Hello, Ms. Mallory; welcome!" Junetta always welcomed Mallory genuinely. "Mr. Levine is already on the massage table."

Mallory walked into the library. Mr. Levine was sleeping. Should she wake him up or not? Mallory hesitated a few minutes; as if on cue, Mr. Levine woke up.

"Hi, Mallory. This isn't some sort of pressure on you to be on time at all. When I lie down here I feel like you are with me, so I am extending your visit by a half hour." John yawned.

"I am sorry; trains are so unreliable these days. We'll make it up at the other end of the session."

They quickly settled into their routine.

"The last time, you were telling me about that Tits bar." Mallory rarely initiated the discussion, but she felt guilty for cutting him off in the middle of his story the previous visit.

Mr. Levine laughed.

"No, no, it's Toots. You know, Mallory, you are a funny girl; Tits bar!" Mr. Levine wondered whether Mallory noticed his breasts had enlarged from the medication.

"Toots Shor's was a sports bar; the hangout for athletes like Joe DiMaggio, Babe Ruth, and Mickey Mantle. Do you know who Joe DiMaggio was?"

"The guy who divorced Marilyn Monroe?" This was Mallory's only knowledge from the fifties, Mr. Levine's era.

"Are you sure it wasn't the other way around? Speaking of wives, Frank Gifford occasionally brought Maxine there. We were all in love with her. She looked like you: beautiful, unpretentious, young. Richard Nixon was in love with both Frank and Maxine."

"Were you a football player?" Mallory didn't think so, but she knew how happy it made men to be thought of as athletes.

"No, don't be deceived by my size; I've been a klutz my whole life. I was there because I knew Toots from Philadelphia back in the day…in

New York he got involved with the wrong crowd and became another 'crumb-bum,' as they say."

Mallory had stopped giving deep massage to Mr. Levine for a number of months now; he didn't need it anymore. She softly touched his back, his legs, and his shoulders—almost caressingly.

Mr. Levine began to cry.

"I am sorry. I don't know why I cry. Every little bit of emotion brings tears to my eyes these days. I cry during old westerns when a brave cowboy's ranch is taken by gangs, or I cry when I see a good man is framed for a crime that he didn't commit; I even cry over good things—a soldier coming home, hugging his wife who is holding in her arms their newborn son. The other day I watched, for the umpteenth time, *From Here to Eternity*...when I heard Montgomery Clift's bugle call after Frank Sinatra was beaten to death, my heart ached so badly that I wanted to die—I was in a puddle of tears. My God, this is like emotional incontinence!" Mr. Levine laughed through the tears.

"Toots was lucky. He died at the right age before suffering all these indignities of getting old. Developers and greedy lenders killed him. He was such a gregarious guy, always joking...I thought nothing could ever take him down.

"I walked in one early afternoon; he was sitting with two unsavory guys at the circular bar, one on each side of him. The place was almost empty. I sat in one corner and ordered my Jack Daniels and soda. After those two characters left, he came over carrying his drink—he liked soda and brandy—and he looked troubled."

"Who were those Mafia-looking guys, Toots?" I asked.

"Well, my future partners," he replied, and took a swig. 'John, I am in financial trouble. How about your becoming my partner? Four million dollars would do it.'

"He was serious and not serious. In those days, the real-estate people were all going bust. He knew that I couldn't even pay my bank loans. Even if I had money, I would never have gotten involved in a bar-restaurant business. My father gave me three important pieces of advice: one, keep your head down and try not to be too interesting; two, stick to roads most traveled; and three, never own something that eats while you are sleeping. I go to bed at 9 p.m. Bars stay open till 3 a.m.; it's the same reason I don't own horses even though I love racing.

"So I attempted to explain, 'Toots, there are three reasons why I cannot be your partner.' He began to have his famous belly laugh, shaking up and down—back to his jovial self as he told a story:

"You know the one about the old Jewish guy who was walking down 42nd Street? A prostitute accosts him: 'Hey, daddy, how would you like to have a good time?' The guy answers, 'Oh, sweetheart, I would love to; but there are five reasons why I can't. Reason number one: I don't have any money; reason number two:... The girl stops him: 'It's okay, man, I don't have to hear the other four.'"

∞

# -XXXVII-

*The only regular activity that my father engaged me in was to go target shoot-ing at Blue Trail on exit 66 off Merritt Parkway.*

We would get up early on Saturday mornings, pack our guns and ammu-nition, and get in his Honda station wagon. We would have breakfast at the International House of Pancakes on Post Road and then hit the road. I never understood why my sister didn't come along if his purpose was to train me in self-defense. I didn't mind that, though; for a change I had him all to myself. Looking back, I understood now, I was assigned the role of the son he never had. Of course, by the time we returned from Turkey, I was taller and stronger than my sister. So maybe it made sense to him.

Dad had his gun friends up at the Blue Trail—mostly early retired officers and cops—from different parts of Connecticut. Their friendship was limited to a few chats on new guns, gun laws, bartering, and exchanging ammo with each other.

We would rent ($15) our paper markers and tape them on a secured wood plac-ard. My job was to place them at various distances from the shooting gallery—for shotguns and revolvers, 50 to 100 feet; for rifles, 150 to 400 feet. Then a shrieking whistle would warn everyone to retreat to their own spots. For a strange reason, I wasn't at all scared at that supposedly scary moment: to run back 50 or 400 feet in an overgrown, uneven land, full of junk thrown in, before the second whistle that permitted shootings.

Then a deafening barrage of gunfire would start. Even though I wore earplugs, my ears would ring for hours afterward. There were two kinds of competitions: the first was who could hit the bull's-eye most frequently, and the second, who could load, reload, and pull the trigger the most within fifteen minutes of the shooting zone. I at least tried to compete for the second challenge, but the gun would get very hot; it would burn my hands.

So I stopped and watched my Dad—the intensity and the fury on his face, a killer's look even, but I wasn't afraid; I was simply curious. Would he "by mis-take" shoot me as I ran back from the gallery during the changing of markers?

*Why was he always holding me in his sight, while other people would be resting or going into the gun shop for coffee or a snack? Many times I thought he was going to kill me, but that never stopped me from going with him to Blue Trail; I think now that on some level, I wished he had shot me.*

*On the drive back, Dad would remain totally silent. He would let me shift the radio stations and listen to whatever was audible without much static. He was equally quiet at lunch in Sherwood Diner, a Greek restaurant...it was the closest you could get to Turkish food in Connecticut.*

Ꮿᴜᴜᴖ

# -XXXVIII-

Today there was a new man at the registration desk; Mallory hated to introduce herself.

"Hi, I'm Mallory Coldwell; I believe Mr. Max Quant reserved a room for me."

The Plaza Hotel's elegant staff was accustomed to wealthy clientele making reservations under false names while giving the real credit card, then later on paying the bill in cash. Most of the staff knew her by now and would rush over and hand her the key without even stopping by the desk.

"Oh, yes, Ms. Coldwell, welcome back. Here is your key. Your room has been reserved from last night so that you can check in before lunchtime."

Within ten minutes the doorbell rang. It was room service. A young Hispanic man pushed in a food cart and set the table for two: steamed vegetables, brown rice, white bean salad, seven-grain bread, and a plate of fruit for Mallory and a seafood tray for Max: oysters, shrimp, scallops, and lobster with two bottles of nonalcoholic beer, Kaliber, on ice.

It was already 1:30. Max was an hour late. Finally he arrived, looking harassed and sweating profusely.

"I am sorry. This has been one of those days where nothing goes right." He took a sip of the Kaliber and sank into a sofa. "Ahh."

"Mallory, have you seen the movie *Ben-Hur*?"

Here he goes again, she thought: "No."

"Well, you should. There is a character in that movie, Simonides, Charlton Heston's accountant; how about Professor Lieberman in *Gentleman's Agreement*?"

"No, again, I am sorry."

"How about Dr. Zorba in the *Ben Casey* television series?"

Then Mallory remembered having read something like that recently in the *New York Times*, about her home state; Senator Lieberman, who was going to be Al Gore's running mate, looked like one of those characters.

"You do sort of look like Senator Lieberman."

"He is a Jewish version of me; I am more a cross between him and Charlton Heston."

"You do have Charlton Heston's shoulders."

Mallory couldn't continue in the same vein because she was afraid of bursting into laughter…she had to change the subject.

"Max, I know people on Wall Street get rich by buying and selling stocks. What exactly do you do?"

Max didn't miss a beat.

"You got another two hours? To try to explain what I really do in less time than that would sound like total gibberish."

He was passing the bottle from one hand to the other.

"I sell short; I sell shares of a company, securities that I don't own, and when the price drops, I'll buy them with other people's money, big money, and I pocket 30 to 50 percent of the profit. You don't become rich by buying and selling stocks with your own money, even if you buy low and sell high, which is not always the case, unless you are an insider; then at best you'll make a few bucks. You make serious money by leveraging; for example, if you invest $100 in an asset and sell it a year later for $120, you have earned 20 percent; right? Not bad. But if you invest $10 and borrow $90, pay 10 percent interest on the debt, your return will be 110 percent. Now who wouldn't give you money if you guarantee 10 percent? That means that you invest conservatively; you don't go for high-risk investments." He took another sip and unbuttoned his shirt.

"I also do pair trading; no, it isn't wife-swapping. Any man who knows Norma would not trade with me… It is a joke, Mallory; here is what pair trading is: I identify two firms in a similar business, and then I buy heavy shares of the better, more solvent one, while betting an equal size against the other.

"This is all active stuff, which requires you to be on your toes. Then there is a quiet, passive way of getting rich while sitting on your ass and moving your lips discreetly—being a feeder. The only requirement for that job is to be ruthless."

Max's long, rambling dissertation left Mallory vaguely scared.

"You look puzzled, Mallory; what that means is I make money from those who make money and from those who think they are going to make money."

"What does a feeder do?"

"All I have to do is to tell people with deep pockets and other hedge-fund managers that I invest a chunk of my money with Mr. Mandrian, for example, for a good steady return—without any expectation of spectacular result—and more importantly for safety; I also add that Mr. Mandrian established a variety of offshore banks.

"The word gets around that Quantum Max trusts his money to Mr. Mandrian; every day I get calls from big shots in the financial world, investors, bankers begging for an introduction to Mr. Mandrian since he never takes calls directly. I eventually and reluctantly agree to do it."

"So, what is in it for you?"

"Oh, I take 1 percent of the money I bring to him. That might not seem too much, but think about 1 percent of one hundred million…yeah? Now you know how the feeder makes money."

To Mallory, this thing made no sense. "I presume he takes some percentage of that money for himself, but how does he make money for an investor to stay with him, never mind getting the new ones?"

"Ahh, that is the heart of the game. First you have to buy into 'malice for all, charity for none.'"

Seeing disgust on Mallory's face, Max offered mock credibility: "It is written on the Lincoln Memorial."

"He would turn in his grave," protested Mallory. "So what does this guy do to provide malice for all and charity for himself?"

"What he does is guarantee to his former investors a few percentage points above the S&P on their money; he delivers that by using an equal percentage of the new investors' money and in return, they all promote him worldwide. So as long as he gets new, new investors (that is where I get in), he could keep perpetuating this promise indefinitely. It is a kind of Ponzi game that never fails."

"But how long could that go on?"

"Well, as long as the market is bullish and the S&P provides about 5 to 8 percentile basis points, the sky's the limit."

"What if the market stops being bullish?" Mallory asked.

"The name of that is bear market. Mallory; you are really smart." He sidled over to her. "If any one of the so-called expert financiers and money managers asked that question, they would never put themselves at such a risk. If I do not anticipate at least a year ahead that the market is going bearish, I'll be in trouble. But even then, the investors couldn't be that sour, at least the older ones, because their interests have been stashed away at offshore banks. They haven't paid diddly taxes on their returns for years; the only losers in this game are the IRS and foreigners—fuck them."

"And if you were able to anticipate the bear market, what would you do?"

"Ah, ha, ha, then my dear, I would sell everything, put the whole money in a Swiss bank, use my Israeli passport, and skip the country. Ha, ha, ha, you want to come along?"

Mallory was fascinated and repulsed by Max.

"But isn't that a rather bad thing to do?"

"Badness is in the eye of the beholder," Max replied with palpable self-importance. "There are some jobs in which it is impossible for a man to be virtuous."

"Aristotle said that." Mallory couldn't resist deflating him a little.

Max's tone quickly turned rancid: "I don't care who said it first; I am saying it now. For some, peddling of flesh wouldn't be a good thing; but for me, it is wonderful. You see, it is a good sin."

Mallory underestimated Max's negative capabilities.

"But isn't it also risky? I mean, how do you know that certain securities are either over- or undervalued?"

"Oh my God, Mallory, you are a smart woman; smarter than half of my partners. I'll tell you the ultimate secret of my business. This is how you secure success: You generate accounting irregularities in a firm, lower its anticipated earnings for one or two quarters, demoralize the management team, and spread rumors of their removal; there, you got it."

Max was smiling broadly.

"Accounting irregularities? That's a euphemism for fraud!"

He hesitated for a moment, then added, "I do not bribe the accounting firms. Now, here is your share for making my life pleasant. Sorry to disappoint you, but I have to go for a meeting; have a great lunch."

He threw a bundle of hundreds on the bed and rushed out.

Mallory was relieved. Did Max really think that she would be disappointed?

⟐⟐⟐

After Max left, Mallory sat on the makeshift dining table and ate her lunch. As she was wondering what to do with the fresh seafood platter, she got a text message from Ham: "Hi, need ne smoke? Sry abt the othr nite."

"Hi yourself, I sort of lost my NYU clients – the new 1's – xcept 1 – r all square – I still hv the whole thng frm last mth. Is bsness bad?"

"I'll srvive."

"Ham, did u hv lunch?"

"No, nt yt, were u offring Chnse fd?"

"No, got smthng betr. Wd u like 2 hv a rl frsh cfood cmbo - r u home - I cud brg it ovr?"

"K"

"I'll b ovr in less thn hlf hr."

Mallory wrapped the seafood in the table cover and got in a cab.

The cab driver sniffed the food: "I do the same. I take any leftovers home from the restaurants for my dog. But at the Plaza, they should have packed it better, you know, some fancy place! Most likely they don't have those aluminum boxes, I bet; no one who eats there bothers to take out."

Mallory tried to read the name of the cab driver through the plastic and overlapping double glass; only a few letters were visible.

"Right."

Some liquid was oozing out of the bag onto the floor.

"It smells good, though; what do you have, cat or dog?"

"Neither."

The cab driver shut up for a while. He was about to enter Central Park from the Avenue of the Americas entrance.

"Hey, don't! Where are you going? I said Amsterdam and 108th Street."

The driver put the brakes on. "Look, Miss, you deliver food, I drive; there is heavy traffic on the west side; so I was going up north from the park and then cross over. But if you don't mind getting stuck in traffic, fine with me."

"No, I don't. Please stay on Central Park South and turn north. Thank you."

There was no traffic jam of any sort. For the rest of the time, the driver and Mallory said nothing to each other.

☙

Ham was waiting by the door.

"What is that? Are you carrying fish in a cloth?" Ham noticed the Plaza Hotel lettering on it. "Where did you get it? Did you lift it from a restaurant?"

"Sort of," Mallory replied.

"Would you like to come in?"

In the past, Mallory met Ham in front of his building but never went in—there had never been an invitation.

"Well, of course," she replied. "We can't eat this on the sidewalk."

"Let me warn you; my room is the polar opposite of yours—the ultimate clutter. But first, you are going to meet Mrs. Vakfiye, a Bosnian lady from whom I rent a room. She used to teach history in Kosovo until the Serbians killed her husband, who apparently got caught in the fervor for independence. Fearing for her life and that of her son, they moved here. Don't be put off with her proselytizing; she is kind and well-meaning. She also speaks good English."

As they entered the apartment, a little overweight woman in her fifties with a pleasant face warmly welcomed her.

"Mrs. Vakfiye, this is my friend Mallory; she is also a writer and a fish thief."

"No, I don't think so. She is too beautiful! Let me put that on a plate."

Ham's room looked like the rest of the apartment. The word *clutter* didn't do justice to the chaotic state of the room: Papers and books were piled up everywhere—Mallory had to carefully navigate around them. Red and blue Turkish kilims were all around—on the floor, on the walls, covering the single bed and the couch, pillows, chairs, and table.

"Is her son in the carpet business?"

"No, silly. This is how Bosnians decorate their houses. Don't you like it?"

"I do, I do, just a little overdone. Have your parents been here?"

"Oh, no, to see how I live? My mother would have a stroke; Dad, I don't know; he gets the life of a struggling artist. When he isn't under mom's pragmatic influence, he really believes in me. He even quotes John Sloane, whom I mentioned in one of my classes, if you remember."

"Yeah, I remember. Actually, you repeated that all the time: 'Though a living cannot be made at art, art makes life worth living,' right?"

Ham nodded.

"Were you trying to discourage us from becoming artists, or were you looking for validation of your life as an artist?" asked Mallory.

Sadness washed over Ham. "Well, if I kept repeating that, obviously I wasn't convinced that I could succeed in either case."

Mrs. Vakfiye returned with a huge, round copper tray. Mallory's seafood, a loaf of bread, and sliced cucumbers were arranged on it.

"I am soaking the cloth in hot water," she said, still smiling.

Ham dragged another chair from the hall and made Mrs. Vakfiye sit down in spite of her protestations: "You eat and talk, you both are young."

Mallory was happy that Mrs. Vakfiye stayed, partly because the dangerous subject of where she got the fish would be off topic and partly because she really liked this gentle woman. Mrs. Vakfiye took a small piece of bread and cut a shrimp in half.

"You are not eating?"

"I had mine already," Mallory replied.

Ham devoured two lobster tails. "You forgot the cocktail sauce. I guess you were in a hurry," he said while chewing.

Mallory dismissed Ham's sarcasm. She was more intrigued by the number of prints in Arabic lettering between the hanging kilims.

"Mrs. Vakfiye, what is written on these? Are these simply calligraphy or some sayings?"

"Actually they are mine," said Ham.

Mallory looked puzzled.

"Do you speak Arabic?"

"No, these are Islamic beliefs that are the essence of Islam. Oh, I may not have told you, but I converted to Islam about two years ago. In fact,

Mrs. Vakfiye was my conduit. She doesn't just clean apartments; she also cleans minds."

Mrs. Vakfiye was listening with a beatific expression on her face.

"And the Purpose of God," Ham continued, having secured the attention of his audience, "is to make humans 'godly' with a small 'g';—humility is one of the requirements."

"How long did it take you to become Muslim?" Mallory asked.

"Two minutes."

"Two minutes?"

"Yes, all I had to do was to recite *Ashhadu enla eliha; Ashhadu enla Mohammadan eptuhu varisuluhu,* which means 'There is only one God and Mohammed is his only prophet,'" explained Ham.

"Are you kidding? That's it? Quite different from how you convert to Judaism. When I was attending Kabbalah classes, I asked them what it would entail to become Jewish. They said it'll take years of training under the guidance of a rabbi, and then you have to pass a tough exam."

"Why would you want to be Jewish anyway?" asked Ham "Every Jew I know seems to wish he wasn't."

Mrs. Vakfiye was listening to these two young, attractive Americans engaged on a subject she had never heard in her own country. Even Ham's explanation of Islam to Mallory was totally alien to her.

"What is Kabbalah?" Mrs. Vakfiye asked.

"The Kabbalah is a sisterhood of goddesses connected by this flimsy string," said Ham and tugged on the red bracelet on Mallory's left wrist, expecting a terse reaction from her.

There was none.

Mrs. Vakfiye picked up the empty dishes from the table and took them to the kitchen.

Mallory also got up and readied herself to leave:

"Thank you, Mrs. Vakfiye, for the cucumbers. You may keep the cloth if you like."

Ham walked out behind her to the door, peering at her curves through her dress; Mallory skipped down the sidewalk. Once she got to the corner of 108th and Broadway, she waved at Ham without turning around.

Did she know he was watching?

⁊ⱮⱮↄ

# -XXXIX-

*N*othing *tastes like itself: Le goût natural of food has disappeared—tomatoes don't taste like tomato; peaches don't smell like peach; genetically swollen grapes don't look like grapes. The natural characteristics of all vegetables, as well as meat, chicken, and fish, are chemically and esthetically altered, and in the process, air and water are polluted with carcinogenic nitrogen dioxide and hydrocarbons, all compounding this maltransformation—even semen has lost its natural taste and smell.*

*We are all genetically deteriorating.*

# -XL-

Max couldn't have found a better-fitting place to live than Manhattan. As a child he was never taught about having an inner sense of right or wrong. His parents, Molly and Harold Goodkind, who had adopted him when he was little older than two years of age, were atheists—though Jewish by heritage—without possessing a fully developed intellectual understanding as to what atheism meant. They mocked Jews, Christians, Muslims, and Buddhists with equal fervor. Although Max didn't understand the intensity of his parents' negations, nevertheless he adopted their view of religion and philosophy of life. Their credos were "Hell and Heaven are transportable to the self-serving" and "Make money, lots of it—however you can—with the proviso of 'just don't get caught.'"

Max's first exercise of this self-serving dictum was to interfere with his parents' attempt to adopt another child. He was only seven years old when a social worker from the adoption agency came for a routine home visit to evaluate the stability of the family. Max, with his eyes tearing, informed her that his parents were beating him every night. "Please don't tell them what I told you. They would kill me!" The social worker was aghast; she quickly reported them to her supervisors. It was only after a long investigation that the city's child protection service figured out that Max was lying. Nevertheless, his parents' chances of adopting another child were doomed.

Max never explained satisfactorily to anyone why he made such outrageous accusations against his parents. He was punishing them because he felt unloved, he said to the social worker. That might have been partly true, but the main reason was that he didn't want to share his potential inheritance with a sibling—though he found out much later that there wasn't much to inherit.

His adoptive parents, the Goodkinds, were in millinery—he bought and sold, she repaired. They lived a modest life in a small two-level house on Allerton Avenue in the Bronx; their 1968 hunter-green Chevy Impala stayed in the garage except on weekends, when Max's father, Harold, would drive them to City Island for lunch in one of the seafood restaurants on the harbor or to have a picnic at Orchard Beach. Harold Goodkind took the subway to his shop on Orchard Street on the Lower East Side. Otherwise the family walked, for everything they needed was close by: shops, grocery stores, restaurants, hair salons, and banks were all lined up along the Avenue from Williamsbridge to White Plains Roads. Jacobi Hospital was just a short distance from their home.

The Goodkinds saved all their money to send Max to college, something that they'd both wanted for themselves but their own parents couldn't afford. Max proved to be worthy of their sacrifice; he won a scholarship to Princeton University and later was accepted to the Wharton School of Business at the University of Pennsylvania. By the time Max finished school, his parents' business had closed—women were no longer wearing hats, except in Easter parades. The Goodkinds were forced to lease the second floor of their house to medical students from the nearby Einstein College of Medicine to balance their budget.

Harold even had to sell his old Chevy—the odometer read only 7,212 miles—to save on the insurance. Al Piccoli, the owner of the body shop on Eastchester Road, asserted that the car wasn't worth even one year's insurance payment. Still, Al was willing to buy it because he could chop it and sell it for parts—he hoped to break even! Harold wasn't that naïve, but there were no other offers. Chopped or not, the day before Al came to pick up the car, Harold spent a few hours in the garage saying goodbye to his only luxury item; he cleaned and polished it and changed its oil for the last time.

Max offered some financial help, but his parents refused—"Son, we are fine; if we are ever in need, we will ask." They never did. That was okay with Max. Even after he became a tycoon, it never occurred to him to improve their living conditions. For him "if we are ever in need" meant exactly that. He never visited them to see how they were living. He was embarrassed of his family, his background, his house in the Bronx, his Jewishness; he wanted to distance himself from his childhood, if not totally erase it—he even thought of murdering his parents.

During his last year at Penn, Max changed his last name to Hathaway; his parents were very impressed with their son's wit and accepted this bittersweet irony. They were only concerned that the Waspish name might backfire because he looked too Jewish with his wavy, dark hair and prominent nose. Fortunately for Max, Molly Goodkind died at the age of fifty-nine from lung cancer and Harold Goodkind six months later from loneliness.

In less than five years, Max Hathaway's hedge fund was a Wall Street phenomenon. His last year's returns broke all previous records. His successes were regularly reported in the business sections of the *Wall Street Journal*, *Financial Times*, and the *New York Times*. He was frequently a guest on CNBC, Bloomberg News, and other television channels.

Max bought a $25,000,000 apartment on Fifth Avenue and then a large house in East Hampton on the shore. Depending on the season, Max parked his wife Norma (the daughter of a well-to-do Jewish family from New Jersey) and their two children, eight-year-old Audrey and fourteen-year-old Robert, while he unleashed himself on everyone and everything with his characteristic sense of entitlement and foxy mien.

Max considered himself a nonpsychological man. He was not interested in his real past, which he had made up of a series of misguided lies anyway; he made up his past anew, as circumstances demanded. He wasn't interested in the future either, having no end product in his mind besides having lots of money; that he already had. His past and the future thus made irrelevant, Max became more intensely aware of the present, if not the moment.

Once he confessed his dilemma to Professor Hamilton Thurman II, who dismissed the whole thing by quoting Donald Barthelme: "A past-less, future-less man (a simple man), born anew at every instant." "You are a condensation of an ordinary person." Obviously Hamilton couldn't tolerate uniqueness in any other person besides himself. So Max tried again to show Hamilton that his simplicity was the deepest level of complexity.

"When I try to think of myself, I find an empty hole; I try to feel myself, I find an inner dryness; I act as others might, including having a job, a family, observing the law, but truth be told, I don't believe any one of those things is really applicable to me."

Hamilton was still unfazed. "Even Warhol once confessed that he looks at the mirror and sees no one, nothing."

Max got the whiff of Hamilton's disdain and gave up. At least with the Warhol analogy Hamilton placed him in good company. Nevertheless, he had to show some backbone: "I hate his Campbell's Soup cans," came out in a strangled voice.

Max grew up feeling that no one gave a damn about him, never did. He believed that no one would come to his help if needed; if he were helpless and hungry, he believed the world would watch him starve to death; so he decided to eat the world, with a particular appetite for women.

A female psychologist whom he had dated briefly told him that his narcissism, mingled with self-hate, was the source of his wanting to be loved without reciprocation. He had told her and many other women that he was getting divorced; when the doctor figured out the lie, she terminated their relationship with a note: "I am reconsidering your earlier diagnosis. I think malodorous narcissism, mingled with hatred of women, is more fitting."

ഐസ്

Max walked up the steps of the Four Seasons restaurant. One of the owners, Julian, warmly welcomed him as Max squeezed a $50 bill into his hand.

"Your guest is already here, Mr. Hathaway; please follow me."

He led Max toward the balcony of the Grill Room. Max had been a regular lunch client of the restaurant for more than three years but had still not been accommodated in the power circle.

At one of the main tables, Revlon's Ronald Perelman looked agitated, sitting with Howard Gittis and Arnold Drapkin. At another table, Blackstone's Steve Schwarzman, Pete Peterson, and AIG's Hank Greenberg were in some dark conversation. At a third table, Lloyd Blankfein of Goldman Sachs seemed to be having a good time with three young recruits. At two tables next to each other, David Rubenstein of Carlyle and Vikram Pandit of Old Lane Hedge Fund were with two older men who looked like investors. Sitting to the left was Alan Schwartz of Bear Stearns with JPMorgan's James Dimon and James Lee. To the right, Sandy Weill and Chuck Prince of Citi were quietly having their lunch. At the next table, the Lauder brothers with Leonard's son, William, were in a heated discussion. In the corner, Mayor Giuliani was holding court with Charles Dolan and his son James.

As he passed them, Max wondered what Carl Icahn and Frank Biondi had in common with Edgar Bronfman that they shared a meal. There were a number of unoccupied tables. Max couldn't understand why Julian would sit him on the balcony.

Max worked the room, receiving his customary mixed reactions: Some people reluctantly shook his hand; some casually waved him off, while others tried to ignore him. For the latter group, Max represented the worst of their industry: He was a coarse, flashy, loud, greedy, unsophisticated newcomer with no breeding, no culture or dignity—too Jewish.

Max's guest, a young and attractive reporter named Clara van Praag from *Forbes* magazine, stood up and enthusiastically shook his hand.

"Thank you very much for inviting me here for lunch. Most CEOs don't even bother to throw a sandwich at you, even if the interview is scheduled for the lunch hour," Clara said with a faint voice.

Max's eyes lingered a little too long on her lips—dark red.

"Well, we've got to eat, right? Why not eat good stuff? I recommend the duck or wild salmon here, or you can have one of each," he laughed.

Max's real intention was to show her off to the Four Seasons lunch crowd: *Forbes* was interested in him.

"Thanks; actually I am just going to have a salad. So the last time we met in your office, you were talking about the wisdoms of your father." She took out her pad. "Can you give me an example?"

Max was surveying the room—no one was even glancing in their direction.

"Well, we walked a lot or took mass transportation rather than using the car. You see, he was ahead of his time—emphasis on physical fitness and environmental protection."

"What about business-related advice?"

"Oh, he *shorted* before such a term was even invented. He bet against his own business—he knew that hat fashions would be declining from their heyday."

"But that makes no sense, Mr. Hathaway. The hat business kept declining and never recovered."

"Well, you are right, Clara; he only knew half of the equation. Not only do you have to know how to take a business down, you must also be sure that it has the potential for recovery once you stop manipulating the price."

"Okay, let's move on. Did your father have any advice for you about the ethics of business?"

Max was wondering whether he could seduce her.

"My father was high on metaphors. He warned me that most crashes occur on straight roads...he had a simple philosophy of life."

Max tried to look yearningly sentimental. "He used to advise jocularly: 'Rise above the principles.' In fact, when it came to business, he was big on loyalty."

"Some people say that you are exactly like that. That you would cut your mother's throat for $1,000,000?"

Max laughed, some lobster escaping his mouth. "I'll kill my mother for less than that—ha, ha, ha, ha. Now these are off-the-record jokes, Clara. As a kid I used to watch Red Skelton: He was hilarious! If I hadn't gone into business, I would have become either a stand-up comedian or a politician."

The reporter's nostrils opened wide...a scent of blood rushed in.

"You have political aspirations?"

"Listen, off the record, right? You don't think that I can wipe both Gore and Bush's asses off in a single debate? I mean, one is pedantic and stiff: He is like a high school principal who bores the audience with every detail and irrelevant facts—a wonk, out of touch with the real people; the other is loosey-goosey with a smirk on his face: a dropout who has no information on any relevant facts. Both of them had mental problems, too, if you know what I mean. They both consulted psychiatrists or counselors or facilitators or whatever.

"You see, when you elect a nut to the White House, you have no idea what he might do. For example, I met Dr. Hutschnecker and Dr. Klein, Nixon's physicians, as well as another psychiatrist—whose name I cannot mention here... They can tell you stories that would make your hair stand up."

The reporter interrupted him: "So why then don't you throw your hat into the ring?"

"No, no. You see, it is better to be a kingmaker than king: You get all the benefits of power and none of its problems. In fact, this coming Saturday, I am having dinner with the future king."

The reporter inhaled Max's hot breath and felt a little nauseated.

"Who is that?"

"No, I cannot divulge his name yet. Have you ever seen me giving a speech on the spot? Don't you think I can be a better president than Bush? Come on. I can talk on any subject for an hour without preparation, without a teleprompter, just spontaneously."

"So you have all the makings of a president, but you don't have such aspiration. So what do you aspire to, more wealth?"

"Look, once you have a G5 sitting at LaGuardia, a one-hundred-eighty-footer sailing between the Mediterranean and the Caribbean at your whimsy, apartments—palaces, in fact—in Manhattan, in London, and in Paris, winter and summer homes in the Hamptons, Palm Beach, the South of France and Greece, you stop aspiring for more money. Two billion dollars is the final equalizer. There is no difference between two billion or twenty billion in terms of someone's quality of life."

The reporter was sure that her editor would love to publish this piece with plenty of innuendos of mockery and contempt.

"Balzac said, 'There is a crime behind every major wealth!'"

Max was caught off guard. The name was familiar.

"Well actually, most of the crimes are perpetrated by poor people. Go visit prisons; not many wealthy people, right? Occasionally you find a few bad apples, in federal minimum security places for tax evasion or insider trading. The rest of us were never caught in such so-called 'white-collar crimes.'"

The reporter jotted down: *Caught* is the operative word.

"Getting back to your personal reputation, how do you react to people who say you are unscrupulous and untrustworthy—a scavenger?"

Max got irritated.

"Who the fuck says things like that? My incompetent ex-partners whom I fired? Unless you give me the source, I would consider that as coming from you or your editor."

"Let's move on." The reporter was not the type to be intimidated.

"Is it true that as a part of your son's bar mitzvah celebration, you flew one hundred kids to Las Vegas for a private performance of Le Cirque du Soleil?"

"Actually two hundred; it was a blast. I always loved circuses and magicians as a child; I can do a few card tricks like a pro." Max took a quarter from his pocket, put it on his right palm showing its head up, pretending to be oblivious to the reporter's noticing it. He flipped the coin to his left hand. "Head or tail? Now be careful, the loser will take the check."

The reporter was thinking, "this man is totally deranged," but to complete this hideous story, she had to find a way out of it. She definitely didn't want to pay for the lunch. She saw "the head" up in his right hand—he wasn't exactly hiding it. If he flipped the coin straight to his left hand, tail would be facing up, but that wouldn't be a trick. Somehow he must have flipped the coin twice while shifting from one hand to the other, but then that would be an obvious trick. So he may have flipped the coin straight, tricking me to think that he was tricking me—son of a bitch.

"Mr. Hathaway, I don't play such games. I am already convinced that you are a magician, but let's move on. How about your personal life? How do you maintain a family life while you are so incredibly busy?"

"For me, the family comes first. I have been married to the same woman for sixteen years, and we have two extraordinarily smart and talented children. My wife is in charge of the internal affairs, and she is very good at it."

"What is her name?"

"Oh, ahh, yes, Norma. Norma. Just for a second I had a junior moment."

"What is that?"

"Well, that is the equivalent of a senior moment in a younger person—forgetting a familiar name or matter."

The reporter felt that this trickster could be pushed to the edge: "May I say that you have been a very interesting interviewee? I really appreciate your answers. May I also ask one more personal question, and the last one?"

"Shoot! I enjoyed the interview as well; you are smart and good-looking."

"Oh, thank you, Mr. Hathaway. Here it is. You have the reputation of being a charming flirt who seeks the company of young, beautiful women. Is this the true description of yourself? You seem to be an eternally young, virile adolescent and a perfect example of what Alice Longworth calls arrested development."

Max, who under his breath was fuming with obscenities, remained silent a few minutes.

The reporter, who feared she had overplayed her hand, clutched her pad.

"Who? Who is that bitch, Alice? I don't know anyone with that name. She imputes that..."

"No, no, no, Mr. Hathaway. She was Roosevelt's daughter—just a little psychology."

Max felt relieved. He thought that some woman from his past had been talking to the reporter.

"Oh, well, what do you expect from a Democrat?"

Max took a sip of water, gargled and swallowed it, and repeated the same once more. He wiped his lips, swiped his teeth with his napkin, and combed his hair back with the fingers of both hands.

"Let me tell you something: If you are asking whether I am a woman-izer, the answer is no. Now, if anyone sees us here and starts a rumor, what can I do? This is obviously a business meeting, and I don't have the need or the time to socialize with other women. Jesus, you are something! Let me ask you something: How would you like to have dinner with me?"

"Well, thank you for the invitation, but I think we have finished for to-day." The reporter collected her belongings, shook Max's hand, and with a well-practiced parting smile, left him sitting there seething.

෩

# -XLI-

*In the egalitarian act of intercourse, hardly distinguishable vaginas are grand equalizers. So why is it that man is obsessed with the beauty of women? I see how they pick me out in a crowd—they take my measure, then their eyes wash over my hair, my eyes, and my face. They like my high cheekbones, I can tell. Then they fix their yearning gaze on my lips, rather my mouth—I know what they are thinking. Rarely do they approach me right away. They keep surveying me (are her breasts real?), then they watch me walk—I can feel it. I stay an extra second on each leg so that my pelvis sways from side to side. Never mind my dimpled smile and my breathless voice.*

*I don't know why I do all this. For attention? I am not at all interested in any particular man; I just want to exceed every man's expectations. So for good measure I pull my elbows in and slip away while jiggling my breasts—exit, stage right.*

# -XLII-

Mallory and Pat got off the Lexington Avenue subway at the 33rd Street station and headed toward their favorite lunch place, Ali Baba restaurant on 34th Street—a hole-in-the-wall, South Eastern Anatolian eatery. A chunky, dark older man with gray hair and a heavy mustache welcomed "the beautiful ladies" back and sat them by the front window.

"Put this in your bag before I forget it," said Mallory and gave Pat an envelope.

"What is all this money that you have been giving to Dad? The first one was to buy the gun, you said, which I think is lunatic. Is he laundering money for you? I mean, all that cash? Mallory, are you doing something illegal? Where do you get so much money? Drugs?"

"I'm a whore, as you always thought I was," Mallory replied casually.

"Come on, Mallory, what is going on?"

The food arrived: a mixed salad, *barbunya*—a cold red bean appetizer—and hummus for Mallory with chicken shish kebab for Patricia.

"No, really. I used to sell pot, but whoring is much more profitable."

Pat put her fork down.

"Are you crazy? You are ruining your body, your life, and for what—to give money to Dad? Are you off your rocker? And he…Dad knows where this cash is coming from?"

"Dear sister, have you yet to dissect the male brain? Do you know what they have in there? I've got this district attorney who is supposed to prosecute people like himself and, of course, women like me, who pays me a fortune for sex, and another client, a Wall Street guy who loves to give me orgasms and showers me with money. They are both married and have children. I am in a very safe, gold cage of lust. You'd think they would be scared of being found out—speaking of potentially ruining one's life."

"Listen, I don't care about their self-destructiveness; I am only concerned about yours. Did Dad ask you for this money for my tuition?"

"Just hinted, and I sort of volunteered, knowing that he is struggling."

Pat looked troubled. "First of all, he is not exactly struggling; not any-more…not only is Mom no longer a financial drain on him, he also got over $200,000 from her life insurance. Furthermore, the next semester I'll be eligible for a scholarship. Do you realize that he is exploiting you, Mallory?"

The owner of the Ali Baba brought one *baklava* and one *kadayif* and two Turkish coffees.

"On the house for beautiful ladies," he joyfully put the tray on the table.

"It is my turn, my dear sister."

"Your turn for what?" Pat asked.

"To be exploited; variation on the theme."

Pat's lip curled in.

"Look, first do not call me 'my dear sister' with this, this patronizing, sarcastic tone. Second, and for the last time, I am telling you that he never sexually exploited me, okay?"

Mallory was coldly staring at her with the patience of a truth seeker.

"I don't want your money," Pat's voice was shrill, "directly or indi-rectly, especially the way you obtain it. I told this, your obsession, to a professor of psychiatry at Yale. He said people could function perfectly well in all areas of life, while sincerely believing the truthfulness of one single unreality. It is called a monodelusion and apparently, it is one of the characteristics of a paranoid personality. Look it up on the Internet! There is a whole description there of you in detail. This psychiatrist says that no reality, no fact, no testimony is ever sufficient to change this delu-sion, unless you get into treatment. Otherwise you are going to destroy yourself as well as the rest of us."

Pat threw the envelope on the table and walked out.

᏶ᎲᎲᎲᎲᎩ

# -XLIII-

*T*he first time Pat and I had an explicit confrontation about her relationship with Dad was following my discharge from Silver Hill Hospital. We were sixteen years old. She had just come back from an additional interview with Dr. Heshe about my original accusation of her sexual relations with Dad. While I was in the hospital, all three members of the family went through some lengthy evaluations.

"How could you? You crazy bitch, how could you, and why would you make such an outrageous accusation? Do you hate me and Dad that much? What have I done to you to deserve that?"

The pain and the agony on her face shamed me.

"I have recanted, haven't I?"

"Yeah, just to get out of the hospital. You still believe that…that it really happened. Look, look in the mirror, look at those paranoid eyes."

"Are you saying that in Turkey, Dad never came to your bed naked and you never touched his…"

"No! Damn it, never!" Pat screamed.

"Are you saying that you never fought him off when he wanted you to play with his penis or…"

"Shut up, Mallory! I am telling you, just shut up! You are insane! I think you should be locked up and the keys thrown away. If you keep saying things like that, I am going to call Dr. Heshe and have you recommitted, do you hear me?"

"I am only asking you to verify what I had seen with my own eyes. I am not talking about this to anyone else, only to you, I promise."

"Are you dense? I don't want you to tell me that lunatic story of yours either. For your information, neither Dad, nor any other man has ever touched me; I am still a virgin. Not like you, who slept with every boy in school! You should worry about your own promiscuity, your lack of dignity; do you know what they call you at Staples High?"

"Wildcat or something?"

"Yeah, you wish."

"Slut?"

"No. Looney."

I *was surprised and troubled. I thought all the kids, not just boys, liked me; they liked my humor, my irreverence, my devil-may-care attitude, and even my sexual freedom.*

"Looney?"

"Yes, Looney."

"And obviously you think so too." *I was hoping she'd recant in spite of all.*

"Well, what do you call someone who overdoses herself and cuts her wrist in a bathtub, almost gets drowned, and gives an even more bizarre reason for her behavior? Let me ask you this question: Am I sleeping with Dad, like you have no doubts?"

"I don't know."

"Isn't that what you said to the doctor in the hospital?"

"I didn't specify the time when it occurred."

"Well, you are lucky that Dad didn't take you seriously. I assure you that he would have killed you. Do you realize the consequences of your accusation? He could go to prison, I'd be branded for life, and the whole family, including you, would be disgraced."

*I had flickering images of Dr. Heshe.*

"Wipe that stupid smile off your face, Mallory! I swear I am going to hit you."

*She didn't. She just turned around and left the room.*

*Is remembrance a choice, or can one specific memory define one's life? I wish I knew.*

⟨∞⟩

# -XLIV-

For the hot and sultry New York summer, three of the four Weisman and Hathaway kids were deposited to the relative safety of their sleep-away camps in Maine (the two young girls, Audrey and Ellen, to Camp Vega in Fayette, and Samantha to coed Camp Laurel in Readfield).

Robert Hathaway, however, managed to spend only one night at Camp Skylemas; the attempt to bribe the camp director to keep him there at least one week failed. The director described him as too disruptive, unrelating, and asocial, which were the same reasons that two other camps had rejected him in the past—Takajo and Cedar. Norma couldn't believe that all these people figured him out in one single day. Max mourned the loss of another $10,000.

The Weismans and Hathaways spent most of their summers in the Hamptons, like most well-to-do Manhattanites. The Weismans summered in their rather modest four-bedroom inland house, while the Hathaways vacationed in their sprawling mansion on Ocean Drive—both in East Hampton.

The whole summer, Norma rarely left the Hamptons; Jeanny spent at least one day in the city—primarily for Mallory's visits and for occasional meetings. Jeff and Max went Sunday nights to Manhattan and returned on Fridays—occasionally on Thursday nights—but their minds never left their work; if anything, having parked their wives in their summer dwellings, they worked even harder with longer hours

Saturday nights, the four of them got together, usually to eat out.

The restaurant, Nick & Toni's, was packed with transplants from the Upper East Side: men in their linen shirts, khakis, and leather driving shoes; women in their summer dresses, four-inch Manolo heels, and sparkling jewelry. They all looked fit and tanned.

As the Weismans and Hathaways entered, Max squeezed a $100 bill into the maître d's hand while shaking it, but still they were seated a little too close to the door—Max wasn't happy. He looked around. The best tables were already occupied by regulars: At one table, Ronald Perelman was laughingly chatting with the sexy actress Ellen Barkin, while at another Ralph Lauren and his wife, Ricky, were lounging with the famous architect Charles Gwathmey and his wife, Betty Ann. At the corner table, Dreamworks SKG founder Steven Spielberg was waving at them, while firmly holding his wife Kate Capshaw's hand. There were two other best tables empty.

Max got up, walked over to the maître d's stand, and shook his hand again. He came back looking disappointed: "You see those two tables? Would you believe they are reserved for the whole season, every Saturday night whether the people show up or not? I had no idea you could do that; that is exactly what I plan to arrange for the next summer, guys." He smiled with glee for having found a solution to this distressing social putdown.

"What do you care, Max, where we sit, since the food is the same?" said Jeanny. "Actually the view is much better from here; you see everyone coming in impeccably dressed, sober, and anxious and leaving disheveled, drunk, and oblivious...plus two pounds heavier."

"Look at these women!" Norma put her hand on her mouth—not clear whether she was surprised, shocked, or embarrassed as two young women with minidresses supported only by their braless breasts stopped by the door; one of them bent over to remove something from the bottom of her four-inch-high heel, fully exposing her skin-colored G-string.

Max, while keeping his eye totally fixed on the women, tried to clear his rattling throat: "What is it with the African governments? They are all down on women wearing miniskirts. For centuries, their women walked around practically naked. Now they are at the forefront of modesty: They claim minidresses are the cause of the rape epidemics!"

Jeff's eyes trembled for a second over the girls' smooth, bare legs. "It isn't just the officials of African governments; even our own Chief Justice Rehnquist thinks that provocative dressing leads to sexual harassment. The old mayor, John Lindsay, once was asked what he thought of miniskirts. He replied, 'That will help women run faster,' and added with a mischievous smile in his eyes, 'and they may have to.'"

Jeanny gave him a frosty look.

The food arrived on large plates containing tiny slices of fish—gray sole, salmon—and a few asparagus tips.

"Why do they put a little bit of food on such big plates? There isn't even enough room on the table for four of them," complained Norma.

Jeanny had her own agenda: "Did you hear that the town is allowing developers to bid on that over one-hundred acres in the West Neck area,

in order to subdivide and build residential lots? Isn't that place a wet-
land? Why is it that the board is deferring the decision to New York State,
for God's sake?"

Both Max and Jeff were still focused on the two tanned young women.
They were both picturing Mallory while maintaining their regular con-
versations. Jeff's reverie was disturbed by his vibrating phone. "Be brief,
I am in the restaurant."

The people at the next table threw disapproving glances.

"Okay, thanks."

"Have you ever visited Shelter Island, with all those thriving eelgrass
beds? Go there some early evening and you'll see for yourself how these
beds are part of the estuary system...you can spot salamanders and hear
peepers."

"Come on, Jeanny, it is just a swamp," said Max.

"What are peepers?" asked Norma.

Jeanny turned to Jeff: "You should know."

"Well, we've got to find out who the developers are first," he replied,
still ogling.

ତ୶ଡ଼ତ

The maître d' gently left the bill on the table, even though they had not
finished their desserts.

Max glanced at the bill and threw a few hundred dollars into the folder.
On the way out, he stopped by a few tables, shook hands, and exchanged
some pleasantries. The other three waited outside in silence.

Jeff pulled Max aside: "The Philip Morris deal got the green light;
they'll acquire Nabisco for $14¾ billion in cash, plus $4.2 billion in debt."

"Wow!" exclaimed Max. "Does John know that?"

"Not yet; I just got the information in the restaurant."

"Oh, I thought, 'Be brief' was sort of a code between you and your lady
friends, like 'my wife is nearby.'"

Jeff gave him a taciturn look.

"Jeff, my boy, don't get frisky: It is a joke. Oh, here's what I'll do. The
time frame is too close. I'll buy heavy both Philip Morris and Nabisco
from London and Israel; you tell John."

"Hello, guys!" hollered Jeanny. "Get in the car; if you cannot talk in
front of us, at least drop us off. It is embarrassing."

Norma protested: "I don't mind, do you? We girls should do our own
talking." Without waiting for Jeanny's reaction, she launched into a long
description of the next summer's Hamptons Designer Show House's gala
cocktail party.

"The exhibit will have all the famous designers' work; you know, it'll help to plan our next year's party."

Jeanny was counting from one hundred down in sevens.

"It is going to be at Villa Maria on June 30th; you've got to come and… and this Sunday Bagels & Books at the Jewish Center? A writer—his name slipped my mind—will talk about his father who was a Polish Jew, but turned Christian and became a Nazi officer; you've got to come to that. It should be really funny."

Jeanny had finally had it: "Norma, how would you like to come to hear James Loewen, who is speaking on how ideologues dictated esthetics and identity to the nation by erecting certain outrageous monuments and declaring them landmarks? As such, they can never be altered, never mind erased? It is on the first Sunday in August at Guild Hall."

Norma's mouth stayed open until the driver closed the doors; Max sat next to him: "George, me first!"

⟊⟊⟊

Max's driver dropped them off, and then took the Weismans to their home.

As soon as they entered the house, Jeanny blurted out what had been bothering her the last few weeks: "Mallory never showed up the last Wednesday! I called and left a message on her cell, but she never returned my call. I hope nothing happened to the poor girl…she is all alone in town! Do you think she could just quit like that without telling me?"

Jeanny was staring at Jeff.

"I don't know. She is a masseuse, after all. What sort of professional conduct are you expecting? Plus, it is summer, Jeanny; she may have gone on vacation."

"You didn't have anything to do with her quitting by any chance, did you?"

"Now, just a moment." Jeff looked deadly serious. "Why would I be against your getting a massage? It is your business whether you are Rolfed or not."

"Jeff, cut the bull. I am asking you whether you tried the same silly game with her as you did with Paula?"

Jeff looked totally indignant.

"Look, that girl practically lived with us, and I treated her like a respectworthy human being by occasionally asking about herself, her family—just to be kind. I had no idea that you two were competing with each other for my affection. You end up firing the poor woman out of jealousy. Have a little faith in your husband, for God's sake…I've got to watch the news."

Jeff picked up a large glass of cognac—he liked Hine Antique—and looking annoyed, went to the living room.

Jeanny joined him to watch NBC's *Nightly News*—they were still for a few minutes; she dialed Mallory: "I'll ask her."

"Hi, you know what to do." The same soft voice with this cryptic message!

"Yes, hi, Mallory; you missed our session. I hope all is well. Please call me back. Oh, yeah, this is Jeanny. Thanks."

She hung up and looked at Jeff, who looked so innocent that he had to be guilty.

ᏣᎳᎩ

# -XLV-

Two years ago, for the night of their fiftieth anniversary, John brought five dozen red roses and ordered Carol's favorite food: lobster ravioli, seafood salad, veal piccata, and tiramisu, delivered from Elio's. He and Junetta set up a colorful table shimmering with five enormous candles. John uncorked a twelve-year-old Chianti Riserva and poured it into a crystal decanter.

Carol, in her second of seven weeks of chemotherapy, was making an effort to participate in the celebration. She had lost so much weight that she looked like a ghost of her former self—her face chalky and wrinkled, her fading hazel eyes buried in their sockets—though they were the only signs of life in her balding head, which she kept forgetting to cover.

Junetta helped her put her wedding dress on. The slightly discolored white dress fell off her—the dress that, even on the day of their wedding, she struggled to get into and, since then, "forget it"—a "consolation prize," she said with a smile, which looked all teeth, no lips.

"John, would you please go into my jewelry box in the safe and take out that Tiffany necklace that I wore at our wedding?"

"Shall I bring the box?" John had never opened her jewelry box.

"No, no it is too heavy; just look for the necklace. It is most likely in the lowest compartment."

John lifted the enormous box out of the safe and managed to carry it to the desk; it weighed a ton. How could she have accumulated so much jewelry? The box was made to look like the first condo he built before he partnered with Gabriel, Jeff's father. Like the building, the box had four floors. The third and fourth "floors" were full of her recent jewelry: expensive pieces like diamond-studded bracelets, rings, and watches. On the second floor, out stretched the diamond necklace, among the colorful beads and glasses strung together with ordinary materials. It looked like a rich American tourist in Mexico.

Still, none of this jewelry could have weighed that much; there had to be a gold bar or something like that in the basement. So he pulled the lowest drawer out—there lay a large book with a fortress-looking thick silver cover and an impressive flap-lock moat securing its privacy. She had been keeping a diary! John's curiosity extended only to yanking the flap a few times. He returned with the necklace and gently put it on Carol's thin neck; it hung down to her belly.

Carol didn't even touch the food; the idea, never mind the sight or smell of it, nauseated her. She took a few sips of the red wine, and shortly after she asked to be taken to bed. As soon as she lay down—still wearing her wedding dress and the necklace—she fell into a deep sleep.

John let Junetta pack the food for herself; he sat by Carol and drank the rest of the bottle. "What could she be writing about?" he wondered; and the key to the lock of the diary? Where could that be? The more he drank, the more anxious he got, contrary to his usual reaction to wine. He had to take a Xanax to calm himself down; eventually he dozed off on the couch.

ᧁᨆᨆ9

For days, John remained preoccupied with Carol's diary. He kept opening the safe, taking out the book, and staring at it. John and Carol were very respectful of each other's privacy. They never inquired about the other's whereabouts during the day, never eavesdropped on telephone conversations, and never read each other's mail. They had implicit trust in each other. But the diary? That was something else, especially because John hadn't known of its existence. How long had she been keeping it? he wondered. Should he read it, and if so, when? Before or after her death? What if there were some terrible secrets in it? Did he really want to know them?

He automatically kept looking for the key; it wasn't on her, as she was more or less naked all the time. She didn't even have a pocketbook by her side; the only thing she had in her possession was her glasses, and he and Junetta even had to keep track of those.

He hesitated to ask Junetta about the key—he felt embarrassed to ask her alliance against her boss. Even Junetta knew that one doesn't have the right to read someone else's diary without permission. He thought of asking the very author herself for consent.

Carol was totally nonplussed—it was in the safe itself. John was ashamed for even having raised the issue. Carol, his dearest wife, obviously had nothing to hide; what an asshole he was. John cursed at and scolded himself for days. Now he was obsessed with having suspected his wife to the point that he had to confess to her. He couldn't even express his remorse clearly because of his torrents of tears.

When he finally calmed down, Carol put her hand on his mouth and gave him one of her dry looks. She said in a wrinkled voice that he was right to be suspicious of her, for she had cheated on him. She repeated herself, noticing the incredulous look on John's face, but this time with an exaggerated air of indifference, as if she was talking about something meaningless.

John wasn't sure whether she was joking or teasing him, or maybe this was one of the earliest signs of cognitive impairment—he had been forewarned about that possibility by her doctor.

John urgently walked over to the safe, then paused a second to catch his breath before he opened it. Inside were their wills, a few thousand dollars in cash, and some Israeli bonds…and a tarnished silver key. With his trembling hands, he tried to open it without success; he came back with the diary in his hand, the key dangling. Carol was deeply asleep.

"Junetta," he said, this time confident in the legitimacy of his inquiry, "my wife wanted to unlock this book; she sent me to get the key that she said was in the safe; but this key…" Before John finished his sentence, Junetta solved the mystery.

"Oh, yes, Mr. Levine, she hasn't used it for months. Let me open it for you; it is a little hard. Mrs. always asked me to help her." And with that, Junetta unlocked Carol's black diary.

John took the diary into the library, sat on one of the uncomfortable chairs around the oak table, and randomly opened it:

> January 1, 1969: I find Gabriel's promises hardly satisfying. For years now, he has been talking about divorcing both his wife and his partner—my guileless John—so that we could finally be free to love each other unimpeded by fear and guilt.

John's hands felt frozen and paralyzed; the book closed by itself abruptly with a sonic thud. Junetta came running—as she always did—to inquire about the noise.

John sat there for hours. He couldn't read any other pages. So Carol had had an affair with his partner Gabe, whom he had brought in; and she had conspired with Gabe to undo her own husband? And this went back to thirty or more years ago? A sinking feeling came over him as he remembered Gabriel's aggressive psychological brinkmanship and his own reticence to take him on. A self-loathing enveloped him in darkness.

He removed all the pages from the diary and threw them into the fireplace; he gave the silver covers and the key to Junetta, who hesitatingly took them.

John went to their bedroom, crawled next to his wife, and kissed her balding head. "Was ever a loved one's dying so innocent and so ferocious?" he howled in choking sobs.

∽✸∾

# -XLVI-

*Hemingway says the truest life must always be hidden; I don't know how one can be a writer and still not be fully transparent. Otherwise what is the point? There are plenty of others, ordinary people providing plenty of life lies— they are either too good or too nice to be interesting.*

*My unhidden, and unhideable, life seems to be always somewhere else, or rather with someone else—mostly men. Well, that isn't exactly right. I live not with man, but "in the other" of man—the one that they deny to themselves.*

*As to my truest life, I live in the hardened stillness of my mind—my native element—in anticipation of man's invisible violence. I live in a rancid listlessness—now second nature to me—in participation with man's savage oblivion. Well, that isn't exactly right either.*

*I live in man's various teeming thoughts of hurting me—to me, the hurt never suffices. I live in man's sordid thoughts to defile me—I am grateful for pain—which takes me almost to the point of total disorganization, but never quite.*

"How is the business, sweet Mallory?" inquired Mr. Levine, who had been dozing off in his customary position on the table. He perked up when he heard an additional pair of steps coming toward the library.

"Good afternoon, Mr. Levine. The business is okay, thanks to your referrals. I already cut down quite a bit, though. I'll be reducing my hours further so that I can have concentrated time to write."

"Are you going to reduce our sessions again?" Mr. Levine lifted his head.

"No, no, not yours, but maybe Mrs. Weisman and others."

"Actually she was asking about you last Wednesday night at the board dinner—whether you were all right. You would call me, right, if you couldn't make it for some reason?"

"Yes, of course. Do you know her husband, Mr. Jeffrey Weisman?"

"Oh, yeah, very smart; I know his father Gabriel—I wish I didn't. He was my junior partner for many years, but that hard knuckle eventually forced me to sell my shares to him. Can you believe this guy's chutzpah? Gabe bought me out from my own business."

"Why did you do it?"

"It is a long story, sweet Mallory. You see, partnership is like marriage: If every day you come home and your wife harasses you, you don't want to go home. Gabriel was determined to be the sole owner of the company. He was younger and more vigorous. He kept harping on how my judgment wasn't good and my decisions were all bad, so much so that I thought maybe he was right. At a certain point, in fact, I became who he perceived me to be: I couldn't make any decision without fearing his attacks. My sweet Carol saw me getting depressed and agitated. It was she who finally said "sell it." We had enough money, no children; why fight? Life's short.

"Look, Carol is gone. I would have given away my entire share to save her. I wish I had died first. I know it is selfish, but at least I could have died with her. What happened to the idea that women outlive men by ten to fifteen years? I am not sure why I am alive, but I don't want to kill myself...I wouldn't even know how. I wouldn't want to make a spectacle of myself by jumping out the window. Oh...I am terribly sorry, sweet Mallory; I didn't mean to dump all this on you.

"Let's forget treacherous Gabriel. You were asking a question about... not about Jeff's father, I am sorry. Jeff is the opposite of his father: He is honest, loyal, trustworthy, and a good family man. Gabriel abused and debased everyone involved with him—his wife, his secretaries, even his own son.

"He emasculated Jeff while pouring affection, praise, and money on Cora, the daughter. You know what he did one day? I was in a dinner meeting with him and a few other guys. This is really a telling story of his contempt for his son. So here walks in Jeff, who wanted proudly to show his first award for 'the student who made the most progress' to his father, who was holding court that day, as usual, in their elegant dining hall. Gabriel told a joke that killed us but also severely injured Jeff's budding self-confidence.

"'In the old country,' Gabe began, gleefully smiling, 'there was once a schlemiel. Everyone knew that he was a schlemiel; his father was schlemiel and so was his grandfather. One day while he was buttering his bread, the slice fell, butter side up; now that doesn't happen to schlemiels. So he decided to present this fact to the rabbi: 'Rabbi, do you think that I may not be a schlemiel after all?'

'The rabbi listened to him carefully and considered the possibility and then reached the conclusion: 'No, son. You are a schlemiel—you must have buttered the wrong side of the bread.'

"Everyone burst into laugher, but Jeff was devastated.

"It is a funny joke, but it is painful if you are the one who is its target. You know what a schlemiel is, right? It is someone who can do nothing right."

Mr. Levine realized that Mallory wasn't laughing.

"I guess this was too Jewish a joke."

Mr. Levine was lamely apologetic, as if he'd failed to entertain her, but wouldn't give up.

"Here, here, you'll love this joke…ha, ha; this is a Jewish joke too, but not too much. This guy is making love to his wife; he makes all the right moves to give her pleasure. As he lies on top of her, he proudly asks, "Well, what do you think?" She says, "I think we should replaster the ceiling, ha, ha, ha."

Mallory cracked a few giggles to please Mr. Levine.

ᘒᙎᙎᖆ

On the way to the subway Mallory checked her messages:

- "Hi, Mallory, this is Jeanny again. Have I done or said anything to upset you? If so, I am sorry. Please call me. I am having double withdrawal symptoms."
- "Hey. This is your favorite Max. How would you like to fly to Paris and London this Wednesday and be back Saturday? I'll work and you can be a tourist, and in the evenings I'll entertain you, of course, pro rata."
- "Mallory, this is your dad. What is going on with your sister? She said I should ask you. What happened to your monthly installments? Now you are two months behind. When are you going to be a responsible person? I have been counting on you. Do you want her to be thrown out of medical school because her jealous sister reneged on her commitment? Call me back soon, and I mean soon!"

The subway came to a halt as it was pulling out of 59th Street. The conductor announced that there had been an accident and they'd be waiting for permission to continue; the doors would be kept locked, as the train was in the tunnel. There was no danger for the riders, and he urged people to stay calm.

Rumors were flying: a terrorist blew up Grand Central Station, a psychotic woman pushed an elderly guy under the train, a man threw himself under…

Mallory's first thought was, that is how Mr. Levine could kill himself. Then she imagined pushing her father under the incoming train. All of a sudden, a soothing feeling came over her, as if she'd taken a whiff of pot. If all goes bad, she could throw herself under the subway. She could get rid of everything that would identify her, carry only one token to get onto the subway station, that's it. The more Mallory delved into the specifics, the calmer she became.

After half an hour, the train began to operate again. She got off the number 5 subway at the 14th Street station; bought a pair of pants, a jacket, underwear, socks, and a belt from an army surplus shop; and walked back to the subway to board the F train to Delancey and Essex Streets. By the time she got to her street, it was half past four o'clock. There was a black four-door car with official plates parked at the corner of Delancey and Orchard Streets. Two black men with shaved heads wearing dark suits, identical sunglasses, white shirts, and ties were leaning on the side of the sedan, smoking. They eyed Mallory quickly. Mallory, who was accustomed to wolf whistles, "hey babes," and other harassing behavior, was surprised at their silence. For a moment, she got scared that they were there for her. Was it the pot? But she hadn't dealt it for months. Was it the IRS? Then she remembered that she had a rendezvous with Jeff today at 4 o'clock.

"Oh, shit," she uttered.

She ran up the stairs and found Jeff sitting on the last step in front of her apartment.

"I am glad you were able to get into the building. I would have felt worse if..."

"Some fat homo let me in, a sticky guy who kept insisting that I should wait for you in his apartment! Never mind that. Where have you been? You are forty minutes late!" He was furious.

"I am sorry. First the subway stalled for a while, and then I got distracted." Mallory quickly opened the door.

"Distracted! You were shopping?" He pulled the plastic bag out of Mallory's hand. "What is this junk? Are you signing up for the Army? You heard that they need a few *good women*?" He took his shoes off.

Mallory got undressed and laid on the mattress facedown. Jeff watched her silent submission; still raging but equally desiring her, he tried to force his penis in without even wetting it.

"So you are not going to let me in, huh?" He hit Mallory's bottom hard a few times, then watched the pinkish imprints of his hand fade away on her porcelain white skin; he hit her again and savagely spread her buttocks.

Jeff didn't hear Mallory softly crying through his own grunting noises. Afterward, he abruptly pulled out and went to the bathroom.

"You know, you could be a little thoughtful and empty out your rectum before my visits. If I ever get an E. coli infection, I'll kill you."

Mallory found her total submission to Jeff's perverse intention very exciting; his wanting her so badly, even at the expense of injuring her, generated a power of its own for her—the power of withholding.

"Sorry, next time I'll have an enema," she joked.

Jeff came back and lay down on his back with four limbs stretched out. He closed his eyes for a second, and Jeanny's image came forth. He felt bad. Why did he need this? How awful it would be if she knew what he had just done...more so if she knew what he had been doing for years— even worse things.

A forceful slap on his face woke him up from his reveries.

"What the...?"

Mallory kneeled at his side.

"My God, you have an iron fist! I think you broke my jaw." Jeff was rubbing his face while looking at her cold eyes. "What did you do that for?"

Mallory kept staring.

Jeff got up quickly and dressed. He took some money out of his wallet, counted it, and put it on the table.

"I am giving you only for one hour because you were forty minutes late and dirty."

☙

# -XLVII-

*N*ow *I understand that pain in pleasure, Mr. Lindeman. I used to miss my school bus on purpose so that you'd pick me up and take me home, and you knew it. I was only eight years old.*

*The first time you took me home, you asked me where my twin sister was. One would think that the two of us would either catch or miss the bus together. No, I was alone and you knew it. When you dropped me off, you noticed that there was no one to receive me. You actually entered the house and hollered, "Anyone home?" Pat must have left for some friend's house, Nana had been bedridden, and Mom was most likely in a stupor. You asked me whether I'd be okay; I said yes, and you hesitated for a moment and left.*

*The second time you picked me up, your eyes looked grayish. You asked me, if there is no one home, would I come to your place to have some ice cream? You lived alone in a small, cluttered trailer house near St. Luke's. You gave me a big bowl of Ben & Jerry's chocolate ice cream and took another for yourself. I have never been allowed to eat that much ice cream.*

*You asked me whether I knew about sex. I said yes. You said, "Well, would you like to have sex with me?" I said yes. I didn't know how, but I knew that the girl had to take her clothes off and lie on the bed facedown, so I did. At first I thought you were tickling me, then I got all wet. I protested, "Why are you peeing on me?" You said, "No, no, that is not pee; it is semen." I then acknowledged, "Oh! Okay, then."*

*Afterward, you washed my buttocks and my legs with warm water; you were very gentle. You told me not to tell anyone about this, for they'll throw us both out of school. I swore that I never would. "Great," you said, "I'll pick you up next Tuesday." We did this at least once a week for a few months.*

*One Tuesday you never showed up; I remember too well, because it was a cold day in March; the rain was pouring. I waited and waited; no silver Volkswagen. I sat by the front door of the school; finally a police car stopped and took me home. I missed our eating lots of ice cream together.*

*The following day there was an announcement: "Two of our most admired teachers—Mr. Lindeman and Ms. Schaffer—tied the knot."*

# -XLVIII-

The Thurmans, a big, patriotic family, had lived in New Canaan, Connecticut, for generations. At one time they were large landowners and major players in the town's financial and political life; they were generous contributors to philanthropic causes, especially in the area of health and higher education: Yale University was one of the beneficiaries of their largess. Hamilton's great-grandfather, Henry Thurman, donated large sums toward the construction of a mental institution, Silver Hill Hospital, complete with a housing complex for the doctors, tennis courts, dining halls, and an elegant library. Patients were brought to adjacent farms for recreation as well as production. Henry Thurman's wife, who was an alcoholic, had lived most of her adult life in and out of Silver Hill.

Over the last century, the family generated many lawyers, congressmen, and state senators as well as its share of psychotics, addicts, and losers. Ham, Hamilton Thurman III, belonged to this latter category. His father, Hamilton Thurman II, had two graduate degrees from Yale—philosophy and psychology—and now was a distinguished professor at Columbia University in New York.

Hamilton Thurman II was a handsome man; he had a carefully sculpted face and carelessly imputing wit. He spent most of his spare time in the library. He loved books. His only other interest, a peculiar enjoyment, was to wander the streets of New York looking for people to be at odds with. For example, he would stare at the windows of shops; then, when the sales staff would encourage him to enter, he would discount them with indignation that he was not a browser—he was a vicambulist and also an excavator—literary, that is, and he would wink.

Actually he had one more enjoyment, a sort of perverse one: Over the years Hamilton developed a great talent for digression. Primarily to stave off his boredom, he would attack innocent bystanders with this literary weapon. Hamilton would describe these encounters in social settings in a matter-of-fact fashion and explain the pleasure he took in generating *kankedort*; and then seeing the discomfort in the eyes of his listener, he would translate the word *kankedort* to simple English, "Oh! It means an awkward situation."

Hamilton Thurman II's wife, Ann (also a Yale graduate, who majored in engineering, with a degree in architecture), has been working for the prestigious firm Swanfort-Bell. Ann had been a brilliant student but was now a less-than-successful career woman. She had a tightly composed look; when not betrayed by the chewing of her lips, she gave the impression of being very sturdy, resolute, and self-assured—an egghead with an antiseptic presence. She always sat in a manly manner with her arms crossed on her chest and her sunken, thin face and mouth downcurved; she would finger point at whomever she addressed. She spoke plainly and with unsparing sternness—barely showing her teeth.

Whoever Ann fixed her light blue eyes on would get a little nervous and quickly disengage from eye contact. Her boss urged her not to stare at clients: "I don't know whether you are tense all the time, but if so, let me tell you it is awfully contagious—people run away from you."

Ann conceded to others that chronic migraines made her somewhat irritable; Hamilton nicknamed her *Sarkazien*—she wasn't sarcastic, she was full of rage; but she didn't know why. Yes, she did: It was marriage to Hamilton and consequently having a child—Ham at that. Because of Hamilton she lacked financial stability. She had to work, most likely for the rest of her life, and probably support him and now his son—yes, his son.

The couple lived in a "traditional six" apartment in a Riverside co-op, overlooking the Hudson River—a (prewar) building mortgaged by Levine-Weisman partners. (Jeff's father was originally a minority holder.) Finally giving in to her husband's plea not to end the Thurman legacy (for his three siblings were all women), Ann had their only child, a son, when she was thirty-nine years old.

She thought she had made it clear to her "husband-to-be" that she did not want to have children. A week after the birth of Hamilton III—Ham—Ann went back to work; she left him to the care of various nannies. Her husband would come home during the day—the university was just a few blocks away—to spend time with Ham; he understood that this was his project; well, his son.

When little Ham began to speak in full sentences, Ann began to have some interest in him. In the evenings and weekends between her work (she always brought some home), she tried to read to him, teach him to draw, listen to music—"Mozart to enhance his left brain development if he were to be an architect"—to no avail. Ham only wanted to be left alone to play with his dolls and their outfits. Ann quickly lost interest.

From then on until his junior-high years, babysitters—rotating female students at Columbia—were his playmates; they built a Barbie-doll collection for him, dressed him like a girl, let him wear their shoes, put lipstick and rouge on him—all never to be mentioned to his parents.

Ham managed to finish Riverdale High School, and his talent in poetry got him accepted to Columbia University—being the son of a celebrated professor helped.

Ham wrote poetry throughout his teenage years—mostly about flowers and nature—that is, until his mother mocked it as "garden variety"; then he began to experiment with free verse. By the time he got to college, Ham looked like a free-verse poet, a little too free perhaps—torn jeans and sneakers, army-navy surplus jackets, and long, beautiful blondish hair; he could easily have been mistaken for a girl if it weren't for his broad and muscular shoulders. In high school as well as college, girls loved him, but his friendly reciprocation drew many of them into despair; some consoled themselves by suspecting him of being gay. He wasn't gay, but he was not heterosexual either. Hamilton was vaguely asexual.

◌⋙◍⋘◌

After he got his graduate degree from New York University (Columbia University turned him down), Ham got a teaching-assistant job in the English Department. His hopes to get a faculty position began to dissipate as he could neither get his poetry book published nor be included in any of the yearly anthologies.

His parents stopped their financial help. Even though he was living in a cheapest-possible way, he still couldn't manage on his meager salary because of his heavy marijuana habit. Eventually his debts to his dealer railroaded him into becoming a middleman for all sort of drugs—NYU students being his main clientele.

Tonight Ham was having dinner at his parents' apartment. They quickly opened various containers of Chinese food and ate—"it gets cold fast." His visits to his parents became less and less frequent as Ham felt more and more alienated from them. His father wanted him to find a tenured teaching position; his mother constantly urged him to quit "this poetry nonbusiness" and get into some real business. This was only making him worse.

As usual, as soon as the first opportunity arose, his mother threw the first salvo. "Son, I work; I've worked all my life," she sliced out the words. "What do you think life is all about? Without work it is all a self-induced miasma; there is no great purpose or meaning to life except to be useful. Even your Miguel de Unamuno says 'work is the only consolation for having been born.'"

"I thought there was no consolation for my being born."

Ann cringed, but that didn't stop her: "We are talking about your own consolation."

Ham turned to his father for rescue: "Dad, didn't you use to say that writers and artists provide moral guidance to societies?... Now that is a useful work, isn't it? Even dictators like Stalin sought advice from Gorky..."

"Son, that example wouldn't bring much comfort, never mind credibility, to the profession. It is better to evoke André Gide, who discouraged aspiring writers even if they were going to be successful because of success's elusive aftermath. An artist never feels useful because he never feels he is working, and if he does, his work is useless. Anyway, what your mother offers is a sense of proportion, which, of course, is thoroughly antipoetic..."

Ham tried to cultivate in his parents a little poetic thinking—it was almost impossible with his mother; with his father it was possible, but he was impossible.

"If you don't jump into your typically molesting comments, I'll tell you about some bad news I just received," Ham said curtly.

Ann protested: "Molesting? If you are referring to our last conversation, all I said was, in your old nature poems, I couldn't identify any sonic or metrical patterns. You kept overlapping the intensity of trimeter—the quick march—with the sedulous pace of tetrameters. You wanted me to be honest, right? You've got to master the science of poetry."

"The science of poetry?" Ham asked menacingly.

"Yes, the vigor of the verse depends on its structure and its architecture. Every soft field, including the arts, has its hard basic science, like mind has brain. For example, Freud, your father's idol, first had mastered biology—he had dissected eels to see if they had testicles—before he indulged in psychology."

Father and son looked at each other mischievously: "Dad, had Freud ever analyzed or dissected an architect?"

"No, son; there was no need. It was well-known that architects have lots of balls."

Both burst into laughter.

"To hell with you two," growled Ann, losing her deliberate composure.

"Let's hear the bad news," said Hamilton.

"I got the rejection from Simon and Schuster as well; and I think I lost my last chance to be on tenure track at NYU..." He stopped for a minute. "I am not as upset as I should be by your principles; for me this is another analogue experience. I am not evading my feelings; I presume that they be surmised."

"Is there such a thing as a digital experience?" Ann asked with an anxious grin.

"Yours," muttered Hamilton, under his breath.

ᴄᴍᴍᴏ

# -XLIX-

The Weismans invited the Thurmans to spend the last weekend of June at their East Hampton house, as they had done many previous summers. Ann looked forward to these invitations, except that she had to endure at least one dinner with the Hathaways—like tonight.

As the four of them entered East Hampton Point, one of the upscale restaurants in the Hamptons that overlooked the harbor, Max waved to them from the far corner of the deck.

Scattered about were a number of female celebrities—Vera Wang, Christie Brinkley, Kelly Ripa, Sallie Krawcheck…and there were even bigger names—George Soros, Martha Stewart, Donald and Melania Trump, Richard and Karen LeFrak, David Koch.

"Hello, Manhattaners, how was the jitney ride?" Max hollered.

Ann saw the disdain in the eyes of the exquisitely dressed, well-tanned "Hamptonians." She wore a comfortable cotton suit in a light gray color—not attributable to any designer, though passable; but Hamilton wore the same white button-down shirt with rolled-up sleeves and brown corduroy long-rise pants that he wore in the winter. She thought she heard some giggles.

"How did you manage to get one of the best tables on a Friday night?" teased Jeff.

"Very simple," Max retorted. "I mentioned the possibility of hostile takeover, and I wasn't joking."

They all kissed each other. Norma was finishing her salad. "I'm sorry, I couldn't wait. I was too hungry; anyway, this doesn't count. I'll order another appetizer with the rest of you."

Max, oblivious to it all, gulped down a few oysters and bottom-upped his Bloody Mary: "Hamilton, you've got to try their clams and oysters, if you got your hepatitis A and B shots! I am personally immune to any shellfish-related disease—you see, I grew up in a kosher home."

"How would that make you immune?" Jeff asked, incredulously.

Norma laughed. Ann and Jeanny looked at each other.

They settled down, but no waiter or waitress was in sight.

"They are just leaving us alone. No pressure," explained Max. "We'll have a leisurely dinner, not like that place, you know, where they bring the check before you order dessert." Meanwhile he was looking around for a waiter. "So what is the weekend program for your guests?"

"Well, tomorrow at five, Peter Matthiessen is speaking at Guild Hall on his book *Tigers in the Snow*," said Jeff. "Jeanny also bought tickets for the exhibition of works by some well-known local architects at the Southampton Cultural Center. You are welcome to join us if you'd like."

"No," said Max, while trying to swallow another oyster. "Actually we are invited to Peter Jennings's house in Bridgehampton—you know who he is, right? The last four years he has been gathering the most important people for his June jazz benefit, for the child care center down there."

"Alan Alda will be there," Norma exclaimed joyfully, "my favorite actor—and Sunday we'll see *Hamlet Comedy*."

"Hamlet is a comedy?" asked Ann, lifting her habitually knitted brows.

A handsome, darkly tanned young waiter came over. Before he took their orders, Max stopped him: "First get us three dozen more of these," pointing to the oysters. "Go, go now."

"How come John never came this year? Every summer he used to stay with you for weeks at a time," asked Hamilton.

Max shook his shoulders: "I don't understand; he uses every excuse to stay home. He wouldn't even come to Dr. Green's workshop; he used to love her. He followed all her eight steps `religiously to improve his memory; now he dismisses them all: 'Seven steps too many,' he jokes. Junetta, his maid, says he is staying in the city because of his massage therapist."

Jeanny's ears perked up. "You've got to be kidding. There are dozens of them here."

"No, no, apparently she is different. John swears by her. She apparently cured his back pain," Max explained while trying to pull a lobster tail from its shell, splashing red and black goo over the table. No one reacted.

Jeffrey was behaving as if he was totally indifferent to the subject, while at the same time trying to figure out what Max had up his sleeve...could he be one of her lovers? Was he trying to out him?

"I think Mallory is a sick girl, if you ask my opinion. She was my therapist too, and one day she just disappeared without even a call to explain why," Jeanny said in an irritated voice.

"What is the massage idea?" asked Ann. "Why do you want someone to manhandle you for a hefty fee?"

Hamilton joined in: "I wouldn't mind being manhandled by a young, beautiful masseuse."

Ann kicked him under the table.

The dinner was finished. Max paid the bill, as usual. They walked out to a warm and humid night in the Hamptons with Max and Jeff trailing behind.

"I am going to go 'long' for subprime mortgages and short for the dollar. Are you in?"

"Max, you are betting against the dollar?" Jeff was puzzled.

"Yes, you see the NASDAQ Compo's upper end could be around 4,200. Tech stocks will be dragging down the Dow, and that would put pressure on the dollar. With the Fed tightening, we are heading for a recession."

"Honestly, Max, long and short of this, I just don't understand. Whatever you are doing for yourself, do it for me too…as long as you know what you are doing."

"What are you guys quarreling about?" Ann hollered.

"Oh, don't pay attention to them," said Jeanny, "they do this after each meal. I guess it helps their digestion."

Norma pulled a few tablets of Maalox from her pocket and began to chew: "We are coming back here on Sunday again for their brunch buffet; it is an amazing spread—and you can eat as much as you can."

"Jeff, will you be coming to Teddy Forstmann's Huggy Bear Pro-Am tennis tournament?" Max hollered as they were pulling out. He saw a thumbs-up from the window.

෴

# -L-

As Mallory walked back from the subway station, she sensed that someone was following her. He seemed to have synchronized his footsteps with hers: When she slowed down, the footsteps slowed down too, and when she walked fast, the footsteps speeded up. It was getting dark, and the street was deserted.

Mallory reviewed her options. She could run to her building, but he might catch her there...what if there was no one in the hall? She could turn around and walk back toward the station, but that would mean passing by him and giving him the perfect opportunity for...Mallory's heart was pounding. Was he a thief, a rapist, a murderer? Her mind was paralyzed, and she couldn't make a decision one way or the other. Her legs were carrying her on their own. She wished the person would do whatever he intended to do now, right now, and get it over with. Her head became numb, as if it were drained of blood and replaced with some toxic juice.

A large and heavy hand touched her shoulder. She froze.

"Yo, soul sister! It's me, Lord Washington! You remember me, right? We met on the train, we talked about the soul book, and you took my card: CEO and president, Universal Escort Service, Ltd."

Mallory looked at him, and a cold sweat rushed over her body.

"I saw you on the subway. I was pretty sure it was you...my, my...you look good, girl...you said you'll call, but you never did. You know that isn't nice...do you live around here? Girl, you got to be totally honest with me, or otherwise it doesn't work. I mean, we could both use some extra pocket money, but to be honest, I only work with clean girls, no drugs, no stealing, and no lying. You know, I mean this is not a good neighborhood for a girl like you. You could live in a luxurious apartment, and I can get one for you, no big deal; what are friends for? Listen, every girl needs protection. Fifty-fifty, I'll throw the rent into the hopper. What do you say, ha?"

The man's hand was still on Mallory's shoulder. Every finger of his hand was ornamented with big gold rings.

Mallory was hoping some people would eventually come by; she needed to delay her response.

"Oh, yes. Now I remember you." She said in a friendly tone of voice. "You invited me to have some soul food, but I am vegetarian. Also, I have a boyfriend, a DA, who wouldn't really appreciate my having dinner with other guys."

"You bullshitting me, girl? A DA boyfriend! My ass, no DA's girl would put a pimp's card in her bag. Tell me the truth, girl. Who's your daddy? You got to have one."

"Of course I do."

"Okay, then, now you're talking. So who is he?"

"Well, my father is a retired Air Force officer."

"Don't fuck with me, girl. I am not asking who your fucking father is, I am asking you, kindly, who is your daddy—your fucking pimp?"

"Listen, Mr. Washington. I think there is a misunderstanding here; I am not a prostitute. I am a teaching assistant at NYU and a writer."

At that moment, Peter and Dave showed up. A little startled with the situation, Peter asked, "What's going on here?"

Mallory, finally able to take a deep breath, replied calmly, "This gentleman thought that I might be a prostitute, that is all. Now that I explained to him who I am, the matter is settled."

Mallory got into the middle of the boys, arm in arm, and headed home. Mr. Washington stood still, watching his catch slip away.

ᏩᎻᏯᎾ

Mallory spent the night with the gun under her pillow. She didn't know whether that man followed them or not—and on the way home, she was afraid to turn around to look back. She was frightened, maybe for the first time in her life, to the degree that she felt she couldn't fight back. That sensation scared her even more: She was totally at his mercy, involuntarily—not like with Jeff, where she chose to be helpless—a willed submission. With this Washington guy, she was a genuine victim. There was not one iota of pleasure in it, masochistic or otherwise; the whole situation was scary and dangerous. She wondered if this was how Pat felt when she was subjected to the abuse from their father.

ᏩᎻᏯᎾ

# -LI -

*O*ne *hot August night at Compo Beach, two of us girls—myself and Ev-*
*elyn—and two boys from Staples High were joined by two little-older guys*
*I didn't know, who brought four six-packs of beer. We drank and swam till late*
*hours—we were having a good time—but when we heard the cops' sirens, our*
*two guys from the school hurried into one car with Evelyn and split; I was left*
*with these two people I'd just met.*

*I had the choice to go with the cops, but that would have meant a long lecture*
*till we got home, or take a ride with these two; I chose the latter—after all, they*
*were Westporters too. They had a small sports car; I sat in the back with the fat*
*one. They drove about one mile or so, and then pulled into the parking lot of a*
*vacant lot by the ocean drive—where once a popular seafood restaurant operated.*
*They wanted to finish the leftover beer and smoke a joint.*

*I was a little apprehensive but also game. All of a sudden the guy next to me*
*pulled my head to his lap. I struggled to free myself, then the other one got out,*
*came around, and put a knife on my neck.*

*"Do what he says, bitch, or I'll cut your throat!" The edge of the blade was*
*pressing on my skin. Meanwhile I had a hard time finding this guy's penis; it*
*was shrunk into his bulging belly—I think he was more scared than I was. I spit*
*on it, jumped out of the car, and ran to the street.*

*I could have easily bitten this guy's penis. Somehow, men do not seem to real-*
*ize the potential danger when they force their penises into a woman's mouth. I*
*would never insert my finger—which has a real bone in it—into anyone's mouth*
*against their wishes; wouldn't a severe injury to the finger or penis be the natural*
*fear of such carelessness? No. Not to men. They are afraid of a purported vagina*
*dentata but not real, thirty-two teeth.*

*Maybe this carelessness is based on some peculiar belief that men may have:*
*a charitable disposition of women toward all penises, or all women "enjoy it" in*
*spite of their protestation, once the penis is securely placed in their mouth…thus*
*there'll be no danger of harming such a precious object of pleasure.*

*For me, it was different. I would have done it voluntarily, if they'd nicely asked for it or bribed me with a little weed or something. I neither enjoyed nor disliked it, but boys wanted that, and I wanted boys.*

❦

# -LII-

Max's visits with Mallory had their weekly irregularity. Their originally scheduled date for Wednesdays, 12 to 2 p.m., was everything but that. Equally irregular was his behavior when he showed up, if he showed up at all. At times, he would just stop by to give money to Mallory and leave. Other times, he would have lunch with Mallory before masturbating her or occasionally be masturbated by her—he rarely attempted to have sex. Mostly he would just talk—talk about himself in the manifest form of talking about everything else.

Today was no different; he came one hour late, threw his jacket on the bed, and sank himself into the sofa.

"Who do you think will be the next president?"

"Al Gore," replied Mallory.

"Ha! You think he should or will be?"

"Both."

"Well, you are wrong; maybe he should but he cannot be." Max spread himself into the sofa, stretched his arms wide, and asked with the look of a teacher posing indifference to a student's answer—in full conviction that the student cannot come up with the right answer: "Do you know why?"

Mallory, always bored with these soliloquies, would usually cut to the chase: "Because of you!"

Max grinned with false modesty: "No, no, I am not that powerful. Gore cannot win because of the Jews!"

"I thought the purpose of teaming up with Lieberman was to win over the Jews."

"Ha! That is how the average mind thinks. It may, in fact, attract some Jews, but most Jews, and the rest of the population, will vote for Bush."

Mallory could usually figure out where Max was heading, but not now.

"Jews are supporting Lieberman's vice-presidential bid so that Bush would become president?"

"Atta girl! Because most Jews are getting rich on low taxes for capital gains, and only Republicans will keep it at the level of 15 percent; to make sure that Bush wins this November, I joined those heavy-hitter Jews to fund Ralph Nader's campaign, just to make sure that Gore's constituency is further eroded."

Max got up from the sofa, self-pleased with his wisdom so much that he didn't even await Mallory's praise; he slowly and deliberately walked over to the desk. "You bring your laptop computer to the hotel? Why? So that the staff thinks of you as a respect-worthy businesswoman or something?" asked Max with a grin.

That never occurred to Mallory.

"No, but we make dates, and you show up for a few minutes or not at all; I wait and waste time, so I brought my work here. The place is nicer, quieter, and better lit than my apartment and it is already paid for, so why not?"

"Yeah, why not." Max went to look at the screen: nothing.

"Do you have writer's block or what?"

Mallory never knew what to do with Max...should she get undressed or sit down and listen?

"What do you want to do, Max?"

"What do I want to do, what do I want to do? First tell me how you would describe me in your book. I don't mean just physically...would you say that I am a strange person—a little nuts, or what?"

Mallory never thought of writing about him or anyone else.

"Well, you know I am writing a novel about my childhood and my family, not about my life now."

Max looked disappointed.

"I see; what if you were writing about me? What would you say?"

"Hmm, I would say, let me think...that you are a complicated person—difficult to figure out; a generous man who is more interested in giving pleasure than receiving it."

"Go on."

"Let's see...an arrivist who is neither totally comfortable with his success nor confident that he'll remain so."

"My, my. You should have become a shrink! What else?"

"Someone who desires compliments and praises."

"Okay." He looked upset.

"Okay, what?"

"Do you like anything about me? No, don't answer."

Max looked sad as he got up to leave.

☙

# -LIII-

*A*fter I was discharged from Silver Hill Hospital, I was sent to outpatient treatment against all my protestations. I was told that I was either lying about the incident or that I had serious character pathology. Either way I needed help. I was assigned to Dr. Kelly, who was a husky, well-groomed Irishman in his late forties; he looked more like a country banker or a lawyer than a psychiatrist. I would have been less reluctant if I had been referred to Dr. Heshe.

Dr. Kelly told me that I needed to talk about my dreams and my fantasies if I wanted to get well and eventually be discharged. Both of those subjects, I thought, would get me into more trouble. I knew that I was a probationary patient and that whatever I told him might be used against me to keep me in treatment forever. I wasn't sure how I could be exonerated and still continue my way of life—forgiveness wasn't one of the therapeutic techniques here. But that is exactly what got me into this trouble to begin with. So I made up a bunch of dreams and fantasies.

In the third session, I told Dr. Kelly that I'd recently begun to remember my dreams, and they were all about him. He wanted me to expand, to give details of my dreams. Then I knew I could get discharged from this treatment thing with his full consent.

I spoke with some "reflective" hesitation: "Last night I dreamt that we were in a boat—a tiny boat; it seemed you were pulling the oars, with a rhythm synchronized to my heartbeats; each time you moved toward me, I expected that you would keep coming and touch me; but just about then, you would pull away with the enormous force of your arms, and the boat jumped forward. This went on and on."

"What do you make of it?" Dr. Kelly asked, in a voice that tried to convey the importance of his intervention.

I couldn't believe that he could buy such a corny dream, never mind my pseudo-innocent attempt to deal with it.

"You are the doctor. You must know what it means; I read somewhere that spider meant mother, but oars? I have no idea."

"You see, Mallory, in the early years of analysis, Freud made such generic symbols available for the beginning practitioners, but what is relevant is your *own specific associations to your dream,"* he explained, all the while pouring his eyes over my mouth.

"I have no gag reflex," I said with a tone of complaint.

"You..." he stammered, "you pick that up with your internist?"

I looked at the painting behind him. I was silent—seemingly in deep thought. I was aware of his staring at me. I crossed my legs and let my skirt slide up a little. The painting depicted a man wearing a red jacket astride a beautiful horse.

"Okay, I guess I want you to sail with me...or ride me."

I wasn't looking at him, but I sensed that he was very pleased with my associations.

"What about the rhythm of the oars?"

"What about it?"

"Well, you said they were synchronized to your heartbeats."

"No, I didn't!"

Boy, he was easy.

"You don't remember having said that?" He sounded frustrated.

"It isn't that I don't remember. I never said such a thing."

I crossed my legs again; this time my skirt went even further up my thighs. Dr. Kelly slumped in his chair to lower his eye level so he could get a better view.

"I drive men wild?"

"How, how..." he stuttered, "how does that relate to what we are talking about?"

"Mallory, the thing you just did is called repression. We suppress unacceptable impulses from our unconscious by using the denial mechanism—a defense against the potential punishment of our superegos."

"Are you saying that I have such a big ego that I..."

Dr. Kelly quickly stopped me.

"No, no. Mallory, superego means conscience—it is the prohibitive, judgmental part of our minds."

"Oh!" I said, sounding enlightened; of course I knew what the superego is.

"Well, maybe you could tell me how you feel toward me."

"Well...you are my doctor."

"Anything personal? I...mean...see..." He was tangled.

I wasn't sure how far I should go with this.

"Well, you are strong and intelligent and most likely a good rider."

"Yeah, ah...riding you?" He asked in a distressed voice.

"What do you mean? I am not a horse!"

I was the cat and the mouse.

"Come on, Mallory, didn't you say that 'I want you to sail me or ride me'?" Dr. Kelly sounded puzzled.

"No, why would I say such nonsense?" I was still looking away.

"I presume we are still in the repressive mode; you are dissociating," he declared.

*"Maybe it is enough for today; we'll pick it up next week."* Dr. Kelly stretched his arms.

I didn't want to go yet; I was having a good time. In fact, the whole thing was creepily erotic.

*"I have a tattoo!"* I said coyly. This time, I looked into his eyes; his pupils looked enormous.

*"What is it?"* he sighed.

I got up, turned around, lifted up my skirt, pulled in the outer edge of my panties, leaned over, and showed him my false tattoo—leaf of a weed—on my left bottom. I stayed motionless, while wondering what Dr. Kelly was thinking or feeling.

*"Okay, fine, well, fine...Mallory, that is fine, now you can pull up—I mean, pull down—your skirt."* He mumbled with a hardly audible, dried-up voice.

⌘

In my next interview, Dr. Kelly announced that he'll no longer be my psychiatrist, but Dr. Greenberg will be—that he spoke with her, that she'll call me, but it would be better if I called her. He extended her card to me.

*"Why didn't you tell me on the phone? It takes me forty minutes to get here."*

*"Well, I wanted to tell you in person, in case you had some questions."*

I was furious: *"You don't think I could ask questions on the phone?"*

*"Well, it is better face-to-face."*

*"Why?"*

*"The nonverbal part of the communication is invisible on the phone."*

*"So now that you have me face-to-face, and all the nonverbal stuff, then what? You want to say something else, or shall I just leave?"*

He was blushing.

*"Well, don't you want to know why I decided to refer you to another doctor?"*

*"No, not really! It is your own business."*

He breathed in long, very long:

*"Well, the thing is, you developed a strong erotic transference toward me—actually bordering on a transferential neurosis."*

*"Fine. Whatever that means—that is one thing, and what is the 'another thing?'"*

Dr. Kelly looked frazzled.

*"You said, 'One thing you developed,' blah, blah, blah, and then obviously there must be another thing."*

Now Dr. Kelly was profusely sweating.

*"Oh, of course; you are a psychologically sophisticated girl, Mallory. As to the other thing, you reminded me of an old flame of mine from college; you see, the therapist must simply be a reflecting screen—without what is called contaminating the process with his own countertransferences."*

I don't know why he couldn't just come out and tell me that he couldn't treat me because what he really wanted was to fuck me.

*"Okay, I understand." I picked up my bag from the floor and headed toward the door. Dr. Kelly was glued to his chair; I turned around extended my hand. "Thank you very much for your help and truthfulness; I'll call the other doctor."*

*Dr Kelly, still sitting, looked at my hand as if it was an object of curiosity and then put his hand inside of mine—it was limp and wet.*

*"When…oh, when you are eighteen, maybe we'll have a drink…a coffee or something."*

*I thought he came down fast from his loftier height: "Goodbye, Dr. Kelly. Yours is a lovely thought."*

*I never called Dr. Greenberg, nor did she try to reach me.*

*Three months later, I heard from Pat that Dr. Kelly's license to practice psychiatry was revoked by the state for having sex with one of his patients; he was also sued by the patient's husband.*

# -LIV-

There were three messages on Mallory's phone:

- "Hi, Mallory; this is Jeanny again. I am sorry for bothering you, but you at least owe me a call—not necessarily to explain why you fired me as a client, but to confirm that you did so, so that I don't have to keep waiting for your call. I am not sleeping well; I lost weight. I don't know. I simply need closure on our relationship. Please call, even only to say that you got my messages. Thank you."
- "Mallory, don't let me come over to New York; I left a message a week ago; don't make your dad mad; call me immediately."
- "Sweet Mallory, if you get any cancellation from any other client, I would appreciate an extra session; yes, this is John Levine."

Mallory had never been pursued by women—for any reason—like she was by Jeanny. She could easily find a masseuse or a supplier...Jeanny's obsession with her had to be sexual. The female body, and for that matter woman, was never of interest to Mallory; she wasn't that enamored with the male body either—she was only interested in their interest in her, and only to a certain point. She couldn't see herself leaving such messages on anyone's answering machine.

She decided to call back her father because she was afraid he would show up at her apartment.

"Hello, yes, Dad, what do you want?"

"Well, finally, Ms. Fancy New Yorker; you don't even bother to return your own father's call?"

"I am, am I not?"

"What, eight days later? Your sister always calls me back the same day."

"So call her."

"Mallory, what happened to you? Is that the way one talks to one's father? I was going to ask you whether you want to come home for Christmas. You didn't come for Thanksgiving, and Mrs. Paterson was very disappointed. She prepared the same great turkey dinner like she has the last few years since your mother got sick. You really should come for Christmas; Pat is coming too."

"Well, your darling Pat is coming; isn't that enough?"

"Since your mother died, you have been talking crazy, Mallory—similar to your junior year at Staples High… Maybe it is time again for you to visit Silver Hill?"

"No, Dad, I think it is your turn now to visit a psychiatrist."

"Well, send the money for that too. Your sister's tuition is due."

"Dad, how is it that her tuition became my problem? The two of you worked out the finances to send her to the medical school."

"Yes, but after your offer, I spent the money on a new car, a few antique guns, clothes, and so forth. Now you are reneging; what am I supposed to do?"

"Sell them."

"Mallory, I am telling you, don't make me come over there!"

"Let me tell you something, mister free spender. If you ever put a foot in my building, I'll have you arrested."

"Your own father? And for what?"

"Ask that of your better daughter."

Mallory had to hang up. Somehow, she couldn't take the next step and accuse him directly of having sexually abused Pat. Was it fear of him? Was it Pat's continuous denial?

⟨⟩

# -LV-

*M*en love to hear that I am aroused by their smell (partly true, if they are not using cologne and deodorant); by their manly demeanors (always awkward); by their intelligence (overestimated); by their knowledge (rather opinionated); by their empathy (mostly self-empathy); and by their love (they are emotional misers).

But what really gives a man pangs of superior masculinity (primarily over other men) is to believe that I have orgasms—multiple times—with him and with him alone. Better yet, I never knew what an orgasm was until I met him (men are ridiculous).

# -LVI-

By now, Mallory was a regular, if not privileged, client of the Plaza Hotel—Max was a big tipper. The staff knew and delivered all her special needs: organic soaps, antiallergenic pillows and covers, and, of course, all vegetarian food for lunch. The air conditioner had to be turned off and the windows had to be open to let the fresh air in, regardless of the weather conditions.

As for Max, he eventually succeeded in obtaining the privilege of intercourse with Mallory, yet he couldn't figure out how to give her an orgasm—nothing would have given him as much pleasure—alas. In those rare times when he didn't have to leave for somewhere else, he would go on and on for as long as he could before Mallory got too sore. Max never got tired or impatient with her nonresponsiveness.

He'd read somewhere that women achieved orgasm when stimulated simultaneously by their clitoris and by their G-spot—it was supposed to be an inch and a half beyond the clitoris—but that didn't work with Mallory. She would neither tell him how to please her, nor would she fake it to satisfy his quest. Max was convinced that she was fully satiated only when sleeping with lots of men.

"Mallory, how many men do you have in your portfolio?" Max asked.

"Why?"

"Okay, let me ask you this way: How would you like to be my girlfriend exclusively? French way: I'll pay all your expenses plus give you a monthly sum. In return you drop all other guys and sleep only with me—at most once or twice a week, but without a condom, which I think is interfering with your having orgasm."

Mallory was surprised by Max's offer.

"You'll live right here or in some other hotel; Carlyle has some nice one-bedroom apartments for long-term lease."

"Where is that?"

"On Madison Avenue, up in the 70s; if you want to live downtown, I could find one there."

"And that monthly sum?"

"You tell me; how much do you make a month?"

"Well, let's see—about $18,000."

"Okay, I'll pay you $20,000 a month."

In spite of Max's predictability and straightforwardness with her, somehow Mallory still had never recovered from her initial reaction to him; she just couldn't trust him.

Max interpreted her silence as bargaining. "$25,000 a month?"

"What if one day you decide to stop the relation and leave me with the hotel bills?" Mallory was embarrassed with her question, but she wanted to ask, at least, to sound professional. "A person who is forced into an inferior position cannot make a safe deal."

Max smiled. "Let me tell you how I could make it safe for you...I'll always prepay three months of hotel bills."

Mallory thought that this was exactly what she had been hoping for. She would finally have enough money to live and to work on her book.

"Okay, give me a little time to put my things in order."

"What things? Dump them. Whatever you need, I'll buy you new ones."

"Well, I've got to talk to the landlord to cancel the lease and..." Max interrupted her.

"Pay the bastard the full extent of the lease or keep the apartment. I don't mind. If you ever let me see the place...why are you so damn secretive as to where you live? Are you hiding an illegitimate child there or something?"

Max's cell phone rang; it was George: "I am sorry, boss; Mrs. Hathaway just called me to pick up Robert from school. Apparently they suspended him."

"George, wait a few minutes. I'll go with you."

He turned to Mallory. "I was suspended at least three times in high school: once for peeping into the girls' changing room in the basketball arena, once for bringing beer to school, and I don't remember the reason for the other time—always by a moronic accusation that I broke some rules of the school. Weren't the rules made for ordinary people to be broken by the extraordinary?"

"You never talk about your legitimate kids—except for getting Robert in the sack; what is the matter with him anyway?"

"Robert is a genius! He cannot sit still when all those morons are lecturing, mind you, on subjects that he knows more about than the teachers; he gets bored. I was the same way, except I knew what not to do. I guess I'd better go and talk to the principal. This is going to cost me a few hundred thousand dollars again."

*Men don't like complex women—neurotic or otherwise. So I present myself to them with highly premeditated simplicity. Men don't want women to know more than they do on any subject; to ask intimate questions; to show any signs of intelligence—there is a thin line there, no flub-dub either—furthermore, no display of frustration, irritation, impatience, or anger. Anxiety and melancholy are not acceptable either; all medical problems are symptoms of female hypochondrias, not to be indulged in their presence.*

*Men don't want women to cry unless it is a part of orgasmic catharsis; to talk, except to praise them; they don't want you to complain—you may shed a few obedient tears; to have any problem, unless it is an opportunity for a man to show off his skills. Actually, they are at their best throwing light upon pseudoproblems. Here, be careful, though, since it may backfire: Never, never be unfit for their lust.*

*It is too obvious that we women are here for men; but what are men here for?*

※

# -LVII-

On the subway downtown, Mallory sensed the steady gaze of some-one…was it Washington? She had lots of money in her bag; "I should have taken a cab," she scolded herself. It wasn't the cost, it was the time; traffic was so heavy in the late afternoons that it usually took an extra thirty to forty minutes to get home by taxi.

As she got off the subway, she quickly entered a grocery store, hoping that he would lose her scent; she went from one aisle to another while anxiously checking out the door; in her frantic activity, she bumped into someone.

"Mallory!" said David. "You seem spooked. What's the matter?"

Mallory's anxiety dissolved right away.

"I think I saw the same guy—the black guy who accosted me the other day that thought I was a prostitute. This time he wanted to rob me. He kept looking at me all the way from the Bloomingdale's station."

David gave Mallory a kiss on the cheek. "Are you done with your shopping?"

"Yes, let's go home."

At the checkout counter, Mallory noticed David's scant purchases: one Heineken Light, one bagel, one orange, one tomato, and one can of tuna.

Mallory grabbed David's arm: "Are you both on a starvation diet? This isn't even enough for one person."

David began to cry.

"Peter left me!"

Mallory had always thought that they were a sort of odd couple; she was surprised that their relationship had lasted that long. Peter more or less supported David.

"Why? How?"

David kept crying. "He…he met someone in a Geoffrey Beene outlet shop in New Orleans…he, he decided to move there."

"Did you see it coming?"

"No, not at all. He told me about it last night, then packed his personal stuff and left."

This is what Mallory was afraid of—that Max would do the same thing to her.

"What will happen to the apartment?"

"Peter was generous about that. He left everything to me. Now I've got to find a job to pay the rent." David stopped crying.

They reached their building, and by the time they got to the fourth floor, Mr. Abrams, the longtime tenant of apartment 3A, opened his door. It seemed like he was waiting for her.

"Miss, may I ask you to please be a little quiet? I don't know whether you are playing jumping-gym up there or whatever, but I am an old man. In fact, I turned eighty-four yesterday; have a little consideration."

Mallory blushed and then mumbled something like, "Yes, sir, I am sorry."

David extended his hand to Mr. Abrams, pulled him out, and gave him a big hug.

"Well, well, congratulations and happy birthday, Mr. Abrams! Boy, you don't look a day older than eighty-four. Come on, Mallory, sing with me." David gave the orange to Mr. Abrams and they began to sing, "Happy birthday, Mr. Abrams, happy birthday to you."

Mr. Abrams beamed with pleasure for a minute, and then his face dropped: "You know, none of my three children even remembered my birthday. Thank you, guys; go ahead, have a good time. I am sorry I became such an old grump; have fun, just don't get old."

Mr. Abrams shuffled back to his apartment.

Mallory and David walked up to their floor.

"Did you say Peter was bored with you? My God, you are so funny and playful."

"Well, I say to you with kind reciprocation, you cannot carry even a simple tune." Mallory laughed, enjoying his trusting intimacy.

"Okay, back to Peter. I think it was sexual boredom; anyhow, do you want to eat with me? I have more stuff in the refrigerator…I could make a delicious rice omelet with tuna: I put in tomatoes, pepper it with paprika, salt, and tarragon and a touch of turmeric; I sauté onions separately with butter in a saucepan until light brown, mix and stir them for two minutes, and then fold over and sprinkle with sprouts and parsley. Voilà!" Dave bowed, arms outstretched.

"Oh, my, I've never heard of such an elaborate omelet! Of course I'll eat with you; anything I should bring in?"

"No, no, I got everything; come in. I'll put some music on; you just sit here and relax. What would you like to listen to?"

Mallory listened to music only occasionally: She never went to concerts or bought CDs, and she didn't even have a stereo. It wasn't that she didn't like music, but she could easily do without it.

"I don't know; anything that you want to listen to will be fine."

David was searching for something. "Ah, I think Peter took a few CDs; in fact all of Elton John's! Oh, you'll love this Dvorak; I got this Hiroko Nakamura's string quartet—it is sublime and also sex neutral."

As Mallory was watching Dave in the kitchen meticulously preparing the omelet, she realized that she felt truly safe only with Dave.

"What is that sexual boredom all about?"

David laughed: "You know, you heterosexuals think of us as a totally different species—not even mammalian—like lizards. Homosexual boredom is like heterosexual boredom: Your partner no longer excites you, you become uninterested to the point that your body becomes uncooperative even if your mind says you should, and the harder you try, the worse it gets. Then mutual accusations, guilt, anger, and avoidance become the foreplay... Now, does that sound familiar?"

"Hm-m-m, not really! Maybe I am the lizard. You see, I never get bored with my partners because I am never excited by them to begin with—I mean as persons. I get sexually stimulated by certain things—anyone could do it if I tell them how, right?"

David looked puzzled. "Right what?"

"Telling your partner how to excite you."

David had never heard this before—a heterosexual woman describing her sexuality in such concrete terms. He thought they were mostly romantic creatures in their sexuality and needed lots of foreplay in the form of attention, affection, love, and especially the prospect of marriage.

"I am sure a little technical teaching would be useful, but isn't it who the person is making love to you rather than what he is doing? Otherwise, the partner becomes interchangeable in the same way that an expert in a field is, like an electrician, a doctor, or a masseuse."

Recognizing his gaffe, David put his hands over his mouth. Mallory wasn't at all insulted: "Well, of course. I think this false idea of lovemaking is what messes up a sexual relationship. You could have sex with someone you love, fine. But sex with someone you love is very time-limited, as the love slowly transforms from 'being in love' to 'loving' and the sex turns prohibitive like an incestuous act."

Mallory was simply repeating what she'd heard from Jeff. "Then the partner yearns to be in love again. They try to 'rekindle' the old flames with romantic vacations, trimming down their bodies, and mandatory roses, wine, and gifts; and if all fails, they consult sex therapists. In fact nothing works. Finally one of the partners finds someone else to fall in love with, and the whole vicious circle repeats itself, if that partner marries again. One of my clients, a wise old man, said the other day: 'It is not the best horseman who runs the farthest but the one who changes the horse!'"

David was aghast: "Boy, you are cynical. No wonder you don't have a steady guy in your life. So what do I do now? Look for another horse?"

"No, what I meant is that Peter is looking for a new horse or found one… You, you should get off his horse."

They began to laugh so much that they fell into each other's arms and then rolled onto the floor.

"Mallory, how about the two of us living together? I'll be your donkey—I'll cook, clean, shop, do all the other chores, and let you write."

౷ൽ౸

# -LVIII-

*T*he *first real conversation I had with my father occurred a few months after I graduated from NYU and came home. Pat was in New Haven, so I went out, picked up hamburgers and fries for him, cheese and crackers for me, and a six-pack of Bud and settled in front of the television to watch* **High Noon,** *my Dad's favorite movie, on Turner Classic Movies.*

*"Isn't this nice, Mallory, to be home, to take care of the house and your old man? Why New York? You already finished college and you can write here. You don't need to worry about supporting yourself. Let Pat be the breadwinner—of course, if she becomes a doctor. I have a good pension, and you could get some part-time job, if you like. You don't have to, just to..."*

*"You want me to be like your housekeeper, a wife of some sort? I think Pat would be more suitable for that role!" I was surprised at myself.*

*He began to feel uneasy.*

*"Mallory, you are really not a grateful child. I am offering you a comfortable situation so that you don't need to struggle in New York. You don't have a job, and this...this Rolfing thing is for chubby girls; you are so beautiful and delicate."*

*I couldn't figure out whether he was genuinely interested in my writing (he never was in the past) or trying to manipulate me.*

*"How much would you pay me for being a housewife?"*

*"What do you mean, pay you? I am your father, and this is your house. I won't ask for rent or anything; I'll buy whatever is needed, you know, food and stuff and your clothes. That's the deal. It would be good for both of us. Why don't you try it for a few years?"*

*He drank two bottles of the beer and ate all the food while talking.*

*"Until Pat graduates from medical school, you mean?"*

*"What has this anything to do with her?"*

*"Well, I presume when she becomes a doctor, she'll work somewhere close, like Norwalk Hospital, or open a private office and live with you. Now that I think about it, it is a great idea. You'll take care of the house, pick up the groceries and beer; she'll bring the bacon."*

161

Dad's eyes sparkled. "Are you kidding? She'll most likely marry another doctor and move away."

I thought I got him.

"No, no, she would never marry a doctor or anyone else; she doesn't date. Dad,
she is still a virgin, she says. I don't know how; she definitely fooled around—I
saw with my own eyes."

His nostrils were wide open.

"When, where? You saw with your own eyes?"

"Yeah, in Turkey."

"In Turkey? You both were kids then."

"Exactly!"

He recoiled: "Okay, listen, I don't want to hear any more. Whatever the two
of you did then is between you. If I were you, I wouldn't keep harping on these
childhood stories. Incidentally, if this is what your idea of companionship is, I am
withdrawing my offer...you can go and do whatever you want. I can manage by
myself."

He got up, took the other two bottles, and handed them over to me: "Now, you
go somewhere else and let me watch the movie in peace."

I thought this was as close to "high noon" as he could tolerate without a
shootout.

࿊

# -LIX-

Mallory listened to her telephone messages:

- "Hello, Mallory, this is Jeanny Weisman. I left a number of messages, and you are not returning my calls, so I presume then my suspicions are right. I didn't want to do this to you, for I thought we had a good working relationship, but you give me no choice. I was calling to inform you that since your last visit my gold Cartier watch is missing. I would appreciate your returning it at once, and if I don't hear from you within twenty-four hours, I intend to call the police. Furthermore, I have told my husband about this; well, let me not go any further."
- "My offer is still standing. Regardless, how about Thursday lunch at the 728?"

"What a vicious bitch," Mallory murmured. "Go fuck yourself." Then she got scared. What if Jeanny gives her telephone number to the police? She had two choices: to call her or to call her husband. She chose Jeff.

"Hey."

"What's up?"

"I want you to hear this message from Jeanny."

Jeff felt the blood drain from his body. He slouched in his chair, hardly able to hold the phone to his ear, until he heard "my gold Cartier watch is missing." He took a deep breath.

⌘

The following morning, Jeff opened the drawer where Jeanny kept her jewelry. There, in the open, was the gold Cartier watch that he'd given her for their tenth anniversary. He took the watch, put it in his pocket without having any clear idea as to what to do with it, and left for the office. It was only in the afternoon when he was on the way to Mallory that the idea of rendering justice occurred to him.

As he walked up the stairs, an uncommon feeling of discomfort came over him. He took the watch out of his pocket, turned it over, and read: "To Jeanny with All My Love." Jeff felt a dull pain burrowing into the deep recesses of his brain. Was that a kind of warped guilt? he wondered—he had never experienced that feeling before. Was sleeping with another woman a transient wrong? Would giving his wife's watch to Mallory be a permanent sin? He rang the bell.

Jeff strutted in cockily. Hand in his pocket, he stood in the middle of the room and looked aggressively into Mallory's eyes: "Ms. Coldwell, yesterday at 4:30 p.m. you played a tape in Jeanny Weisman's voice to her husband Jeff Weisman, is that correct?"

Mallory, a little puzzled, answered, "Yeah."

"Well," Jeff continued in the same prosecutorial tone, "is it also correct that in that above-mentioned tape, Mrs. Weisman accused you of stealing her gold watch made by Cartier?"

"What is this nonsense, Jeff?"

"Miss Coldwell, please answer by 'yes' or 'no'!"

"Yes."

"By playing that tape to Jeanny Weisman's husband you were intending to blackmail him, is that correct?"

"Stop it, Jeff. It is not funny."

"Miss Coldwell: 'Yes' or 'no,' please."

"No."

"I am in possession of a court order to search your apartment...do you object to the process?"

"Do you really think that I stole her watch?"

"Let me repeat the question, Ms. Mallory. Do you object to the search of your apartment for the purpose of recovering foresaid gold watch, belonging to Mrs. Jeanny Weisman, per order of the court?"

"Fuck you!"

"I presume that means yes."

Jeff went straight to the middle drawer of her desk, quickly opened and closed it, and turned around with the watch hanging from his hand.

"Aha! The prima facie evidence."

"Oh, Jesus!" Mallory let it out: "For a moment I thought you really believed Jeanny's story. So where was the fucking watch?"

Jeff, pleased with his performance, kept laughing until Mallory asked again, "Where did you find it?"

"In its regular place."

"So it was never lost?"

"No, don't you see, she was scaring you to call her back, but now...," he took Mallory's hand and put the watch on her wrist, "...now it is yours—fully justified."

Mallory looked at the shining watch; she had never seen a watch like this. The gold band, intertwined with her Kabbalah bracelet, looked out of place, so she took the watch off and handed it over to Jeff.

"No, thanks anyway."

"Mallory, this watch is worth $12,000!"

"It is not to my taste."

Jeff couldn't believe his ears: A call girl who allows herself to be fucked for money just refused such an expensive gift! She was full of riddles.

"You can sell it."

"No, really. I don't want to be a party to her sick game and your...ah... your peculiar sense of justice."

"I see. Well, I was also hoping that the watch would pay for a few sessions. Anyway, I am sorry, that is what I thought, so I didn't draw any cash this week...I'll leave the watch with you until the next week when I bring..."

Mallory's green stare got even harsher.

"Mr. Jeff Weisman, do I understand that you do not have money for the transaction that you are here for? Is this correct?"

"Yes, ma'am."

"Is it true that you stole your wife's gold Cartier watch, worth about $12,000?"

"Yes, ma'am."

She was plowing on: "Mr. Weisman, you are introducing stolen property into this transaction, thus trying to render the other party to become a coconspirator in your crime. Is that correct?"

Jeff was enjoying Mallory's line of seductive reasoning.

"Well, the other party didn't actually..."

"Mr. Jeff Weisman: 'Yes' or 'no,' please."

"Yes, ma'am."

Jeff found her provocative sternness (no matter that it was an act) very erotic.

"Thus, Mr. Weisman, you plead guilty for above-said crime."

"Yes, ma'am, with explanation."

Jeff was impressed by the intelligence and the wit coming from a woman he considered just a sex object.

"No explanation needed; you are guilty, double guilty, okay? Now then, let's fuck." Mallory dropped her skirt to the floor by jiggling her hips.

಄

# -LX-

*M*en will do anything for sex, the kind of sex that delivers aching lust: They would fall in love for sex, they would marry for sex, they divorce for sex, they'll pay for sex—that is the least of all. They'll offer jobs, positions, and other privileges for it. In the process, they'll risk their own careers, their reputations, and their families; in short, they barter their lives for sex.

The Tertullian declaration was wrong; not woman but man is the gateway through which the devil comes.

# -LXI-

"Oh, shit! I forgot to turn off the phone," Mallory screamed. She looked at the number: It was Ham's. One o'clock in the morning? "Ham! What's up?"

"No, miss," said a woman's voice with a heavy accent, "it is me, Vakfiye, you remember in Ham's place, yes? You brought fish and I made cucumbers? Yes?"

"Well, of course, I am so sorry, it's late."

"I use his telephone. I dialed all his fast-dials. Two hours ago I left message with his parents; now I got you too. Miss, he is not waking up! He has been sleeping since this morning and maybe from last night. I don't know."

"Vakfiye, did his parents come?"

"No. What do I do, please?"

"Look, I think he should be taken to a hospital emergency room. I'll call the ambulance. They most likely will take him to St. Luke's. I'll be there as soon as it's daylight—in a few hours, anyway.

"Thank you, Miss; şukran, şukran."

In the morning, Hamilton went to check out the message: "Ann, there is no message on the answering machine. Did you not mention last night about rent, or something that Ham's landlord was calling us for?"

Ann was on her way out. "I must have pushed the delete button by mistake; sorry. I am late to work. Call Ham and see what is going on again; there is no respite from this kid. Bye."

She left in a huff.

As Hamilton was about to pick up the phone, it rang: "Is this Mr. Thurman?"

"Yes?"

"Mr. Thurman, I am Dr. Shapiro from St. Luke's Hospital. Your son was brought here by ambulance around five o'clock. The information we received from the landlord was that she couldn't wake him up, and the toxicology report shows high levels of heroin and marijuana; we are about to..."

"Excuse me, doctor; you said St. Luke's?"

"Yes, St. Luke's emergency room."

"I'll be there in a few minutes."

Hamilton grabbed his coat and rushed to the hospital, which was just five blocks away from their apartment.

The emergency room of St. Luke's looked like a disaster center. The waiting room was packed with patients, mostly African American and Latino. Doctors and nurses—mostly white—were weaving in and out of this cloudy chaos, while shouting orders to each other.

A male Hispanic clerk at the information booth couldn't understand Mr. Thurman's New England accent and asked him to write down the patient's name and surname. Then, not being able to decipher his handwriting, he asked him to print it. Meanwhile, Hamilton noticed a tiny light wave in the dark sea; he walked over. Two women—one scantily dressed young woman and one head-scarf-wearing older woman—were talking to a police officer. Another cop was pacing up and down the hall.

Hamilton pulled the sagging curtains aside and found Ham in an ill-fitting hospital gown, lying on a stretcher.

"Hello, Mr. Thurman, you look like your son! Your son is okay; he spoke to me. By the way, I am Vakfiye."

"Thank you for calling us. We didn't come earlier because my wife misunderstood your message. You said he spoke?"

"Yes, you got to pinch him to speak, doctor says; it is okay to pinch him."

A young Indian doctor gently pushed everyone away and pulled up Ham's eyelids. Ham tried to turn his head away; the doctor put his knuckle on Ham's sternum and pressed: "Ouch!"

The doctor wasn't sure whom to address: He shifted his eyes from one to another and finally settled on Hamilton. "Are you all related to the patient?"

Without waiting for an answer he continued: "You are all very lucky people. If you had brought him one hour later, even I could not have saved him. As soon as there is a bed available, I'll admit him to Bellevue Forensic for a week or so. After that, you should find a long-term rehab hospital for at least thirty days—if he's released; after that he could come back to our After Care Clinic. Let me also warn you, most insurance companies don't cover all this, but the Bellevue part is taken care of."

Hamilton looked at Mallory for a full minute, thinking she was a harmonious sample of his own tribe.

He turned to the doctor: "Why are you sending him to Bellevue instead of here, and what does 'if released' mean?"

"Oh, no one told you?" the doctor replied. "Your son is under arrest for possession of a large amount of marijuana and heroin. Apparently at the time of admission—I wasn't here—they found bags of narcotics in his pockets, and the police were notified—it is the law."

"I thought he wasn't admitted here. Why was he searched?"

"Well, sir, when a patient is in semi-coma, he is stripped of his clothes, and his belongings are collected and given to the administrative clerk for safekeeping."

Hamilton put his reading glasses on and leaned over toward the doctor's chest to read his name tag—he took his time: "Dr. Cur...Curhani, would you consider my son safely kept when you function as an informant for the police?"

The doctor's self-confidence and mildly condescending attitude dissolved.

"Sir, I didn't do it."

"Dr. Curhani, I used the word 'you' here as a plural pronoun for indirect object of the function of the verb."

As if looking for help, the doctor's eyes moved to Mrs. Vakfiye, whose head was by now totally buried in her scarf.

Mallory was thinking what an unbearable father this man might have been to Ham.

One of the policemen, who was eavesdropping on their conversation, approached Hamilton.

"Are you the father of this gentleman?"

He pulled out a pen and a booklet from his belt pocket while Hamilton nodded his head affirmatively.

"Give me your full name and your address and your daytime telephone number."

Hamilton opened his wallet, took out one of his cards, and gave it to him.

"Hm-m!" The officer took down the information and gave back the card.

"Officer, I gathered from the doctor..." Hamilton turned around looking for him—Dr. Curhani had slipped away. "Yes, the doctor said that my son was arrested and will be transferred to Bellevue. What will happen to him?"

"Well, sir, that is up to the district attorney's office. It will have all the evidence for prosecution. In New York State he could get a long...," the officer stopped himself. "I think you should hire a lawyer."

Another officer came over, and the two conferred in a corner.

Hamilton nervously searched his pockets for his cell phone but couldn't find it.

"Do you ladies have a phone that I can use?" Hamilton took a long look at Mallory.

"Are you Mallory, Ham's highly talented student?"

"Well, thank you. He is just being kind." Mallory offered her cell phone. He dialed Ann.

"Ann, what is Jeff's private number? No, no, I'll talk to you later. Ah, okay, yes Ann, *later* is an indeterminate adverb."

He shook his head and dialed the number.

"You must be very horny or hungry. You never call," came the self-satisfied voice of Jeff.

Hamilton, who was already shaken by Ham's situation, got a little confused—obviously, Jeff's private line must be primarily used by his wife.

"It is me, not Jeanny, you...you optimistic nerd."

Now, it was Jeff's turn to be confused. He couldn't figure out how Hamilton could've gotten Mallory's phone...did he misread the number? He hung up.

Hamilton dialed again. "Were you insulted by the noun 'nerd' illegally qualifying your optimism, or did you just hang up on me?"

"Oh, hi, Hamilton. I am sorry. We must have gotten disconnected. What is up in your abstract mind at such an early hour?"

"Yeah, I am sorry to disturb you so early. It is Ham again. He was found in an intoxicated state in his room and brought to St. Luke's emergency room, where he was searched, found in possession of a large amount of drugs, and arrested. Two police officers are waiting for him to wake up now so that they can transfer him to Bellevue's forensic unit."

Jeff exhaled with audible relief.

"Okay, okay, Hamilton. That...that is okay; let it be. Just call your Silver Hill and secure a place."

Hamilton, still a little disoriented, gave back Mallory's phone, looked at his watch, and said, "Oh my God, I have a class in ten minutes! Would it be possible for you to stay till noon? I'll be free after. I'll come and release you," he laughed nervously.

"I am sorry, Miss, I got to go too, so sorry," Vakfiye said as both left the ER in a hurry.

༺☙

Mallory pinched Ham's arms as instructed a few times; clearly, he wasn't happy about it—he seemed to be cursing in his sleep. A Hispanic man with a square body, in his forties, swaggered into the ER like he owned the place. He talked to the other two officers, eyed Mallory, then waved them away.

"Hi, I am Detective Salvador Alvarez. You are his girlfriend or something?"

A lascivious smile pulled his lips apart.

"Yes."

"Why do you hang around with a drug addict? He is hopeless; we arrested him a few times already; believe me, he is no good, unless you are a druggie yourself. What do you take?"

"Nothing."

"Do you help him sell the stuff?"

"No, of course not!"

"I don't believe you." Detective Alvarez stepped closer. "One of these days I'll catch you too. Look at yourself. You are a beautiful young lady, but you look like hell: hair is uncombed, your dress is all wrinkled... Do you sleep with your clothes on after you get high?"

"I told you I don't take any drugs."

"Do you have an ID?"

Mallory searched her green bag and pulled out a badge.

"A student at NYU, huh? That is more reason that you should go with clean-cut guys...but this is an old ID—it expired a year and a half ago."

"Yeah, I just forgot to renew it."

A series of beeps took over; a nurse came running. She wiggled the IV poles, tied Ham's arms to the stretcher, and left.

Ham screamed, "Fuck!"

Detective Alvarez threw a disgusted look at Ham: "Foulmouthed too; we'll keep him here for a while and then book him. You shouldn't wait here all alone; it could be hours or days."

"Why do all that? He is not a criminal; he was suicidal—he took all those drugs to die. Most likely he passed out before he took them. That is why he had all those drugs in his pocket."

"Yeah, yeah, yeah; is he that good in bed, that you would tell such utter lies to save him? Listen, sweetie, lies won't save him, but you lie under a real man, now that might. Where do you live?"

"Downtown."

"Okay, I'll give you a ride home. We'll talk about it."

"No, thank you. I have to wait for his father to come."

"All right, give me your telephone number and I'll call you."

"Look, officer, I appreciate your help, but I am engaged to be married so I don't..."

Detective Alvarez interrupted her: "To this loser? Gee whiz. Okay, here is my card. If you change your mind, give me a call." He walked over to the two cops; they talked a few minutes, and as he left, he turned around and blew a kiss to Mallory: "You'll not regret it!"

*⌒〰〰〵*

Mallory stayed with Ham till his father showed up. At about the same time, a private limousine sent from Silver Hill Hospital arrived. Ham was semiawake and physically unstable. The physician assistant, who came with the limousine, was familiar with Ham from his previous hospitalization. He reassured the family that they didn't need to accompany him to the hospital—all would be taken care of.

After the limousine pulled out, Hamilton and Mallory stood awkwardly in front of St. Luke's main entrance: "I should have gone with them," said Hamilton.

"We just met, but let me give you some advice: Don't get married, and if you do, never have children. Anyway, that's what my wife says, and I repeat it when I feel particularly depressed."

A cold breeze whipped the rain across their faces. Hamilton decided not to venture out. "If I may paraphrase Oscar Wilde: Advice is never of any use to anyone. The best thing you can do about it, is to pass it on." And then he laughed; "Wilde didn't realize that his was also an advice."

He watched Mallory, her white skirt becoming see-through, dissolving into the gray, wet day.

*⌒〰〰〵*

By the time Mallory left Hamilton, she hadn't eaten for over twelve hours, so she bought an apple on the street and dialed Jeff.

"Hello?"

"Jeff, it's me."

"Mallory, what is going on? How did Hamilton get your telephone? You almost blew my cover."

"How do you mean?"

"Well, thinking that it was you, I made a joke."

"Such as?"

"Mallory, is that important? How do you know him? Please tell me you don't..."

"No, no. Don't worry, he's not my client. His son was one of my teachers, and now we are just friends. His father used my phone because he forgot his at home. Manhattan is a small town, huh?"

"Yeah, a little too small. Thankfully, he is a naïve character. Anyone else would have figured it out."

"I knew that you knew Ham's father. You bailed him out at least once that I know. Are you going to help him?"

"I already did, but you know, Mallory, the best help one can give Ham is to let him go to prison for a year or two, to dry up, and learn a lesson or two."

"Anal kind?"

"The best kind, simultaneous and sequential. A good-looking blond kid like that... Hey, are you getting a little stoked? I could provide a modest version tomorrow around four o'clock."

"See you then."

⚬〰〰〰⚬

Hamilton called his wife after the doctors at St. Luke's had reassured him that his son would be fine. "There are no residual effects of the overdose." Ann cut him short, "Fine, fine; well, I don't have to hear every gory detail of it. This is another chapter in your wreckage of a writer son. For me, it is really getting boring. Listen, Hamilton, I have a dinner meeting with clients; I'll join you later."

Hamilton sat by the lobby to wait out the rain. "Too horny or hungry?" he replayed Jeff's remark in his mind. That made no sense.

⚬〰〰〰⚬

# -LXII-

*T*here was a boy with whom I used to hang around—Eliot. He was one of the most talented and the smartest kids in our class; he wasn't very attractive, but his South African accent made up plenty for it. His family moved to the United States after they began to feel increasing anti-white, anti-Jewish sentiments there.

Eliot was sort of a curiosity. He didn't know how to play baseball, hockey, or football. He was too short to play the other games common in both countries—basketball or volleyball—and he couldn't recruit other boys to play soccer with him. So isolated from other males, Eliot made friends with certain girls—some nerds and me. Nerds showed him off to their parents while I tried to corrupt him.

I introduced Eliot to beer, to marijuana, to oral sex, to cursing, and especially to pickup drag racing on the Merritt Parkway—on his sixteenth birthday his father, a diamond dealer, gave him a sporty red Mazda. The trick was to accost a young male driver who was either alone or preferably with a girl and tease him by driving next to him long enough to force him to speed up, to break the parallel run. We would chase him for a while, catch up with him, then I'd pull out my T-shirt to show my breasts—occasionally my ass—then peel off and leave him in the dust, so to speak. Only rarely a guy like that would give up, slow down, and let us go. Usually they'd enter into a testosterone race with us, until we either lost each other or pulled over somewhere and made new friends.

One Saturday evening as the sun was setting, we picked on a bulky guy in his thirties. He was alone, cruising sixty miles per hour on the Merritt Parkway going south; he was driving a four-door black Ford, and we began to drive on his left, not passing. He looked at Eliot a couple of times like saying, "Okay, fellow, pass already." He even slowed down a little to make it easy for us, but Eliot also slowed down. I could see the guy was getting irritated, so I gave him a head signal like "race us"; he shrugged his shoulders, kind of like "get lost, kids." I unbuttoned my blouse and turned to him, jiggling my breasts; that was our regular signal for Eliot to zoom away. In five seconds we hit seventy-five miles an hour, weaving in and out of lanes.

*The guy in the black Ford was hooked! I was watching from the side mirror; he was having a hard time negotiating the traffic. Then I saw him reaching out of his window and putting a light on his roof—though not flashing. I said to Eliot, "Slow down; the guy is a cop. He put a light on his rooftop."*

*"Don't be silly," he replied. "What color is the glass of the light?"*

*It was too dark to tell.*

*"It is most likely a yellow or blue—one of those auxiliary worker's cars, like road construction, blood transportation, or something. Do you want me to lose him?"*

*I said, "Yes, he is a little creepy."*

*Eliot accelerated to eighty-five miles an hour. A few minutes later, a red light began to flash on the black Ford, while a screaming siren scattered the cars to the right; the guy was on our tail.*

*"Oh, my goodness, an unmarked car!" Eliot was shaking.*

*"No, idiot! It is more like: 'Oh, shit! I told you the guy was a cop!'"*

*"Drive up to the side-road exit," a voice boomed.*

*A few miles down Round Hill to exit 28, there is a service road that runs into a few acres of land with an abandoned building on it. We pulled over to the edge of the road.*

*The unmarked car stopped a few feet behind us—the red light flashing.*

*"What is he doing? Why is he not coming over?"*

*"Eliot! Shut up!"*

*"My parents will kill me! What am I going to do? Listen, Mallory, can we change seats? I'll pay you $1,000. You see, you are a girl so he would let you go. But me? What do you say? Please."*

*"Are you crazy? He saw you driving. Don't you remember I was showing my boobs to him? Hello-o-o!"*

*"Maybe I should go over to him," Eliot said and opened his door.*

*"Stay in the car!" an even more stern voice ordered.*

*I had been in a similar situation before, so I knew the cop was writing us up. I buttoned up to my neck.*

*Finally, the cop left his car and walked over toward Eliot's side with one hand caressing his gun on his belt and the other holding a booklet. He knocked on the window.*

*"Lower it. Your license and registration, please."*

*"I am terribly sorry, officer, but she just..." The officer cut him off.*

*"Your license and registration, please."*

*Eliot tried to open his alligator-skin wallet, but all his papers and a few hundred dollars fell out. He was shaking uncontrollably. I picked up his license and registration from the floor, wrapped them in with all the money, and gave them to the officer.*

*He stared at me. "You realize that you could be arrested for trying to bribe an officer?"*

Eliot shouted, "I didn't, officer! You saw her do it. She gave you the money. I would never insult a police officer."

"This license is only valid until 7 p.m. What time is it, sir?" The cop asked in a pseudo-polite voice.

"I am so sorry: That is why I was hurrying to go home."

"Your address says Westport, sir. You were heading south. Would you insult an officer's intelligence?" he said with glee.

"No, officer. I beg you..." he cried out weakly.

"What is the speed limit here, sir?"

"Sixty-five miles per hour?"

"No, sir, fifty-five; and how fast were you driving?"

"I am not sure."

I smelled urine from Eliot's seat.

"Eighty-five miles per hour!" The cop was dragging this thing out.

"I'm sorry, officer...please let me go." Eliot began to cry.

"And you?" The cop turned to me, steeped in testosterone. "You could be charged for indecent exposure, endangerment of public safety, and trying to bribe me."

I hated both of these men—their unbending arrogance and crawling impotence. At that moment, I hated all men.

"Drive the car behind the building," he ordered.

Eliot looked paralyzed.

"Hey, you knucklehead, I said drive the car behind that building! Are you deaf?"

We jerked forward. Was he going to rob us or kill us? I wondered. When we stopped in the back of the large barn building, the officer turned off his lights and approached my side of the car. He opened the door.

"Now your girlfriend has to suck my cock, or I'll take you downtown!"

"Go ahead, Mallory," replied Eliot.

"You must be kidding! Is it up to you, Eliot, to give consent?"

"Please do it for me; I don't want to go to jail! Please, Mallory, I'll make it up to you; what is the big deal?"

"What is the big deal? You suck his cock."

Eliot looked at the officer to see whether that would be an acceptable alternative, but the officer spit at him: "Are you a homo?"

"Please, Mallory, do what he says! You do it to me, so what is the difference?"

Eliot was wiping the spit off his face with a perfumed handkerchief that he took out of his back pocket.

Meanwhile, the cop leaned against the open door, unzipped his pants, pulled out his penis, and put it in front of my face—it was small but wide; his crotch smelled of pastrami. As soon as I touched him, he ejaculated all over my face then wiped his penis with my blouse.

"Okay, now scurry off and don't let me catch you again."

"May I have my money back?" Eliot said.

He looked at him in disbelief and threw one of the bills at me.

"One hundred dollars for five seconds? Not bad!" he smirked and left in a hurry. Eliot casually took the money from my hand and stopped crying.

 measure

# -LXIII-

The day after Ham was sent to St. Luke's Hospital, Vakfiye and her son, Ahmed, were awakened by steady knocks on their door at five o'clock in the morning. They looked at each other—what could that be?

"Open up, FBI!" A harsh voice reverberated through their small apartment.

Vakfiye quickly got dressed and put the cover on her bed while Ahmed, who always slept fully dressed on the floor, slipped his mattress under her bed—they were tidying up the place to be respectful.

"Open the door, FBI!"

The moment Ahmed took the chain off the door, three tall men—two young, one middle aged, all in dark navy suits—barged in. They pushed Ahmed's face against the wall, kick spread his legs, frisked, and hand-cuffed him.

"He is clean, Richard," one of the men said.

"Are you Vakfiye bin Hakim, the occupant of this dwelling?" the older one asked.

Vakfiye slumped into a chair. "Yes, please don't hurt him...we both have green cards."

"This is a search warrant," explained the agent, Richard Brown. "Answer my questions truthfully and neither of you will get hurt. Do you have any guns in the house?"

"No, why should we have guns?"

"Do you have any explosive material in the house?"

"No, sir. We are very good Muslims."

"Yeah," he snickered. "Did you know that your son raises money for Palestinian terrorists?"

Ahmed protested: "I work for the Islamic Brotherhood charity organization."

One of the younger agents was walking around the apartment, randomly opening closets and drawers.

"Well, isn't it the same thing? What are all these green books?" Agent Brown picked up one from the pile.

"They are Korans, sir."

"Why do you have dozens of them? Are you proselytizers?"

"Sir?"

"I said why so many?"

"Oh, we give them to friends; they are signed copies of Imam Abdullah."

"Is he the guy running that mosque in New Jersey?"

Ahmed was pleased that his boss was so well known.

"Yes, sir, I translate for him and Hamas corrects my English."

Agent Brown looked at the younger two officers, who were collecting papers, notes, books, and lithographs and putting them in large boxes.

"Did he say 'Hamas'?"

"Yes sir, our American brother; Hamas is his Muslim name. He lives here in that room...his American name is Ham—Ham is a poet."

"I see; this is getting more and more interesting," murmured Agent Brown. "I was wondering who was writing such heart-tugging letters in perfect English. After having read one of them, I almost decided to volunteer myself for their Palestinian causes, never mind sending some money."

Again the other two laughed.

"Let me get it straight: You rent out this other room, and where do you two sleep?"

"My son usually stays with his friends in New Jersey. Occasionally he stays over; then he sleeps on the floor."

"Get those friends' names and addresses later," Agent Brown addressed the young ones. "So where is the poet?"

"In the hospital, St. Luke's, overdosed."

"Overdosed with poems?" All three chuckled.

"Drugs."

"Drugs, huh? Is that how he is paid for his rhetorical service, Ahmed? Ahmed is your name, right?" He turned to his associates: "They are either Ahmed or Mohammed."

All of them laughed.

"Sir, Muslims don't use drugs," Ahmed replied.

"I am not asking whether you use drugs, idiot. I am asking whether you are his supplier. Aren't all those fucking Muslims from Afghanistan major suppliers of heroin?"

"No sir, I don't supply drugs," Ahmed asserted.

"We tried to stop Hamas," joined Vakfiye, "especially after he accepted Allah as his savior. We told him that if he wants to go to Heaven, he has to be clean."

"This is getting even better," Agent Brown smiled. "So the poet converted to Islam, I presume with your help. How did you recruit him to be a jihadist?"

"Sir?"

"I mean, what is in it for him, like four hundred virgins?"

"No sir, that is a mistranslation of the Koran…it is four hundred pigeons," Ahmed explained.

"Four hundred pigeons? What the fuck does one do with four hundred pigeons?" All five looked at each other.

Vakfiye took her old teacher posture: "No, no, in Syriac, it is four hundred raisins."

"Whatever, what is the last name of Fatass? We owe him a visit and 'get well' wishes."

"Not Fatass sir, it is Hamas. I don't know his last name."

"You don't know Fatass's last name? Does he pay the rent in cash? So you also cheat the IRS. What does he look like?"

"Like him." Vakfiye pointed to the blond guy.

"Okay, I'll find him. There couldn't be too many blond kids overdosed at St. Luke's. You two," he pointed to his guys, "take all the evidence and book him. I'll just take a look at the poet. Don't forget his computer either."

"Please don't take my computer, sir. It is my butter and bread."

The blond guy already had disconnected Ahmed's and Ham's computers.

"Don't worry; the government will provide your butter and bread for a very, very long time. As for you, lady, do not leave the city. Here is my card; if you decide to cooperate and give us the names of those members of the jihad, call me; that would make your and your son's lives easy. Otherwise, I'll have all those pigeons shitting on your heads in hell."

As the agents took away Ahmed and boxes full of their belongings, Vakfiye began to cry: "Oh, my America, my dream America."

☾⟗☽

Agent Brown pushed aside the woman on the line and showed his ID to the male Hispanic clerk at the information booth in St. Luke's. The clerk went into a total panic: "What do you want?"

Agent Brown wasn't interested in a potential immigration situation, but he just wanted to intimidate the clerk, so he jotted down his last name: Ruiz. "What does 'J' stand for?"

"Juan."

"Okay." The agent wrote down the name. "Where is that blond kid Ham, whatever his last name is, the guy with the drug overdose?"

"Thurman. He was discharged, sir." The clerk looked into his notes: "He came in at 2:34 a.m. yesterday and left at 1:30 p.m."

"An overdosed person is discharged within eleven hours of admission?"

"I don't know, sir; let me get you the doctor."

The clerk announced in a loud voice: "Paging Dr. Curhani. Dr. Curhani, FBI is here."

Dr. Curhani arrived, looking exhausted and scared.

"So, fellow, where are you from?"

"I do have a green card, sir."

"Yeah, why were you so nervous?"

"FBI? Sir, it is like seeing a snake! Oh, sorry, I didn't mean in a bad way; it is just scary." Dr. Curhani's dark face turned all white. "How can I be of some help?" he mumbled.

Agent Brown wasn't offended by the snake analogy at all—he was comforted by his effect on the doctor.

"I ask you again, where are you from, doctor?"

"I am a third-year resident with a J-1 visa, officer. I got eleven more months on it."

"Doctor, I asked 'where you are from?'"

"Oh, I am originally from Pakistan but trained in India."

"That is why you are so reluctant to tell me where you are from, huh? How wonderful!" The agent took a friendly attitude, smiled, and shook his hand. "I have been to both countries. Are you Hindu or Muslim?"

"I am Muslim."

"Well, fine. A couple of questions, doctor..." The agent resumed his cold expression. "I gather you discharged your fellow Muslim, Ham Thurman, somewhat prematurely."

"No. I had no idea that he was Muslim. Actually, he was guarded by the police until he was to be transferred to the Bellevue Hospital forensic unit... Then a detective..." the doctor searched his pockets, "yes, a detective signed him off by order of the district attorney's office."

"DA's office, huh? Do you have the detective's name and telephone number?"

"Of course, it's in Mr. Thurman's chart: all official. You know, I need fifteen months, just four extra months after my J-1 expires, to finish my residency in medicine and to qualify for my board exams."

"Good, good luck. Let me see that chart."

"I'll give you the information about the detective, but as you may know I cannot show you the chart without the patient's written permission—it is the law."

"What do you think I am? I am the law! Bring the fucking chart."

The doctor quickly left to fetch Ham Thurman's chart.

ᘓᙏᙡᓓ

# -LXIV-

When I sobered up in the Silver Hill Hospital following my suicidal attempt—I guess that is what it was—I asked the nurse in charge who brought me in. She didn't know, nor did the social workers or doctor on the unit. Apparently, the admission sheet had only the police report with my name and address on it, as if I were found on the highway. The space for the "next of kin" was empty. The working diagnosis was severe depression, paranoid personality, and substance abuse. The source of information wasn't identified—obviously I wasn't.

When I repeated to the chief of the unit what I had been telling everyone the last two days, that whatever I had said on admission was to be discounted because I was intoxicated, he smiled broadly—the sleek guy: "What were those things you said under influence that should now be discounted?"

"I have no idea what I might have said or done."

"What brought you to the point of desperation that you had to overdose yourself with a mixture of pills and then cut your wrist in a bathtub?"

"Nothing. I am a very happy person. I had a severe headache, so I took a bunch of Tylenols and a couple of beers and decided to take a bath and shave my legs. That is all I remember."

"Hmm. You shave your legs with a razor blade?"

"Yeah, with my father's old razor. It does a better job than all the fancy electric shavers."

"Hmm, but you took the blade out of the razor?"

"No, I was putting a new one in."

"Hmm, are you right-handed?"

"I can use both of my hands equally."

"Hmm, can you write with your right hand?"

"Not that well."

"Hmm, then you are left-handed?"

"I don't write that well with my left hand either." I almost laughed at my own witticism."

"Let's move on. You don't remember cutting your right wrist?"

"No, I don't."

"Hmm. Is it possible that someone else cut your wrist while you were dazed with Tylenols and alcohol?"

"Of course, that is what must have happened. My God, doctor!" I thought he was in the wrong business.

"Hmm...who do you think might have wanted to kill you?"

"That I don't know. Definitely none of my family members; we are a very close-knit, loving family. None of us would ever think of harming strangers, never mind each other."

"Hmm, that is what your parents and your sister told us. How about someone outside the family?"

"I have to think about it; lots of girls are jealous of me, and I must confess, I broke a few guys' hearts too," I whispered with theatrical embarrassment. "Dr. Watson, you are..." Thankfully, an old nurse loudly barged in, interrupting my best line: "Dr. Waltzman, Mrs. Reingold is having seizures!"

The doctor, helter-skelter, left my room to follow the nurse.

A few hours later, the same nurse brought my clothes to my room and gladly informed me that I was being discharged; that in the team meeting Dr. Waltzman dismissed Dr. Heshe's working diagnoses. He stressed that I was neither suicidal nor depressed enough to justify my incarceration (yes, incarceration), that I was either a victim of intoxication or a victim of foul play, so that either way, I was a victim; that the case should be referred to legal authorities for further investigation.

"Please call home; someone should come and fetch you," said the nurse and looked around "Where is your luggage? No one packed an overnight bag for you? You didn't even change your underwear the last two days."

She opened and closed the bathroom medicine cabinet. "Not even a toothbrush?"

"Of course not," I said, sounding indignant. "We all thought I'd be brought to the Norwalk Hospital emergency room, have my stomach pumped, and I would go back home. I guess whatever nonsense I uttered on the way landed me in the lunatic asylum. I really deeply apologize for wasting your time."

"No sweat," the nurse replied. "Will you be calling home or should I do it for you?"

"Oh, no, I'll do it right now."

The discharge paper and the follow-up information in my hand, I stood in front of the main building of the hospital as if I were awaiting my parents to pick me up. Of course, no one was going to show up, as I didn't even bother to call them.

It was a cold, rainy day. I didn't even have a coat with me, but I didn't want to hang around too long, in case the doctors changed their minds. So I began to walk toward the exit of the property, and by the time I got there, the rain had seeped through my dress, my underwear, my skin, my muscles...now it was soaking my bones. I began to shiver violently.

A small truck pulled aside. "You running away from the nuthouse, are you?" A man in his thirties leaned over and opened the passenger side door. "Get in, even if you are."

*I squeezed myself to the edge of the door, but the wetness from my hair, my clothes, and my shoes began to leak toward the driver's side—the floor and the seat.*

"If you drop me off somewhere in town, I'd appreciate it," I said, while watching the flood extending outwardly.

"No, no, young lady, I intend to take you home. Just relax. I don't remember your name, but I have been to your home a few times—your father and I volunteer for the firehouse."

"Mallory."

"Oh, yes, of course! So Mallory, what happened? What were you doing there?"

"I went to visit a friend of mine—just missed the bus."

"You know, they should have a shelter or something at the gate... You just relax, we'll be there in no time." *He turned the heat up.*

*As he dropped me off, my father pulled up next to him. The two of them began to chat from their cars.*

*I walked in. Only my mother was there, and she behaved as though nothing had happened.*

"Hi, Mallory; is it raining?"

"Mother!"

*I took a shower, changed my clothes, and came down. Dad, without uttering a word, handed me a bottle of Bud and a can of peanuts.*

⌒◝◟◞⌒

# -LXV-

Mallory woke up at noon the following day. She turned her phone on: six missed calls, two voice messages, and one text message. Only Ham could have texted her, so she opened that first.

- "Hi Mal, 10 am -- S H very accomm -- legacy? I embarrassed TY 4 caring, I shouldn't b here 2 long, c u soon."

Mallory wondered whether she really cared for Ham. She needed and liked his editing, but to get him to return a few pages a month was an ordeal. She should just write and finish her book, then hire a professional editor. Mallory dismissed any other aspirations about him, like getting married—whatever that meant—as total nonsense. He was unreliable, unstable, and sexless. She erased the message: "I am not visiting you there; no way!" She said loudly.

- "Hello, Ms. Mallory, this is Vakfiye. Sorry to bother you again. This morning FBI agents came and arrested my son and took his and Hamas's computers and all other papers and signs. Please help me! I heard that Hamas was sent somewhere else, so you are the only one who could help. I called Hamas's parents too, but they didn't call me back…please, I beg you."

Mallory pushed the delete button. "Damn! Am I a nurse for Ham or a social worker for his landlord?" she screamed.

- "Hey, I presume you are still considering the exclusivity offer, but how about tomorrow at the Plaza?"
- "Hello, Mallory, Mr. Levine would appreciate if you could visit him sometime today…what, I cannot hear you…anytime, he says."

She screamed again: "My nipples are bleeding, people!"

"Too dramatic," she concluded, and sat at her table and began to reply:

- "Yes, tomorrow noon at the Plaza."
- "Yes, Junetta, I'll come by around four o'clock to visit Mr. Levine."
- "Vakfiye, I am not sure how I can help; you should call the police. Well, I am sorry, I guess you were looking for some help against them. Let me think about it. I'll call you back."
- "Hi Ham - U r lucky - cops were trying 2 get u arrested - did ur angel bail u out again? They arrested Ahmed --FBI-- according to Vakfiye nd took his and ur pc's - so call her ok - now u have lots of time on ur hands nd ur mind is free of dope. Sit down nd write, I, no longer need your editorial help, so don't feel u've got to avoid me, get well."

There was a knock on the door: "Hi, Mal." It was Dave.

She opened the door and Dave walked in carrying two large bags. He put them on her kitchen table and spread out their contents—oranges, bananas, cashews, macadamia nuts, raisins, a large cut of Gruyère, and a box of whole-grain matzos.

"I may have a job; we are celebrating."

He hugged her long and hard. Mallory was genuinely happy to see Dave and hear his good news.

"Actually, Peter got me the interview through his connections. You are looking at a potential store manager of Monica in SoHo."

Mallory, who had heard so many false alarms, couldn't totally get excited. Nevertheless, she behaved as if she was.

"Wow, that...that definitely deserves a celebration. So much food though, Dave! And what is this? Matzos?"

"Don't pronounce the 's': matzo—it is just wheat and water—your kind of bread." He opened the box and pulled out one square, split it in two, gave one half to Mallory, and began to eat the other.

Mallory cautiously bit into this strange cracker: "It sticks to the roof of your mouth. Do you think it is stale?" she asked. Dave laughed.

"Well, that is for sure; it was made about five thousand years ago."

Mallory, who didn't get the joke, was trying to dislodge a piece from her teeth.

"Let me lend you some money, Dave. You'll pay it back when you get your first check."

"Thank you, Mal. I am really embarrassed! I am already three months late. You have been extremely generous and patient; I don't know what I would do without you. I could not have even kept the apartment. I am keeping track of your loans, and I'll definitely…"

Mallory interrupted him: "I know, I know, Dave. Don't worry about it. Let's eat quickly because I have an appointment with one of my clients this afternoon... He is an old man, and I don't want to be late."

❦

# -LXVI-

❧✦❧

"Oh, sweet Mallory, thank you for coming." Mr. Levine greeted her and extended an envelope.

"I put in a little extra for you for Christmas. So what do you think? Clinton's leaving in a few weeks and Bush's kid is becoming president... You know, we used to idealize the presidents, as they were a symbol of benevolent fathers. There were occasional abuses like the Teapot Dome, but by and large, the government elected by the public served them in good faith."

Mallory didn't want to ask what the Teapot Dome was. She kept massaging John's cervical vertebrae.

"Clinton was smart, but so nakedly into money and power or sex. Maybe it has always been that way...if so, at least it was clothed in romance—like Gary Hart's dalliance with a beautiful woman in the Caribbean or Eisenhower's relation with his aide or Kennedy's affair with Marilyn Monroe."

"Ouch! Mallory, I am an old man. You see, I never had sex with some other woman throughout my marriage except once. Not that Carol was a hot kitten. No, she was like the best sister one could ever have, someone you could have occasional awkward sex with—you see, I felt like I was violating her, like there was something wrong in having sex with her, ouch!

"I fell in love, passionately, once in my life. She was my secretary and twenty years younger, rather a girl. She wasn't Jewish; she had your accent, and she wasn't needy or demanding. She wasn't interested in my money; she just wanted me as a man. I got an erection the moment we were alone—only in the office, mind you, never going to motels or anything like that. It was always a quickie and totally satisfactory for both: She would have an orgasm by simply touching me. Mallory, did I tell you all this before?"

Of course he did, and many times, but Mallory never said so. She wasn't bored with John's repetitions. In fact, they were not that repetitive—there were always some nuances coloring the picture differently.

"What happened to her?"

John began to cry: "You see, no one knew about her relation with me, least of all Carol. Then, one day she came in and gave notice for her resignation; I felt like all my world collapsed. 'Why?' I asked. 'What can I do for you to stay?' She sweetly answered that she wanted nothing and that she had decided to go back to her home state of Minnesota. I offered to buy her an apartment and give her a high monthly income without even being my secretary anymore. She just smiled and said, 'You gave me everything I needed and wanted. Now it is time to go.'

"After she left, for two years I was depressed; I even had to go to see a psychiatrist—a kind of Dutch-uncle guy—who told me that a part of me must have died with her departure but that I shouldn't allow the rest to go under. I wasn't going to kill myself, because I wouldn't do that to Carol, but I couldn't lift myself from the depression either. The good doctor said that I was treading on the surface, that I should let myself get really depressed—that is, hit the bottom and then kick up. I was too cowardly to do that…what if the bottom were so deep that I could neither reach it or kick back from it?

"Mallory, have I told you this before? So my long depression gave Carol her cancer: It was supposed to weaken my resistance and give me cancer, but I think I was more resilient. I've been told that depression is contagious, so Carol got depressed and her immune system collapsed.

"Why am I still alive, Mallory? I have lived enough. I've seen the world, I ate at the best restaurants, I slept in the most luxurious hotels, I traveled first class, I read a lot, I drank the oldest whiskies, I smoked plenty of Cohiba Reserva, and I was really loved by one woman, Carol, and genuinely desired by another…"

John grew silent. His eyes looked humid and hollow. For a moment he seemed bereft. Then he tried to recover; his wilted smile drifted away as some seemingly involuntary words began to drizzle out: "The truth is, I really haven't seen much of the world, the food was just okay, I hated hotels, whiskies were stale, books taught me nothing, Cohiba burned uneven…"

His voice trailed out with a faint moan.

"The worst of all, Carol didn't love me; she loved Gabriel, Jeff's father. My Carol—sweetest of all torments."

His mood grew darker.

"My secretary? Once she realized that I am not going to leave Carol to marry her, she stopped desiring me."

He continued with a pensive voice.

"Time has savaged my mind and my body. I am simply the decrepit remnants of myself, waiting to dissolve into oblivion."

Mr. Levine looked at Mallory with faltering eyes:

"You know, Mallory, it has been a long time since I felt as good as I do now. I think a malignant truth is better than a benign lie. By telling you all this, I feel almost intoxicated with the intimation of a real self. My secretary, ah... Oh my God, I cannot remember my secretary's name! Mallory, have I ever mentioned her name to you? Please, do you remember what it was?"

"No, Mr. Levine, this is the first time you have ever talked about her."

Mallory, with a sad patience, allowed Mr. Levine to tell it again.

"Okay, let me focus. I can visualize her face; just a minute, just let her knock on the door and I say 'come in.' I see her smile—she is like a ray of sunshine slipping through the dark clouds. As she approaches me, I feel her warmth. Her lips are moving... 'I cannot hear you,' I say, 'please come closer...closer, closer.' No, I cannot."

"Well, you remember what is important." Mallory tried to put him at ease.

"Sweet Mallory, how did you learn to be so kind and gracious? Maybe you should talk a little about yourself. It would really give me pleasure to hear about your life. Mine doesn't really exist anymore... You see, I am again converting the subject to myself.

"Why don't you get married and have children, Mallory? You will have beautiful children... I am so sorry that Carol and I didn't have children. When you get old, you realize that there is no one to really care about you, or even bury you or read Kaddish for you. 'Here I go again,' as President Reagan used to say. Now, about you... Tell me about writing... Why is it so hard? You said you have been working on it for a number of years."

"The message, Mr. Levine...the difficulty is in sticking a subtle message within a story that is original, powerful, and still subtle enough to hold the attention of uninitiated readers." Mallory was just making that up, to avoid what she was writing about.

Mr. Levine was giggling.

"What is so funny, Mr. Levine?" Mallory asked.

"Well, sweet Mallory, your words—sticking, holding—that you are using remind me of a joke, a little off-color, but you are grown-up girl, right?"

Mr. Levine's mischievous smile was showing signs of fatigue.

"What is the difference between a stickup and a holdup, Mallory?"

Mallory struggled for an answer. "The degree of literacy?"

Mr. Levine laughed: "No, the age; the age."

Mallory was amazed by this old man's sense of humor: He sexualized every subject.

"I know I am boring you. I am like the character in Wood House. The eldest man, whenever he was called upon to say something, only spoke about his age."

Mallory had no idea what Mr. Levine was talking about. He kept laughing.

Mr. Levine's laughter got drowned in his coughing spells. Junetta rushed into the commotion, and she and Mallory watched him with frightened expectation. Mr. Levine slowly recovered. Exhausted, his head leaned to one side as he fell asleep.

൙

# -LXVII-

FBI agent Richard Brown called the 24th Precinct on the Upper West Side and asked for Detective Salvador Alvarez.

"Hello, Brown, twice in one month? What is up this time?"

Richard Brown intensely disliked Alvarez's casual and effusive informalities, since they had never been social together.

"Mr. Alvarez, I gather you let go a certain young man, Ham Thurman, even though he was in possession of a large quantity of heroin and marijuana."

"Why? Are you interested in his cute fianceé too?"

"Mr. Alvarez, I don't know what you are talking about. I gather from his hospital chart that Mr. Ham Thurman was arrested, and while he was waiting for his transfer to the forensic unit at Bellevue, you came in and summarily discharged him on his own recognizance?"

"Brown, Brown, my man, it turns out that he is just an ordinary junkie. DA's office dropped the charges."

"Why?"

"Because he was illegally frisked."

"Which DA's office?"

"Jeff Weisman's. Listen, Brown, just some friendly advice: If I were you I wouldn't fuck with him."

"Yeah? We'll see." Agent Brown just hung up the phone.

# -LXVIII-

Exactly at noon, the doorbell of the hotel room rang softly. Mallory knew it was the driver because Max never used the bell. He always knocked on the door with his fingers—one single tap, followed by three consecutive taps, then one more single tap.

"Who is it?" she asked.

"George. Mr. Hathaway's driver, Miss."

Whenever Max couldn't make their rendezvous, he sent George to deliver her money. However, Max would always call and warn her first. Mallory opened the door.

An overweight boy was standing next to George.

"Oh! This, ahh, you must be Robert?"

Robert stood silent.

"Yes, Miss," said George, and gave an envelope to Mallory. He then gently pushed Robert into the room. "I'll come to pick him up at two o'clock," he said, and hurriedly walked away.

For a long, seemingly very long minute, Mallory didn't know what to do, or say, except silently curse at Max.

"Come in, Robert; would you like to have a Coke or...ahh...Coke?"

Robert shook his head no.

"Okay, let's see...would you like to watch TV?"

Robert was still standing where George pushed him in, looking at Mallory's feet.

"Actually, I don't even know how to turn the TV on, but how about some nuts and fruits? Did you have lunch?"

Robert opened his mouth: "It is easy."

"It is easy? Oh...you mean the TV. Well, can you show me how?"

Robert picked up the remote, sat down on the bed, and turned the television on: Hotel services came on the screen. He surfed the channels in rapid pace and stopped on the Bloomberg channel: A series of scales, numbers, lists, abbreviated names of companies and stocks, and fast-moving crawl tickers lit the screen. Robert pulled the two pillows from the bed and put them behind him, muted the sound, and settled to watch—totally indifferent to Mallory.

Mallory sat on a chair perpendicular to the bed, from where she could see both Robert and the television. She was fascinated by the intensity of Robert's engagement. He couldn't have an attention problem as Max insinuated.

"Are you checking out how your investments are doing?"

Robert closed his eyes tight for a second and then opened them wide, never blinking. Simultaneously, his lips twitched a few times then locked silent.

How was Mallory supposed to seduce him? The kid seemed to be utterly uninterested in her. What did he think he was here for?

Mallory slid her skirt up a little and kicked her shoes off.

Robert's eyes were glued to the screen. She took her skirt off, dropped it on the floor, and sat back, spreading her legs. For a single second Robert looked at her shoes and her skirt before shifting back to the TV.

It was 1 p.m., and there wasn't much time for anything to happen. Mallory pulled her panties down to her ankles. Robert again looked at her panties and went back to the screen. Something is definitely wrong with this kid, she thought. One last attempt: She unbuttoned her shirt, unhooked her bra, and threw them on the bed. Robert looked at her shirt, picked up her bra, smelled it, and put it back exactly where it had been on the bed. Again he turned his eyes to the TV for the rest of the hour.

The doorbell rang. Mallory quickly got dressed and opened the door. George, with a crooked smile, asked, "Is Robert ready?"

Mallory pointed at him. Robert didn't move, as if he were totally unaware of these two people's interaction about him.

"We've got to go now, Robert," George said very loudly.

Robert, without looking at him, got up and walked to the door.

"Good-bye, Robert; it was nice meeting you."

Robert walked away without saying a word. George shook his head and followed him.

Mallory went back to the bed, sat where Robert had been sitting, and looked at the screen—the numbers, names, scales, and crawlers kept coming and repeating in certain intervals without much change, or at least that's how it appeared to her. She tried to keep her eyes from blinking without success.

"Fucking asshole, Max!" she screamed.

ᏏᎷᎷᎤ

# -LXIX-

When Mrs. Vakfiye came back from work, she found the door of her apartment wide open. She wondered if she'd forgotten to close it when she'd left earlier that morning. She walked in with some apprehension, tripped over a broken chair, and fell on the floor. All the kilims from the wall were pulled down, all her Arabic-lettered, glassed-in prayers were broken and strewn around, and the drawers were emptied out in the middle of the room. All the mattresses and pillows, as well as the sofa, were slashed haphazardly. All the clothes (hers, her son Ahmed's, and Ham's) were piled up in a bathtub full of water. The refrigerator's contents lay in front of it, melting.

There was a piece of paper nailed to the kitchen cabinet: Ham Yu owe us 5 G—nex mont ve kill yu.

Vakfiye collapsed on the floor wailing, "Oh, God, why, what have I done to deserve all this?"

It had been five days since they'd taken Ahmed away. He called twice on the second day and said that he was being treated well, that there was nothing to worry about. He wasn't allowed to tell her his location, but said he'll soon be coming home—he was cheerful. Since then, there had been no other information, and now this.

Vakfiye dragged her bed against the door and crawled in, exhausted. Should she call the police, the landlord, or Hamas's parents? She got up. "Pull yourself together, Vakfiye," she scolded herself. "This is not the time for self-pity; Ahmed and Hamas both are in trouble and they need you. Allah is merciful and all powerful. You are not alone. Only He will determine the ultimate fate of everyone, but He also demands that I do my best to be helpful." She dialed 911.

"Yes, may I help you?"

"Some people broke my door and destroyed the furniture in my apartment."

"Slow down, ma'am; first of all, what is your name and your address?"

"My name is Vakfiye bin Hakim."

"Talk slowly, ma'am. How do you spell that?"

195

"W, a, k, f, y, b, e, n, h, a, k, i, m"

"Am I supposed to learn these people's language?" The dispatcher was speaking to a colleague on an open microphone.

"I think she's been calling once a day—a mental case. What's her name?" the other dispatcher asked. "I don't know…If you go by her spelling it sounds like 'what the heck.'"

Both burst into laughter.

The first dispatcher: "Ma'am, what kind of name is that?

"Bosnian."

"Come again?"

"Bosnian!"

"Okay, what is the address? This time, slowly."

"228 West 108th Street."

"So, what is the problem?"

"I came home, the door was broken, and …"

The dispatcher interrupted: "Well, ma'am, you don't call 911 in this country for a broken door; you call the manager."

"It is not repair thing; they destroyed the whole apartment."

"Do you know who did it?"

"No, but they left a note for the young man who rents one of my rooms that says we are coming to kill you."

"Oh, why?"

"It says he owes them money."

"Who owes the money? Ma'am, please speak English and slowly."

"No, Hamas owes them the money."

"Hold it, hold it. Listen, I am going to dispatch an officer within half an hour, okay? You explain to them the whole story, okay, ma'am? Are you listening?"

Vakfiye couldn't talk from sobbing, and the phone fell to the floor. Holding on to her head tightly with both hands, she began talking to herself: "We should have never come here, they don't like us; we would have been better off killed by Serbians. At least it would have been done and over; here there is no end to it. Oh, Ahmed, my poor son, what have I done? I know you came because you trusted my judgment; these people don't believe in Allah."

"Ma'am, ma'am, I cannot hear you." The dispatcher turned to her colleague again: "Woman doesn't even know which side of the phone is the receiver and which side you speak to. Listen, Greta, I got to take my break…could you dispatch someone there to see what is going on? It is a slow day anyway."

⚬ↄ∭ⅇ

# -LXX-

By the time two police officers came to Vakfiye's apartment, the landlord of the brownstone was already there, trying to evict her.

"What is going on here?" the officer asked, and then recognized Vakfiye. "Were you not at St. Luke's ER the other day with that overdosed kid, what's his face, Ham?"

The landlord answered, "These people are trouble, officer. They have to leave."

"Take it easy, man," the officer replied.

"They sell drugs, jihad books, brainwash kids to Islam, you name it… They are gangsters and terrorists. Look at this threatening note."

"I said, take it easy. Are you the landlord?"

"Yes, sir. FBI arrested her son, Ahmed."

"Why?"

"I don't know…and now this."

"Please help us, sir," begged Vakfiye. "My son is a good boy, he is no terrorist! He is just a fund-raiser for the Islamic charities."

The two officers went out to consult with each other: "Should we call Alvarez?"

They were on the phone for at least fifteen minutes before they came back. "Ma'am, fix the place up—and you," he turned to the landlord, "you fix the door. She isn't moving out. We'll be back."

One of the officers picked up the note, and they left.

Less than half an hour later, Detective Alvarez showed up at Vakfiye's apartment; the landlord and she were still trying to put the place together. The detective dismissed the landlord and sat on the windowsill:

"Listen, lady, and listen carefully… That kid, Ham, got off easy on drug charges, but this, this is a different ball game. I understand the FBI arrested your son for his connection with some Islamic fund-raising organization?"

Vakfiye tried to protest: "Sir, he is never…"

"Listen, listen, I came here to help you. I don't work for the FBI, I work for the City of New York. I want to find out who did this damage and left that note. Otherwise I cannot protect you. So you have to help me find these people; your cooperation will also help your son, eventually."

Vakfiye was standing in the middle of the trashed room, shaking: "Can I get you some coffee, sir?"

"No, no, thanks. Do you have any idea who might have done this? Did some drug dealer kind of characters come to visit Ham regularly?"

"Some Ispanyols came once or twice a month, and once in a while his girlfriend, that is it."

"Is that the cutie who was in the hospital with him?"

"Yes, sir."

"What is her name again?"

"Mallory, sir."

"Does she have a last name?"

"That I don't know, sir."

"Do you have her address or her telephone number?"

"No, sir." Vakfiye lowered her eyes.

"Lady, you are lying. Hand over her telephone number. Otherwise, kiss your son goodbye."

"I had that from Hamas's phone; she never gave me the number. She was on his automatic dial."

"So now you have it… I don't give a fuck how you got it, just write it down here." He pushed his pad into her hand. Vakfiye went back to the room and came out with Mallory's telephone number.

"Please don't hurt her; she is totally innocent."

"Lady, in my business no one is considered totally innocent, including myself. Now, here is my card; call me immediately if any of those Hispaniols," he chuckled, "shows up."

෴

As soon as Detective Alvarez got into his car, he texted Mallory's number to the central office. "Hey, check the address of the cell # and call me back a.s.a.p."

He drove down Broadway and double-parked in front of Zabar's; he wanted to grab a turkey sandwich. A long line was spilling out to the street. Discouraged, he got back to his car, where the phone was ringing.

"Yeah?"

"It is a business address on Wall Street, a hedge fund firm—Hathaway Group."

"You're kidding! Okay, thanks."

෴

# -LXXI-

Mallory had no credit cards, no savings accounts, no investments any-where except a small checking account at Chase Manhattan Bank, left over from her NYU years. That was the only mail she'd get once a month—and some junk mail. Today there was a real letter—a small en-velope from her father.

Dear Mallory:

Good news! I don't know whether Pat already told you or not—I met a great lady at one of the Sunday bake socials. Susan is divorced; she has two won-derful teenage daughters and works part-time as a real estate agent. You'll like her and your stepsisters. Yes, we just got married, quietly, with just a few friends who attended the church ceremony. I didn't want to burden you or Pat, for I know how busy both of you are.

Anyway, I sold the house and am moving in with them—they have a nice small house in Wilton. You'll like it. I hope you'll be happy for me, as be-ing old and alone is not fun. I look forward to your call. Let me know when you'll be visiting us and get to know your new family.

Father knows best, as always.
Matt

The words "two teenage daughters" (wonderful) were the only thing that got Mallory's attention—one or two more potential victims.

She dialed Pat: "I'm sorry. The mailbox for the number you have dialed is full. Please try again later, thank you," came the automated answer. This had never happened before, so she called again and got the same recorded message. Who would leave so many messages for Pat? Mallory couldn't figure it out. After the third attempt, she just gave up. She tore up the letter and threw it into the wastebasket. "I've got to warn them somehow."

# -LXXII-

Max, Jeff, and John had a lunch date at the Four Seasons. "John, how is it that today you are able to walk up the stairs of the restaurant? In fact, you're skipping every other one! Last dinner we had at Hamilton's you couldn't even get up from the sofa," asked Max.

"Well, son, there are times that a man can get it up and there are times that he is all limp."

"Yeah, yeah, you are always trying to get away with some smart-alecky statement," Max slurped his lobster bisque. "You know, we should meet more often, just the three of us, without wives and without Hamilton. I know Jeff doesn't want us to talk on the phone about certain confidential stuff, and I agree. With them around us at the famous round table, we never have sufficient time for serious matters. Before we break up for Christmas, we've got to make some decisions. Okay?'

"Hit us," said John cheerfully.

"John, this is serious. Bush's thirteen trillion proposed cuts would definitely help us—if he can push them through Congress—but the boom is about to bust. The Federal Reserve raised short-term interest rates five times during the last sixteen months, and there is no way that the NASDAQ's gain last year of 85 percent is sustainable. I know Paul O'Neill; he ran Alcoa well, but this is over his head.

"I suggest that we go cash for a while—either six-month treasuries or money market—that is just the seasonality of the trading system…the alternative in such a bear market, so pick your choice. If I don't hear from you within twenty-four hours, I'll choose for you."

Jeff scratched his head and said, "Max, honestly I don't know whether you pretend that there is some sound science behind all this economic jargon, or is it just like a three-card monte?"

Max smiled: "You don't think the three-card monte has its own iron-clad rules? Let me give you a simple example of the science of macro-economics. The long-term bond market determines interest rates. If the government lowers interest rates, the bond market smiles, which in turn stimulates borrowing and spending."

Max's phone rang. His secretary Kimberly was on the line.

"I am sorry, Mr. Hathaway; you told me not to interrupt your lunch meeting, but I have a detective on the phone who demands to speak with you."

"What about?"

"He wouldn't tell me, sir."

"Okay, put him on."

Max got up from the table, walked across the Grill Room, and waved at John Varriano—the veteran bartender—who drew many sketches of him.

"Yes, yes I am, just hold on; let me get to some quiet place."

He walked down to the lobby on the first floor. "So officer, what seems to be the problem? Is it Robert?"

"Robert? No, Mr. Hathaway. We have traced a telephone number that might have been used in some illegal activities. It turned out that it belongs to you. We just want to confirm that the telephone is not lost or stolen."

"What sort of illegal activities?"

"Don't you want to know the telephone number, Mr. Hathaway?"

"Listen, officer, I run a multibillion-dollar business, and I have a few phones. I don't waste time remembering all the numbers. Give me your name and your badge number. Hello, what is your name? Hello, hello... son of a bitch hung up."

When Max returned to the table, John was ready to tease him: "Was it Bush, that you so quickly jumped to answer?"

"It was some sort of hoax; a guy pretending to be a detective was asking whether I lost my phone."

"Did he have a Nigerian accent?" Jeff asked.

Max gestured with his arms dismissively while wondering whether Mallory was involved in some illegal activities; but if so, why did the man hang up? The whole thing made no sense. He cut the lunch short and hurriedly left the restaurant, leaving Jeff and John a little puzzled.

Once he got into the car he called Mallory, only to get her voice mail.

"Hi, it is me; did you by..." Mallory picked up. "Oh, hi, Mallory, I was just leaving a message, but it is...it is, by the same logic it couldn't be... Listen, some detective called and informed me that the user of your phone—I presume you—is involved in some illegal stuff, and then he hung up. I think he was fishing, but I don't want to be blindsided. If you are involved in some shit, you'll tell me, right?"

"I'm not involved." Now it was Mallory's turn to be puzzled.

"Well, maybe it was some kind of practical joke... Are we getting together tomorrow?" Max asked.

"First, let me tell you something, you son of a bitch. Do you realize what you did to Robert? Don't you have any common sense? The kid is not only young, but I think he is also retarded."

"You mean you didn't fuck him?"

"Fuck him! Max, he couldn't keep his eyes off the television, on some money channel all the time while he was with me. It is a cruel thing to do that; he has no idea of women or sex."

"He watched the Bloomberg channel the whole hour? That is my son; he'll go places, this guy. You see, at this age he already understands the ultimate priority of life—money. If you don't have money, you won't have women and you won't have even a TV to watch, ha, ha, ha. I never knew he followed the market—sneaky kid."

"Well, I think the whole thing was awful. Don't you ever do that again."

"Fine, fine, see you tomorrow."

෴

# -LXXIII-

Monthly dinners at the Weismans had the orderliness of a courtroom: The guests, the same five people—the Thurmans, Hathaways, and John Levine—were expected to be on time, exactly at 7 p.m. for cocktails, to be followed by dinner at 8 p.m. and be recessed by 10:30 p.m. At the dinner table, Jeff would hold court, but then the somewhat-inebriated guests would veer in different directions; Jeff would try to recruit Hamilton—the wrong person—to rescue the evening from deteriorating into a free-for-all and reassuring its failure.

Jeff couldn't wait for people to finish their appetizers:

"I would like each of us to tell about a book we read recently, okay?"

A chorus of no's burst out from the other six.

Hamilton's ill-suppressed mockery crept in: "Just declaim a few lines from Othello and they'll think you are a hell of a fella."

"Cole Porter, Cole Porter!" Norma screamed unmusically, clapping her hands—half afraid that she might be wrong. When she saw the surprisingly pleased expression on Hamilton's face, she repeated again, "Cole Porter," this time in the daintiest of tones.

"Yes! Yes, we have a winner!" announced Hamilton, with his familiar fecund mercilessness.

"It is definitely more interesting to talk about the books we have not really read—from cover to cover. All you have to do, in anticipation of such an event, you peruse, skim, skip, glance at a book written by some canonical heavyweight such as Stendhal, Maupassant, Proust—especially Proust, who himself believed that you can open a book somewhere, anywhere, and read, really read. There you have it: The interest of the book lies in its fragments."

Ann looked at Hamilton longingly.

"I am sorry the meat is a little too tough. I thought the filet mignon is supposed to be the softest of all the cuts," Jeanny said, noting John's struggles with it.

Hamilton took exception: "Actually, the softest meat is the buttocks. Did you know that cannibals first went for the buttocks? They get even softer with age."

Jeanny shook her head in disbelief—she was thinking of her sagging derrière. The men looked at each other, expressionless, not wanting to be the target of the women's rage.

"Is there a difference between cows and bulls?" asked Norma.

"Cows tend to be warily reticent," answered Hamilton.

Jeanny's anger at Hamilton's transgressions never lasted too long. She liked Hamilton's playful bantering and eloquent repartees, and she preferred his well-disguised aggression to her husband's naked one, though both fed on emotional havoc. She couldn't help comparing them. Hamilton's mind was discursive and abstractly remote. Jeff's mind was linear, topical, and plodding. Hamilton's rejoinders seemed to be unsullied with intentions—the targets of his witticisms were random and opportunistic; he had no secondary agenda—except to enjoy the company of himself.

How did Hamilton escape becoming the victim of traditional education and upbringing? She lived in a world where everything, even social situations, was cleverly calculated by a self-serving array of computations. An excessive demand on her to grow up and be successful left her feeling immature and insecure. Hamilton's presence forced her to confront her own limitations and her fixed ordinariness.

"Hamilton, you are sort of an Oscar Wilde manqué," she laughed coyly. "But as long as we are talking about food, there is a saying that too many raisins will sink a cake."

"Raisins?" Norma looked puzzled.

"The wit, the wit! You dimwit," Max scolded her.

Hamilton smiled. He should have married someone like her.

As the dinner was ending, Jeff proposed that each should tell an interesting thing that they had done during the last few months.

Jeanny hated that: "Couldn't we just relax and let people be?" she begged.

Norma jumped in: "I saw a great movie, *The Family Man*; you've got to see it."

"I heard that it is a schmaltzy version of *It's a Wonderful Life*," said Jeff.

"It is about deceiving one's wife and being outed by the kids," said Hamilton.

"You went to see a movie, Hamilton?" asked Jeanny in mock amazement.

"No, I just read the review in the *Times*. I no longer go to movies or theaters, except occasionally to off-Broadway shows. They all become a distraction, full of synthetic emotions—phantom feelings."

"Characters, in the works of classical dramatists like Ibsen and Shakespeare, were thoroughbred neurotics—their audience cried. In the hands of absurdists such as Beckett and Albee, characters were lost in existential isolation—their audiences experienced confusion and despair," Hamilton continued.

"Now, in the movies and on television, characters are primarily narcissistic sociopaths who swim in meaninglessness while indiscriminately inflicting pain and harm on other people, while we, the audience, laugh and vicariously enjoy their pathologies.

"Ah, I went to see the Flamenco Festival with a Spanish friend. Ann wouldn't come; she gets upset with the sounds of stamping feet, red colors, and lustily strummed Andalusian guitars. Back to you, Ann."

"If you insist. What's interesting is 'the emergence of the crystal as an emblem of new architecture in New York,' as Herbert Muschamp describes two residential buildings that become reality on the Lower East Side. Can you believe that Philip Johnson, at the age of ninety-four, is still at it? It's the ultimate example of contextualism, if there were one... Well, I guess I lost my audience."

Max and Norma already had their coats on.

ᏯᎷᏯᎾ

After the guests left, Jeanny put the dishes in the sink and said, "Maria is coming tomorrow; she'll do the rest." She kicked her shoes off and sat next to Jeff, who was intensely reading an affidavit.

"Jeff, may I interrupt you for a few minutes?"

Jeff took his glasses off.

"I've been meaning to talk to you about John for some time... I am really worried. He seems to be falling under the spell of that bitch."

"Why is that bothering you?" asked Jeff tersely.

"He is wearing pink shirts, purple ties, Gucci glasses, eats only organic... He stopped drinking, he practices yoga, he hired a trainer."

"So?"

"Can't you see, Jeff? She is taking control of him."

"So?"

"Isn't John one of our closest friends? Don't you care that he is making a fool of himself?"

"Look, Jeanny, before Mallory, he was always a depressed and unhappy man who was slowly dying. Now he came alive! What if he is having a little fun with her? I don't see any harm. He is still as sharp as ever when it comes to finances. You should see how he dances circles around Max."

"What if he marries her?"

"Well, we will put one more chair around our round table."

"You can't be serious, Jeff. I wouldn't allow that whore in my house. I don't care whose wife she is."

"Jeanny, do you realize the intensity of your reaction? Can't you recover from being rejected as a client? This happens in every profession."

"Don't insult professions! She is just a masseuse, and Rolfing therapy is not a professional line either. In fact, the whole psychotherapy field is open to any current or ex-patient, who could hang out her shingle and say, "I am a psychotherapist," period. This girl manipulated John to fall in love with her; are you going to watch this disaster play out?"

"Jeanny, I believe you are the one who is in love with this bitch-whore of a woman—I think you should call some therapist with proper credentials. I mean it; you talk with so much venom! Anyone who heard this litany would think that she harmed your child or destroyed your reputation… All she did was no longer come to give you massages. Come on, Jeanny."

Jeanny was sobbing.

"And why do you defend her? You always defend other people against me."

There was a knock on their bedroom door: "Mom, I am back; good night."

Jeff looked at his watch.

"It is almost one o'clock. What happened to the 11:30 curfew?"

"I can't handle Samantha, Jeff. You go talk to her; she doesn't listen to me."

"I will, tomorrow. One drama at a time."

⌒▨▨⌒

After they left the Weismans, Norma asked whether John was going to get married to his masseuse: "What is her name; is it Melanie?"

"Yes and no," replied Max.

"No and yes?"

"In sequence of your questions."

"Oh, well. Max, did Robert tell you that he now has a new friend—a girl, finally."

"You are kidding."

"No, no, her name is also Melanie. Isn't that funny?"

Max turned his back, thinking, "Oh, shit!"

"She even let him smell her bra. Can you believe that? Boy, times have really changed… I didn't even let anyone see my bra until, I don't know, my senior year."

"Norma, you shouldn't talk to Robert about girls and sex; that is a father's job. Equally, I will stay away from that subject with Audrey."

"I didn't start talking with Robert. Max, I know that. He demanded to smell my bra! When I said no, he let out such a metallic scream, you would think someone was cutting his legs or something."

"So did you?"

"Yes, what am I supposed to do? Get evicted from the building? As it is right now, both floors—above and below us—are complaining that he's making too much noise. This is a small building, and everyone already thinks he is a rude kid: He never says "hello" or "good morning" to people, he rushes in and out of the elevators while he pushes others as if there is a fire or something..."

Max thought maybe Mallory was right. This scheme of his might not have been the brightest idea. He'd have to talk to Robert.

ᏩᎳᏍᎤᎩ

As soon as they got into a cab, Ann said, "Do you think John's Mallory is the same Mallory that Ham is dating? Wasn't she making money by doing Rolfing therapy to support her writing career? Rolfing is a sort of massage, right?"

"Yes, it sounds like the same girl."

Ann's voice darkened: "I wonder whether Ham knows her connection with John."

"What is the connection, Ann? You mean the marriage? There is no such possibility. I saw the girl in the ER of St. Luke's Hospital. She is young, pretty, educated, and seems devoted to Ham. When I had to go back to class, she stayed with him for hours. She didn't look like a gold-digger type to me. She may not have told him about John, or about any of her clients... After all, isn't that supposed to be confidential?"

"Yeah, I guess. Anyhow, Ham isn't such a catch either. I wonder what she thinks of him: a jobless poet-manqué who is half of the time drugged out."

"Oh, that reminds me, I got a call... Ham is ready to be discharged. The hospital's administrator left a message that someone, I guess me, has to come to pick him up. So tomorrow afternoon I'll go to Connecticut... Do you want to come along?"

"You know the answer to that, Hamilton. How is it that he is so quickly cured?"

"One gets cured from illness, not from the indignities of having a creative mind. Your relationship with him needs to be cured; you value only the informative mind—the mind with its 'from without' language that produces differentiated things. Ham has a creative mind; the mind with its 'from within' language that generates only undifferentiated emotions; that is to say, nothing. But that's what the magic is all about, right? Creating something from nothing. While pragmatic scientists move in small steps, intuitive/creative artists make quantum leaps."

"Total gobbledygook! The only leaps I know that poets make are from high-rise buildings," Ann replied tersely.

○〜〜○

# -LXXIV-

To celebrate their son's quick discharge from Silver Hill, the Thurmans ordered not only Chinese but also Indian take-out food; it was a feast that Ham enjoyed and also dreaded.

"Have you written any poems while you were at the hospital?" Ann asked.

"Psychiatric hospitals have been rather inspirational venues for many poets. Mom, I have failed as a poet. Even you say so too—that I don't get the science of it, that my poems have no structural stability—why should I keep writing?"

Hamilton, seeing his wife's jaw muscles tighten, tried to prevent her from replying.

"Ham, what your mother meant was that in your earlier poems, your ideas and their musical echoes didn't resonate with the structure. You need to cultivate the art of sonnets, sestinas, villanelles, and other prosodic and stanzaic embryological patterns to bring the form and content together—the art of poetry—that strange flow between shapes of stanzas and metrical variations. The corollary notion, namely that ideas may occur in freestyle verse, but not in their enactments, is a total fallacy."

Ham listened to his father with a dry impatience. He was the only man he knew who was more abstruse than himself. After his father spoke, he was speechless because he didn't understand what the hell he was talking about. Was his father smart to the point of nonunderstandability, or did he have a highly pixilated mind?

Ann made a dismissive gesture to Hamilton: "That is not what I am saying at all. Son, you don't have to be a poet! All we want is for you not to deviate from real life—a productive, self-sufficient, normal life; maybe even get married. You desire a stable, healthy, and successful life, don't you?"

"Mom, being a poet is a deviation by definition. As for 'desire,' I have long escaped from its coercion."

"Son, I think you are forcing yourself to convert a real loss to the semblance of loss… The real loss is hellish and…will not remain indefinitely alive. The semblance may help you rouse against it temporarily and maintain certain exaggerated profundity, but it'll not relieve you from all consequences of its *logo Daedalus* web," Hamilton added.

"There is no such word," Ann said. "Hey, listen, the two of you. Are you for real? What the hell are you talking about? Ham will be out of a job, and there are no plans for him to take charge of his life! The two of you are blubbering about something that a normal person would not even understand."

"It is Dad who always reduces every conversation into linguistic quarrels. Mom, you don't want me to feign lucidities or deform my uncertainties. There is no other tolerable definition of a poetic state."

Ann was getting impatient: "No, no. I want you to be lucid and be certain—no feigning, no deforming."

Hamilton tried again to reconcile them.

"Son, what you call linguistic quarrels are designed toward clearing the verbal confusion generated by terminological dissonance. We all, including your mother, have the poetic instrument within us. But you don't even have reflective hesitation in your production of absent things. How do you expect a philosophy teacher and an architect to organize their unconscious to receive your undifferentiated exchanges? You use a language that we don't speak and then accuse us—mostly your mother—for the imperfect misapprehension of you?"

"Dad, I don't speak that language either—it is the language felt within; it is only spoken when someone resonates with it. The sender and the receiver need to synchronize their unconscious to reach the indissoluble strata of a poem and its revelation of the finest misapprehension of the unreal. You taught me that."

Ann put her hands up: "I cannot even tell whether you two are psychotic or not, and I really don't care anymore! I am going to bed. Your inexhaustible incoherence is giving me a splitting headache. Damn, I am beginning to talk like you."

Ann left without saying good night.

The two men looked at each other.

"Please, would you just let me be myself?" pleaded Ham. "I cannot be otherwise and even then, being myself only takes me so far. I cannot please people's prosaic leanings and still remain poetically meaningful."

"Son, you don't get published because of this, this...your sense of arbitrariness." Hamilton's voice sank to a lower key: "Furthermore, the poet has to deliver something more than phonetics, metrics, rhythmics, semantics, and syntax."

"Such as what?"

"Well, let's say some logic, and maybe knowing yourself and not being satisfied with search alone."

"Dad, I am really surprised! For years, I coveted your sensitivity to the ring of language. Now you are asking me to be logical! The essential element of being a poet is to oppose thought …if I knew myself, I would no longer need any inner labor; no longer worry about the imminent danger of audible shapes… I would simply kill myself."

"Ham, I am not talking about your not writing poetry, I am talking about why it may not be working well for you. Poetry is not unstudied indolence. If your poems can speak only to you and have value only for you, they have no value at all. Even in speaking the language of gods, you must subordinate to that of humans."

Ham looked lost.

"No, you are not getting it! Son, I'll be more specific… Give me a stanza and I'll show you what I mean."

"What do you mean by 'give me a stanza'? I cannot give you a stanza. What if I asked you to give me four lines of philosophy? At times, ideas flow through me with their own voice, which preexists in my mind. Its auditive appearance becomes a poetic event, in a form of a stanza or not."

"I could give you four lines of philosophy… I am not saying write now a new stanza… Just read one that you have already written."

"I am not sure which one of you is worse, Mom or you. She kills poetry by dismissing it, while you torture it by means of imparting poetically perverse transgressions."

Hamilton knew and felt bad about his role in Ham's striving toward the unattainable: the timelessness, the eternal presence in fleeting moments. "Well, I grant you…"

Ham interrupted his father. "No Dad, you don't! I cannot write better poems. Well, I would if I were a better poet. Actually, a better poet said that. You gave me my wings—urging me to write what flows through me. But maybe those wings were built from feathers and wax."

Ham left his father aghast and walked over to knock on his mother's bedroom door. "Mom, yes there is such a word as *logo Daedalus*… A historical colleague of yours, the architect Daedalus, built a labyrinth to imprison his illusionary evil king and scared his son Icarus to death! Good night."

He walked toward his room, the literary agent's comments still ringing in his mind. Well, maybe she and his parents were right, albeit for the wrong reasons.

Ham couldn't figure out how others played the game of life so well while he couldn't even figure out what the game of life was. Did he just bluff his way into poetry? He used to quote Sartre to his students at NYU: "You've got to choose: Live life or tell about it." He had neither.

He was up against his limited gifts and more so against the limitations of himself. For the former, his poetry—milking iambic parameters out of the vernacular of drug culture—was not a totally authentic work. Was anyone else's? Had there not been a ceaseless thievery and plagiarism in the field since the time of Ovid? Contrary to the self-aggrandizing opinions of his teachers, he knew that literature was not a moral force—definitely not for himself. If anything, literature subverted his mind—well, at least reinforced its already subversive disposition.

As to the latter—the limitations of himself—once he was a poet (however judged), he could do nothing else. Everything bored him now, even teaching poetry. Was he condemned to die as a poet? What did Macbeth mean by "jump the life to come"?

ᏬᛟᛟᎡᏬ

# -LXXV-

"Fuck, fuck, fuck!" Mallory cursed loudly. She forgot to turn the phone off again. It was only eleven o'clock.

"Hello, Mallory."

"Who is this?" She asked in harshly scolding voice.

"Oh, sorry. I hope I am not interrupting some fun. Hey, this is Detective Alvarez; do you remember me? You were supposed to call me."

"How did you get my number?"

"Oh, that is from Mrs. Vakfiye, who voluntarily confessed everything."

"Whatever. Listen, I am busy, and please don't call me again." Mallory was about to hang up.

"She confessed that you and her son, that dopey boyfriend of yours, were in big business—drugs and money laundering among other things."

Mallory had to sit down. Her knees were shaking.

"Detective Alvarez, I have never met Vakfiye's son in my life. I don't know what you are talking about. There is nothing she could confess that could implicate me."

Alvarez noticed the change in Mallory's tune.

"Well, that is Mrs. Vakfiye's word against yours. You see, it isn't going to be so easy. It is too complicated to explain on the phone. We either have to pay a visit to your home or you have to come to the 24th Precinct to give a deposition."

There was a long silence on the phone as Mallory considered all her options. She'd stopped dealing pot more than five months ago... Why was this becoming an issue now?

"Are you serious?" she decided to bluff it out: "If so, I have to check with my lawyer and call you back. I still have your card."

"That is fine. Let me hear from you within the next forty-eight hours. Incidentally, do you work for the Hathaway firm?"

"Detective Alvarez, I told you I'll speak to my lawyer and call you back."

"Fine, fine. No need to be so snippy... Señorita, you are going to need me...and need me bad," said the detective and hung up.

Mallory was stunned. He'd actually hung up on her! Did that mean that he wasn't simply trying to pick her up and that she was actually being legally pursued by a detective for drug and money laundering charges? What about the "other things"? Obviously, he must have discovered her relation with Max. Should she really find a lawyer or should she call Max or Jeff?

The phone rang.

"Listen," came the detective's voice, "I want to give you one more chance because I like you… I don't want you to get into serious trouble. Let me meet you somewhere for a coffee and I'll tell you a little bit more of what you are up against, and then you'll have something to discuss with your lawyer."

Mallory felt relieved.

"Well, thank you, detective. Friday on my lunch break we could meet in my neighborhood Chinese restaurant. It is on the southeast corner of 98th and Broadway—Hunan Balcony."

"See you there at 12."

After they hung up, Mallory texted Ham: 'Ham I thnk cops r on ur case. I'll b able 2 tel u mor about it Fri. ttyl.'

ᏟᎷᎯᎾ

# -LXXVI-

Hamilton Thurman double-parked his old Honda in front of Ham's apartment, grabbed one of the two bags, and followed him into the building. This was Hamilton's first visit to his son's place and also Ham's first since he was discharged from the hospital.

As they entered, a smell of rotten cheese and fruit overwhelmed Hamilton's senses. He had to step carefully around empty beer bottles and soda cans strewn on the floor with garbage from torn bags. He felt sorry for his son.

How did this happen? His chest tightened—his golden boy living in such a squalid environment.

Ham opened the main door; stale air rushed out. Ham noticed a new unpainted wood door frame. His key slid easily into the lock, but it wouldn't turn. He tried again and again—unsuccessfully.

"Are you sure you have the right key?"

"Dad! I only possess one single key."

Hamilton's heart sank.

"There is something wrong with the door itself. It seems like some repair was done while I was away."

Ham went across the hall and knocked on the door of the building superintendent. A balding Hispanic man in his fifties wearing a white shirt half covering his bulging stomach opened the door and growled, "What? Oh, you! You owe me a month's rent." He pulled up his pants, swallowed the contents of his mouth, and held on to Ham by his jacket's lapels. "*Caramba! ¿Qué se cree?* You disappear the whole month and now show up with your luggage to move in…"

Hamilton interrupted. "Excuse me, sir; I am his father and will be happy to pay all his debts… Can he just get in?"

"Okay, señor, you the boss. It is $600."

"I only gave Vakfiye $200 per month," murmured Ham.

"*Si*, but she left the apartment to you and I kept your stuff in there, holding the place for you, *comprende*? So it is $600 or no key."

Some woman was screaming from the inside, "*Pedro, no dejes enfriar la comida!*"

"I got to go. You either pay or I'll sell your things and sue you for the rest. *Punto!*"

Hamilton pulled out his checkbook.

"Listen, I'll give you a check of $300 now and I'll get the rest of it by Monday…is that okay?"

"Well, you look like a gentleman. I will take your word."

Ham protested, "Dad, I have nothing there that is worth $600, nor can I afford to live here, so let's go."

"Son, we owe the man the rent for last month. We'll pay that, pick up your stuff, regardless of what it's worth—then leave. Of course you cannot stay here… You'll stay with us until you find another suitable place."

Hamilton gave one of his cards and a check to the super, who unlocked the door and quickly retreated back to his apartment: "Turn the lights off and close the door on your way out… *Es un escándaloso!*" banging his door shut.

The front room of the apartment where Vakfiye lived was empty, except for a bed and a couch—both covered with torn plastics—and a round wooden table and four mismatched chairs. The walls were scarred white from the removal of artworks and other items. The empty closet was wide open.

They walked through the kitchen—there were a few rusted pots and pans left hanging. When Ham opened the door of his room, he screamed. Hamilton's jaw dropped. All Ham's clothing was piled up in the bathtub, exuding a molding smell. The rest of his belongings were left on the top of the sliced mattress in the middle of the room. All his books, his computer, his radio, stereo, and CDs were gone. Could Vakfiye have stolen them? But why destroy his clothes and underwear?

"I think there is something seriously wrong here, son. Did you owe money to the woman?"

"Just one month's rent. She wouldn't do this kind of ugly thing."

"Do you have any enemies, like people that you buy drugs from? You can be straight with me… This is dangerous, son."

"Ahh…yeah. I guess…yeah, but…"

"How much?"

"Ahh…well…it is hard to say…they expect more than I actually…"

Hamilton glanced at his son—his handsome son looked old and beaten.

"We'll talk later. Let me find out from the super who did this."

He knocked on the door many times, but there were no sounds from inside. He kept knocking and knocking. All of a sudden, two policemen appeared with the super trailing. Both officers launched at Ham and his father.

"What are your names?" they screamed at the top of their voices. "Oh, you are that overdosed kid, right? You look much better," one of them sneered. "You are under arrest. You have the right to remain silent. Anything you say can be used against you in a court of law. You have the right to have an attorney present now and during any future questioning. If you cannot afford an attorney, one will be appointed to you free of charge if you wish."

"I am sorry, sir," said the super sheepishly. "I was ordered to call the police anytime anyone came to this apartment."

One of the officers quickly put Ham's arms in handcuffs. The officers looked at Hamilton and put away the other handcuff.

"All my computer stuff was stolen," said Ham softly.

"Oh, no, it was not; it is with the FBI. Mrs. Vakfiye and her son were deported after they cooperated with the FBI. They implicated you, among others, in certain activities that are not our business for the moment... You'll have to deal with them eventually."

"Why would the FBI trash his belongings?" Hamilton asked incredulously.

"Actually, that was done by his own drug gang. Apparently, he cheated them for some big sum and then fled the city. We caught one of them too; it turns out that your son is the ringleader. Anyhow, we have to take you both to the precinct."

"What is the charge, officer?" asked Hamilton politely.

The blasting sound of a police siren getting louder and louder drowned out his question. A police car stopped in front of the building, and the red, blue, and white flashing lights rainbowed the hall. The front door was kicked wide open, and Detective Salvador Alvarez lumbered in. He looked at Ham and Hamilton, shook his head, and walked out while signaling the officers to follow him.

"Did you not recognize the kid? He is the one whom DA Weisman stopped us from charging in the hospital with packs of heroin falling out of his pockets."

"Yes, we did, but you told us to arrest anyone who came to this apartment."

"Are you morons? What would you charge him with now? Visiting his old apartment? It is the other three Colombian guys we hoped would show up. Anyhow, you go in and apologize to them for the misunderstanding and let them go."

The detective got into his car in a hurry and sped away, this time without any lights or siren.

⟨≡⟩

When Ann came home, she found her husband and son moving her desk and files from Ham's old room, which she had converted to a home office for herself.

"What are you two doing with my things?" She was furious.

"Ham lost his apartment...too complicated to explain right now. He has to stay with us for a while until he finds another place."

"At my expense! Do I have to empty out the closet too? I am storing my outfits there."

"Actually, you are lucky on that ground," Hamilton regained his ironic self. "He has absolutely nothing to move in with. His room was flooded and nothing was salvageable, so we left everything there for the super, who was extremely cooperative with us, and also with the law. I just need a check for $300 from you to finish the deal."

"What deal?"

"I said the ordeal."

"Incidentally, I called you both on your cells a number of times... I got a sound of a click, then your voice mails. Are you two hanging up on me after recognizing my number? Did you think, Ham, that I wouldn't let you come to live with us here temporarily if you consulted with me first?"

"Actually, I thought you are the one who does that to me when I call home, Mom. I hear a click and then an answering service... Of course, I wouldn't dare call you at work."

"Now that's settled," said Hamilton, smiling. "Obviously we don't want to talk to each other, so let's quietly finish the work and make the room relatively, and, of course, temporarily livable (stressing the temporary, imitating the frosty voice of Ann)."

ᕙᕤ

# -LXXVII-

"Agent Brown, Agent Brown. You guys at the FBI fucked us again, right?" said Detective Alvarez.

"What are you talking about, Detective Alvarez?"

"Don't insult my intelligence, Brown. Where are the Bosnian lady and her son? We were counting on the Colombians to pay them a visit. Together, we would have broken up the largest drug ring in history. I informed you of the cartel's activities, as I am obligated to, but weren't you supposed to coordinate with us if you were going to act on it?"

"Detective Alvarez, these people were under surveillance for terrorist activities for many months, long before your report on cartel stuff. Anyhow, are you suggesting that these people left that apartment without your permission?"

"No, shit! They were taken away by your people, Brown, without our consent."

"Well, you are wrong. We paid a visit to them and had a little chat. It turned out that both had nothing to do with terrorism or interstate drug trafficking, and we just left."

"The super said you broke their door to get in."

"Well, yeah. They wouldn't open the door and I warned them three times... What else did that scum tell you?"

"Nothing. He got so scared that he didn't even come out to see what happened until the following day."

"So, is the case then closed?"

"Brown, Brown, my man. You cost me a promotion! I should never have let you in on the case... 'Cooperation' my ass."

# -LXXVIII-

Jeff's visits to Mallory were rigidly scheduled and acted: He would call twenty-four or forty-eight hours before, give the time of his arrival and departure, and comply with it to the minute. He rarely talked about himself or about anything else, for that matter. His conversations were limited to gross erotic utterances that bordered on obscenity. He never asked much about her life, her interests, her background, her mood or state of mind; not that Mallory was interested in any intimacy or even social intercourse with him. But today it was a little different.

After they had sex in their highly routine order, he strutted around and returned to the bed: "Earlier you looked sad; I thought that maybe after sex you would feel better, but I see that you are still depressed... Is something wrong?"

To Jeff's amazement, Mallory entered into a long litany against the Taliban.

"Oh, it is about Afghanistan. I cannot believe those savage animals of the Taliban are destroying ancient Buddhas in Afghanistan, under the misguided edict of discouraging idolatry: Those gigantic statues hewn from sandstone embedded in cliffs."

"And that depressed you?" Jeff kept looking at her, puzzled. "Are you a Buddhist? I thought you are Kabbalist." Seeing a displeased expression in Mallory's eyes, Jeff backpedaled.

"It made me sick too, looking at them being blasted away, these hundreds-of-years-old, priceless artifacts. On the other hand, the Taliban government has been able to eliminate the entire poppy industry, cutting down two-thirds of the world's opium production."

"Are these Taliban Afghans?"

"They are a mixture of Shiites, Hazara, and Sunni Pashtun ethnic tribes."

"Wow." Now it was Mallory's turn to be impressed. "How do you know all that? That is a much more specific answer than I was expecting."

"You thought I was just a..."

"Horny DA!" Mallory finished Jeff's sentence.

"Rather, a poor public servant."

"So, where do you get all that money?"

"Well, that is a long story... First, may I ask what you do with all that money?"

"Mine is a short story. I live off it. Incidentally, I don't make much money. You are one of my three clients."

"Hard to believe, but it is okay. John being one, me two... Who is the third?"

Mallory looked at her watch: "Ah, you are breaking your own rule!"

Jeff was out the door.

⚬ﾐﾐﾐﾐ⚬

# -LXXIX-

Ham was unhappy living in his parents' apartment, what with his mother's unrelenting demands that he should find a job, settle down, grow up, and not to get them into trouble. Their discussions on poetry and his poems were particularly unbearable.

Today was his birthday. His father gave him $100, which he took gladly, while his mother offered him lunch at her office—which he declined. In the evening, he was invited for dinner with Mallory and Dave.

Dave prepared the birthday dinner—vegetable lasagna and salad—served with dark Heineken. He had been told Heineken was Ham's drink of choice. As they sat at the table, Mallory toasted to his long and healthy life (Ham flinched). She and Dave sipped while Ham drank.

"Happy birthday, Ham, happy birthday," they sang. Mallory gave him a book: *Collected Poems of James Merrill*.

Ham looked pleased and embarrassed.

"Wow. I am sorry, Mallory, I don't even know your birthday, never mind getting you a gift."

"Don't worry; I thought you might enjoy a little something. Well, of course you must be familiar with Merrill. I read a little about him, and he is described as some sort of alien being—someone with superior talent and looks, but detached, thus possessing rather a book-learned view of the world."

There was a long, searching look in Ham's eyes.

"Ham, have I offended you?"

"Oh, no. I was just thinking of your adjectives: 'talented, detached, a sort of alien being…' That is how I would have described you. Well, do you know what the difference is between Merrill and me? He has won every award given to poets."

"He was also mega-rich and gay," added Mallory.

"I am neither, and that is not a poetic distinction."

"Rich? Forget rich, never mind mega-rich… What about gayness?" blurted out Mallory. "How do you know you are not? What if you are just suppressing it, and that might be interfering with your creativity? Don't you see? Highly creative people are all gay!"

Dave, who hadn't expected this turn in the conversation, got excited, though he was concerned about Ham being "outed." He had seen guys get scared when pressured too hard and too fast, so he jumped in to rescue Ham: "I sort of understand how someone can write a story or a novel—I don't mean to diminish the talent required to write, Mallory—but I am awed by poetry. I mean, how does one even get to that? You have to be a genius."

Mallory smiled. Ham looked unconvinced: "Being a poet is much easier than writing prose. Once you master the form of formlessness and believe that the content will simply emerge within the readers' minds, you have it! The underlying weakness and banality of poetry are generously forgiven, if the metrical structure is not explicitly laid out."

"Ham is being very modest. I read only a few of his published poems—he never let me read his whole manuscript—but he is definitely a major poet," said Mallory.

Ham changed the subject. "How is your own work coming along, Mallory? You never talk about it anymore. Have you found an editor?"

"No, it is going okay. I decided to finish the book before getting involved with an editor. It is a little slow going."

"How come?"

"Well, I got involved with some groups. One is trying to do something about the destruction of the sculptures of Buddha in Afghanistan and the other is about the environment. Can you believe the president of the United States votes against the Kyoto Treaty while the rest of the world is willing to sacrifice what is necessary to improve the air quality—to slow down the melting of glaciers?"

"He is a moron," said Dave.

Ham looked puzzled: "Who is destroying Buddhist temples? What is this Kyoto business again?"

"Not the Buddhist temples; gigantic Buddha sculptures carved on the mountains in Afghanistan... The Taliban is destroying them with explosives while the world is simply watching."

"Taliban?"

"Some Islamic tribes in Afghanistan."

"Mallory, I am surprised how engaged you are with worldly affairs; it's remarkable! Of course you can't write; writing is an inner communion. It excludes even the slightest attention to outside matters, never mind external communion."

Mallory's phone rang.

"Hi, Mallory, I am glad I got you... Your sister is in Yale New Haven Hospital. I called and left at least five messages the last two days and I said call me urgently, you, you..."

"Dad, slow down; if you had left messages that Pat is in the Yale New Haven Hospital, I would have returned your call; your urgent messages have been all about you, which honestly, I am tired of. Hold on for a second."

"I'm sorry, guys, I've got to take this call from my apartment. You go ahead with the dessert; I'll join you as soon as I can, okay?"

Dave looked at Ham with some apprehension. Ham kept eating.

Mallory walked over to her place. "So, what is wrong with her?"

"Doctors say she is depressed."

"Why?"

"They don't know."

"So what do you want me to do? Send her antidepressants or send you money to pay the hospital bills? What exactly do you want?"

"You are a heartless kid, Mallory. She is your sister! Your stepmother and I visited her twice already… Don't you think you should go and visit her?"

"Okay, first I'll call her. Is that it?"

"Don't hang up. Listen, yes, we could use some money. We had to bring things to her. Furthermore, you promised that…"

Mallory hung up, and when the phone rang again, she turned it off. Mallory went back to Dave's apartment. She told them her sister's situation and excused herself.

"Well, you'll get to know each other better without me anyway."

Neither Dave nor Ham looked happy with her departure.

ᏬᎻᎵᏅ

"Yes, this is the nursing station. No, you cannot talk to her, since it is dinnertime. After that your sister has to attend her group therapy."

"So when would it be a good time to call?"

"Tomorrow, after lunch, is your best bet."

The place sounded worse than Silver Hill, thought Mallory.

"Well, may I at least leave a message?"

"No, ma'am, I have thirty patients and I cannot play personal secretary to all of them, so call tomorrow." The nurse hung up the phone.

ᏬᎻᎵᏅ

# -LXXX-

*I think I was severely depressed since my early teens; I just didn't fully recognize it, nor did anyone else. It was always, "She is angry; she is wild; she is jealous of her sister; or more benevolently, she is just a typical adolescent and will grow out of it." I never did. Yes, I was angry; yes, I was jealous; but I was also unhappy. Our minister once scolded me for looking too gloomy: "Melancholia was one of the original ten sins," he instructed me. "It was only replaced by gluttony in the last century." I kept eating.*

*No one even asked me if I was depressed and why. Nor did I—I thought that is how everyone felt. Even my doctors didn't use the word* depression. *According to them, I was acting out my "borderline personality."*

*"Borderline" was explained to me as somewhere between neurotic and psychotic; they warned me that it wouldn't take too much of a push to put me on the psychotic side of the fence; like with sex, drugs, and alcohol—I was doing all that to feel a little better, but they only worked for a little while, and then sadness came back with full vengeance.*

*I wasn't wild. I was desperate! But no one saw it; I was told by my family and even by others that I was a bad girl; I wasn't. I was simply hurting, but no one paid attention. If one person had said "I love you," I would have stopped all that behavior. How come no one loved me?*

*Why would Pat be depressed? Dad always loved her.*

225

# -LXXXI-

A gent Richard Brown was on the phone with the FBI's regional director.

"We got the court order from Judge Cohen to wiretap Jeff Weisman; Hamilton Thurman and his son Ham Thurman; Imam Abdullah; and two of his lieutenants."

"That is fine, but why did you deport Vakfiye bin Hakim?"

"Well, first, she had nothing more to offer. Secondly, she was becoming a nuisance, going around and trying to recruit help to find her son. Sooner or later, that could have become a problem. She had access to Professor Thurman—you know how those liberal bleeding hearts are… They could have gotten the newspapers involved."

"So she just left without any fuss?"

"No, she thought she was going to join her son back home."

"Where is, what is his name, her son?"

"Ahmed, he is in the detention center. He confessed easily that Imam Abdullah and those two others were raising money for Palestinians, and that Ham Thurman was their translator. Yet he is still denying that they were all part of a larger plot, in spite of all the evidence."

"Such as what?"

"Well, one of Imam's assistants owns a farming equipment and supply store in New Jersey, and the other sells used cars."

"Are you drawing a parallel with all those characters in prison involved in the Twin Towers' garage bombing? Richard, those horses already left the barn."

"Not all the horses… I believe we have a sleeper cell. They live at Nicole Pickett Avenue—the same street where Ramzi Yousef, the guy who drove the truck to the WTC, used to live. We got all their telephone bills for the last year: They called that blind Muslim cleric, Sheik Omar Abdel-Rahman, a lot in jail and also the bomb maker Abdul Rahman Yasin, the one who fled to Iraq—thanks to another leftist DA.

"Boss, these people have easy access to urea nitrate–hydrogen. They can make and deliver Semtex explosives; hear this out, boss: According to our bomb experts, only Bosnians, Palestinians, and Colombian drug traffickers use these plastic explosives, and what do we have here: a Bosnian guy, Columbian drug dealers, and Palestinian sympathizers—bingo, right?"

"This sounds a little too far-fetched, Richard. To me, this is likely a legitimate fund, raising money for displaced Palestinians for humanitarian purposes only. After all, they have reported the amount of money they collected and where it came from—isn't that enough?"

"Boss, I don't want to contradict you, but you got to meet these guys to see the evil intent and the hatred deep in their eyes."

"Richard, I don't mind being wrong, so please feel free to contradict me... I am just a little concerned that we might be making a simple drug bust and legitimate fund-raising into a major terrorist plot, and we'll end up with egg on our face, especially now that you are wiretapping three Americans, including one who is an assistant district attorney—a bulldog DA at that. Do you know what sort of wrath you may be inviting on us if you are on the wrong track?"

"Boss, believe me, I am on the right track! The DA dismissed an open-and-shut case against a terrorist without any hearing... He didn't even allow the kid to be booked."

"Richard, I thought this Ham kid was caught with some heroin on him. He wasn't considered by anyone as a suspected terrorist."

"Sir, with all due respect, we thought he was, but Weisman didn't even give us a chance to interview him... He let the suspect leave the hospital, and he interfered with any informal access to him because there were no charges against him."

"Richard, calm down. I understand your frustration; but I gather all the material you collected from his and the Bosnians' rooms shows no evidence that these people were plotting or even capable of anything of this sort?"

"Boss, we do have plenty of evidence: There were over two hundred Qur'an and pamphlets and slogans in Arabic letters."

"Yeah? If you find two thousand Bibles in someone's house, would you go after him?"

"Sir, I don't mean to be disrespectful, but are you equating God's word with that of Allah, who is the ultimate jihadist? It is in their Qur'an: It says Allah is the Supreme plotter."

"Richard, I really don't know how to answer that... All I want is for you not to jump to any conclusions prematurely, period. Oh, one more question. Why is Professor Thurman being wiretapped? What has he got to do with these questionable allegations?"

"Well, sir, we have audited some of his lectures. He spoke openly against us, saying that we had unlawfully broken into the houses of private citizens and took their belongings without returning them. He quoted Detective Alvarez—you remember him from his last fuck-up— that we (just to be intimidating) ransacked his son's apartment. Last week, he gave a lengthy sermon on America's enabling Israel to imprison, deport, and kill innocent Palestinians and appropriate their lands. He accused us of…let me find the right quote…just a second…yeah, here, 'the relative morality, and the ambiguous sense of truthfulness.' The following day, he devoted all his time to the subject of 'Deconstruction of the Western Belief System.'"

"*Deconstruction* is a philosophical term, Richard."

"Yes, but that is how white-color jihadists work: They don't go around with explosives wrapped around their bellies, they carry igniting books in their pockets. Within the last three months he took out more than a dozen books from the Columbia Library, all on Islam—Islamic art, Islamic culture, on Mohammed, and so on. Converts are much more dangerous than native Muslims, as our old boss used to say."

"Hold on, hold on, Richard… Our old boss gave the FBI plenty of black eyes. Listen, I have a call coming in from Washington, so just take it easy and keep me posted before you take any drastic action, okay?"

They hung up.

"Fucking asshole," Richard muttered. "They go to law school and turn holier than thou… That's why the country is in trouble." He called the FBI's detention center.

"Hi, yeah, it's me. You got to make that terrorist Ahmed talk, do you read me? He has to give us a written and signed affidavit in front of witnesses, saying that Ham and his father were supporting Palestinian jihadists, if he wants to see his mother again. Otherwise, I'll have him rot there for the rest of his life. Is that clear? Tell him that they have already confessed anyway, so this is just procedural, to show us that he is in good faith with us. Now it is all in your hands. Let's see how good you are. Okay, go get him; I know you can do it."

ᏬᎢᏗᎢᏬ

# -LXXXII-

Patricia was crying on the phone.

"Mallory, I have been in the hospital for two weeks and you are just calling to say hi? I almost died! Don't you care at all?"

"I called a few times, but those cuckoo's-nest nurses would neither get you nor take messages…and your cell was full."

"You could have come, Mallory."

"I gather Dad and our new mom visited you frequently?"

"They came once. I didn't want to talk to her. She looked like Mom and was drunk. Can you believe that?"

"Well, it is a perfect setup for incest."

Patricia stopped crying: "You heartless bitch. Is that the only thing you are interested in? You don't give a damn whether I am dead or alive, do you?"

"I would if you were totally truthful with me. Now why did you try to kill yourself?"

"Mallory, please show some affection, some sympathy; I have no one else. Mom is dead, Dad is gone… It is only you and me."

"But it never was before. All those years when I was cleaning Mom's drunken puke, you and Dad had no sympathy for me. Now that he betrayed you too, you are looking for someone else, right? So you got depressed because he deserted you and had chosen two new young victims… Is that right?"

Patricia began to cry again: "You are a monster, Mallory."

"Well, why don't you just say that dad sexually abused you and get it over with? Then I'll be your sister, your friend; I can't do it if you maintain this horrible lie and crime… I saw you two in the living room in our house in Turkey. You were both naked; your head was on his lap, bobbing up and down.

"I am not crazy, Pat. Please tell me I am not crazy! You two put me through hell. Tell me that he forced you to give him a blow job, that he molested you. Tell me that you didn't want to, that you were a victim of

229

his. Tell me that you didn't enjoy it, that you suffered to keep peace at home, that you were trying to help Mom… Please, Pat, tell me you tried to kill yourself because you feel guilty and are suffering from keeping the secret—that unspeakable secret to protect this real monster of a father."

The phone was silent.

"Hello, Patricia? Hello…fuck!"

Mallory didn't know when the phone went dead and how much of what she'd said was heard by Patricia. She dialed her phone again and got her voice mail: "I've said my piece and now it is your turn." Mallory recorded her last message.

⚭

# -LXXXIII-

Junetta was pleased to see Mallory: "Mr. Levine not feelin' well, but he'll be happy to see you, Mallory. He is in his bedroom."

She found Mr. Levine lying on his back on the bed, staring at the ceiling; why wasn't he waiting for her as he usually did in the library? Mallory wondered.

"Hello, sweetheart. You are the only bright spot in my life," he managed to say before closing his eyes.

"Mr. Levine, shall I help you to turn over?"

"No, sweetheart. I think I've had enough massages. Now what I want is to die. No fanfare, no goodbye speeches, no funeral or memorial, but quietly disappear, as if I had never existed. I want to die without pain, without becoming needy of others, and without anyone's sympathy. You see, sweet Mallory, the future holds no promise for me—only further handicaps—illness and suffering and aloneness. Why should I continue to perpetuate this life—a postponement of the inevitable? I go to some social events; they all want my money. I go to some dinner parties—well, you know some of them—they just tolerate me; and you, sweet Mallory, I know you pity me… Why otherwise would you visit me? You can get the same fee from anyone else—someone who could reciprocate and feel better.

"Someone should put me out of my existence," John groaned. "I was going to say misery, but it isn't misery; it is worse—nothingness. I mean nothing to anyone, and especially to myself. There is no medication for this; only death—the best antidepressant.

"Oh, Carol, oh, Carol. Why did you die before me? I wish I believed in an afterlife. What a curse that I believe in nothing! There is no meaning to my life, no purpose, no reason to be alive. Oh God, oh what? Well, please bring an end to this soon."

Mr. Levine stopped talking. He let out a few inarticulate sounds, but his lips were still moving. He took a long breath, waved his right hand, and softly went to sleep.

Mallory watched as Mr. Levine's shallow breathing became even less noticeable. Did she have a responsibility to help him die? she wondered. Was he indirectly asking her to do something about it? She stared at the large green pillow next to his head, Carol's pillow. Mallory had heard or read somewhere about merciful staff in nursing homes putting pillows on patients' faces and freeing them from prolonged sufferings. Mallory leaned over him to get the pillow; Mr. Levine's lips moved—she held the pillow against her chest and remained motionless. Would this be a genuinely altruistic act or an act of murder? she considered. Would she like someone to stop her misery if she were that old, alone, and in pain? Thoughts roared through Mallory's mind; she squeezed the pillow.

"Ms. Mallory!" Junetta's voice brought her back to reality, but she couldn't turn around. "I got to go out for a while if you don't mind; I have to buy a few things. You are welcome to help yourself to coffee and scones if you like. They are in the kitchen."

"Okay, Junetta, thank you. See you later," Mallory responded loudly.

Mallory's clothes were soaked in sweat. "Now I have a little more time"—this is a good omen. As soon as she heard the apartment door shut, Mallory positioned herself over Mr. Levine's head. Again she squeezed the pillow between her hands. It's light and airy; it must be goose feathers, she thought, putting her left knee on the bed while standing on her right leg. She slowly lowered the pillow, centering it on Mr. Levine's mouth. She hesitated for a moment a few inches away and then pressed the pillow tentatively onto John's face. Mallory closed her eyes until she felt Mr. Levine's head moving violently from side to side. She pressed a little harder, but couldn't take the gargling sound coming through the pillow—she wanted to cover her ears, but her hands were on the pillow—she pressed even harder; the whole bed was convulsing. Mallory's mouth dried up. She wanted to cough but couldn't. She felt something stuck in her throat, and her eyes were getting watery... Had he died? She slightly released the pressure. Her hands still on the pillow, she began to cry—tears were cascading down her face to her neck.

All of a sudden she got thrown to the floor—Mr. Levine's body jolted with incredible force when his defibrillator discharged. Mallory lost her balance and tumbled down.

"What...the...hell...are you doing?" John's voice was drowning in intermittent coughs.

Mr. Levine sat on the bed, still holding the pillow tightly, with his eyes wide open. He was inhaling long and deep. The whistling sounds of his breathing were only interrupted by hard, scratchy coughs. With his eyes tearing, he stared incredulously at Mallory, who was still on the floor.

"What—the hell were you doing?" he repeated again with glaring eyes. "Why were you trying to kill...me?"

"May I get you some water?" Mallory got up, her whole body shaking "Oh, no, no!"

The sound of the front door opening and closing heralded Junetta's return. Hearing the harsh coughs, she rushed to the bedroom: "Are you okay, Mr. Levine? Let me get you some water."

She returned with a glass of water and handed it over to Mr. Levine.

"I am okay, Junetta; you can go now."

As she left she threw a suspicious look at Mallory. Mr. Levine passed the glass to Mallory.

"Sit there. Drink some water and explain yourself."

Mallory took a sip and sat across from Mr. Levine. "I thought you wanted to die, Mr. Levine," she managed to say.

"Yes, I wanted to die, but I didn't mean to be killed… Can't you see the difference?"

Mr. Levine's breathing turned normal with only occasional coughs interrupting. "And why are you crying when I am the one who almost got suffocated?"

Mr. Levine got up from the bed as if nothing happened and came over to Mallory. He put his hand on her head and said: "Listen, listen…it is… ahh…ahh it is, it was just a misunderstanding. It happens between good friends; believe me, it is okay. I am alive, so it is all right."

Mallory was inconsolable.

Junetta stuck her head in and quickly pulled it out.

Mr. Levine dragged a chair over and sat next to Mallory: "Look, I really know that you did it in good faith, so stop crying, for God's sake! Maybe I should have just let you finish it; I swear, no bad feelings. Next time, though, ask me what I might want you to do and be very specific—like how do I want to be killed; definitely not by suffocation; I want to go easily, like with some injection of morphine or something like that, like going to sleep and never waking up; I don't want to experience my own dying." Mallory kept crying.

"Look, please stop crying. This is actually funny—*komisch*, if you think of it. That was the last word of Otto Rank before he died; comical, yes?"

Mallory glanced at him. "Otto Rank?" Mr. Levine's striations of self-presentations puzzled her.

"Aha. You see, I looked up your professional ancestors. Let me let you into one of my secrets, something that I have never shared with anyone else. I did something similar to someone I love the most in my life—I killed Carol."

Mallory was deeply touched that this elderly gentleman would forgive her for trying to kill him. Now he was confessing that he killed his wife?

"You see, at the end, Carol was a tired and faded woman who had a meaningless grin on her face, which lingered long after an exchange of pleasantries. That was the extent of our conversation the last few years! She had physically and psychologically 'gone to seed.' You had to coax her into any meaningful conversation. I asked her a few times: Do you want to live like this or would you prefer to end it all? I know it was sort of heartless, but I also believed that it was truthful. Even to a question as harsh as this one, she would twitch her mouth and shrug her shoulders. 'Well, is it yes or no?' I would ask, and she would just keep staring at me."

Mr. Levine stopped talking a few minutes. "But in her last days, she was in so much pain that she begged doctors to end her life, and they wouldn't do it. But they told me that if I wanted, I could... All I needed to do was open the morphine drip wide and slow her down into a coma."

He began to cry. "You see, I killed Carol, my dearest wife... I didn't want her to beg strangers to kill her." Mr. Levine got up and walked to his bed.

"I think I'd better lie down." Smiling mischievously, he put both of the pillows under his head. "Did you ever see that cartoon—well, it was a long time ago—this old guy, a really old, sickly-looking guy—someone like me—lying in a hospital bed? He had a sign pinned to his cover that read 'Asleep, not a heart donor'...ha, ha, ha." Mr. Levine began to have one of his belly laughs, in between coughing spells.

Mallory got up, wiped his eyes, picked up her bag, and ran out.

That night, Mallory broke her abstinence—not counting occasional slip-ups—she drank lots of vodka and smoked pot until she was out cold.

⚬〜〜〜⚬

The following day Mallory woke up groggy but feeling better about John's situation. In fact, she felt strong enough to take on the next challenge: Detective Salvador Alvarez.

Mallory walked into Hunan Balcony; the place was empty except for two attractive young men by the entrance. They were sitting close to each other and holding hands under the table. They were both in blue jeans and polo shirts (one in purple and one in pink) with identical brown-colored jackets hanging from the back of their chairs. They didn't even look at Mallory... What a shame, she thought; all handsome guys were gay in the city.

Mallory saw Detective Alvarez sitting at the corner of the restaurant. He got up, shook her hand, pulled her chair back, and helped her be comfortable.

"Detective Alvarez, what are all those accusations about?"

"Call me Salvador, please; you see, this is an informal meeting...what would you like to eat?"

"Actually, I am not that hungry, so I'll just have a cup of sweet and sour soup."

"No, no, you've got to eat to maintain that beautiful body of yours," Detective Alvarez said appreciatively. "Are you looking at someone outside?" He noticed Mallory's eyes were staring out into space. "Are you being tailed? You are not going to double-cross me, I hope."

"Okay, I'll also have some cold noodles." She turned to look at him.

Detective Alvarez ordered kung pao chicken and then leaned over.

"I think the FBI took Vakfiye and her son from that apartment, although they deny it vehemently. How else could these two people disappear into thin air? Now, it is possible, but unlikely, that the cartel gang got to them...but that is not how they operate."

"I hope they are okay...but what does all this have to do with me?" she pressed.

The detective flashed a wide smile.

"Well, you enter the picture if we consider the third possibility, that these Bosnians are smarter than we are, and that once they realized that they were in trouble, they picked up and went into hiding until things cooled down a bit.

"Because of the fact that your boyfriend, sorry, your fiancé, is intimately involved with the case, whether drug dealing or money laundering or, as the FBI suspects, involved with the Palestinian terrorists..." The detective stopped for a minute and searched Mallory's eyes, which were gone again, fixated on a point somewhere outside.

"You helped them to get away! You see, they neither had the means nor the wherewithal to pull something off like this... Hamilton was incarcerated in the hospital—not that he is cured or anything—so that leaves only you... You're smart, you have the money, you know the important people in this investigation and have an interest in their disappearance—you wanted to remove any potential witnesses against your boyfriend and any access by us or by the FBI, right?"

"You could write for *Law and Order*."

The detective spread his legs: "Funny you should mention that; my high school English teacher in the Bronx, Mrs. Cantanelli, used to say, 'Salvador, your problem is you got too much imagination,' and she would pull my ears. I didn't mind... These days, you touch a kid's hair and the parents will sue you.

"So, Mallory, where did you send them? You see, my whole career is at stake... I told my boss that if we got one of you, the others would follow naturally. Their loyalty to each other is paper thin. Actually, the kid we picked up in the neighborhood turned out to be a small-time crook, unrelated to this situation. I've got to crack this case and you...you are my only hope."

Mallory felt relieved: "Salvador, I am sorry that your whole career is dependent on this case, but I assure you that I neither helped these people escape, nor do I know where they are. Furthermore, you have Ham! He may help you find their hiding place—if, in fact, they are hiding at all—but he could help you find those gangs, especially if you give him immunity."

"Immunity! You talk like a lawyer—working for the Hathaway Company."

Mallory didn't want to show any reaction. She was forcing herself to think of the young couple she saw across Broadway the last time she was in this restaurant, kissing each other and later engaging in some intensive conversation. How different her life was compared to normal people's… Here she was sitting across from a buffoon of a man whose intention was, one way or another, to hurt her.

"Yes, freelancing."

"How free?" the detective asked with a crooked smile. "You know what freelancing is?"

Mallory figured out that the detective had fired his last bullet: "Mr. Alvarez, I have given you the informal interview that you demanded. I want you to know that I didn't tape our conversation (stressing the *didn't*) because I don't want to ruin your career that you are so intent on promoting. If you have any case against me, you have to deal with my lawyer. Otherwise, I can assure you that a tape of our conversation may surface and will put your precious career into jeopardy."

The detective was startled: "Now, just a moment, did you or did you not tape our conversation?"

Mallory got up, said "You can have my cold noodles," and walked away into the tumult of Broadway.

Mallory couldn't wait to call Jeff and tell him the whole story—except for the Hathaway part.

Detective Alvarez signaled the "gay lovers"; they bolted out of the restaurant.

"Wait, the bill!" hollered the waiter, who was running after them in a frenzied speed. "Don't worry, man. I'll get her too," replied Detective Alvarez and threw down a $20 bill.

෴

# -LXXXIV-

This was the third Wednesday in a row that Mallory had been waiting hours for Max, who only sent George with an envelope full of cash, far exceeding the sum they had agreed upon in the past—with notes saying things like "If you lived there you would be home now" or "If you lived there you could see me more often." It was the second of these messages that stopped her from accepting Max's offer… Otherwise, she could have used a little more comfort and a little more time to write.

She ate the leftovers of her lunch, then put on her ready-made "stay-away-from-me" face, and walked out of the Plaza.

After she got off at her subway station, she picked up two bottles of Absolut from the liquor store and headed to her apartment. She saw the pleading eyes of one young man, in dirty, torn clothing and without shoes on this cold March evening. Why were all these young men choosing the Lower East Side, where people weren't all that well off, for panhandling?

In the last week alone, two more vagrants had made this side of Delancey Street their home. They never accosted her, but she felt obliged to give them some money, at least occasionally. They were always polite and grateful, but nevertheless it was a nuisance to run into them day and night—each time she passed them, they asked for help in a hardly audible voice—jobless, recovering from alcohol and drug addiction, in poor health—though they all looked rather capable, for at least some kind of manual work. The unpleasantness and danger of the encounters with Lord Washington added to the mix, and she was already considering moving elsewhere… Max's proposal began to sound more and more attractive.

She stopped in front of one of the young beggars, who was busy rubbing his feet to warm them up.

"How much do you expect to make from now till dark?" She asked.

The young man lifted his head, clear blue eyes looking surprised and scared. "I don't know, ma'am."

"Well, $5, $10, $20? How much did you take home, let's say, yesterday?"

The young man lowered his head.

"Please, I am cold and hungry. I just left the hospital… Anything you can give, I'd appreciate."

Mallory took a $100 bill out of her wallet and handed it over to him.

"You cannot make more than that… Now, I want you to go wherever you live and buy yourself a pair of shoes. Otherwise, you'll end up in the hospital again."

The young man hesitantly took the money, gathered himself, and ran away.

Mallory laughed, "So much for the sickness and the handicap!" He hadn't even wasted a minute to say thank you.

⌒∞⌒

Mallory listened to her messages.

- "Hello, Ms. Mallory, you didn't come last week. Mr. Levine got worried… Are you coming tomorrow? Please come, Mr. Levine is missing you; oh, this is Junetta."
- "Hi, it's me. I'll be there between two and four on Friday." It was Jeff's stern voice.
- "You bitch, you killed your sister! Now I hope you are happy… She overdosed again yesterday—a day after her discharge. Okay, what are you going to do now? What did you tell her that she had to…"—he was cut off.

Mallory opened the window. Could this be real, or was it just another attempt from her father to have her call back so that he could extract some money from her?

Mallory dialed her sister's number… This time there was no answer—not even an automatic one. She got scared then and reluctantly, she had to call her father.

"Hi, what is that nonsense message?"

"Nonsense, huh? Your sister, your beautiful sister, a Yale medical student dies, and you call that nonsense? You horrible creature; don't you have anything else to say?"

"Is she dead?"

"What a cold way of asking, as if you are asking if she is pregnant."

"Who is the father?"

"No, fuckhead, there is no father… I was just commenting on your matter-of-factness."

"If you don't answer my question I am going to hang up… Is she dead?"

"Don't, for God's sake, yes, she is, and we want to bury her tomorrow next to your mother."

Mallory put the phone down. She sat on the bed and put her head between her hands: Pat is dead?

"Are you still there, Mallory?"

"Oh, yes. You said the funeral is tomorrow, right?"

"Right."

"Of course I'll come. You said she'll be buried next to Mom at Willowbrook Cemetery?"

"Yes, if we can gather enough money to buy the plot."

"Son of a bitch," Mallory thought, in the midst of "his sorrow" he's angling for money.

"How much is a plot?"

"Well, it is $2,500, but there are two side-by-side, and they won't sell just one of them."

"Who do you have in mind for the third plot?"

"Me, of course."

"What if I kill myself also?"

Mallory felt her father's calculating silence.

"Please, Mallory, you are the only daughter I have left... I want you to live a long life and give me a few grandchildren."

"Okay, then buy your own plot. What did you do with the money you got selling the house?"

"Mallory, I have a family to support now!"

"Okay, let me ask you this question: Do they ever bury people on top of each other? Like one six feet down and the others four or eight?"

An agitated voice blustered: "Fine, fine. Don't come to the funeral. I don't want you to be there, anyway. I'll sell the car and pay for the expenses. One of these days I'll visit you when you are least expecting and break your neck."

Now he was screaming at the top of his voice: "Furthermore, you are a jealous bitch of a girl! You must be happy that she is dead because you always knew that I loved her and despised you... Your mother and your sister never loved you either."

Mallory wasn't outwardly disturbed by his confession. She decided to take advantage of it. "As long as we are being honest with each other, come clean. Did you make Pat another wife to yourself?"

"I didn't make her anything, you horrible person. She took care of me when your Mom was incapable, while all those years you were fucking every man, married or single, in town. You! You are the one who wanted to be my wife! Now you tell the truth... You hated me and your sister because you couldn't get me to bed, right? You little whore. I'll come one

of these days, grant your wish, and tear your ass, you, you little cunt!"
he hung up.

Mallory was stunned with his explicitness but also felt good. Now it
was all clear who was what and where she stood with the family, especially with him. Now it was all transparent...or was it? Was that a confession of some sort? Did he mean that Pat made herself a wife to him? She
tried to remember every word of his litany... Did I want him, as he accused me of doing? She was strangely aware of herself...and she wanted
very badly to lose that awareness of her awareness. She wondered if
perhaps she had invented his relation with Pat.

Mallory put two ice cubes into a glass, poured vodka over them, and
drank it down in one gulp. Then she poured another one.

৩৸৲৩

# -LXXXV-

*I was in my senior year at Staples High, the Thanksgiving night I came home around 2 a.m. Mom and Pat were sleeping, but Dad was up… Empty beer bottles and half-eaten turkey sandwiches were piled up on the coffee table. Dad was wearing only pajama bottoms, and he was slouched in front of the TV as he watched a tape.*

*"Come here, you little slut, maybe you can learn a few new tricks."*

*I sat next to him on the sofa. A beautiful blond was giving a blow job to an older white man reclining on the floor, while a young black man was fucking her from behind.*

*"Dad!" I protested. He turned his face away from me. "Yuck, your mouth smells of sperm. Don't you wash it down with beer or something afterward?" He handed me a half-empty bottle of Budweiser.*

*"Why do you watch pornos when you have a wife and…" I couldn't finish my sentence.*

*"You must be kidding."*

*He looked deep into my eyes, maybe the first time he ever really looked at me, his heavy-lidded eyes pleading helplessness—an impotent man, defeated by life and fate. Is this what Pat had seen? If so, I almost could understand her. I drank some of the vodka left in a bottle while watching the tape.*

*The porno actors were at it for over ten minutes until finally, both men began to masturbate together and ejaculated all over the girl's face. She couldn't open her eyes from the smear and was trying cheerfully to redirect the semen toward her mouth. I looked at Dad. He was half-asleep.*

*From the front opening of his pajama, I saw his graying pubic hair and his limp penis. I extended my hand and slid it into his pajamas—he turned his eyes to the TV, seemingly oblivious to me. I lightly stroked his penis inside the pajamas until a mild erection filled my palm.*

*I put my head on his chest, but he didn't move. I heard his heart beating faster and faster, and I lowered my head onto his lap… He was still motionless. I pulled his semierect penis from his pajamas. His crotch smelled a disgusting composite of beer, turkey, and cheese.*

*He turned the TV off, gently pushed me away, pulled himself together, and walked away without saying a word. I heard his wobbly steps going up.*

*Was I rejected? Did he not like it? Wasn't I as good as Pat, or was he totally disapproving of my behavior? What was it? A mix of anger, doubt, and nausea took over. I drank the leftover vodka and beers and turned the tape back on: There were no new tricks to learn. I was more intrigued by the fact that men like my father would pay for these tapes to watch women bringing someone to orgasm... What was the big deal? Provide enough friction to a man's penis with your hand, mouth, vagina, or anus and voilà: He is in seventh heaven and he'll sell whatever he has to pay you.*

*Another ten minutes into the tape, it got repetitive and boring; I turned off the television.*

☙

*In the morning, Dad behaved as if nothing had happened between us. He was in his usual indifferent attitude toward me while overly solicitous of Pat—had she slept well? Did she want more orange juice?*

*Was he guilty of cheating on her? We sat down to have a late breakfast that the two of them had prepared. Mom kept asking why we weren't at school, but no one bothered to reply to her.*

*"Did you all see those wild turkeys on the lawn this morning?" Mom asked.*

*Usually during breakfast no one talked besides Mom—she just rambled—unless some tasks were to be distributed.*

*"We cooked one of them yesterday," Dad replied, laughing.*

*"I saw the turkeys: There was a mother and three youngsters," I said, looking at Dad and Pat with disgust.*

*"Are you serious?" Pat asked. "You really saw wild turkeys?"*

*I stared at her—I could have strangled her.*

*Mom got up and went to the living room, while cursing at something or someone.*

*"Okay, I am off," Dad turned to me. "The next three days, your job is to clean this place thoroughly. It is a pigsty... And you, Pat, finish your damned college applications." He banged the door closed behind him.*

*"I'll help you, Mallory," Pat said. "Don't worry."*

*I walked into the living room. Mom must have turned the TV on, and the porno tape was running. She was watching it, glued to the screen, but without any expression.*

*"Do you like watching it, Mom?"*

*"I did that," she said.*

*"To whom?"*

*"To your husband."*

*"You mean Pat's husband."*

"Pat!" *Mom screamed.*

*Pat came running in.* "What is going on here?" *she looked at Mom and the TV. Horrified, she turned it off, pulled the cassette out, and threw it at me.* "Take your dirt somewhere else! Don't you have any shame, Mallory? What are you doing to this poor woman? I don't understand."

"It is Dad's." *I tried to explain the situation and gave the tape back to her.* "She just happened to turn the TV on. He left the cassette in the player for you to see and learn a few new tricks, I guess."

*Pat looked at Mom, then me.*

"You are the one who turns tricks, Mallory. You could probably teach porno stars a few techniques of your own."

*She walked away with the cassette.*

"Turn tricks? Whores turn tricks."

"Yeah," *she turned around,* "where did you get those brand new $20 bills?"

"What! You go into my things now?"

"Of course not. Whenever we go shopping or to Sherwood Diner, you pull out those twenties... Where do you get them? Dad wouldn't give them to you."

*I thought I got her:* "Yeah! How do you know? Do you mean to say that he doesn't give you money?"

"He does, but for something specific, and his bills are always old and crumbled... Yours look like someone just printed them."

"Those are from Dad too, for something specific."

*Why was I playing this game? I just couldn't stop now, even though Pat was getting agitated.*

"Don't say stupid things like that. You think you are getting me jealous? He can give you whatever he wants, I don't care...but I know you are lying. I happened to search his pockets too, and he never has that kind of money."

*That was news to me.* "Why do you search his pockets?"

"That is not your business," *she replied tersely and closed the door.*

*Anytime I thought the family picture was getting a little clearer, it quickly turned muddy again. Could the truth be found anywhere? There was still something going on between them, but what? Was she keeping him in check, but was he aware of that? Did she ever find something, and if so, what was it? Oh! All of a sudden, the pieces fell into place: Of course, Pat was the suspicious wife, searching her husband's pockets, looking for evidence of infidelities—a paranoid, possessive child-wife. Immediately I felt better—now I understood why he couldn't accept my offer... He wouldn't dare! It wasn't that he didn't want me; it was too dangerous, period.*

*From that day on and for months onward, I too began to search Dad's pockets. There never was anything worthy of interest: small bills—yes, rumpled—change, loose bullets, lotto tickets, a few telephone numbers that turned out to be for nursing homes in Fairfield County. These same items remained in his pockets for weeks until his clothes met his own criteria for dirtiness and were sent to the dry cleaners.*

*Amazingly, the few times I put a $20 bill in one of his pockets, he neither looked puzzled nor inquired about it. Pat, who claimed that she searched Dad's pockets regularly, never asked him or me about them (they were crisp bills)... If she were not searching his pockets, why would she tell me that she was, especially in a confessional tone? I stopped putting $20 bills in Dad's pockets... Again no reaction from either one of them.*

*They were gaslighting me! Again I would be identified as the crazy one and be discredited, while my real accusation would simply be dismissed.*

◠◠◠

# -LXXXVI-

"Hi, Salvador, we followed the chick all day. After she had lunch with you at the Chinese restaurant, she went to the Plaza Hotel. She took the elevators to the seventh floor, and two hours ten minutes later she emerged—the same outfit, the same hairdo—walked to the 63rd and Lexington Avenue subway station, and took the F train to Delancey Street. There, a tall, black pimpish fellow began to follow her at a distance. She entered the liquor store and exited with a small brown bag—it had to be hard liquor. She gave $100 to one of our undercover guys and then she quickened her pace, sped to her building, and climbed up to the fourth floor… Guess which building and whose apartment?"

"Come on, man, I don't have time for that."

"Salvador, do you remember five years ago a young prostitute was killed? That crime is still unsolved… She entered the same apartment."

"Was this pimp ever questioned for that murder?"

"No, I've never seen him before."

Detective Alvarez, who was removed from that very same case for failing to find the murder suspect and demoted down to drug enforcement division, saw a window of opportunity to hit two birds here.

"Can you bring him in for a background check?"

"Are we not overstepping our…"

Detective Alvarez cut him short: "No, no, we are still after the Colombian gang. The chick and the pimp may be the main distributors… On second thought, let's just watch them for a while to see who is coming and going."

"Okay, Sal. Sorry, one more thing… There are some homeless guys hanging around, besides, you know—ours. They look real, but you never know. I just thought I should mention it. Should I shoo them away or…"

"If you can't tell whether they are really homeless or not—then they are. We don't need some hysteria from those downtown commies now, to mess up our scheme, do we?"

Detective Alvarez pulled out a Cohiba and lit it: "Les mostraré."

# -LXXXVII-

"This is what we got so far, boss," said Agent Brown in a confident voice. "Professor Hamilton definitely is a pro-Palestinian agitator. We have recorded a number of his lectures, and his followers are growing. It would be important for Columbia University to silence him first before we'll see his true colors. I venture to guess that he'll have private meetings in his apartment and without protection from the university; we'll be able to nail him then. The kid, Ham, is an important instrument of the terrorist cell. His computer is full of self-indicting declarations."

"Such as?" an impatient voice came back.

"Well, such as 'Infidels' days are numbered,' 'Kill infidels whenever you find them,' and…

"Brown, Brown, aren't those quotations from the Qur'an?"

"Yes, boss, but I cannot arrest the Qur'an."

"But you want to arrest Ham on what charge?"

"Well sir, you name it. Ahmed, the Bosnian guy, more or less accused him of writing the English version of those inflammatory pamphlets and using the U.S. mail to distribute them while he extracted money from others by blackmail. I am not even going after his drug-dealing and his association with the cartel… So you just say the word."

"Brown, are you not skipping one person?"

"You mean the DA, sir? Well, you were right… Not much came out of it. He is just an ordinary john banging a whore," the agent said apologetically; "and the only thing a little peculiar is that he is always talking about some financial deals with two other guys; so we dropped him."

"He picks up prostitutes?"

"No sir, just one ass he visits weekly. The two guys whom he speaks to regularly are both loaded—one is in hedge funds, Max Hathaway, the other in real estate, John Levine. Incidentally the hedge fund guy owns the building at Orchard that cutie lives in."

"Did you find out who she is?"

"The girl, boss? Yeah, she isn't a regular. We were just wondering whether he is passing some insider information to those business guys— I wouldn't put it past him. If you want, we could go back in and listen again, because we didn't pay much attention to money discussions... maybe we should have. I am sorry, boss. You think he is related to the Palestinian terrorists—the money behind it?"

"Brown, what on earth are you talking about? Stop that nonsense. The guy is Jewish. Listen, the girl—the girl...you said she isn't regular... Then what is she?"

"Well, she is a cute pothead, I would say in her twenties. Within the last six weeks, only our DA visited her. There is a sloppy gay neighbor and her druggie boyfriend, Ham."

Brown interrupted himself: "Oh, oh, I know what you are getting at now. Sorry, boss, I didn't connect the dots... So you think she is the front in laundering money under the pretense of making it through prostitution? That would be why she has no other customers, of course... Boss, you are a genius. I should have thought of it myself."

"Brown, listen, that is not what I had in mind; I was more interested in Weisman. You told me that he let that kid Ham go, according to Alvarez."

Agent Brown jumped in again. "Oh, now, now I understand: The DA is on the take from these drug traffickers, and the kid Ham and Weisman aren't really into the girl. She is just a conduit! Sons-of-a-gun, they really fooled me... I must say, that never occurred to me."

"Brown, Brown, please let me finish. I don't think Weisman's on the take. The man is already filthy rich. That is not it. He is banging the girl for sure, and so is Ham, in exchange for drugs...the question is whether we should out him?"

"Boss, we got bigger fish to fry here...why bother with a sexual affair? The girl is not a pro."

"It is okay; we got a small fish, so let's fry it. Check her out thoroughly and find a hook to hang her with if she doesn't go along with us."

"Boss, I don't mean to be disrespectful, but what do you want her to do for us?"

"I don't know yet... It may be as simple as her outing him by our blackmail, so just lay the groundwork for the moment."

"Yes, boss. Incidentally, I think there is around-the-clock surveillance of the building by some shabbily dressed guys. I think they are NYPD officers."

"Richard Brown! What is wrong with you? For half an hour you have been chewing my ear off, and only at the last minute do you casually drop the most important information... While you are preoccupied with catching the biggest fish, we are going to miss a reasonably-sized one and go hungry!"

"I am sorry, boss. What do you want me to do?"

"Look, weren't you trying hard to convince me that we have a terrorist cell situation? So shake one of them, for God's sake, and see what spills out. Or just shoo them away…this is now a federal case."

"Shake down one of the cops in civilian clothes, sir?"

"Not shake down, for God's sake, just rattle. Find out what they are after. Do you want to lose another major investigation to local jerks? This is big, Brown! Take over, and don't let them snatch it away from you."

"Sir, yes sir."

After they hung up, Agent Brown was shaking with fear and anger. He jotted down the gist of his conversation with the boss. "He is giving me lip service about the terrorist issue. In reality, he seems more interested in the sexual life of the DA rather than pursuing a major lead to arrest terrorists. He also wants me to confront undercover cops about their activities on Delancey. I'll obey the order, but I'll make it clear that this is not why taxpayers pay the FBI—our job is to protect the country from terrorists, first and foremost."

He carefully put his report in the dossier of the "sleeper cell at Nicole Pickett"—his private file.

⚬⟆⟆⟆⚬

# -LXXXVIII-

*A*fter Mom's funeral, Mr. Lancaster, the minister of our church who never hid his disapproval of me, approached me to offer a few accusatory condolences. Then, with an "it is hard to believe" attitude, he explained that my mother had spoken to him about the distribution of her personal belongings, however little they were, and that she wanted me to have her diamond ring. The minister said he had also conveyed Mom's request to my father.

"Should you decide," the reverend added, sneering, "to donate the ring to the church, we would be happy with our blessings to give you an appropriate receipt for your tax-deductible contribution."

After that, I never heard about the subject from my dad or from the minister. The only question that lingered in my mind was, why should Mom leave her single valuable possession to me? Was I the least harmful member of the family to her? I presumed Dad would have given the ring to Pat—I felt less guilty.

# -LXXXIX-

"Ham, hey, how would you like to hang out?"

"Listen, I am sorry, Mal, but things are not really…well, I have not been out for a… I'll tell you about it later… Also I am looking for an apartment."

"Ham, I am asking you out!"

"Ah, you are asking me out? Ah…like a date?"

"Yeah, like a date! Gosh, Ham, you are embarrassing me."

"No, no, I am sorry, of course…the thing—you know, we never dated before…you know, we are sort of friends, you know editing and shit."

"We could be like Dante's Paolo and Francesca."

"But they fell in love over tales of Lancelot…what they actually loved was the compatibility of their literary taste. You don't care about poetry—the aimlessness of it; and I don't like novels, for they strive for an end product. One is like dancing around in circles and the other is like walking on a thin line."

"Ham, do you want to date me or not?"

There was a long silence, and Mallory was getting irritated.

"Ham, are you gay? I asked you the other day, and you evaded the question. So please level with me."

"No, I am not… How many times do I have to say it? Okay, let's have a date. How does one go about it? Mallory, I have no money to take you to the movies or dinner."

"I don't care about that kind of stuff. If you got some crystals, that would do. I am on my way home now, and I'll prepare some food."

"I thought you stopped all those years ago because it was eroding your nostrils?"

"Well, can you make it about sevenish?"

"Yeah. Okay."

Ham thought that Mallory was trying to exorcise herself from her childhood, but instead she was marinating in it. Her memory seemed dimmed and blurred with irrelevant obsessions that overstated the truth. Well, are we not condemned to be what we are?

Ham knew that. Nevertheless, he didn't want to be part of this girl's life—her wobbling thoughts, her inexhaustible incoherence, interrupted only by muted reproaches, her unpromising credulity, her spiritual self-sheltering as a substitute for emotional honesty, her ups and downs on a progressive scale, and her odd transgressions with infinite overtones—all were just too much…even for him.

⟨⟨⟨⟩⟩⟩

For a moment on the subway, Mallory thought she saw Lord Washington. A chill came down her spine, and she kept looking around anxiously: No. Maybe she was getting a little paranoid, but then again she saw him, or she thought she saw him, and again he disappeared.

At the grocery store near her station, she picked up a six-pack of Bud Light—the only cold beer left—and headed to her apartment. She pulled the place together a little, put her computer into the closet, cleared the desk of her papers, and set it as a dining table. She prepared a salad with lettuce, tomatoes, olives, avocado, Gruyère cheese, and hard-boiled eggs.

This was going to be awkward, she thought. She has not dated for a long time either… She went out with many boys when she was in high school, but they were mostly hanging out in a group. She even went to the prom with a bunch of guys and girls together—the sex meant nothing.

Mallory's doorbell rang. It was exactly 7 p.m., and Mallory smiled—Hamilton was on time for a change. She buzzed to unlock the main door, left her apartment door open a crack, and went back to prepare her salad dressing.

There was a timid knock on the door.

"Come in, I am in the kitchen."

"Well, well, well…you are also a cook, ha, Ms. Soul?"

The voice! The voice! Oh, that frightening voice! Her heart jumped inside her chest.

Mallory turned around—Washington was closing the door behind him.

Oh, my God, please Ham, hurry, please—Mallory was drenched in cold sweat.

"Why are you here?" she managed to utter.

"Why am I here?" Washington took his purple jacket off and hung it on the back of the chair as he languidly settled down.

"Why am I here? Let's see…sit down. I am here because you have been a bad girl. I have been extremely reasonable so far. I offered you a very good deal, including moving you out of this dump, but no, you want to be in business all by yourself. You have been selfish and inconsiderate and you lied—you lied to me! No one, believe me, no one ever lies to Lord Washington."

"Look, Mr. Washington, I am not lying to you. I am not a prostitute. I am not. I have a steady boyfriend, and in fact, we are engaged. Ham is a professor at NYU and he should be arriving anytime now, so please… leave before it gets ugly."

Mallory, her heart still racing, felt her strength coming back once she realized that Washington wasn't about raping or killing her. He wanted to use her. She could somehow maneuver herself out of it today, even if she kind of agreed to some arrangement…then she could move out and lose him forever. Where the hell was that Ham? This wasn't the day to be late again.

"Ham, Ham, ha! Not the pastrami? Ha, ha, ha. Look girl, what is your name?"

"Ma…Molly."

Washington went to the window and closed it.

"No, no, no. That is not a good name for a girl of your quality. How about Dolly?"

"Dolly!"

"Now you are talking. I like cooperative girls. Dolly, I have a sense that we'll be good friends—soul friends, if you learn to share the goodies. I'll bring lots of money to the table and I'll be honest with you… My job isn't easy, but I'll do my part, if you do yours. If any john hurts you, I'll break their bones; that, that you can count on. No one can slice my girls or give 'em a black eye. One guy used to kind of strangle girls—not to kill, just make believe—but one of them got her pipe broken. I would not stand for that…a little playfulness, okay, but severely injuring and putting a girl in the hospital? No sirree. No money is good enough for that."

Ham, where the fuck are you? You son of a bitch!

"Unless, of course, the girl is not truthful with me. Then, not only will I let the worst guys do whatever they want with her, but I myself will crack a few bones. The last girl who pulled a shit like that on me is still missing."

Washington was shaking his head up and down while talking.

"Dolly, let me put my cards on the table. The last month, the pastrami came here three times…he is that asshole Jewish assistant DA. I spoke to Harold, his driver…he lives in the same block where I live in Harlem. He didn't know who he was visiting here so often, and he didn't even know which building the DA was going into. I must say on his behalf that he didn't want to find out—I knew it was you. Am I clever or what? Anyway, I knew that you were a high-class whore, but I had no idea how high, you girl. Plaza Hotel! Fifth Avenue apartment! I have been on your tail for weeks now. You fuck really fancy people, girl! I am not saying nothing."

The doorbell rang. Mallory jumped up, but Washington grabbed her firmly and forced her to fall back on her chair.

"Please let my friend come up! We'll work out some arrangement," Mallory pleaded.

"Who is this guy, Ham, whatever. How much do you charge him?" Washington asked while still holding onto Mallory's arm.

"I told you, he is a teacher at NYU. I don't charge him; he is my boyfriend."

"Okay, now Dolly, from now on we charge everyone. There will be no free fucking; this is a business, girl. Does Kentucky Fried ever give free chicken to friends? No! I am the only one who gets free fucking. You can totally trust me."

The doorbell rang again.

"Please, Washington, I'll do exactly what you said, I...please."

"No, no, no more Hams, only Pastramis." Washington unbuttoned his vest. "Now get your daddy a cold beer."

Mallory felt she got a lucky break then because her Beretta was taped behind the refrigerator—fully loaded. However, she was in Washington's view and not far enough away... She needed him to be distracted elsewhere, or at least to turn his back, for her to pull the tape and free the gun.

She brought the beer.

"Bud Light? Another thing, don't fuck sissies...or charge them double. They are a pain in the neck, and they cannot get it up! If they do, they cannot come, and if they come, half of their junk goes back to their bladder, making them feel bad, and they'll blame you for all that."

Washington took a sip of beer, put the bottle on the desk, and began to pull open the drawers one by one, throwing their contents on the floor: some letters, blank paper, envelopes, stamps, sunglasses, hats, panties, bras, socks.

"Where do you hide the fucking dough? Don't let me strip search you."

"It is in that manila envelope."

Washington tore open the envelope. Dozens of $100 bills fell out.

"Oh, oh, oh, not bad, not bad at all."

Mallory was watching Washington picking up the money from the floor. "Please God, turn him around." Washington was always keeping an eye on her, even as he was carefully counting the money.

"Forty-two hundred dollars. I presume this is one day's take; not bad, but we can do much better, Dolly, you'll see."

Washington put a $100 bill on the desk and pocketed the rest. "It is stupid to hide the money in a desk drawer. From now on, I am your safe. I'll keep the bills for you and I'll give you $200 a day. I think that is a fair pocket money, and as for the rest, I'll keep it for whenever you need something—you know: shoes, clothes. I want my girls to be classy.

"Now, you'll give me your phone, I'll give you mine until we totally trust each other. If you get a call, say 'Mr. Washington's office' and take the message. Now, this is how it goes: I'll make the deals, secure the money, and you'll await my call. I'll tell you where to go, the name of the guy, what he expects, and how long. You'll let me know when he arrives at the appointed place and when he leaves. Also, give me some idea whether he is a creep or not, you know what I mean. Then you leave and come directly home. Do you understand? It is very simple…if the guy asks something quirky and pays you any extra dough, you'll bring it to me, okay?"

Washington's phone rang. "Yo! Hey beauty, yeah. You are still there? Well wait for another half an hour…what? Why do you give a shit, he already paid… What? Am I a fucking weatherman? So take the train."

Mallory was slowly backing toward the refrigerator.

"You can drink mine, it tastes like shit." He pushed the bottle toward her direction. "No, no, moron, I am talking to someone else, a new girl… what? Her name? Dolly…why? Here it is, be nice, though."

He gave the phone to Mallory and stayed close to hear the conversation. "Listen, Dolly, Washington is the best daddy money can buy. His clients are all fancy people: money guys, lawyers, doctors, judges, congressmen, ambassadors. All clean guys, all married, family men. Listen, Dolly, would you like to live with us in Chelsea? We have a great condo—me and Latifa—Georgy, the third girl, had to leave, so we have an extra room. Did you hear about her? Poor girl…"

Washington pulled the phone from Mallory: "Okay, that is enough." He buttoned up his vest, put his jacket on: "I got some business tomorrow. In fact, another Pastrami put me up to it—this is the second time. If he pulls one more shit like that, I am going to cook his goose. Anyway, I'll call after the deposition, so keep the phone on all the time. Oh, here is the charger."

Washington hauled himself up out of the chair and prowled around a little. He put his phone on the desk and extended his hand to Mallory for her phone. Mallory felt paralyzed. He emptied out her bag on the mattress and took her phone. "Oh, we got the same Samsung, girl—so you don't need my charger!"

☙

Washington left casually, as if this was all in a day's normal work. Mallory heard his heavy footsteps down the stairs and the slamming of the front door… She couldn't believe that he was gone and she was alive, but she felt like he was still in the room. The image of the gold teeth in the back of his mouth was locked in her eyes. A hot stream ran down her legs. The image of her father threatening Pat flashed through her mind. She ran to the door, locked it, and then stumbled into the kitchen, where she tore out the tape holding the Beretta and turned off its safety. Her hands were shaking so much that she couldn't even hold the gun; she had to put it on the desk.

"What shall I do, oh God, what should I do?" She kept asking herself. Whom can I call? Max, Jeff, Ham? All three? She dialed Ham, but she had to leave a message: "Ham, I have been through hell. Please call back. When you came...I was held up by this, this awful big black guy. Please, Ham, I am so scared! I don't know what to do."

After she hung up, she realized that if Ham called he'd get Washington.

"Hi, me again, don't call, the guy took my phone and gave me his. I'll keep calling. Please turn your phone on."

She put her ear on the wall of David's apartment: not a sound. She was afraid of going out of her place. She banged on the connecting wall, hollering, "David, David!" She heard a knock on the door. Mallory froze again.

"Mallory, open the door; what's going on?"

Hearing David's voice, Mallory began to cry hysterically. She let David in and locked the door again.

"What happened?" Mallory was holding on to him tightly. Listening to fragments of the story, Dave offered for her to spend the night at his place. Tomorrow she could look for another place.

Mallory took her computer, gathered a few things, put the gun in her bag, and followed Dave out the door.

Dave offered Mallory one of his Valiums, poured her some Chardonnay, and sat next to her.

"Why not call your boyfriend?"

"Ham? I did, his cell was off."

"No, no, the hunk that visits you often...what is his name—the Weisman guy."

"Oh, I didn't know that you knew his name." Mallory was taken aback.

"Yeah, I saw him a few times, entering or leaving the building. I recognized him from his picture in the newspapers. Once you were late, and I let him in. I presumed both of you kept it a secret because he is married, so I didn't ask you. But now it is different: His being a DA could really be of great help, but if you don't want to involve him, just call the police. For now just go to sleep; I insist that you sleep in the bedroom—I'll change the sheets. I'll sleep on this gorgeous sofa."

Mallory lay down on the bed. The Valium was working. She felt safe here. She took the gun out of her bag and aimed it at her reflection in the mirrored ceiling. This time, her hand was steady.

༺༻

# -XC-

Norma was determined to celebrate their anniversary in some festive surroundings and with good food, not the way it was at the Thurmans' last year—in their dreary apartment with take-out food. She made the reservation at the Four Seasons weeks ahead of time and sent the invitations to their same friends—the Thurmans, Weismans, and John Levine—no gifts, please—so that there would be no misunderstandings... No one protested.

Although the private dining room of the Four Seasons—a few steps up from the Pool Room—was a little too big for their private party, Max didn't want to change the tradition they had followed for years and invite more people. Norma didn't understand why the Weismans always traveled during their own anniversaries. The Thurmans never celebrated theirs, and John, poor John, had been without a partner since Carol got sick—and now dead. So her own anniversary became the only one that was celebrated, but always with the same people. Regardless, she made sure that Max also lavished her with jewelry, designer outfits, and trips to Palm Beach the weekend afterward.

The Weismans came with John, the Thurmans a little later. During the cocktail hour, Max, John, and Jeff were huddled in one corner of the long rectangular room. They were discussing the upsurge in energy stocks, especially coal.

"On the twenty-first of this month, Peabody will be offering an IPO: They need to raise about a half-billion dollars," said Jeff.

"Shall we?" asked John.

Max shook his head: "No, it is too late."

In another corner, the ladies were discussing the collapse of privacy in the lives of public figures.

"I hope Jeff decides not to run for office," Jeanny said. "I dread that we'll see our names and pictures in the tabloids, especially the children."

Meanwhile, Hamilton was talking with the waiters—there were more of them than diners. He was eating hors d'oeuvres and drinking Veuve Clicquot Ponsardin La Grande Dame Rosé, 1995.

Finally they all gathered around a side table, decorated with crystal glasses.

"Take a sip, Norma. This champagne costs a fortune," Max prodded her.

Norma always refused to drink wine: "Champagne and wines taste like vinegar to me, even the most expensive ones. I don't understand how you could drink that."

"Oh, no, Norma, wine is a uniquely complex drink. You've got to focus on its discernible properties, such as the aroma and flavor that wine imparts," said Hamilton, smirking, and in a condescending tone of voice. "You've got to engage the wine, the way that you listen to Schubert and Mozart or take in paintings by abstract artists, such as Klein or Rothko."

"Actually, I hate abstract paintings and I can't stand that 'high C's' classical music, replied Norma. "If I can't hum the tune, I am not interested, and if I cannot identify the objects on the painting—whether it is a human face, a house, or an apple…I just get nauseated."

Hamilton gulped down half of his glass: "I take it back. In truth, I am guilty of and grateful to the rhetoric about the aesthetics of wine, since it gives a pretty look to sloppy drunkenness." He already was tipsy.

"Furthermore, at least you can hum some tunes. Although she sings in St. John's Chorus, my wife is as unmusical as Ulysses S. Grant, who apparently knew only two tunes: One was *Yankee Doodle Dandy* and the other was not."

"You lifted that from somewhere," said Ann. "I sing only at Christmas."

"Hamilton, do you sing too, in Jesus's birthday celebration?" Norma asked.

"Hamilton sings only on his own birthday. He might be the only New Yorker who never stepped into St. John's Cathedral," Ann said with a disapproving voice.

"How come, Hamilton?" asked Norma. "Aren't you a goy yourself?"

They all laughed. "What, what is so funny?" Norma turned to Jeff.

"Is Samantha going to have her bat mitzvah next year?" she asked confidently.

"Yes," replied Jeff, "not that she wants to. In fact, she is into Waspy boys! Nowadays she is dating a Baptist kid from a very prominent family, mind you."

Mr. Levine woke up. "Samantha is dating a Baptist boy?"

"Oh, my," said Jeanny. "I thought you were in your transcendental state of oblivion; and what do you have against Baptists, if I may ask? Your Mallory is Christian."

"No, no," a mischievous smile glimmered on John's face, as was always the case before he delivered his punch lines: "As the detective Kinky says, 'I have nothing against Baptists; I just don't think they hold them under water long enough.' Ha, ha, ha!"

No one else laughed. Such unresponsiveness usually prompted John to increase the rowdiness of his jokes.

"So, have you heard this one? A goy, a schvartze, and a yid enter a bar..."

"Oh, no! Please no, John," jumped in Ann.

They settled down for dinner—abundant and ostentatious flower arrangements obscured their views of each other. Asparagus soup, wild salmon, and Caesar salad were all accompanied by miniature croissants. Chilled Cousiño-Macul Sauvignon Gris complemented the food. Then came perfectly cooked ducks (the skins had no fat) and filet mignons for Chateau Lafite, Rothschild Pauillac 1970.

Hamilton thought that if any god has ever dined, this would be the chosen place.

"The world lied to us," he whispered to Ann, who winced: "Stop drinking, Hamilton!"

Hamilton kept savoring the red wine, and the waiters were more than obliging... They were enjoying him.

He laughed: "There is a time to sin, and a time to sin!"

"Max, how come we come here so often?" John asked. "Do you have some special arrangement with this place? We have lunches here, dinners, celebrations—do you get some discount?"

"He is trying to win the privilege of being seated at one of the center tables at the Grill Room," joked Jeff.

Ann chided John: "You know, John, you did the same thing last year when we were celebrating Max and Norma's anniversary at our place, when you questioned how come we—only us—get together and whether we had any other friends. Now you are questioning why we always come here—don't we know any other restaurant?"

"Oh my goodness, what a memory. I am sorry; I had no idea that I have become such a cranky old man. But in my defense, I am just asking questions! I am not criticizing... Actually, I like the fact that I am part of this small, intimate group, and I love the food and ambiance at the Four Seasons."

"It is the absence of Carol," said Jeanny. "When she was alive, you never raised those questions... As long as Carol was there, you didn't mind who was at the dinner party and where it was held."

John looked at Jeanny with glistening eyes and stayed motionless. The arrival of the quirky headwaiter Giuseppe, accompanied by arrays of coffees and desserts—chocolate soufflé and fruits—interrupted the awkwardness of the situation.

"Jeff, you've got to go for the governorship," said Max. "You could beat Giuliani, hands down. The man cannot shut up! He is his own worst enemy... Even though Judge Gische imposed a gag rule on Donna's request for a restraining order that barred Judith from Gracie Mansion yesterday, Rudy kept blabbering. He even contradicted Felder, his own lawyer."

"His mind is on beavers," joked John.

"Please, John, not again," pleaded Jeanny.

"My college wants to change its name—Beaver College—it is getting embarrassing," said Norma.

John attempted to protest.

"You have dirty minds of your own, ladies," interjected Hamilton. "John is talking about the mayor's fight against ferrets, those small, furry, adorable, but smelly creatures. Yesterday the city council failed to pass a bill legalizing beavers...oh, sorry, ferrets, as pets by a veto-proof margin."

"Isn't this a ridiculous subject for an anniversary celebration dinner?" protested Jeanny. She got up, pushing all the flowers to one end of the table.

John, now feeling exonerated, stood up and cleared his throat: "Listen, I am a little tipsy, and before it gets worse, on behalf of all of us, let me congratulate you on your anniversary and wish you both a healthy and lengthy life."

"That is it?" joked Ann. "You volunteered to speak for us all so that we don't keep repeating ourselves and bore each other stiff, but healthy and lengthy?"

"I think it was too lengthy a toast," joked Jeff.

"The 'lengthy life' is a misnomer... You can say a long life or lengthy talk but not lengthy life," said Hamilton.

Norma was close to tears: "You know, I don't mind if you repeat each other. I would rather have that than your criticizing John. At least he got up and said something nice. If you can't say something nice, my mother used to teach us, don't say anything."

"Well, that is why," inserted Hamilton in a muffled voice. Ann kicked him under the table.

"Speaking of that," Jeff took his typical take-charge attitude, "I suggest that each of us say one nice thing about ourselves and one thing that is not so nice. Then the rest of us will comment on both."

"Oh, no! Not tonight..." All seemed disturbed by the idea.

"What? Are you trying to destroy our friendships?" asked Jeanny. "How about we all tell one thing about you that we consider not so nice."

"If you really want to destroy our relationship, we should each take a turn and hear what the rest have to say about him or her," offered Hamilton.

"You know, you are ruining our celebration," complained Norma.

"Hey, hey...this dinner is already costing me a lot," joked Max.

Norma got up and brought the flower arrangements back to the center of the table.

John put his coffee down and spoke in an uncharacteristically serious tone: "One thing that is not nice about me—in fact is quite awful, is that I refuse to die, in spite of my frequent declaration that I wish to be dead.

"I never told you this, but Carol, during her last month of life, suggested we die together. She suffered so much that she no longer wanted to live, and she couldn't stand the idea of my being old and alone in the world afterward."

A heavy silence enveloped the table.

"She even obtained more than enough potassium and morphine from her doctor… All we had to do was to start an IV line, something our regular nurse volunteered to do." He smiled: "A few million dollars' contribution to a hospital secures a lot of cooperation from those usually reticent doctors. The nurse was to teach me how to connect and disconnect Carol's IV—ostensibly protecting the doctors from those zealots of the legal system," he looked at Jeff.

A howl of laughter quickly turned into bewilderment.

"Oh, I am sorry, Jeff; this was supposed to be about my own shortcomings."

Jeanny couldn't listen any longer: "So, at the last minute you chickened out. That is normal… Okay now, tell us something nice about you, or shall I do it for you while you finish your soufflé?"

Ann grabbed her bag from the floor: "Actually, it is getting late, and I have an important breakfast meeting tomorrow. We already know how wonderful John is."

"Oh, no, it isn't just chickening out; that would have been understandable," John said in a wavering voice.

They saw John's eyes watering; Ann had to sit down—now they had no choice but to hear the rest.

A cold anxiety suffused John's face.

"I lay down next to Carol; her IV was set to run twenty drops a minute. The nurse hooked up my IV—tears falling from her eyes to my face and arm; she kissed us both on our cheeks, collected her stuff, and left crying.

"As soon as I heard the door of the apartment shut, an involuntary trembling took over me. I began to stutter: 'Carol, I am going to open wide your IV drip and turn mine on. Is that okay?' She turned her head toward me… An unfamiliar smile flashed on her face—she looked at peace. She kept blinking to stop her tears from falling. 'However—whatever—my love; but if you don't want to do it, it is okay, I understand. Just let me go. I would be grateful for that alone. You don't need to die with me,' she said tenderly.

"Did she read hesitation in my voice? We kissed; our lips were cold and dry—she gave me the same unfamiliar smile again—a strange expression. I felt breathless." John stopped breathing, as if to get the feeling right.

"I opened her IV. Now death was running full speed into her vein. I reached to open my IV—there was no rush, though—I waited to see her a little more. Why not witness her last moments on this earth? I sat on the bed next to her, watching. Her breathing was getting shallow. I put my head on her chest, and I heard no beating of her heart. I murmured in her ear: 'Goodbye, sweetheart, goodbye. I loved you so much. You were the best thing that ever happened to me.' The smile, that unfamiliar smile—a sort of disbelief—I wanted to stop it. I tried to pull her lips together, pressing her cheeks on both sides toward the middle, but they seemed frozen in time. What did she mean? The first time in her life she was not trusting me? I kissed away her breath."

"Hamilton, please say something," Jeanny begged.

"'The beginnings and endings of all human undertakings are untidy,'" says John Galsworthy, "but in fact, in between, things are no better."

Ann gave Hamilton her knitted-eyebrows scold.

John began to tremble as he took a mouthful of wine.

"By the nurse's advice I was to slow her IV back to twenty per minute after she died and before I opened my own. Now it was my turn. I lay down again next to her and turned the knob to ten, twenty, thirty, forty drips per minute. I held her hand—it was cold and stiff. A panic came over me and without thinking, I got up and pulled the IV from my arm with such urgency that the needle tore my skin. I was bleeding all over the bed. I snuggled next to her, and I made no attempt to stop the bleeding... That way of dying, I didn't mind. My eyelids were getting heavy.

"Did I really believe that I could bleed to death? Not really, but I don't know, it was a pleasant feeling—dreams rushed in. I was a toddler trying to run away on all fours from a horse-driven carriage. I should have bought those shares of Federal Express... How could I be sleeping and awake at the same time?"

Jeanny and Norma were sobbing.

Ann held John's arm. "John, please don't torture yourself. You did what any one of us would have done."

Max made a gesture of a gruff lack of interest. "I always had a large position at Federal Express."

"Look, otherwise we would have missed your company," said Jeff.

They all agreed and made a move to leave.

John was undeterred: "That is not the worst yet. I had another opportunity to redeem myself, and again I flunked."

They all looked at him with quizzical puzzlement—what else could he have done?

John tried to take a sip from his wine glass, but a spasm blocked his throat. He broke off and then smiled: "Yes, that sweet Mallory offered me the second chance, and I again forfeited."

Jeanny stopped crying: "Did she offer you to die?"

Hamilton's eyes sparkled: "She must have offered him 'une petite mort.'"

Ann pulled her hand away. Max and Jeff were quiet. Norma's eyes were pleading.

"I told her I didn't want to live. She offered her help."

"How?" Jeanny asked.

His eyes glazed, John's lips moved sideways, as if he were imitating Carol's last smile. "She knew that death would absolve me. Unfortunately I didn't trust her."

Drenched in sweat, John pulled his frail body up and with faltering steps left the room. The rest were paralyzed in their seats.

"Please, someone go after him!" screamed Norma. No one moved.

"Let him be. He needs to take revenge on himself," explained Hamilton.

The waiters entered the room to collect the remnants of the celebration.

☙〰❧

The doorman of the Four Seasons opened the door for Max, with an exaggerated courtesy; he was ahead of the others.

"Mr. Hathaway, George is right at the front."

George, who was standing by the car, swiftly opened both doors of the Mercedes for the Hathaways and Weismans.

Ann and Hamilton said goodbye to them and walked toward Park Avenue.

Max, who was sitting in the front (Norma, Jeanny, and Jeff sat in the back) turned to the driver: "George, did you see Mr. Levine leaving the restaurant?"

"Yes, Mr. Hathaway, about ten minutes ago. I thought he was going back with you, but he waved me away. He took one of the limos and left."

"Did he look okay? I mean was he a little drunk or…?"

"No, Mr. Hathaway. He walked straight and even opened the limo's door himself."

Norma was leaning over to hear their conversation: "One of you should have gone after him."

"I think he wanted to be alone," Max defended himself, "after such an emotional turmoil. How could he sit and have a regular in-car conversation?"

"That is a rationalization for your laziness," Jeanny accused him. "We could have all sat together silently. Besides, what is an 'in-car' conversation anyway? I've never heard of that."

"What was Mallory doing to John exactly?" asked Norma.

"In-car means the partition is down," explained Max, signaling George with his eyes.

After they dropped off Jeff and Jeanny, Max moved to the backseat of the car and pulled up the partition.

"Norma, don't you know anything? It is embarrassing... At times you ask such stupid questions... I mean, what could a woman be doing to a man?"

"What?" Norma asked in a shrill voice.

Max pulled down the partition.

⟨ఱఱ⟩

Jeanny and Jeff took their showers in their own bathrooms. Each separately stopped by the children and said their good nights. Jeanny paid the sitter and joined Jeff in bed. He was watching Jay Leno—with a hardly noticeable smile.

"Is he not funny tonight, or are you not in a light mood?"

"Both," Jeff kept watching the TV.

"What do you think happened between John and that bitch of a girl? Hamilton hinted that they had sex and something about it upset John to the point of wanting to die. Is that it?"

Jeff sounded uninterested in the subject: "It could be."

"It could be? You seem a little too indifferent." Jeanny's sarcasm was mixed with irritation.

"What do you want me to say, Jeanny? Why speculate as to what might have happened between an old guy with prostate cancer and a young beautiful woman?"

"Oh, she is now a young beautiful woman? Not a whore masquerading as a Rolfing therapist? Why don't you come out and say that you, too, are attracted to her. Do you realize that since she discontinued our sessions, you have made no attempt to make love to me? It is almost ten months! Tell me the truth if you are fucking her; I don't care anymore... If not her, you'll find someone else anyway. Just be honest with me. What I cannot stand are the lies, lies, and more lies!" Now Jeanny was screaming at the top of her lungs.

The door of their bedroom flew open. Samantha and Ellen, half-dressed in their pajamas, rushed in—"Mom, Mom!"

Jeanny wrapped her arms around the girls: "Oh, it is okay. I am sorry. Parents do occasionally fight, and it is a good sign." She turned to Jeff. "In what story was it that a person asks a couple whether they ever fought or not and they answer, 'No, we are not that close!' Ha, ha, right?"

Jeff pulled the bedcover to cover himself. "Oh, yeah, I can't remember that either... Your mother and I are very close, and at times too close, so go back to your beds."

The girls hesitantly moved toward the door. They looked back a couple of times before they left.

Jeanny got into the bed, softly crying. She tentatively snuggled up to Jeff, who was still watching TV—muted.

ᏝᏝᏝᎧ

The Thurmans had difficulties finding a cab. They were standing on the corner of Park Avenue and 53rd Street, and every passing cab (there were few) was either occupied or off-service.

"It is the weather," said Ann. "Even in a drizzle, cabs disappear."

The rain picked up in intensity before it turned to sleet and then hail.

"So unusual for late March!" She put her handbag on her head.

"I think it is the 'Thursday night' phenomenon—the Muslim Sabbath," Hamilton replied.

"You are making that up."

A gypsy cab stopped: "Where do you want to go?"

"Riverside Drive and 94th Street," said Ann.

"Twenty dollars."

They jumped in.

"You are lucky, because I am going home to the Bronx. You are my last customers."

"Sir, what does that sign say?" Ann pointed to the Arabic letters engraved on the mirror.

"It says 'God Is Great.'"

"May I ask a question? Is there a Muslim Sabbath?"

"Muslim what?"

"Like, do you stop working on Thursday nights?"

"I don't know anything about that. I am not a Muslim myself. This is someone else's car... Listen, just because I am dark-skinned with black eyes and a beard doesn't mean I am a Muslim."

"Oh, no, no," Ann quickly agreed. "Anyhow, there is nothing wrong with being Muslim; our son is. What religion do you practice?"

"I don't talk religion," the driver replied.

A cold silence fell in the car until they left the cab.

Ann asked, "Why was the cab driver denying he is a Muslim?"

"Every Muslim in the country is scared of persecution since the '93 World Trade Center bombing, except Ham, of course, who goes out of his way to convert to Islam at the worst possible time," replied Hamilton.

"Incidentally, Hamilton, what was that 'the world having lied to us' comment? Furthermore, it is impolite to whisper in an intimate setting."

"It is equally impolite to be always right," Hamilton replied, unperturbed.

"And how is it that the world has lied to you?"

Hamilton was trying to get his clothes off. He got tangled on his pants and fell on the couch.

"Oh, that… You know, like austerity, education, simplicity, selflessness, altruism, modesty, truthfulness, genuineness, with which we were hammered on… You know that the light travels at the same rate? Aha! But not the darkness!"

"I think you are drunk, Hamilton. You are not making any sense. No one ever told me that poverty is a noble thing to aspire to. Don't blame the world for your misconstrued certainties."

After they got into bed, Ann continued her old litany against the Thurmans and Weismans: "How come your friends never consider giving us a ride home? We go out of our way to appear wherever they want. Afterward, they get into their limousines and go home, leaving us stranded in the rain!"

"That is how they are."

"What about their attitude toward poor John? Why would they let him go off by himself in the middle of the night, especially after such a difficult confession? I think both Jeff and Max are selfish, egotistic characters. Incidentally, what was that Mallory issue again? Did she offer John death or mini-death—I presume it meant sex?"

"After age eighty, both mean the same thing."

Ann wasn't happy with Hamilton's reaction, but she also knew that "this was how he is…" She pulled the covers over her head and turned her back to him.

〇〰〇

# -XCI-

It was about 9 p.m., and Mallory's phone rang—the phone was in Lord Washington's pocket.

"Dolly's line," he answered, trying to hold on to the subway's hanger. He was on the number 2 Seventh Avenue Express that he had boarded at 14th Street on his way to his apartment in Harlem.

"Who is this? Did you say Dolly or Mallory?"

"Both; it depends... Are you one of her regulars?"

Matt Coldwell wasn't sure whether he misdialed so he hung up and redialed.

"Dolly's line."

"Listen, I am her...ah...how is it that you are answering her phone?"

"I am her new manager. My name is Lord Washington. Whom am I speaking with?"

"I am her dad... What does she need a manager for?"

"Ex-daddy?"

"What are you managing? Are you in the book business?"

Lord Washington chuckled, "Come on man, level with me... What fucking booking business? Dolly never told me that she had a daddy. Even if you were, bad luck fellow. Now I am the new daddy. If you try to get back to the game, I'll fuck your ass... Do you read me? You sound like a nice old white pimp. Let me tell you, if you want to work for me, I'll cut a deal, provided you bring your other bitches to the kennel... What do you say?"

Matt Coldwell, who always suspected Mallory's involvement in some form of masseuse–call girl scheme, never imagined her being with a pimp and all.

"Yeah, I would be interested."

A young Hispanic couple gave Washington a disgusted look and moved away. He, in turn, shook his gold pendant at them.

"That's good; I like cooperative people... So what is your name—your real name, now?"

"Patrick O'Donovan."

"Okay, Patrick. Now your new name is Rich. Ha, ha, ha...it just came to me. I was going to say Rick but it came out Rich... We'll both be rich! Now where do you get your girls from?"

"In Connecticut, mostly."

"Good, good. I met Dolly on Metro North when I was coming back from Bridgeport after I visited my old mom. That is good, very good. Girls from Connecticut are whiter and cleaner and also very cooperative. I like cooperative girls... Blacks and Hispanics are too bitchy. You know what I mean? So how many girls do you have?"

"Oh, about six."

"Six? You got to work a little harder, Rich. You know what I mean? I like hard workers... How much do you charge johns per hour?"

"Ah, ah...four hundred per hour."

"Are you out of your fucking mind, Rich? White girls from Connecticut? I'll get $1,000 per hour, trust me!"

"I guess I got lots to learn... Can we get together, have a beer or something, somewhere?"

"Are you crazy? You son of a bitch. A black and a white pimp walk into a bar, ha, ha, ha; what is the name of that fucker? The...comedian...gee... you know, come on, the old white guy...don't you watch cable, man?"

"I..."

"Listen, listen, we'll walk and talk. Come to meet me tomorrow afternoon about 5 or 6 at the corner of Delancey and Orchard Streets."

An uncontrollable anger began to boil in Matt's chest. Lord Washington waited for a minute or so.

"Hello! You got a problem with that? You're worried that your bitch will see you with me? Fuck her! We'll go and pay her a visit together. It is not her business... Okay, okay, then; I'll see you tomorrow."

Matt Coldwell paced his living room for a half hour after Lord Washington hung up. Then he went upstairs, opened the cabinet where he stored his guns, and took out his .38 Smith & Wesson from its holster. He loaded it with six silver federals and put it back. "Tomorrow is the day of reckoning with both of them," he muttered, seething with rage.

⊙━━⊙

# -XCII-

In the morning, Mallory opened her eyes to a full view of herself on the ceiling—she kept staring. Is this how men saw her lying under them? She turned over and stretched her neck to see her view from the back, pulling her buttocks apart—a passive, receptive, and helpless female body...irresistibly powerless.

A man could do whatever he wanted with it. She was paid to be absent as a person—her needs, her wishes, her thoughts were to be suspended, that is, until he had an orgasm. Until then, she was not to do or say anything to interfere with his aloneness in her presence. It must have been like a virtual porno, wherein the spectator joins the action. "Is there a book here?" she wondered and then quickly dismissed the thought—there must have been too many already.

She picked up Lord Washington's phone and pushed the send button... A bunch of numbers lighted up. "Oh, shit!" she yelled. What if that Washington does the same thing?

She dialed Max. "Hi, I lost my cell. Just letting you know you may want to cancel it... See you tomorrow at noon."

"Jeff, hello. I...I am surprised to get you in person. Listen, I lost my cell, so you cannot call me at that number...well, of course I'll get a new one after I cancel the old one...today, well...oh, listen, my apartment is in terrible shape...I'll tell you more about it later. I am staying in the next apartment, Dave's...yeah, 4B. You met him, don't you remember? Yeah, yeah...no, no, he is totally safe...oh...see you at 3:30."

Hi Ham, sry bout last nite - went thru a terrible ordeal. Some1 held me up in my apt while waiting 4 u. I am staying @ Dave's place - pls...I was going 2 say call - but that man took my phone - maybe u could stop by sometime.

She turned off Washington's phone.

Mallory heard the front door unlocking. Her heart began to beat against her chest so hard and fast that she thought it might burst. The pounding went up to her ears.

"Hello! It is breakfast time!" Dave knocked on her door. "I have fresh flaky croissants and organic honey."

Mallory glanced at her watch. It was almost eleven o'clock, so she quickly got dressed before she sat in the eat-in kitchen with Dave and devoured two of the croissants.

"I've got to rush, Dave. Would you mind if my hunk, as you call him, visits me here this afternoon? I'll sort things out tomorrow. Obviously I have to move out, sorry. Oh, maybe you and I can find someplace to live together?" Mallory wiped the crumbs off her chest.

"I would love that," said Dave. "Until then, use the place like your own." He smiled. "That is hardly a generous offer anyway, seeing as how you have been paying the rent... Have one more croissant."

Mallory cut the last croissant in half and took it with her to the bathroom.

"Dave, did you see anyone out there?" she asked.

"No, no one suspicious, just the same few young alcoholic veterans of the Gulf War. I think someone is watering them. You aren't the one by any chance, are you?"

"Not anymore."

Mallory came out with her face washed and hair brushed, still chewing her last bite.

She gave Dave a $100 bill in spite of his mild protestations and tentatively opened the door.

"Do you want me to come along?"

"No, no, Dave. I'll be fine; see you tonight for dinner."

"Oh, goody—I'll make your favorite vegetable lasagna right now."

Mallory was already out.

ᏩᎻᎽᎾ

"Boss, the 'pigeon' is on the move."

"Who is the 'pigeon,' Brown?"

"Boss, the pigeon!"

"Is that a code name for the DA?"

"No, sir, the girl."

"Richard Brown, don't you think you should first let my office know that you are giving a code name to someone? Furthermore, why are you giving a code name for an ordinary whore?"

"Well, sir, you have been emphasizing her importance, and we don't know whether terrorists are listening."

"Terrorists are listening to us?"

"Just being cautious, sir, as you always advise us to be. So, another thing… One cop in civilian clothes is following her, and two are staying put. I am following them. She is walking down to the subway station, over and out."

꧁꧂

# -XCIII-

"Good afternoon, Ms. Mallory," the concierge greeted her with a lascivious smile. "Mr. Hathaway is already in his room, and I took the liberty to add a few new items on your lunch tray. I hope you'll like them." He looked for the key. "Is there anything else I can do for you, Ms. Mallory? Anything at all?" his grin widened.

"No, thanks." Mallory took the key, wondering why Max chose to arrive early.

The concierge ogled Mallory as she sidled toward the elevator. He let out a sigh and grinned dreamily. Meanwhile, he noticed a shabbily dressed man at the registration. He rushed there, intending to drag him out, but pulled his hand back in time when he noticed the man was flashing his FBI badge to the clerk behind the desk.

"Who is the woman who just walked in, the one in the navy raincoat and sandals—mind you, sandals in this weather?"

"Officer, I have to bring the manager; I am not allowed to give any information to anyone about the clients."

"Even to the FBI?"

"Let me get the manager, sir; I am too new here."

The manager gently touched the agent's shoulder. Richard Brown jumped back and squatted down, his right hand reaching for his belt. He quickly recognized the absence of any immediate danger, so he slowly stood up, looked to his left and right, then turned around and casually put his hands into his pockets.

"Don't you ever touch an FBI agent from the back!" His eyes were bulging from their sockets.

"I am terribly sorry," stuttered the manager, his blood draining from his face." "If you don't mind following me, we'll talk in a private place."

They passed through the scattered clientele and entered an office behind the reception area.

"May I get you something to drink? Coffee, soda?"

"No, I'm fine. Now bring me the registration of that young woman in the navy raincoat."

"She doesn't register, officer. The room is registered under the name of one of our regular customers—her lover."

"What is her name?"

"Ms. Mallory."

"Does she have a last name?"

"We are told to mind our own business, officer, and not to be too intrusive."

"So, you are not going to tell me the name of her lover either?"

"Officer, I don't want to get fired."

"No, I don't want that either. This is just an informal chat between us. What does he look like?"

"In his late forties, of medium height, dark complexion with curly hair—though balding."

"Is he from the Middle East? I don't mean to profile."

"If he is, he must be second generation. He doesn't speak with an accent, but I think he is Jewish."

"Does he have a Jewish name?"

"No-o-o."

"I see. Do lots of Middle Easterners patronize your hotel?"

"Yeah, some."

"Do they ever get together either with Mallory or her lover?"

"That I wouldn't know, officer. This is a big hotel."

"Okay, listen, pay a little bit more attention to that and call me when they huddle here with her. Here is my card. I don't mind your intruding into my privacy."

Richard Brown left the lobby, walked across the street, and sat at the edge of a fountain facing the hotel.

✧✦✧

Even before Mallory could use her key, the door opened. Max must have been warned that she was on the way up.

"Hi. Surprised?" Max managed to say, his mouth full of chocolate. "I see the concierge knows a thing or two about you," he said, waving a big bar of organic Lindt chocolate. He wiped his muddy teeth with his tongue—drops of brownish spit fell on his shirt.

"John died," he said casually.

"Mr. Levine died?"

"You look scared."

Mallory couldn't answer… Yes, she was scared but didn't know why.

"Come sit here. Apparently, he died in his sleep; his live-in maid, old Junetta, found him dead in the morning. Now the interesting part: I just came back from a meeting with his executor, whom you know—your client, Jeanny's husband, Jeff Weisman. Guess what?"

Max bit hard into the chocolate bar, grinning ear to ear.

"You won't believe this: The old goat left you $5,000,000..." Max waited for a reaction.

Mallory swallowed softly, and her head dropped.

"What...are you disappointed? He left the rest of his money to various charities.

"Hey, what is that dark face? Look at me." Max held her shoulders. "You are now a multimillionaire! Do you understand that? You don't have to massage anyone anymore... Hell, you don't even need me—I hope you will, but...is something wrong, Mallory? I guess you are shocked. I don't blame you... Here, take some chocolate."

Mallory began to walk toward the door.

"I killed him," she said with a fearful whisper.

Max chuckled. "What are you talking about? He was with us at the Four Seasons until 10:30, and Junetta says he arrived about 11 p.m. and went to bed... No one came afterward. Where are you going, Mallory? Ah, you don't...let me...I couldn't get...I mean I didn't have time to get a new phone. George will bring it to you. Just call me and let me know when."

Mallory extended her hand to open the door, but Max rushed to block her exit. "Listen, one more thing. Let me manage your money, okay? I make killings on CDOs, collateralized obligations. I package these debts, slice pools of loans into tranches."

"He owed me nothing," muttered Mallory.

Max continued with glee on his face: "Credit derivatives insure debt holders against default... You couldn't lose if you wanted! Do you understand?"

Max stopped for a minute and followed her eyes, which were fixed at a distance beyond the closed door. "What is it? Are you seeing a ghost or something?

"I can see the skepticism in your eyes; you may be saying to yourself, how could that be? What if everyone joined the same deal? This is, after all, a zero-sum game... For us to win, someone else must lose. Well, there you got me, but here are the secrets of this scheme—I must be honest with you, it is a scheme: First you've got to have big money to participate. Your average shlomo, as Jews call it, cannot get into the game. At best, they invest in the S&P and beat inflation by one or two points, if they stick to it for ten years—most cannot.

"Here is the real beauty of genius: If—and that is a big 'if'—we cash out too much of a profit, the financial system becomes undercapitalized, and then the government has to step in and bail us out—forcing every taxpayer in the country to share the pain of Wall Street. After all, we may not be all on the same street, but we are all in the same boat. And…and in return, we'll help the government, meaning the president, senators, and Congress, to get reelected. This whole thing—scenario—is repeated every ten to twenty years. You see, it is the money that safeguards the democracy."

"That is the justification for social pathologies?" Mallory asked in a lacerating voice.

"Why? This is America—the land of Amerigo Vespucci—the notorious huckster, sociopathic spinner, spin doctor, deceptive scientist, and shameless bluffer himself! And you, you are America—the feminine Amerigo.

"You see, we both try to figure out what the other person wants and then present it to him in the form of a beautifully wrapped illusion, right?"

Mallory made a lifeless attempt to get around Max; this time he let her go.

"Listen, Jeff will be in touch with you. Don't tell him about our relationship; otherwise he'll not let you invest with me—he is such a stickler." He put an envelope of cash in her bag.

Mallory passed the concierge, who looked a little surprised, on her way out:

"So soon, Ms. Mallory? Did you like the organic 80 percent dark chocolate?"

He rushed to open the main door, but Mallory entered the swing door and exited. The concierge, feeling a little dejected, noticed the grin on the old doorman's face. He stopped to enlighten him: "Ahh, hers was not a well-fucked daze."

Mallory summoned the image of Mr. Levine into her mind, as he was when he tried to make her laugh… A sad cheerfulness swept over her as she ran into the street.

⊙⟋⟍⟍⊙

Richard Brown began to tail Mallory as she left the Plaza Hotel. Mallory, in a sleepwalker's inattentiveness, almost got run over by a cab. She headed toward the 59th Street/Lexington Avenue subway station, where she boarded the number 6 train.

The train was packed. One young, short black guy, holding on to the same bar as Mallory, was rubbing himself on her back without even being subtle about it. She looked totally unaware and vulnerable. The agent felt compelled to protect her, but by the time he got close to them—in the midst of grunts and displeasure from other passengers—the train stopped at the 42nd Street station. Agent Brown saw the guy put his hand in Mallory's handbag, pull out an envelope, and run out of the train. The agent followed and caught up with him before he could go through the turnstile.

"Stop! FBI!" he shouted.

The kid turned around, saw a big guy with a gun pointing at him, threw the envelope at him, and jumped the turnstile. Dozens of $100 bills scattered between a crowd of commuters. Richard Brown hesitated for a minute, deciding whether to pursue him or not. In the end, he decided to pick up the money. A number of passengers were helping to collect the bills.

He announced loudly: "They are not real—counterfeit. Thank you, all." He secured his gun back on his holster and put the envelope in his pocket.

As he left the station, he called the office: "Hi, it's me. Anything? Good. Have someone pick me up in an hour, from the Oyster Bar at the Grand Central Station."

Richard Brown sat in a corner and ordered a dozen oysters and a bottle of Buckler nonalcoholic beer. He opened the envelope, quickly counted the money—$3,900!—and called his supervisor.

"Boss, the Gordian knot is untying itself, as you always say, urging us to be patient. The pigeon, as I suspected, is the carrier. She went to the Plaza Hotel to meet someone with a Middle Eastern background."

"So? She's just a whore. Does it matter whether she's screwing a guy from the Middle East or from the Midwest?"

"No, boss, but she stayed in the room only for twelve minutes, came out with a devil-may-care attitude, and walked to the subway carrying $3,900 in her handbag! She didn't even take a cab. You see, she is clever; she didn't want to generate suspicion."

"Uhh...did you say $3,900?"

"Yeah, boss; the whole thing in twelve minutes? Obviously, the money was not for sex, and it wasn't for her; otherwise she could have taken a limousine, never mind a cab, like other girls—they love limousines."

"Richard, slow down. How do you know she had $3,900 in her bag? I hope you didn't frisk her."

"No, sir; a punk pickpocketed an envelope from her and ran out of the train. Once he saw me coming after him, he dropped the envelope on the platform."

"There was $3,900 in it, and you have the money in your possession?"

"Yes, sir."

"Hmm. Okay then...maybe...well, you might be right, I guess; the threshold for a meaningful suspicion of wrongdoing is reached, to justify the request for wiretapping and an undercover operation—ex post facto—okay. We'll present all this stuff to the central office. Meanwhile, do me a favor and keep watching the DA. Open a separate dossier and also take a few time-lapsed shots of him as he enters and exits the girl's apartment and include a few nice pictures of her too."

"I've already done so, boss. I...I really appreciate your confidence, and believe me, I'll not embarrass you there. We got a big fish, though. Thanks, thank you, sir."

"Fine, fine. Just one more question: The girl didn't realize that someone stole her money and didn't notice all that commotion on the platform?"

"That I don't know, sir. Initially, she was totally oblivious. Whether she saw me running after the guy and that whole scene, I don't know. By the time I turned around, the train had pulled out already. Sir, you don't want me to return the money to her, do you?"

"No, no...we'll see. Just file a report and include that."

"Sir, yes sir."

෧෩෧

# -XCIV-

*I* presume one day I'll die—*a vaginal death. I'll no longer be an object of desire—I'll take my leave from sex. I'll be perceived as the dried-up remnants of a woman, and eventually my cries will thin out as I feast on my loneliness.*

*Then one day I'll die again—a literary one. I'll no longer be read. I'll take my leave from prose. I'll be thought of as an anonymous author, and eventually my cries will dry out as I feast on my failings.*

*One day I'll really die—a literal death—I'll no longer be. I'll take my last leave from reluctant stares. I'll not be looked at—a time-eaten corpse—cries? No, just a massive silence in a barren void.*

*Here I have some talking points, far in advance, for my eulogist—a wild optimism—most authors do not have an audience, even in their funerals.*

*First, stammer a little, like the exploratory tones of an orchestra. I read somewhere that it prompts the audience. Then inhale my absence—please, no quivering lips, and speak with a mournful vagueness:*

*"Mallory was fucked, literally and symbolically (a short pause for a few giggles). She looked at the world from the prism of sex and literature—too elusive—(have a half a cough). She couldn't put a leash on either of them (continue in a contemplative tone)—two of the wildest beasts.*

*"How do I know her? Well, how does anyone know anyone? (look at the guy at the last row) Yes, I knew her once—not in the biblical sense (try to blush as if you were lying). By way of sex and letters, she sought enlightenment. Alas, she fell upon their thorns and bled to hollow sadness (a hardly visible grin here will do it).*

*"She refused to learn from her pleasures and her sufferings—'learning,' she said, 'deprives people of their deep authenticity.' Living and writing were two major mental strains for her, so she protected herself, or she thought she could (a sarcastic pull of your mouth to the left), by displaying profound ambiguity that confused her more than the people she was fiercely trying to confuse.*

*"She lived in servitude of an aimless will and plunged the depths of incestuous gloom. The meaning of her existence was about to take over, but by then, the dance was over—a thick blame. Only death could have contained her silence, and it did—roughly and quickly.*

"She was bred at battles of her own making; she precipitated nameless wrongs—a form of love, she schemed to stain the time—only to discolor her own unconscious.

"She bristled at the saying that 'it is better to have loved and lost...' She thought that was very wrong, if not a perverse paradigm. Love—the gift of the god of narcissism—can lead to the worst kind of loss one could imagine: the loss of one's self. She never fell in love, but she still lost herself.

"In one of her sweet moments, in a fit of innocence, she confessed that she wasn't free to love—she was lacking the moral frame for it—and most likely, she would plunder even her own wild-nest. 'Because,' she said with her usual pensive sigh, 'my star is unstable'—not that her earth was any less so. As if that is not bad enough, her body mutinied against the tyranny of her cobwebbed mind.

"Toward the end, her voice was blithe—she wanted you all (all six of you) to know that she loved at the times of herpes, chancroid, chlamydia, warts, and HIV. She wanted you all (if they are still there) to think of her as a sadly pleasing, forgotten melody! She didn't want you to shed any sane tears—sympathy is an immoral sentiment—she didn't die, for she had never lived."

Now, collect your papers, get ready to step down from the podium, and then stop, as if you forgot to say something; then say with a sense of exasperation:

"I wrote her epitaph: Mallory—For fuck's sake."

൭ᴍᴍᴑ

# -XCV-

The doorbell interrupted Mallory's writing; she buzzed Jeff in.

"Wow! This is some gay apartment," he noted as he briskly walked into the bedroom. "Come on, get undressed."

Mallory stood by the door. "I heard from Junetta that Mr. Levine passed away!"

"Mallory, I neither cry nor do I howl over dead bodies, okay? John was a very good friend, but he was a sick and old man. His prostate cancer invaded his pelvis and backbone, and in the end, he lived long and well. So are we going to sit shiva now?"

"Shiva?"

"Like sort of talking and mourning about the dead while gorging on lox and bagels... I think he would have preferred that we fucked... You know he was a dirty old man."

Mallory kept waiting for Jeff to confirm what Max told her about Mr. Levine's will. Meanwhile, Jeff was totally naked, lying on the bed and admiring himself on the mirrored ceiling.

"Junetta said that you are Mr. Levine's executor. You would know whether there'll be a service or not and where."

Jeff was relieved. "No, he wanted no service—a simple burial (which will be expedited tomorrow) next to his wife. He specifically requested no one to attend, except me and Max. Not even spouses were invited."

Mallory wondered whether Max was lying or whether Jeff was withholding the information. Why would Max make something like that up?

"I cannot today," she said softly.

Jeff found her reticence intensely exciting.

"What kind of unprofessional attitude is that? You never heard of the 'show must go on' dictum?"

"Yes, the show."

"Mallory, are you really that affected by John's death? Come on, you never mentioned having some special relationship with him except an occasional massage."

"Will you be taking care of his affairs?"

"Yeah, I'll set up a foundation and all that. Did he promise you something?"

"No."

"Okay, then. Let's not talk about the dead but about the live one," pointing to his erect penis.

"Sorry, I can't."

Jeff jumped out of the bed and quickly put on his clothes. "I am not paying for this visit, you know. Call me when you recover from your mourning."

Mallory cocked her head: "Jeff, are you familiar with Marquis de Sade?"

Jeff quickly protested, "Am I being sadistic? I don't get a kick out of hurting women. Only once, I guess, I was a little rough, but you know why... It is usually not my nature."

"That is not all what de Sade is about. He wrote about people reducing each other interchangeably to their sexual organs and copulating anonymously and without restraints."

He slammed the door and left, not hearing her last sentence: "That is all we are."

∾

As soon as the sounds of Jeff's steps silenced, Mallory took a bottle of Absolut from Dave's freezer, poured it into a large glass, and returned to her computer.

"Is betrayal the essence of all relationships?"

Mallory kept looking at the sentence, as if someone else had written it. If so, self-betrayal cannot be that far behind, she thought. Now everything began to make sense to her: her mother's alcoholism, her father's incestuous transgressions, Pat's suicide, Max, Jeff. She smiled. How about Dave and Ham, and what about herself? She contemplated for a while—whom had she betrayed? Well, the answer was she betrayed everyone she met, for she was never real; and of course, by the same criteria—unrealness—she betrayed herself the most.

∾

# -XCVI-

"Hi, Salvador. Nothing is happening here. A white guy in his fifties hung around for a while, stood outside of the building, and then went into the hall. He must have tried to get in—unsuccessfully—then he came out and looked up at the windows for about a half hour before he left… He must have been one of the johns who got stood up, because the girl wasn't even in the apartment."

"Where is she?"

"She left around 4 o'clock, not even carrying a bag. I guess just to stroll, I don't know. She was sort of leisurely walking toward Essex Street. I stayed put as you told me, waiting for Ham and his pursuers to show up… Salvador, may I…if you don't mind, suggest that we are wasting our time here? She is not really part of anything, just a simple whore, and Ham is never going to show up here. Even if he does, the Colombians are not going to be on his tail… They lost his tracks. Ham never comes out of his parents' house, and the drug dealers are not staking out his parents' building… There you have it."

"So you think we should just quit this?"

"Yeah, I think so."

"Okay then, let's have a breather."

"Do you want me to harass the white dude?"

"Listen, I never accept a consolation prize. Fold it in; we are done there."

"Salvador, I wasn't offering a…"

"Oh, shut up."

The FBI's Richard Brown was never confused, but if he was ever made to feel that way, it was because of those "fancy lawyers" in the central office.

"Boss, the pigeon is taking a walk in the neighborhood. She is in her navy raincoat—unbuttoned—and no handbag, so I don't know. There is an NYC detective hovering over a middle-aged guy who is trying to get into the building. I am not sure whether he is related to the case. The black pimp was around for a while, and then he disappeared. They are a team, all right.

"Now boss, I understand why you wanted me to stay with the DA. In addition to a terrorist cell, I think we stumbled into a major prostitution ring. We have been tapping the pigeon's phone: Outgoing calls from this line go to a few women and lots of men."

"Who are the incoming calls from?"

"Funny you should ask, sir…there are none! A different number must have been given people to return calls to. Of course we checked that out, but you always get the voice mail… The voice is the girl's—she says: "You know what to do. Wait for the beep.""

"Richard, you are tapping the girl's phone, right?"

"Yes, sir; it seems confusing. The girl must have gotten suspicious, so she is trying to throw us off the scent. She obviously got another phone. I've got to arrest her for something to get the number of her other phone and figure out the telephone issue."

"Off the scent?"

"Yeah, the scent of a terrorist investigation… But I don't believe we need to keep surveillance of the building… Wiretapping these people for a while, that would be sufficient."

"The next time put the horse in front of the cart, Richard. Suspend the on-location surveillance and limit all activities to electronic surveillance and please stick to it."

"Sir, yes boss."

# -XCVIII-

That night, Mallory never returned. Dave stayed up till 4 a.m., kept checking her apartment, and then coming back to his—anxiously waiting. Anytime he called her cell, he got Lord Washington and hung up. Maybe she was with Jeff, he thought to comfort himself, and eventually fell asleep.

When he woke up, he ran into the bedroom, but it was untouched. Why would she not call me at least? he wondered and again dialed her number: This time there was not even voice mail.

Dave waited all day and the next night, then the next day and next week: Mallory never returned. He checked all the newspapers daily, looking for an accident report or something to explain her disappearance—nothing.

Dave didn't know much about Mallory's family; he had no one to call except Jeff and Ham. Jeff's secretary refused to connect him directly and tried to pass him to one of his associates. He demanded to speak to Jeff since "it is a private matter."

"Yes. What is this all about? I gather you have been harassing my secretary?" Jeff said tersely.

"No sir, I just wanted you to know… Mallory has disappeared, it is almost ten days…"

"Who is Mallory, sir?"

"You know who she is! I am her next door neighbor. You used my apartment. She's missing!"

"Sir, I don't know anyone with that name. I don't know what you are talking about, but if you ever call again, I'll have you arrested—you do know who I am, right?"

"Yes… no… I'll not bother you again, but do you know where she could be?"

He heard the bang of the telephone receiver.

David dialed Ham.

"David? Oh, yes, yes. Mallory is missing? May I remind you that she is a novelist?"

"But Ham, she left her handbag here, her ID, her money, a telephone, a gun, everything! It's as if she walked out naked."

"Gun, Dave?"

"Ham, I'm worried about her life. This is totally out of character for her. Furthermore, I have to vacate the apartment—tomorrow is the last day of the month—I cannot pay the rent. Do you mind stopping by and picking up a few of her belongings, especially her computer, for safekeeping?"

"Only the computer… I cannot take her clothes, shoes, or gun, for God's sake."

"Ham, she has no shoes; only a few dresses, that is all."

"Okay, okay, I may stop by today."

ᏊᎲᎲᎾ

During the next few weeks, Ham kept checking the newspapers for any story that might throw some light on Mallory's disappearance. He regularly read the Doe Network—the New York City Police Department's case files of missing persons and/or unidentified remains. Ham was convinced that Mallory had been killed. He was surprised at how many unidentified young women were found dead in the city. Finally he found a file that totally fit Mallory's description.

**The Doe Network**
Case File: 1337UFNY

**Unidentified Female**
- The victim was discovered on June 18, 2001 in Manhattan, New York
- She was a victim of homicide; the cause of death is believed to be asphyxia, possibly by strangulation
- The time of death: sometime within March 2001 and June 2001

---

**Vital Statistics**
- Estimated Age:          22–30 years old
- Approximate Height:  5'6"–5'8"
- Approximate Weight: 110–125 lbs.

---

**Other Distinguishing Characteristics**
- Hair Color:       Light, possible blond
- Eye Color:        Unknown
- Nose:             A mildly deviated and perforated—¼" irregular hole

- Ears:            Both ears pierced; left ear double pierced.
- Dental:          Available. Teeth near perfect, no fillings. Might have had expensive cosmetic dental work at one point in life.
- Marks/Tattoos:   A 1½" horizontal old scar, two inches above the left wrist.
- Clothing:        Wearing ¾ length light blue skirt; sleeveless off-white cotton T-shirt, both from Army/Navy; brown leather 1½" high heel sandals with plastic soles, size 6, made in Taiwan. Scraps of a white underwear and white 34C bra were in the pockets of a navy raincoat—in which she was wrapped—its manufacturer was unidentifiable.
- Jewelry:         None. An orange-colored wool bracelet was on her left wrist.
- Fingernails:     Unpolished; had been bitten down to her flesh.
- Other:           Possibly of Irish or German descent, the victim may also have abused drugs and been a prostitute.

**Case History:**
- The victim's badly decomposed remains, which were wrapped in a navy raincoat and stuffed inside a large black heavy-duty plastic bag, were found in the basement of a run-down vacant boarded-up residential building. There is strong possibility that the victim was murdered at some other location and subsequently transported to this abandoned site of the Hell's Kitchen section of Manhattan.

A construction worker who was clearing the building discovered the victim. The killer had bound her hands and feet with an extension cord and circled it around her neck. Wide, commercial-size duct tape tightly sealed the victim's mouth.

**Investigators**
If you have any information about this case, please contact:

> New York City Police Department
> Midtown North Detective Squad
> Detective: Salvador Alvarez
> Telephone: 212-767-8415
> Agency Case: 1337UFNY
> NCIC: 0002001-45

Please refer to this #1337UFNYwhen contacting any agency with information on this case.

"A poetic disobedience," declared Ham.

> What was exactly between us?
> Tearing each other to shreds—
> Line by line—
> Till nothing remains, except
> Broken sounds of
> Discordant cries.
> Still drooling blood and
> Feeling a strange high
> Only the need to forget
> In a flare of time
> A vague regret.

Ham went back to reading Mallory's autobiographical novel.

∽⟡∾

# -XCIX-

Tonight, the dinner was held at the Weismans. The menu included organic steamed mussels, broiled wild salmon, and pecan pie.

"This is the first time we are meeting without John," said Jeanny. "I wanted to serve what he would have liked to eat."

"Did you know that John left the bulk of his money to the New York Hospital–Cornell Medical Center?" Max said. "Only a few million for his maid and his masseuse."

"His masseuse?" Jeanny's face reddened.

"Didn't Jeff tell you? He is the executor. I am simply one of three—of course, now only two—members on the board's foundation."

"Well, it isn't that simple," Jeff stuttered. "He made no provision for gift taxes. Furthermore, he must have changed his will the last week. I am not sure why and how, but you all know toward the end he was *non compos mentis*."

"He is simply *non veritas menti*," Hamilton threw in casually.

"Are we not all?" said Jeanny, staring at Jeff.

"Please stop being such an annoyance," said Ann. "People are talking about something very serious. Was John really mentally incompetent for all these months that we had seen him, including the very same night before he died?"

"Well, you all know that the last two years John was simply a ruin of himself—a ruin in the prosaic sense. Someone that time and circumstances had left severely damaged. He used to be extremely proper. He had a refined sense of humor, but recently, I am sure you all noticed, he was grossly sexual and inappropriate, which is one of the signs of dementia," said Jeff.

Ann rebuffed him. "I think that is an absurd conclusion. Yes, he was fond of sexual jokes, but he explained why, lucidly and eloquently. Do you remember, about a year ago, when Jeanny confronted him with that? No? You don't? Huh. Incidentally, I wonder how judgment is made about his right mind and by whom, especially when such a large amount of money is involved?"

"Well, that is usually the responsibility of the executor. I hope you would consider me a trustworthy lawyer," Jeff said in a hurt voice.

"Of course, of course," came the chorus, minus Ann: "Jeff, if John is considered mentally incompetent to will a few millions to his maid and to his masseuse, would he not be equally disqualified to make an even larger donation to UJA or NY Hospital?" she stopped short of accusing him of dishonesty.

"True," said Jeff, irritated. "Except that John's intention to leave his estate to Cornell was a longstanding one."

An uncomfortable silence followed. Jeanny got up.

"Anyone for coffee and John's favorite pecan pie with vanilla ice cream?"

They were all relieved.

Max took his coffee and pulled Jeff aside. "What are you doing? Are you not going to give the $5,000,000 to the girl? What if she finds out that John willed it to her and takes you on? John's mind wasn't dysfunctional. On the contrary, he kept all his marbles till the day he died."

"Look, should a whore get that kind of money? Max, we could put that into the foundation. You manage it, and together we would put the money to some good use."

"What if she finds out?"

"You keep saying that, but how could she have access to John's will? She may never even find out when and how he died. According to Junetta, he had not seen her for weeks. For what reason would she even expect anything, never mind $5,000,000?"

Max found himself in the unenviable situation of having to confess his relationship with Mallory and having told her about the $5,000,000. He tried to wiggle himself out of this dilemma: "Why not give the poor girl what rightly belongs to her? I am not that interested in getting an extra $5,000,000 to manage or receiving kudos from some charities, especially from UJA, if this is going to be nonkosher."

Jeff was listening to Max with total disbelief. He thought that it wasn't beyond the realm of possibility that Max was one of her clients.

"Well, okay then. I'll get her phone number from Junetta. In fact, Jeanny may still have it."

"Hey! Hello, Masters of the Universe! We are getting ready to leave," hollered Hamilton.

The dinner came to an abrupt ending.

❦

Jeanny couldn't wait for the guests to leave, "You aren't going to give that bitch millions of dollars, are you?"

"Well, we've got a problem. Max is taking this unusual moral stand that the money was willed to her and it is hers. I tried to appeal to his greed, but to no avail. He didn't even want to manage the money! Go figure. Do you still have her phone number?"

"No, I don't. I threw it away."

"I guess I'll have to get it from Junetta."

"Ah, she called to say goodbye yesterday. Apparently, you gave her $10,000 and had her sign a bunch of papers, and with that, she left the country."

"Well, we'll find the girl."

"What if you can't?"

"Well..."

"What if you can't?" Jeanny's eyes were cold and harsh.

"Well, the money will remain in the foundation until she shows up and claims it with the compounded interest."

"For how long?"

"Until...until she is dead. I don't think there is a statute of limitations."

Jeanny walked out of the room, restless.

◌▨▨◌

In the cab home, the Thurmans were unusually quiet. Finally, Ann broke the silence: "Why was Jeff trying so hard to get us to believe that John was mentally incompetent?"

"No, no, no. He was trying to get us to confirm that John was mentally incompetent."

"Hamilton! That is what I just said."

"No, you said why was Jeff trying to get us to believe, not why he was trying to get us to confirm."

"Whatever. Oh, for God's sake... So why? Is he planning to discredit John's will and then what? He cannot pocket the money."

"He most likely will get the board—the same board, just he and Max— to donate the money to his future campaign."

"Well, that will not fly, especially if this is the same Mallory that our son is dating. Don't we have some fiduciary responsibility to make sure that she gets the money?"

"Rather prejudicial; we would be more interested in our Ham's getting a rich wife, and thus be off our payroll, than in increasing Jeff's chances of political success."

"Well, of course."

"Loyalty, even in those who hate moral relativity, like Evelyn Waugh, is determined by expedience," said Hamilton.

Ann burst into laughter. "Hamilton, unless you talk plain English, I am not listening."

Ann walked over and put her ear on Ham's closed door—the television was on. She knocked: "Ham, could you come out for a few minutes? We need to talk to you about something."

She came back and joined Hamilton in the living room, where they silently waited for Ham. About ten minutes later, Ham emerged totally red-eyed and rumpled from sleep.

"I cannot stay here any longer; you are driving me crazy! I would rather live in a shelter and even get killed by gangs than be under house arrest in your place. The fact that I occupy a small room at the end of the corridor and eat your leftover pizza and stale Chinese food doesn't mean that you have the right to wake me up in the middle of the night to talk...and what is it that you want anyway?"

"It is only eleven o'clock. Are you drunk, son?" asked Hamilton.

"Where did you get the alcohol? Did you go out? Oh, no! Don't tell me you drank that bottle of expensive Cabernet that my client gave me?" Ann was furious.

Ham sunk into the sofa, put his feet on the coffee table, and closed his eyes.

"Ham, take your feet off the table!" She screamed.

Ham opened his eyes for a second. "Some things!"

"Ham, was your girlfriend Mallory treating Mr. Levine? You know, the old fellow with a sense of humor whom we talked about occasionally."

Ham yawned wide, "She is not my girlfriend."

"Well, she is a friend and she is a girl, right? Anyway, that was not the essence of my question."

Ham had to be awakened—Ann pushed his legs off the table.

"What the fuck!"

"Was Mallory a sort of therapist, Rolfer, or masseuse, something to Mr. Levine, damn it?" Ann kicked his foot.

"I don't know. She never talked about her patients."

"Well, if she was, she just got millions of dollars."

Ham dozed off.

Ann and Hamilton headed toward their bedroom, leaving him there.

"The kid is hopeless," declared Ann.

"No. Actually, I was impressed with his indifference to the subject."

"If he weren't simply blacked out! We'll see tomorrow how indifferent he is to a sizable amount of money."

"I said to the subject."

Ann threw a disgusted look at him and closed the bathroom door.

⚬⚬⚬

# -C-

Today was the first day of the month—the day of rent collection. Mr. Lazarro began at 6 a.m., starting with the fourth floor—this was where his least favorite tenants resided. First he glanced at the door of 4A, before he knocked at David's apartment.

For David, the dreaded moment had finally arrived. He couldn't sleep all night in anticipation of Mr. Lazarro's visit. He had no money, Mallory had never returned, and to top it all off, Peter never replied to his calls and letters. Only his divorced sister in New Jersey was willing to help by offering him to live with her and her two children for a while.

"Open the door, you fat faggot!" Mr. Lazarro banged on the door.

David rushed over to unlock the door, but he tripped and fell, bruising his knee.

"Oh, Mr. Lazarro, I am so sorry; I didn't mean to keep you waiting. Please come in… Would you like to have a fresh cup of coffee? I just brewed it—it is French vanilla."

"Stop bullshitting me and give me the rent."

"You see, Mr. Lazarro, I would love to, but Mallory was supposed to bring it yesterday… She must have forgotten." Dave began to cry. "Actually, Mr. Lazarro, she disappeared! It has been over three weeks; I am afraid for her life."

"You mean to say that I won't have her rent either? Is she not in her apartment?"

Mr. Lazarro's mouth was foaming. "And you didn't tell me. You cocksucker!" Mr. Lazarro ran out and tried to unlock Mallory's door—it was unlocked. He rushed back to Dave's, saying, "Where is her stuff? She actually moved out without paying the rent? You know, I do have her and your deposits. Right now, at this moment, both of you are ex-tenants. I consider your behavior as criminal because the deposits were not supposed to cover the debts of deadbeat tenants who skip town. It is against any damages. Furthermore, I don't know how long it'll take to find new tenants… Therefore, I am taking possession of everything here. You can take your filthy clothes and get out, right now."

Mr. Lazarro went to the bedroom and opened the closet: "Whose dresses are these and this bag?"

"I'll take them with me, if it is okay."

"Don't fuck with me… It is okay with you? My ass."

Mr. Lazarro turned the bag upside down on the bed. A few dollars, a bunch of papers, a notebook, a pen, and a cell phone scattered on the bed, followed by a handgun.

"What the…!" Mr. Lazarro picked up the gun. "A Beretta! What the fuck is this? Whose gun is it? I am sure it isn't yours… So that bitch carried a semiautomatic in her bag all the time! Jesus, the safety isn't even on."

He took the cartridge out and put it in his pocket. He began to wave the gun at David.

"Mr. Lazarro, I am getting a job; I can easily pay the rent on the other apartment. You could have everything here and rent as is; no sweat."

"Listen, little shit; I wasn't born yesterday. Get your ass out of here or I'll make another hole on it. I took the cartridge out, but there is no way of knowing whether there is one bullet lodged in the chamber unless you pull the trigger, and I am going to do it if you don't get out of this place now."

Dave threw a few things in his carry-on and hurried out, his whole body shaking.

ᏝᎠᏝᎩᎾ

# -CI-

"Mr. Weisman, Detective Alvarez is on the telephone," announced Jeff's secretary.

"Hi, what is up, Sal?"

"All is well. We gave up on that drug gang for the moment; the trail got cold once we took the kid Ham off the hook. Now I believe his family is keeping him under close watch and the gang will move to somewhere else... We'll see.

"But that is not why I called. A few weeks ago our guys coincidentally arrested a black pimp, who had solicited one of our undercover ladies downtown and offered her a crisp $100 bill. When we booked him, he spilled all sorts of beans: that he is the procurer for wealthy men and that he had powerful connections. He threatened and demanded to be released."

Jeff couldn't follow where the detective's story was heading.

"Sal, could you get to the punch line?"

"I am getting there, sir. He had a fancy phone among his other confiscated belongings. After he jumped bail, I got curious with his phone... I used its speed dial, and guess what? One of the numbers was yours."

"What? Who is the guy?"

"Well, he calls himself Lord Washington, but his real name is Tyrone Washington. He is from South Carolina, a small-time pimp with a few whores, in and out of jail for drugs, but no other major crimes."

"Who were the other numbers?"

"One belongs to a businessman, Max Hathaway, and the other was a disconnected number of someone with the name of John Levine. The third was that same kid Ham... I don't know what to make of all this."

"Sal, is the pimp still in your custody?"

"No. Believe it or not, some young black woman bailed him out the following morning—$5,000, all in cash."

"And the phone?"

"We'll hold it until his court appearance."

"He must have stolen someone's phone."

"Yeah, the phone is registered to the Hathaway Company."

"Sal, could that phone be misplaced and get lost by any chance? You would be doing me a great favor."

"Of course, Mr. Weisman. He'll never show up anyway."

"Well, I appreciate it."

"No sweat, Mr. Weisman."

"Sal, do you think this guy robbed the woman—the owner of the phone? Where else would he get so much cash overnight?"

"There is no robbery filed within the last three weeks. We don't even know who the owner was. You are right, it is a woman or at least the outgoing message is that of a young female—all she says is 'after the beep, you know what to do.' Do you have any idea who might have your number in her speed dial, as well as the other three?"

A cold sweat ran down Jeff's back.

"Mr. Weisman...hello...are you there? Hello. Yeah, could it be that young lady, Ham's girlfriend?"

"Yeah, that is possible."

"Should we pursue it, or just wait for a report of a robbery or something?"

"Yeah, let's wait. She must have just lost her phone and this guy picked it up and used it. I am sure it is as simple as that."

"Okay, done."

꧁꧂

# -CII-

Max and Jeff sat across from each other at corner table #89—the quietest spot in the Pool Room. Max ordered a Bloody Mary, Jeff plain tomato juice.

"I wanted to talk with you, Max, on a somewhat sensitive matter. That is why I chose here rather than the Grill Room, so as not to be interrupted by regulars."

Max gulped down his drink and began to chew an ice cube.

"So, the...let's see... how to put this? I do have a hunch that you know this girl Mallory. A year ago, John mentioned that he gave you and Jeanny her telephone number, in case you needed a masseuse. Mallory dropped out with Jeanny after a few months—and I have no idea why. I don't know whether you ever used her services. If you did, obviously it wasn't in your apartment; otherwise, Norma would have known about it."

Max fished out the remaining ice from his glass.

"Are you now, or have you ever been, fucked by Mallory? Is that what you are asking, Jeff? Come on, cut to the chase."

"No, well, yes that too, but you could simply be having a massage at her office, her place."

"Jeff, am I a kind of guy who gets massages? I took the name from John, in case Norma wanted it. Then I forgot even to tell her about it. Jesus, this was a year ago, Jeff."

"Listen, Max... Actually, I am not really interested in whether or how you are involved with this woman. There is a much more serious problem. The woman has disappeared into thin air. One of our detectives found her telephone in a pimp's possession, but before they figured out their relationship, someone bailed him out with lots of cash, and he, too, disappeared."

"There must be a pony in this pile of shit," Max grinned.

"No, Max. Actually, there is no good news here. Not only was the girl's phone registered to your firm, your private number was in her speed dial!"

There was an awkward silence.

Max spit the last piece of ice into his empty glass.

"Why are you fucking with me, Jeff? Why didn't you just come out and say this in the first place, instead of beating around the bush? Why would you expect me to volunteer to tell you whom I fuck? So there you have it... Yes, I do fuck her; that is, I used to. I've had no contact with her for over three weeks.

"Now I understand why she doesn't return my calls. Your people have absconded with her phone! Why don't you guys mind your own business? The girl is a legitimate masseuse and an honest writer. She told me, and I believe her, that she had only three customers: John, obviously before he died, your wife, and me. Now she has disappeared, and you are asking me whether I stashed her somewhere all for myself. And what is that to you? Were you also fucking her? Now it's your turn... Come clean, Jeff."

Jeff looked straight into Max's eyes... He was deadly serious.

"Max, I don't cheat on Jeanny. As Paul Newman says: 'I have filet mignon at home. Why should I go out to eat hamburger?'"

"That is a strange thing to say, Jeff. He said that, Paul Newman, the actor? No wonder he's into all that food business. You know, half-Jews are really a confused bunch. The choice isn't just between filet mignon and hamburger... There are also ducks, dumplings, peaches... Anyhow, to answer your second question, I have no idea where she is."

Max's voice took a sarcastic turn.

"Are you desperately looking for her in order to give her that money? You put me through all that so she'll get her $5,000,000?"

"Well, that too, but she is also a missing person."

"So put the money into escrow and then wait. Sooner or later, she'll pop up... They always do... That is, when they run out of money. Listen, I've got to go. These shrimp are too good to waste."

Max signaled the waiter to package his leftovers. "Ah, there are also shrimps, honeys, and *mon-chou*; in case your French is a little rusty, it doesn't just mean my cabbage."

Jeff sat there watching him walk away with his casual attitude. The only other person who might have shed some light on the subject was David, Mallory's neighbor, even though Jeff had treated him harshly on the phone.

As he was muttering, "I guess there isn't much to do except to wait, as Max suggested—too bad she was a perfect sex partner," Jeff's eyes met with those of a young blond woman sitting at a table by the pool. She smiled, and whatever she said to the woman sitting across from her, that woman turned around and looked at him—a plain look.

Julian, one of the owners, came around.

"Well, hello, Mr. Weisman. I heard you and Mr. Hathaway were here, so I thought to stop by and say hello."

"Listen, Julian, who is that young lady—no, don't turn around yet. I think the mother is getting up. Maybe she is going to the restroom... now!"

Julian turned around, looking at them with his knowing eyes.

"I've never seen them before... Not our typical clientele, either."

Meanwhile, the young woman—she seemed to be in her early twenties—got up and walked over to Jeff's table.

"Hi. I hope I am not disturbing you. You were looking at me. It was sweet! I thought you may be too shy to come over. My mother—well, she isn't exactly my mother—and I would be delighted if you could join us and have your dessert with us." She had a Russian accent.

Julian was shaking his head side to side, trying to discourage Jeff from accepting the woman's invitation.

"Thank you, Miss; I have to go back to work... Maybe some other time?"

"Okay, here is my card if you ever...just ring." The card must have been in her hand all that time. She put it on the table and swung around toward her table—bouncing her hips with each step. Twice she turned back, though it was only a short distance, and smiled again.

The card read: Ms. Salina Salinowskowitz, Parapsychologist–Tarot Card Reader, telephone number, and a Queens address.

Dismissing Julian's disapproving glance, Jeff securely placed the card in his pocket.

"Julian, please charge our lunch and that of the ladies to Max's account."

He saluted the young woman goodbye and briskly walked out. "One vagina closes, another opens," he consoled himself.

ଚ୍ଚ୍ଚ

# -CIII-

"You could have either of the apartments. One is a studio and the other is a one-bedroom," said Mr. Lazarro, out of breath from having walked up the four floors.

"You are very lucky. Apartments like this don't come on the market often."

Mr. Lazarro was showing the two apartments to a potential new tenant, a young brunette in her late twenties. He unlocked the door of apartment 4B.

"Step in. As you see, this one is totally furnished, elegantly, if I may say so. I'll have to paint this wall. It looks like chicken pox because the previous owner, an artist, had covered it with fancy pictures, but they left all their marks. What color would you like?"

The woman walked into the bedroom, "Do the bed and the mattress all come with the apartment?" she asked sheepishly.

"Yes, and sheets, blankets, pots and pans, vacuum cleaner, and mirror…no, no look up…the ceiling, yep."

"Ohh, interesting!" She blushed. "What is the rent?"

"I'll give it to you for $2,000 a month… You look like a nice girl. Incidentally what do you do? I don't mean to be intrusive, but…?"

"No, no. I am an actress; well, I am studying too. I was sharing an apartment with two other girls, but now I got a job as a cashier in a restaurant. May I see the other apartment?"

Mr. Lazarro, a little disappointed, walked over and opened the unlocked door of 4A.

"This is not fancy, but you have a mattress, a table, and a chair. Everything in the kitchen is in working condition. This place needs a little feminine touch, but it is small and cheap. I'll give it to you for $700; believe me, it is a bargain."

The young woman opened and closed the refrigerator's door: "Why is it making so much noise?"

"Oh, because it is empty. Fill it up with stuff, you know bread, bologna, whatever, and it'll calm down to humming. A lady like you, who lived here till a month ago, used to invite me to dinner occasionally... She made mean mac and cheese. I would bring a six-pack, well she... Anyway, finished her school and she became a teacher herself and left for a job back in her home town in Ohio; yes, Ohio. It is a lucky apartment! All the other previous tenants got rich or married."

"What happened to the tenant of the other apartment, the artist?"

"You know, these creative people are funny... He decided to move to California. I gather he has someone there, so he left all his furniture to me as a gift for being a very good manager."

Noticing the continual hesitation in the woman's eyes, Mr. Lazarro dropped his charming facade.

"Lady, make up your mind. I don't have all day. Here is my card... Take it or leave it, no later than tonight."

The young woman was startled with the change of tune in the man's voice. "I'll, I'll...take it," she said, even though she still wasn't sure. She took out her checkbook, looked at his card, and wrote $1,400 to Goodkind Realty: "$700 as a deposit and $700 for the first month's rent," she said and handed him the check.

Mr. Lazarro pocketed the check and abruptly gave her the key. "I'll come the first day of every month, early in the morning, to collect the money, all right?"

He left her standing in the middle of the room.

# -CIV-

Sunday night, as Hamilton, Ann, and Ham were finishing a meal delivered from a new Chinese restaurant, the phone rang.

Ann answered.

"May I speak to Ham, please?" a cheerful female asked.

"Who, may I ask, is calling?"

The Thurmans had more or less quarantined Ham. Furthermore, he wasn't allowed to give their telephone number to any strangers. The police warned them about the possibility of the gang's accessing them, using various ruses.

"This is Christine Rivers. Is this Ham's mother? We spoke a few times in the past. His literary agent... I have good news for him."

"Oh, of course, just a minute."

Ann passed the phone to Ham with incredulity. "Your agent, Ham!"

Ham lumbered reluctantly to the phone.

"Oh, hi. Ham, I hope I am not disturbing you. I read your novel; well, I actually devoured it, this weekend. I just couldn't put it down until I finished! What a page-turner. Listen, I know I didn't do well with your poetry—the field, as you know, is a dry well—but this, this is a gem! I have no doubt we'll get a large advance. I already spoke to a friend of mine at Simon and Schuster, and she is very interested. She is even willing to consider a multibook contract, but I am not going to let my friendship interfere with that... I told her I want a bidding war. Ham, I cannot believe this! I never knew that you also write prose... My God, you are some multitalented guy. I loved the ending: 'Is betrayal the essence of all relationships?' WOW!"

The blood drained from Ham's face.

"I know how traditionally trained you are Ham... That is why your defying typical fictional form, with seeming informality and violating nearly all writing-school rules, including being against the writer as protagonist, is so extraordinary. And the language! Sonority of your prose is overwhelming—its exactitude draws no pity for the character!"

Ham turned his back against his parents and pressed the receiver to his ear.

"I see a National Book Critics Circle Award lining up for you, Ham. Ham, may I ask a question? I mean, how were you able to capture a female voice so accurately? I guess you tapped your very inner woman—*anima* so to speak. I guess that is why you want to use the first-name initial—a sort of *nom de plume*; H. Thurman—H. could be Harriett, Holly, Haley, Helen, anything—no one would believe that a man can have such an access to the female mind. However, well done, Ham. It is amazing. I am still reeling with emotions.

"Actually, it isn't the first time a presumed author's sex is identified by the opposite sex. I am sure you know that when *Frankenstein* was published, everyone in London believed that it was by a man, even though her name was on the title. Closest they guess was that the writer was Percy Shelley, but in fact it was his wife, Mary Shelley."

Christine Rivers was speaking so fast that she became out of breath. "And isn't it ironic that Percy Shelley was also a poet like you."

Ham had not forgotten their last conversation, when he tried to please her by being agreeable and flexible while she demolished his poems for being without iambic pentameter and internal rhymes. Now, it was her turn to suck up to him. Of course, this was a counterfeit victory.

"I loved the simplicity and the directness of the language you use, as if this is a genuine diary of a somewhat less-talented young woman—I mean in the literary sense, of course—rather than a well-crafted piece of literature by a seasoned writer like yourself. And the randomness of your character's associations—seemingly haphazard, breaking the chronological order—put the reader in a constant state of anticipatory failing. Bravo, Ham, bravo!"

Ham sensed his father's curious gaze at the back of his neck.

"So I'll send you a new contract. I couldn't find the old one; I must have misplaced it... Anyway, it would have required updating. I am so excited. Let me know when you get the contract, and then we should celebrate with a lunch on me. Oh, I almost forgot, it is finished, right?"

"No, simply abandoned."

"Whatever...I need a page or two summary of the novel by tomorrow. Ciao."

Ham got off the phone, wobbling.

"What is that gray face? I thought she said she had good news." Ann looked puzzled.

"Oh, yes, it is good news: She loved my work and thinks that she will get a publisher and even an advance."

"But Ham, you are talking as if you lost a dear friend! You have been dying to see your poems in print for such a long time. In fact, you thought your career as a poet was over. Well, congratulations. Incidentally, didn't I tell you that one day someone would discover you and overnight you'd be a published poet?"

"Well actually, I may become a published author. She liked my novel," Ham managed to say.

"What?" Ann jumped. "You have been writing a novel? Since when?"

"Since I have been interred here."

Hamilton got off the sofa and opened the window. "One cannot be both truthful and seem so."

"Hamilton, please join the conversation, relevantly," Ann scolded him.

Ham sensed a slow-motion tumble in his father's doubts.

Ann continued in her righteous tone.

"You see, Ham, if you buckle down and put your mind to it, there is nothing that you can't accomplish… It is just a matter of discipline and motivation. You had all the ingredients of being successful; all you needed to do was apply them to a field where there is a demand. You see how easy it is? It is a matter of finding what people want to buy, not what you want to sell them. I am so glad that you'll be financially independent finally, because since Columbia refused to give tenure to your father, I am not sure how long he'll have the job or whether we can keep supporting you."

His back against the open window, Hamilton looked at Ham, who was still standing by the phone with a dazed look. Hamilton pulled himself up and sat on the windowsill.

"You wrote a novel within two months?"

Ham stammered: "Well, it has been germinating for a while. I am sorry, when did you hear about your tenure's being rejected? Didn't the dean, as well as all senior faculty, think that it was a shoo-in for you?"

"Yes, but apparently the school considers me too controversial. No need to panic, since I am not fired yet. Let's get back to your novel writing—you distill beer now?"

Ann interrupted: "Are you trying to spoil this too? What are you insinuating?"

Hamilton jumped down from the windowsill: "Do we get to read the manuscript or wait for its publication?"

"I'll have to write a brief summary of it in a form of a proposal to-night… Mrs. Rivers wants it by tomorrow. I'll leave a copy for you with your breakfast, if that doesn't upset your stomach as beer seems to do. Now, I must just go in and do my damn homework."

After he left, Ann scolded Hamilton. "Please leave him alone. The kid, for the first time in his life, comes up with something that has any commercial value, and what do you want? I am not going to support you two for the rest of my life."

"Don't you find this a little peculiar, Ann? I mean, have you seen him writing the novel? What could he be writing about anyway, that it is so well received by his cantankerous agent? Has he been writing about growing up with us and all that? Why would that be of interest to anyone? Let's say if you receive a brief summary of a book that more or less says the following, would you publish it?

"I am the only child of a reluctant mother with a highly practical mind and a determined father with a peculiar mind. I grew up to be an unpractical, undetermined person with a poetic mind—and took my unholy vengeance upon them. I think Hitler said something like that at Ham's age in Vienna, when he failed as an artist."

☙

The following morning, Hamilton found the summary of Ham's novel at the kitchen table; it was just a few lines.

*'The Litter of Betrayal'*
*A Novel by H. Thurman*

*This is the first person narrative of a twenty-two-year-old, semi-delusional woman, obsessed about her father's incestuous transgressions with her twin sister. She is a writer-manquée, an Id-therapist, and a call girl, who revenges men by exploiting their bodies for money and by excavating their minds for literary material.*

Hamilton remembered his son mentioning to him a few months ago of the disappearance of Mallory, his novelist friend. As he glanced through those lines again, he felt a tender confusion and wobbled into a chair.

It did not take too long though for Hamilton to recover from his initial shock. He got up briskly, walked up to the window that overlooked the Hudson River, turned around, and pulled himself up to perch on the window sill, his favorite pulpit. In a self-pleased tone, he muttered "My son is a 'perfect mistake,' as it is said of Cy Twombly. Okay, let me lower the bar a little: Every literary work represents an intellectual heritage; that is to say, Ham is a thief, as it is said of every author."

☙

# About the Author

**T. Byram Karasu**, M.D., is the Silverman Professor and University Chairman of the Department of Psychiatry and Behavioral Sciences at Albert Einstein College of Medicine/Montefiore Medical Center, and the editor-in-chief of the *American Journal of Psychotherapy*. He is the author or editor of eighteen books, including a novel, *Of God and Madness*; a book of poetry, *Rags of My Soul*; the seminal *Treatments of Psychiatric Disorders*; and two best sellers, *The Art of Serenity* and *The Spirit of Happiness*. Dr. Karasu is a scholar, renowned clinician, teacher, and lecturer, and the recipient of numerous awards, including the American Psychiatric Association's Presidential Commendation. He lives in New York City and Connecticut.